MW01258216

THE
RIFTS
— OF —
PSYCHE

THE STARSEA CYCLE BOOK THREE

KYLE WEST

Copyright © 2021 by Kyle West

All rights reserved.

No part of this book may be reproduced in any form or by any electronic or mechanical means, including information storage and retrieval systems, without written permission from the author, except for the use of brief quotations in a book review.

Cover Art by Deranged Doctor Design.

1

LUCIAN HAD BEEN WALKING for hours, and night was falling.

He stumbled on a rock, almost face-planting on the rugged ground. The only reason he caught himself was due to Psyche's lower gravity. He panted, trying to catch his breath. The air was thin up here, but maybe it would be thicker at a lower elevation.

He was following a trail, but it was impossible to tell where it was leading. For now it led up a set of broken steps carved into a cliff. Those steep, shattered stairs would have been impossible to climb in standard gravity.

Climbing hand over hand, his muscles strained under the exercise. He had done nothing for months besides sitting in his cell. Coupled with the low transit gravity of the prison barge, he was the weakest he had been in his adult life.

Pulling himself up the final step, Lucian gasped for breath. Once standing, he peered beyond a precipice before him. It fell hundreds of meters, the trail crisscrossing down before it was lost to darkness. Even in low gravity, it would be hell going down that. But there was no other way to proceed. And the lower he descended, the darker it would become. He just couldn't catch his breath. He needed to find shelter before night fell. And he needed to find water.

Wherever his escape pod had landed, it was far from any sort of life, human or otherwise. Maybe this part of the moon was isolated, and he was the only living person within a thousand kilometers. If that was true, then it almost certainly meant his death. He would be doomed to wander this moon until he collapsed from thirst, hunger, or sheer exhaustion.

He tried pushing these dark thoughts from his mind, descending deeper into the rift. He tried not to think of what threats might be lurking in the gathering darkness.

One thing was sure. The further he descended, the dimmer the sky grew. Was that due to the onset of evening, or the twisted mountains blocking more sunlight? Those mountains didn't look right, anyway. Through the violet mist, they were warped like some lurid vision of hell. Even Volsung hadn't been as bleak as this. The only life were low, stunted trees clinging in rocky crevices. There was no wind whatsoever, while the air was cool, dry, and . . . *dead*, for lack of a better word. If there was water, it had to be at a lower elevation. And with water, hopefully, there would also be life. And where there was life, there was food.

The mere thought of water made his throat feel even more parched, but it was almost too dark to proceed. Of course, he could stream a light sphere and search late into the night. But light might attract unwanted attention. It would be better to find water without it, but for all he knew, that would be impossible. And of course, it would mean dismantling the block he'd formed around his Focus all those months ago. Lucian had never been afraid of the dark, but the darkness of this moon terrified him. Anything could be lurking behind the copious boulders, crevices, or pits he passed.

In the end, Lucian had to stop because he was tripping over

every stray rock and crack. And now, the trail was skirting the edge of a mountain, and one false step could send him falling hundreds of meters. He needed light, but first, he had to see if it was even possible to stream.

He reached for his Focus. There was no sentimentality as he worked to dissolve the block. It was a knot he had practiced untying countless times in his head during the long journey here.

And just as it had been in his imagination, the block was unraveled with a simple streaming of Psionic Magic. A strange heaviness departed him. It would take some time to regather his ether, so to stream a light sphere, he would have to over-draw. There was little choice unless he wanted to stumble over the side of the trail and into the fissure.

The image of his focus, the Septagon and its seven colored points, formed perfectly in his mind. He reached for the Radiant Aspect.

He siphoned ether directly from the Manifold. The energy that powered all magic entered him, shocking him like cold water. But it also burned him at the same time, as if there were acid mixed in. He hadn't expected so much ether to enter him so quickly, especially being out of practice so long.

There was little time to wonder at it. He created a thin stream, and a dim light sphere manifested before him, illumining the area up to five meters.

Now, he had to get that light to follow him. And for that, he would need to test his Binding. His heart pounded a bit, not knowing what to expect. He would have to stream Binding at *some* point, so he might as well do so now, when he wasn't under any immediate threat.

While holding the Radiant stream, he reached for the Binding Aspect. He bound the light sphere to his right shoulder so it would follow him. He didn't notice any discernible use of ether – it was as if his pool had remained at the same level.

Granted, such a simple tether didn't use a lot of ether anyway, but at the same time, it should have used at least some. It was evidence that the Orb of Binding was real, and the Oracle had not been lying to him.

He kept the luminosity of the light sphere low, just enough to see by. He wasn't sure how long he could hold it. He was tired, weak, and didn't relish having to draw more ether than he already had.

The light revealed the trail sidling down the mountain range on his left. It dropped deeper and deeper into the rift with no sign of ending.

This was some mess he was in. Would they really have dropped him on some random part of the moon? Or would they have put him where there was at least some human habitation nearby? He thought back all those months, to what that prison guard had told him. The Treaty of Chiron stated the League only needed to get the exiled mage to the surface. He'd said the Treaty had ensured nothing about the mage's survival, so Lucian had to take that into his own hands.

Lucian's train of thought was broken when he stepped on something organic and squishy. He pulled his boot away with a squelch, looking down at what appeared to be a pile of mud. A pile of mud that was warm.

That was when the smell hit him.

His mouth twisted. "Disgusting."

He wiped his boot on a nearby rock but couldn't get the residue completely off. There were two piles of it, not quite steaming, but hours-fresh.

He supposed that answered his question about whether there was animal life on this moon. This observation was not helped by the fact that the creature was bigger than him. Far bigger, and nearby.

Shelter was sounding like a better idea every second. Turning back wasn't an option. Up above were only dry wastes.

The area he had come from hadn't held so much as a snowbank for water, despite the freezing temperature. That told him little precipitation fell here.

Whatever life was here had to live below, between the mountains. But other life also meant competition for resources. He had to be prepared that the natives were not friendly.

Lucian proceeded cautiously, rounding a bend that wrapped around the mountainside.

That was when he saw a light in the distance, the unmistakable orange glow of a fire.

He immediately cut off both of his streams and crouched. His mind hummed with the positive afterglow of magic. How he had missed this feeling. And because of that, Lucian understood more than ever why magic was so dangerous.

He kept his attention on the fire. It might have been a hundred meters away, but he couldn't see anyone around it. He thought about reaching for Radiance to home in on the infrared spectrum. Doing so would allow him to see any heat source besides that fire. A heat source like another human. But he already felt strained from holding his light sphere. If there were people around, he needed enough magic to defend himself. It was a risk he couldn't take.

The best way to proceed was to move carefully, to watch his steps, and not make any sound.

He edged along the trail, keeping the rock wall on his left. If he veered too far to the right, he would fall into the rift. Even with the lower gravity, a fall from this height would be fatal.

As he approached the mouth of the cave, there didn't seem to be anyone within a few meters of the fire. But from the even burn of the flames, it was clearly manmade. The only question was, where was the man?

Lucian crouched in the shadows, waiting for what seemed half an hour before moving in. He felt exposed, stepping into the light like this. He reached for his Focus; he needed to be prepared for the worst. He stood a few meters from the fire, which was almost burned down to coals. Beyond the firelight, he could see the cave went even deeper.

What was he doing in here? Half of him wanted to turn around and head back out into the night, and the other half wanted to explore further.

A sudden crashing noise emanated from deeper within the cave, like metal falling on rock.

"Hello?" he called.

He winced. Why had he given himself away? After a few seconds without a response, he creeped deeper into the darkness of the cave. He really should be turning around right now, but there was no way he was going to spend the night out in the darkness. Not with whatever had made that gigantic pile of crap. He needed shelter, or at the very least, directions on where to find food, water, and his own safe place to hole up.

At a bend in the tunnel, he heard a woman's voice, singing softly. He strained his ears to listen, the hairs on his arms rising. If there was anything he'd learned from watching horror holos, now was the appropriate time to leave.

As soon as he started backing away, there was a witchy female cackle. "Leaving so soon? We haven't even started, yet."

Lucian ran, but tripped over a rock. Footsteps approached from behind.

He tried to get up, but he was so heavy, as if he weighed ten times what he should have. The ground below him glowed silvery. With horror, he realized it was a gravity amplification disc. As the disc pulled him down, hard, it was impossible for him to budge. Even his lungs fought for breath.

Well, he'd made a poor showing of it. After only a few hours on the surface, he was going to die.

2

IT WAS Lucian's first fight with a rival mage with his life in the balance. And from the way things were going, it was probably going to be his last.

If he wanted to survive this, then he knew he needed utter calm and to reach for his Focus.

He reached for Gravitonics, fumbling for a counterstream to extricate himself from this situation. But he couldn't even *feel* his ether in the first place. Whatever this mage was doing, it was far beyond his abilities to fight against. He realized he knew nothing, that he had had barely any training at all.

He was completely at this woman's mercy.

Still, that didn't stop him from trying to reverse the Gravitonic stream. He tried to brute force through the block around his Focus, but again, there was nothing. He struggled to lift his arms but gave up after a few seconds. They were like leaden weights in Jupiter's gravity.

"Let me go," Lucian managed, fighting for breath. "I won't hurt you."

From the sound of her breathing, he guessed the woman

stood about a meter behind him. A strange chortle escaped her throat.

"You're a rotting poor Hunter," she said. Her voice sounded young, probably around his age. From that earlier maddened cackle, he had expected an old hag. "Either that or you're fresh off a barge. Either way, if you don't cause any more problems, I might not kill you."

Lucian had no choice but to be at her mercy. She ran her hands over the length of his body. He tried to squirm away but couldn't; she didn't avoid the areas he wished she would. Those probing fingers were like eels, seeking any sort of weapon. He groaned as he fought to escape.

"Now, now," she said. "Can't have you stabbing me with a surprise shockspear, can we?"

"Hands off," Lucian said. "I don't have any damn shockspear."

The sheer weight of his body was almost enough to suffocate him on its own. His vision was getting dark – blood and oxygen were not reaching his brain efficiently. If she didn't let him go, and soon, he would pass out. And if he passed out, he would never wake up again.

The weight suddenly released, and Lucian scrambled free. He whipped around to face the woman and was surprised by what he saw. Even in her raggedy clothing cinched together with a rough piece of rope, she cut a striking figure. Her pale, blonde hair fell just past her shoulders, while her eyes were intense and blue. Her bare feet were filthy and heavily calloused. How she got around on these rocky trails, Lucian couldn't begin to guess. She looked the part of the quintessential cavewoman, and the local make of her clothes told him that she was no prisoner from a barge. She was most likely born and raised here.

Last of all, he noticed part of her left arm was mottled with sickly pink patches. He couldn't tear his eyes away from that skin, of which he had only read and heard about.

She was a fray.

"Don't mind my arm," she said. "I'm not far gone, yet, whatever the Elders of Kiro would have you believe. I've still got my mind, of that you can be sure."

Lucian backed up a step. Any moment now, she could lash out and end his life. She had so easily overpowered him. Worse, he couldn't even stream his own magic to undo her block.

"If you unblock me, I won't hurt you," Lucian said.

She seemed to consider for a moment. "Not a chance. Of me unblocking you, or *you* hurting me."

Lucian hadn't expected that to work, but it had been worth a try. "I was only looking for a place to stay. I can leave you in peace."

"You *are* fresh off a barge," she said. "No fray-hunter would be as incompetent as you."

Despite the insult, Lucian almost breathed a sigh of relief. She no longer saw him as a threat, which was exactly what he needed.

"I just landed here. So what?"

The woman rolled her eyes. "How long have you been here, exactly?"

"Six hours, maybe? It's hard to say."

Lucian wondered why she was asking him all these questions. She probably wouldn't be going through the trouble if she planned on killing him.

"That explains it. Being fresh off the barge is the only reason you'd be dumb enough to go out there at night. I'm just trying to help."

"*Help?* You almost killed me!"

"I wasn't sure of you at first, but I'm reasonably sure you can't kill me. I can't let you go back out there. It would be irresponsible of me."

"Okay. Well, why would you want to help me?"

"Well, why wouldn't I? You're a lost little puppy out in the wilds. I'm not a cold-hearted bitch."

"Sorry. I guess I'm pretty cautious after you attacked me."

"You were trying to run. I thought you were here to kill me. And if I'd let you go, that would've been the end of you."

"Why is that?"

"Wyverns." The firelight lent her blue eyes an intense appearance. "They hunt the rifts at night. Doesn't matter if it's pitch black. They have large eyes that catch the smallest amount of light, and where there's *no* light, they can smell your warmth. Failing that, they can use their shrieks to find their prey. They always hunt in pairs, husband and wife."

"That's romantic," Lucian said. The joke didn't do much to take away the sick wrenching in his gut.

"Only caves are safe, with a bright enough fire to keep them away. They hate the light and will only fly in it if you *really* piss them off."

"I thought you said they like warmth. Fire means warmth."

"Aye, that it does. But light blinds them something fierce, and they won't attack into it unless they are truly desperate."

The woman suddenly approached. Lucian tensed, but she only walked past him and took a seat on a rock by the fire. There, she warmed her hands. "Have a seat. Looks like you've seen better days. I don't have much, but there's food and water."

Lucian approached the fire cautiously and sat on the ground. He felt a curious pressure release in his mind. When he reached for his Focus, he had access to his magic again. He watched her for a moment cautiously, suspecting some trick. But it seemed her unblocking him had been intentional. It was her way of showing good faith, so it was on him to match that.

Lucian watched her from across the fire. "What do these wyverns look like? I found a steaming pile of crap up the trail, so they must be big."

That got her attention. "Quite early for them to be active, but it's not unheard of. They have big wings, big teeth, big claws. Trust me. You'll know one when you see it, and there's a good chance it'll be the last thing you see altogether."

"Lovely."

She watched him. This was Lucian's first real conversation in months. Did people *always* stare like that when they talked? Perhaps they did, and he had just forgotten.

"Is there something in my teeth?"

She broke into a smile that seemed a bit too wide. "What do you mean?"

Maybe that idiom didn't exist on this world. "You're staring."

"I know," she said. "Just sizing you up. If you lost that beard and got some meat on you, you might even be passable."

Passable? What was she getting on about? Lucian decided that comment was best ignored. Her poking him just showed how little she thought of him as a threat. That alone was humbling.

He cleared his throat. He had to admit she was a good-looking woman, but besides their obvious differences, that skin of hers freaked him out a little. She claimed to have her mind still, but of course, she could just be saying that. Normally, fraying began its work by rotting skin and organs before spreading to the brain itself. It was hard to tell whether her eccentricity was due to the fraying, or from living alone. And why *did* she live alone, for that matter?

Whatever the case, he couldn't ever forget that she had manhandled him like a child. Or rather, *woman*-handled. Whatever happened, he needed to avoid going toe-to-toe with her.

"Quite the conversationalist," she observed. "Who are you? Where are you from? How'd you come to be here?"

Lucian warmed his hands a moment, considering his response while ignoring her jibe. "My name is Lucian. I'm from

11

Earth. I . . . attended the Volsung Academy and failed out. That's why I'm here."

"Volsung," she said. "Never been there." She gave a short, somewhat bitter laugh. "Then again, I've never been anywhere but Psyche."

He was right about her being a native. "What's your story, then? And your name?"

"I'm Serah. Serah Ocano, if you care to know my family name." She looked him over. "You're the first off-worlder I've seen in a long time."

"Are there a lot of Psyche natives?"

"Well, there was a colony here before the Mage War. And the other Worlds have been sending their own trash here for a while, along with the mages. And of course, people have needs, and those needs make more people. Not a lot of folks live here in the Riftlands, but go to the Golden Vale in Dara and you'll find cities so big they'll make your eyes pop out." She shrugged. "Or so they say. Never been there myself. But they say Dara has a population of one million."

That had to be an exaggeration, but Lucian didn't want to openly disagree with her.

"My mother and father were both mages," Serah went on. "I guess that's where I got it from."

What were the odds of that? Being a mage was supposed to be random, or from the Manifold, or whatever one wanted to call it.

"Why're you looking at me like I'm strange?" she asked.

"It's nothing. I've just always been told genetics had nothing to do with magical ability."

"Genetics?"

Maybe that was a word she didn't know, either. "The bloodline. You said your parents were mages, and that's the reason you're one, too."

"Yeah."

"That's . . . different from what I've been told."

"You've been told wrong. Children of mages aren't *always* mages, but they are more likely to be."

"And that's . . . common knowledge here?"

She gave a lopsided smile. "What, they don't let mages couple off-world?"

Lucian was about to protest, before he realized that they *didn't*. Well, the Volsung Academy didn't, at least. Could *that* be the reason? If the League didn't want extra mages on their hands, they would certainly discourage mages coupling. Or force sterilize them, but that wasn't a practice as far as Lucian knew.

There was something more to it than that. Vera herself had acknowledged magical ability had nothing to do with genetics. There was a missing component, but it wasn't worth arguing about.

Of course, if Serah knew something that everyone else outside Psyche didn't, that knowledge would be useless. No one left this world.

"I guess you know a lot about surviving here, Serah."

"You don't live to be *my* age without that."

"You can't be *that* old, though. You seem close to my age."

"About that. Maybe a bit older. Fifteen or sixteen."

Lucian looked at her blankly. There was no way she was *that* young.

"Psyche years," she said. "Sorry. We don't go by the Earther calendar here, but I understand the years are shorter there. I'm not even sure what I'd be in that. Twenty-five or twenty-six, I guess."

"And you really live on your own?" He watched carefully for her reaction.

She poked the fire with a stick, her expression unchanging. "No. I've got a friend in the back of the cave there. He's asleep, so no need to worry about him. He's got the fraying bad, but it makes him melancholy. He's not a Burner."

"A Burner?"

"Wow, you really do know nothing. That's what we call the ones who go crazy. They burn up all their ether, trying to kill everyone and everything. Until they kill themselves, at least. That's maybe a quarter of frays. The rest just sort of . . . lose themselves, I guess. Slip through the cracks of sanity." She sighed sadly. "That's Ramore right there."

"Ramore's your friend's name?"

She nodded. "I know, it's a weird name. Don't really know where it comes from. Me and him go way back. Both exiles from the Deeprift villages. I'm from Kiro, he's from Fira." She sighed heavily. "He was once a wyvern hunter, taught me a lot of what he knows. Without him, I wouldn't have survived the Upper Reaches. Now, he needs *me* to survive."

"That must be hard."

"Yeah, it is. What can you do, though? I stick by my friends, even when they aren't convenient. Makes the living twice as hard, but without him, what do I have? Maybe one day, he'll get better. Not likely, but there's always a chance. Most would have left him for the wyverns by now. Not me, though."

"I take it survival isn't easy here."

She cast him an annoyed glance. "You're one for making obvious statements, aren't you?"

"Sorry. It's all I've got right now."

"Well, just shut up and listen. You don't have to have some rotting remark to everything I say."

Rotting? That was the second time she'd said that. It seemed like a local profanity. He wanted to ask about it, but figured it would be best to keep quiet.

She nodded in satisfaction. "That's better. First thing you need to learn – get inside before nightfall. If you don't, there's a good chance you won't live to see the morning. There are plenty of caves in the rifts. *Don't* go in the ones that are too high up. That's where the wyverns like to nest. For that matter, you shouldn't *ever* go to the very bottom of the rifts, the part where you can't really see the sky anymore and it's dark all the time. At some point, all the rifts go low enough and join up in this place called the Darkrift. That's where you'll find a lot of nasty creatures, and a lot of frays, too. And with frays, you'll find Burners."

"How far until the bottom?"

"There's no *real* bottom," Serah said. "It just keeps going down and down until you realize you're not in the open air anymore. And it keeps going down below that, as far as we know."

"How long's a day here, anyway?" Lucian said.

"Well, a day's a day. From what others have told me, Psyche's close to Earth standard. Don't know if anyone's measured it properly, though."

"I see. So, it's just you and Ramore in here?"

She nodded. "It's a bit too close to Kiro for my liking." She held up a finger, staying Lucian's next question. "Kiro is a day's walk down the trail. Keep going down and you'll find it. Big cave mouth, big wall, always guarded."

"Why aren't you living there?"

She laughed at that. "You kidding? I used to live there." She held up her frayed arm. "The minute they see this, they send you packing."

"That's harsh."

"That's the rules," she said. "Can't let a fray wind up a Burner one day. It can happen at any time. Even if I don't blame them, I don't like them."

"So, when someone frays, they just get banished?"

"That's the modus operandi," she said, mispronouncing things epically.

It sounded harsh, but if there was a better solution, Lucian didn't know what it was.

"Well, it's getting a bit late," Serah said. "I should probably check on Ramore." She stood and seemed to consider for a moment. "Tell you what. Tomorrow, I'll take you down to Kiro, see if they might let you in or at least give you a chance."

"Why wouldn't they let me in?"

"You're a stranger. Usually, you can't get into a Deeprift village unless someone vouches for you, first."

"Can you vouch for me?"

"I would, but I don't know how far that would get you. Kiro and I have something of a . . . strained relationship."

She went off to check on her friend. Lucian wondered how bad Ramore's state was to be isolated back there.

Whatever the case, tomorrow he would wake up and hopefully reach this Kiro Village. He was nowhere near fraying, so maybe this place would accept him if he were willing to offer something in exchange, like work.

And always, Lucian had to remember his ultimate goal: escape. He recalled his audience with the Oracle all those months back on Volsung. She had entrusted the Orb of Binding to him. He didn't even know what to do with that, and he didn't know how any of it worked.

For a moment, Lucian doubted whether it had even happened. It wouldn't be the first time. The question was probably pointless, anyway. He had to survive the night first, and every night after that. Then, he could worry about the Orb, along with the Oracle's worrying encouragement to locate the rest of them.

When Serah's footsteps approached the fire, a series of high shrieks emanated from outside the cave. Just hearing that gave Lucian chills.

"There they are," Serah said. "Just pretend it's a lullaby and you'll fall right asleep."

"I don't think that's going to work."

"They're checking us out all right. But with the way I built this fire up, we can sleep as safe as two mud-sallies during hibernation."

"Whatever that means."

"Goodnight, Lucian."

Lucian lay down, being sure to keep the fire between himself and the cave entrance. More shrieks echoed from outside.

This was going to be a long night.

3

LUCIAN AWOKE TO A GUTTURAL YELL, and was pushed by some unseen force across the rocky cave floor. He scrambled up and found himself face to face with a shambling corpse of a man dressed in rags.

It took a moment for things to register, but when they did, he reached for his Focus.

It was going to be a fight.

Ramore's deadened eyes did not match his wide, mad smile. He'd lost most of his hair, while his pink, mottled skin hung from his face like melted wax. His flesh was cadaverous and decaying, covered with open sores. He extended a trembling hand, which became wrapped with reddish light.

Serah scrambled up, her eyes widening. "Ramore, no!"

Lucian had time enough to wrap himself in a Thermal shield, countering the incredible blast of heat directed at him. Even with the shield, he felt as if he were standing in an oven. Ramore's nightmarish face strained as he streamed more Thermal Magic. Lucian felt his shield buckling while his reserves of ether burned away at an incredible rate. Thermalism was not his strength, and this would be a losing battle the longer it went on.

"Get out of here!" Serah said. "He's too strong!"

Ramore's stream strengthened, and there was nothing Lucian could do to defend against it. Ramore's expression was one of twisted, murderous rage.

Serah was trying to pull Ramore away, but he shook her aside with unreal strength, sending her sprawling to the ground. Lucian edged away from the cave while concentrating all his ether on maintaining the wavering shield. If it cracked, he would be immolated in seconds.

When he reached the cave mouth, Ramore was still in pursuit. Lucian had to do *something* to keep the frayed mage from following him, but what? All his ether was tied up in the shield's upkeep, and if his concentration slipped, even for a moment, it would mean his death.

Suddenly, the heat dissipated, and Ramore keeled over with a groan of pain. Serah had clearly done something to distract him, but Lucian didn't have time to speculate. He ran off into the darkness, leaving the frayed mages behind. Serah screamed something after him, but Lucian wasn't sure what. The only thing he *was* sure of was that there was no way in hell he was taking his chances back there. Not when he could be murdered in his sleep.

He had to find his own cave, somewhere. Serah had said there were plenty of them. The only question was, could he find one before the wyverns smelled him out?

Serah had also said the wyverns hated light. So, he streamed a light sphere to illumine the path ahead, tethering it so that it floated about a meter ahead of him. As before, streaming Binding seemed to make no impact on his ether at all, even when he was dualstreaming. All he had to do was keep up Radiance, which thankfully used less ether than the Thermalism.

The trail snaked down into the rift. Due to the low gravity, Lucian wasn't really sprinting, but loping. He forced himself to slow down before he careened over the edge. It didn't seem as if he were being followed.

Not ten seconds after streaming the light sphere, bloodcurdling shrieks echoed from the rift, causing the hairs on his neck to stand on end. Lucian picked up the pace, glancing behind to see the cave mouth he'd just escaped, where two human silhouettes blocked the interior light. They both disappeared, likely seeking shelter from the wyverns that were surely coming.

He had to find a cave, and enough fuel to make a fire. The shrieks sounded again, closer now. Would he have the time?

The path made a bend, weaving between two clefts of rocks. It had to be the entrance of a cave. If he could just get inside, find some fuel, and light it with a Thermal stream, he'd be safe. Probably.

Lucian went inside, following the trail until it reached an open area surrounded by high cliffs. No, this was most *definitely* not a cave. There was no discernible escape, though of course it was impossible to tell in the darkness.

Lucian's blood went cold when he realized the truth. He would have to fight for his life again, but this time, there was no Serah to bail him out.

The first thing he did was deepen his Focus, streaming the light sphere as bright as he could manage. Doing so burned his ether at an alarming rate, but there was no other way to counter what was coming. He needed not only to see his surroundings, but to inhibit the wyverns before they got too close.

Lucian didn't have to wait long. Two massive, dragon-like creatures with wide, leathern wings and long, snake-like necks emerged from the darkness above the cleft. Their forms were long and scaly, while massive black eyes reflected the light of his sphere. In tandem, they opened their gaping maws, revealing rows of needle-like teeth, and let out discordant shrieks that sounded demonic as they flapped toward him. The light sphere had little, if any, effect on their aggression.

Lucian reached for his shockspear, only to realize he had no weapon at all. He had only his magic and his wits to rely on. And of course, the Orb of Binding. If everything about what he'd experienced on Volsung was a dream, then he would be dead within seconds.

But he would not begin by streaming the Binding Aspect. He reached for his Focus, only to find that the light sphere had eaten up all his ether. He had no choice but to overdraw from the Manifold itself. A sweetly poisonous infusion of ether entered him, leaving him shaking and exultant. It was a fiery power that demanded immediate release. He reached for the Psionic Aspect and began to direct every bit of that ether into a stream designed to push the two wyverns back as far as possible. He needed to create some space, enough time to figure out how the Orb of Binding worked. And a kinetic wave would give him that space – assuming his stream was powerful enough.

The hardest part was waiting for the right moment, watching helplessly as the wyverns dove toward him. They seemed to move in slow motion, a side-effect of being so deep into his Focus. All that training on the prison barge had given him a concentration greater than he would have ever thought possible.

And he would need every bit of it as he waited, patiently, for the right moment. He had to wait until they were just meters away ...

The wyverns' shrieks pummeled him then, drowning him in a wall of sound. The time had come to create his *own* wall. He finally let go of his stream, unleashing a massive, kinetic wave. His entire body shone with violet light as the shockwave emanated outward. It blasted the wyverns, who shot away as if knocked with a gigantic and invisible bat. They tossed and tumbled in the air, shooting into the distance. Lucian had hoped the lower gravity would make kinetic force even more powerful, and it was a bet that was paying off. The wyverns screeched their dismay, but they spread those wings wide and were slowly regaining control.

It would only be a temporary reprieve. It gave him time, nothing more. He could not indefinitely overdraw from the Manifold, as the poison of ether would make it impossible to remain conscious.

So, he cut off the Psionic stream, his chest heaving. The power felt sweet, but at the same time, gut-wrenching with the nausea it had introduced. His skin prickled with fire. It was almost as if he could *feel* the poison of the Manifold rotting him from the inside out. The taste on his tongue was acrid and foul. If he drew any more ether, he would be in dire danger of fraying.

He had to figure out how to use the Orb. And he had to figure it out now. Nothing else would save him.

The words of the Oracle returned to him. The Orb of Binding would allow him to stream the Binding Aspect without fear of overdrawing. While its power was theoretically unlimited, it was still constrained by the strength of Lucian's Focus.

His heart pounded, not knowing what to expect. Using this Orb might even kill him. But he was dead anyway, and there wasn't a moment to waste. He sought the Binding Aspect, only dimly aware of the flapping of leathern wings accompanied by monstrous shrieks.

He opened himself to the Binding Aspect. And beyond even that in his mind's eye was the Orb, waiting and thrumming with potential power. He reached for it with his Focus, and streamed.

And gasped as the Orb siphoned an insane rush of ether into him.

He had never known such pure, unadulterated power. And within the ether given by the Orb, there was no hint of the foulness of the Manifold's toxin. It was as if it were naturally accrued ether, although even compared to *that*, it was purer. It was magic as it was meant to be, as it had been *designed* to be. And he could drink of this well as deeply as he could control it. In his mind's eye, the Orb of Binding's radiant blue light pulsed with seemingly endless energy. He had the power to Bind entire worlds, crash them together, rip them apart . . .

It would kill him, but it was a possibility. If only he knew how.

That power needed an outlet. Now, those wyverns would die. He had no doubt about that. He knew that as surely as he knew his own name.

He began by streaming a focal point on a nearby stand of sharp rocks, and the focal point held with ease. As the wyverns entered a dive, he created two more streams, anchor points, one for each wyvern. These two streams held as well. That shocked him; the greater the mass of the bound object, the more magic required to complete the anchor point. Magic rippled through him, his hands emanating blue light. And still, the Orb pulsed, an endless fountain. He strengthened the energy in each of the anchor points, allowing more and more magic to stream into them. The rate of his magic flow doubled. Then tripled. And then quadrupled. The Orb opened further, allowing more ether to flow. The tethers connecting the wyverns to the rocks grew brighter, and brighter, until Lucian could hardly look at them.

The rush of magic burning through him was unreal. It was like blue magma, and he knew without the Orb, it would have frayed his mind and body to a crisp. Even *with* the Orb, he could hardly control the two tethers, such the power behind them.

And if he lost control, he died.

The Orb pulsed like a beating heart. With every pulse came more ether, more power, more magic.

And that magic had to go *somewhere*.

With a guttural yell, Lucian released the tethers' tension, which had become a laser of blue light connecting the wyverns to the sharp rocks. The wyverns shrieked as they shot with incredible speed along those lines, the change in direction so fast and sudden that their bodies ripped apart in midair. Most of the wyverns' remains were pulled along toward those rocks, where they were impaled, while the rest of the bloody bits and viscera had been obliterated into a fine, red mist.

Lucian had no time to wonder at this power. To be *horrified* by it. The Orb was still beating like a heart, spewing more and more ether into him. Did this thing have *brakes*? He couldn't hold it in, and it had to go somewhere. He set a new anchor point on some nearby cliffs, in the direction he had come from, and a new focal point on the cliffs opposite those.

There was no time to think. He simply had to *do*. Holding this amount of magic for any longer would end him. He could feel the power of the Orb ebbing, the force of its pulses fading. He had to make sure every bit of it was streamed into the new tether.

Lucian held the tether as long as he could, until he could no longer maintain the stream.

He released, and with that action came a deafening crack. In a single moment, metric tons of rock ripped from the two cliff faces, guided by a crackling blue energy tether which looked more like lightning. The bright blue tether spread, diffusing into random rocks and debris, creating a storm of floating boulders that crashed into one another with thunderous booms. Small bits of rock rained from the sky, pelting Lucian's back.

He ducked behind a nearby boulder. For minutes, that rock rain fell in the slow motion of Psyche's gravity. His chest heaved, and though his eyes were open, he couldn't see a thing. When he tried to stream a light sphere, he didn't have a drop of ether left. Minutes later, the cliffs were *still* collapsing. He could only hope he was far enough to not be buried.

It was probably fifteen minutes before things settled down enough for him to poke his head above the boulder. He tried streaming a sphere again, but he could only do so long enough to see his immediate surroundings.

What he saw looked like a war zone. Blasted cliffs, craters, ground up rock about a meter deep in all directions, the tinge of ozone, as if that massive storm of tethers had burned the air itself. When his light sphere winked out after using the last of his ether, he was left in darkness under a star-filled sky.

All he could do was hope that such a raw display of power kept other wyverns away, rather than draw them like moths to a flame.

He reeled in disbelief, knowing he had done something that no mage could ever hope to do. None of it had been a lie or a hallucination.

He held one of the seven fabled Orbs of Starsea.

4

LUCIAN FORCED HIMSELF TO STAND, his legs shaking. He felt as if he were coming down off the hardest of hard drugs, every neuron fried to a crisp. An impenetrable fog made it hard to hold onto any thought for long. Despite feeling completely empty, he still needed shelter, and fast. He would not be able to handle another outburst of magic, and more shrieks were already echoing in the distance. It was impossible to tell just how far away they were, but he had no doubt they would be upon him soon.

He began searching the piles of rock and disintegrated boulders for somewhere to hide. Surely in all this mess, there was some hole he could crawl into. He'd have to risk it collapsing on him, because sleeping out in the open was simply not an option. He had to find a crevice large enough to fit into, but small enough that the wyverns couldn't reach him with their long talons.

After a few minutes of aimless searching, he found something that would suit well enough. He got on his belly and crawled inside like a worm, going as deep as he could until he was sure nothing from above could follow him in. Serah had mentioned they could sense heat, so he needed to go deep enough for them not to detect him. He couldn't create a fire, so he'd have to rely on the shelter of the rocks themselves.

There was always the danger he could be buried alive, and he didn't relish the thought. But as he saw it, this was his only option. He was simply too exhausted to run any farther.

Once deep enough, about five meters beneath the surface, he closed his eyes. Until he heard the crunch of feet on the rocks above.

"Lucian? I thought I saw something over here."

Serah? How in the Worlds had she found him? He remained as still as a mouse, unsure of where he stood with her after the Ramore incident.

"I can feel you around here," she said. "Too tired after your fight for a concealment ward, eh?"

Concealment ward? Lucian had never heard of such a thing. "What do you want, Serah?"

"Prickly, aren't you? You buried alive or something?"

"Something like that. Where's your friend?"

"I left him back in the cave. Sorry. He must have gotten jealous or something. He doesn't really have much impulse control these days, and it's been a while since I've seen how he acts around others."

She waited a moment, apparently waiting for him to accept the apology. He remained quiet.

"If you hold on a minute, I can lift up these rocks with an anti-grav disc. It'll probably kill me, but . . ."

"No!" Lucian said. "I'm not buried. Just hiding."

"Oh. Well, coast is clear for now. Can you get out of there so we can talk?"

Lucian considered a moment whether he could trust her. It didn't make sense that she would risk her neck just to hunt him down. So what *did* she want?

Lucian shimmied up through the rocks. The squeeze was so

tight that for a moment, Lucian believed he might be stuck. He could see Serah's bare, dirty feet above him, illumined presumably by a light sphere. He sucked in his breath, and pushed upward, scratching his torso in the process. The next moment, he was standing in front of her.

She gaped at the surroundings. "*You* did all this?"

Lucian looked around at the devastation, which was made even more apparent by the light of Serah's sphere. "Seems so."

"I saw the blue light from the cave," she said. "Either you're the best Binder this side of Sol, or the dumbest one."

"Probably the second."

"There's bloody bits of what looks like two wyverns on the rocks over there." She pointed with her chin.

"You'd be right about that. That was the focal point of the tether I made."

"How'd you manage to bind *two* beasts that size?"

Lucian decided to ignore that question. "Why did you follow me?"

"Well, I risked my neck to see if you were all right. As to the why, I don't know. I just follow my gut, and my gut said to come check on you." She smiled sheepishly. "Sorry again about Ramore. Like I said before, I guess he jumped to conclusions when he saw us together."

"Don't worry about it. Look, are we sitting ducks out here or what? What should we do? Because I'm not heading back to the cave."

"I don't know what sitting ducks are, but I think I know what you mean. I don't think getting us both out of here tonight is in the cards. Besides, the pass is buried now."

"Then how did *you* get over here?"

"I'm nimble as a rift goat, and my primary is Gravitonics. I'm almost good enough to fly." A shriek sounded in the night, to which Serah rolled her eyes. "*Great.* They got the scent of us now. You think that gap can hold us both?"

"Probably. It'll be tight, though."

"We've got to get in there before . . ."

Two more shrieks sounded.

"Rotting hell. Get in!"

Lucian let her go first. With the benefit of her sphere, it would be easier for him to make his way down. Serah wriggled quite adroitly, and he was soon following her path. She went to his former spot, as deep as it was possible to go. If Lucian followed her that low, they'd be rubbing elbows. Well, *more* than elbows. He was face-down in the tunnel, though, with no way to reorient himself so that he was facing above.

"You're too close to the surface," she said. "One of their claws might stick you."

It seemed there was little choice. He wanted to be as far from the surface as possible, and if that meant risking it right next to Serah, then so be it. Besides, if wyverns could truly detect body heat, he needed to be as low as he could get.

Lucian wriggled his way down, until he and Serah occupied the same cavity. He tried to create as much space as he could, but they were still shoulder-to-shoulder, lying on their backs in the gravel.

"Don't be bashful." He could hear her smile. "I won't bite."

Lucian ignored her. She let the sphere wink out, likely to conserve her ether. Lucian knew if those rocks above so much as shifted a centimeter, it could cause a chain reaction that would bury them both.

Even as Lucian tried to create more space, Serah didn't seem to be one for modesty. If anything, she snuggled *closer*. He almost told her to cut it out, but he had to admit, it was a cold night and all he had on was his prison jumpsuit. Sleep would come easier if he were warm.

They lay there in silence, with nothing but the sound of their breathing and the fading shrieks of wyverns. After five more minutes passed, it seemed the monsters had lost the scent, because there were no more shrieks.

Serah let out a sigh. "I think they're gone."

Lucian moved to head up to the surface but was restrained by Serah.

"Hold up! What're you doing, trying to get yourself killed?"

"You said they're gone."

"If you go back up there, they'll come back, mudbrain! You can't keep me warm if you're a dead body."

Lucian settled back. It appeared that this was reality, at least for the rest of the night. It was too dark to see her, anyway. Thankfully, she didn't smell too bad, mostly of smoke and earth. He was probably far worse. They only showered them on the *Worthless* once a week, and it had been a few days since his last one.

"I guess what they say about Earthers is true," she said.

She left that hanging, likely to get him to bite. "What do they say?"

"That you're all a bunch of prudes."

Lucian scoffed. "I'm no prude."

She gave a short laugh. "It's all right. Maybe you're just shy."

"I'm not shy."

She sighed. "Well, you're no fun. That one you can't argue with."

"This isn't a vacation."

"You're telling me. This is the first conversation I've had in months outside of Ramore's grunts and groans. Can't you indulge me just a *little* bit?"

Lucian was too exhausted for this back and forth. Then again, it didn't seem she was going to relent unless he gave her something.

"Sorry. Just not sure what to talk about."

"Tell me about Earth."

"What about it?"

"Paint me a picture. If you paint a picture nice enough, maybe I'll fall asleep."

Lucian had to repress a sigh. "I'm from Miami. It's a city in America. Lots of water, tall buildings. And people. Lots and lots of people."

"How many? A *thousand*?"

"Millions. Most of them clawing and fighting for survival, but some of them living the good life."

"Which one were you?"

"Clawing and fighting, of course."

"Good. That's the more interesting answer."

She scooched closer to him, until the entire sides of their bodies were touching. Lucian didn't stop her. They lapsed into silence for a while, and Lucian found himself getting a bit more comfortable. Even if she was fraying, she didn't seem dangerous.

"Tell me more," she said.

Lucian almost told her "no," but he found himself talking about home and himself and how he'd ended up at the Volsung Academy. She got bored of that pretty quickly, and asked him instead to describe various things about life on Earth. What people did, what they ate, what the men looked like there, what the women wore. Her questions were exhaustive.

"Let's just get some sleep, all right?" he said, once he'd had enough.

"I can't fall asleep next to a stranger. You're a dangerous prisoner, after all. An exile of the prestigious and exclusive Volsung Academy."

"I'm not dangerous. In fact, I was one of the worst Novices the Academy has ever seen. That's why they sent me here."

She laughed at that. "Really? The weakest mage of the Volsung Academy can kill two wyverns and bury the Snake Pass? Then I would like to see what the strongest could do."

He somehow had to get her off the scent. If she even

suspected what he had, he didn't know how she would react. "I don't know how I did what I did. Pure luck, I guess."

"Lucky *and* dangerous. I think you might have a secret."

She couldn't possibly know about the Orb. Then again, she had managed to detect him simply because he didn't know how to stream a "concealment ward." Was it possible she could detect the Orb, too? Was that the reason she was flirting with him, to lower his guard and try to steal it? To Lucian, it didn't seem likely, but he knew not to trust anyone.

"Remind me how it is you found me," Lucian said.

"I followed the light. And I followed the ripples in the ethereal field, which got me close enough to find you."

"The ripples? What do you mean by that, exactly?"

"So *demanding*. I might tell you. But you must promise to be nice from now on."

"I *am* being nice."

"Men always think they're being nice. But I regret to inform you that you're an unrefined brute, Lucian. You must listen to a lady when she speaks and give the appropriate response to whatever she says. You might be surprised how far that gets you."

He suppressed the urge to growl. Doing that would only make him sound like an unrefined brute. "Well, you're full of surprises. I'll give you that."

Her posture seemed to thaw a bit. "That's better. Well, Seeking is rather simple. Using Radiance, you can learn to feel flows of ether accumulating into a mage. Some are better at Seeking than others. When a mage doesn't want to be found, they can stream what's called a concealment ward, also using Radiant Magic. Done right, it keeps the mage from being sensed ethereally."

"I see," Lucian said. "Thanks for explaining."

"You're welcome." After a moment of silence, she continued. "I feel like I need to explain something else to you. You're from a warm climate, right, so customs are different. Here on Psyche, in the Upper Reaches, there's little firewood. All you have is warm bodies to keep from freezing. So, this is very normal to me. In fact, it's highly offensive to sleep separately from someone. It means you greatly dislike them, or you're mad at them, or you're just trying to insult them in some way."

She snuggled even closer. Well, now there was nothing he could do. If he tried to create some space now, then he would be "insulting" her.

"I think you're just making that up."

"Not at all."

"Then if Ramore were to see this, he'd be fine with it? Were you guys together or something?"

She giggled. "Well, I admit he probably wouldn't be fine. Then again, it's hard to live with someone who's in his state. He's . . . not right in the head anymore."

"Sorry about that."

"It's life," she said. "Well, thanks for humoring me. I think I'm ready to sleep now."

Her breaths were almost immediately even with sleep. Now that she *was* quiet, Lucian found he had a million questions for her, mostly about Psyche itself. Such information could save his life down the line.

But he was also tired. He closed his eyes, the warmth of her body lulling him to sleep.

———

WHEN THE MORNING'S rays illumined the underground shelter, he and Serah had somehow ended up holding each other, to the point where there was plenty of available space in the cavity. The air around them was cold, so the surface had to be even more frigid. After Volsung, though, nothing would ever feel truly cold to him. He had to admit her warmth felt good, but at some point it had to come to an end. He couldn't let himself enjoy it too much. He still wasn't sure of her, and likely wouldn't be seeing her again after today if she was still keen on leading him to Kiro.

Her eyes lazily opened, blinking in the light of the dusty sunbeams falling between cracks of rubble. She looked at him a moment, registering he was there, before shifting to stand and boost herself out of the hole. In a moment, all the warmth between them dissipated.

"Can't we sleep in a little longer?" he asked.

She gave a short chuckle. "Can't get enough of me now, huh? I would, sunshine, but we've got a long day ahead of us. Unless you intend to join me and Ramore back at the cave."

No, he most certainly didn't intend on that.

"We need to get moving. It'll warm you up, and it's coldest in the early morning, especially here in the Upper Reaches. The mountain air is thin. But we've got to get moving if you're to make Kiro before nightfall. And I'll need to find shelter for the night."

Lucian followed her out, finding that the gray daylight of the surface was indeed cold. They stood close, and despite her lack of layers, she didn't seem affected by the chill. A mountain woman, or perhaps a cavewoman, through and through.

"Are all women here like you?"

She laughed. "No. There's no one like me, not in all the Rifts of Psyche." She pointed toward the pass, which was now a mountain of rubble. "Today's task is getting out of this pass and on your way to Kiro. Thing is, they don't let just anyone in."

"So, how do I get let in?"

She pointed toward the sharp rocks Lucian had used to skewer the wyverns. He could see what remained of the wyverns' twisted, mangled corpses in the violet morning light.

"If we harvest a trophy from those, it might be enough to convince the Elders you're worth it. The venom in their fangs is especially prized. Not every mage can kill one of those things, after all."

"You have a knife to cut it?"

She produced a dark, obsidian knife. "This'll do. Once done, we'll be on our way. Ramore should be good on his own till tomorrow, and I know how to take care of myself. You don't live as long as me unless you know what you're doing."

"All right, then," he said. "Lead the way."

They began by hopping along the broken boulders toward the wyvern carcasses, a sort of dance in the low gravity. Though Serah never explicitly said, it seemed she was racing him. She was always one step ahead, adroitly leaping from one broken boulder to another, her blonde hair streaming behind.

"So, you still haven't told me," she called back. "How does a little mage boy like you tear down cliffs like this? If the Elders of Kiro ever hear of it, they'll think you're mad with the fraying."

Lucian stopped and feigned the need to breathe, to have more time to prepare his answer. "In life-or-death situations, people are capable of incredible things."

"That's a slippery answer if I've ever heard one. What'd they teach you on Volsung, and might I learn it?"

Lucian laughed, but thankfully, Serah seemed to tire of the subject soon enough. She was scaling the cliff leading up to the wyvern remains. Lucian took note of her path and followed her.

Despite where he was, and how dire the situation, he couldn't help but smile. At least here on Psyche there was some measure of freedom, even if he had almost died twice by now. At this rate, he wouldn't last long.

He knelt next to Serah, who was slicing off a fang with gusto. It was at least a full meter long. Lucian's stomach churned just watching.

"Try not to poke yourself with it," she said, handing it to

him. "Just a drop of that venom will paralyze you for hours. Two drops will kill you."

"What about the other fangs? Should be three more, right?"

"Well, if you wish to search for them, you are welcome to it. I'm not allowed to trade with the Deeprift Villages. Not officially, anyway. I'll come back later to harvest them." Her nose wrinkled. "For now, though, I'd rather step away from this stink."

They made their way down the cliffs, and Serah shared her water and food with Lucian. He marveled that she had thought to bring both with her last night; she likely never went anywhere without them, and for that he was grateful. He drank deeply from her canteen, while eating some mystery meat wrapped in some flatbread. He didn't want to ask what it was, but at this point, he didn't care. He was starving.

"Helpless as a babe," she said, her eyes playful.

"Would a baby have killed two wyverns?"

"No, probably not," she admitted. "It's just so easy to make fun of you. You rise to the bait every time. We should keep moving."

They picked their way over the boulders, taking most of the morning to get through the buried pass. It got a little brighter, and the clouds never really went away. Serah would stream antigrav discs for them to cross gaps more easily.

"Thought you said you could fly," Lucian said.

"*I* can. But I wouldn't want to leave you behind."

"Oh, I see. Well, why don't you give your arms a few flaps?"

She just gave a secretive smile. "Doesn't exactly work like that, but maybe someday."

They had now reached the same trail Lucian had followed last night. The sky, like yesterday, was filled with those strange, violet clouds, so thick that the sun was not visible.

"Does the sun ever come out?" Lucian asked.

She laughed. "If you go high enough. Of course, I hear the skies are clearer if you go Planetside."

"Planetside?"

"Psyche is tidally locked. You know what that means, right?"

"Of course."

"Well, we're Voidside right now. Psyche's atmosphere is thick, so you can't see the sun unless you scale the highest mountains. Which is impossible to do, as the air's only truly breathable in the rifts."

"So where are we in relation to all that?"

"Here, we might be a third of the way from the bottom." She pointed to the ridge behind her. "That might not look too high, but behind that ridge is one taller. That's how it is here. You can only see so far because of the haze. I don't really know what it's like on other worlds. I've only had it described to me."

"I wish I could show you South Shoal in Miami."

"I remember. Lots of sun and a whole ocean of water, right? Almost enough to make me think you were telling tales."

"Oh, it's very real." He noted her pale skin. "*You* would roast alive."

"Sounds lovely. Are there mountains in Miami, too?"

"It's flat," he said. "Lots of buildings and people."

She shuddered. "Oh, I would *hate* that. Sounds like Dara."

"Dara is the city you talked about, right?"

"Yes. The seat of the Sorceress-Queen of Psyche. It lies in the Golden Vale, just before the Mountains of Madness. You should be careful with anyone from the Golden Vale, Lucian. Their slavers sometimes come into the Riftlands, and you'll know them from their spears and armor of bronze. And their Mage-Knights wear colored robes and carry spears, too. If you see anything like that, you should run."

Lucian clearly had a lot to learn. "There's a queen here?"

She sighed and shook her head. "You ask too many questions. Just stay away from the Queen's slavers. They aren't often seen in the Riftlands, especially this deep, but we are eternally at war with them."

By late afternoon, Lucian could better see the interior of the rift plunging toward the fathomless depths below. Even in full daylight, that bottom was lost to distance. Looking upward, he could see the steep slopes of the mountains blocking out most sunlight. The terrain rose impossibly high until the tops were lost in a violet haze.

He could discern trails crisscrossing down each side of the rift, though there seemed to be no clear way across. There were trails hundreds of meters above and below them on both sides. Even some greenery was beginning to cling to the rift's sides, with tiny waterfalls that were quickly reduced to mist and cloud.

As they walked down the trail, Lucian couldn't help his curiosity. "Is the entire moon like this?"

"Hardly. Voidside is mostly mountains and rifts, like this. Usually there's a deep lake at the bottom of those rifts. They say the land gets flatter the farther Planetside you go. Once Planetside, you're beyond the Mountains of Madness and Dara, in what's called the Westlands. Beyond that, they say there's lands called the Fire Rifts. And beyond even that, with the planet Cupid taking up almost all the sky, is the Burning Sands. They say it's a hellish wasteland with no trace of water, with open cracks belching smoke and lava. Nobody in their right mind goes there."

"So, what you're saying is that *this* is the most habitable part of Psyche."

"No. That would be the Golden Vale, where Dara is located. It's warm enough from Cupid's extra light, with flatter land to build on and farm, and has some rivers. These are wild lands here. But it's here that we're safe from the Sorceress-Queen and her slavers."

Lucian wanted to ask more, but Serah seemed melancholy.

So, he was content to be quiet and take in the new world with his own eyes. After his cell on board the *Worthless*, Psyche might as well have been paradise. The land was harsh, but that harshness also had breathtaking beauty. It was the last thing he'd expected. He'd imagined something much like the Isle of Madness on Volsung, only worse.

But he knew for all its beauty, there was even more danger. The wyverns and Ramore were evidence of that, and that had only been his first day.

"Can I ask you a question?" Lucian asked.

"You just did."

"Why are you helping me? It has to be inconvenient, right?"

She sighed. "I have my reasons. Besides, no one survives here on their own. Not for long."

"*You* have."

"Not without help. People have taught me. My father . . ." She trailed off. Whatever it was she had been about to say, she decided it was better not to say it. From the prickly look on her face, Lucian didn't prod further.

They walked all afternoon, descending deeper into the rift. The gathering darkness was more due to the rift's sides blocking the sun than the onset of evening. Only a thin sliver of sky remained. Lucian wondered how *anyone* could live in such darkness. Perhaps there were fewer wyverns down here.

Serah was whistling a merry tune when Lucian spied two human forms round a bend. She gave no reaction, so Lucian figured it was safe. Lucian watched as they approached the two men, old, wizened, and weather-beaten. They each had a curious tattoo on their forehead, and his hackles rose at that. But Serah was still acting as if everything were normal. The brand was in the shape of a snake, or perhaps an eel. The old men stood aside to let them pass without a word, their wrinkled faces cautious and eyes suspicious.

"Good afternoon," Lucian said.

One shook his head disapprovingly, while the other clenched his jaw.

Once out of earshot, Lucian looked back. "Not friendly, are they?"

"No," Serah said. "Technically, you shouldn't even be speaking to me."

"Why is that?"

"Frays are outcasts. Shunned and forgotten. We can't speak to Rifter folk, nor can we trade with them. The Snake Rifters abide by the same laws as the Deeprifters. Most of them, anyway."

"That's harsh."

"In short, it would look bad if you were seen with me, so I'll let you go when you're close enough to be safe."

"When will that be?"

"Oh, about an hour or two. What, missing me already?"

But Lucian's mind was on other things. "You're taking a risk by helping me. What if those two men tell their rift about you and me?"

"They're from Snake Rift. Not really my concern."

"What are they doing out here, then? This is the Deeprift, right?"

She shrugged. "Not my business."

Lucian looked over his shoulder, but the two old men were lost to view. The mist had shrouded them.

It was hard not to feel bad for Serah. He kept that feeling to himself, though. Serah would be none too pleased with that sentiment. She walked proudly, almost *too* proudly, as if she were aware that Lucian saw her differently now.

"The social system here makes no difference to me," Lucian said. "In fact, it sounds a bit unfair. I'm not going to shun you, no matter what people say."

"If you want to be accepted by Kiro, then you must." They

walked a few steps more. "Let me tell you, I did my share of shunning in my day. Maybe I deserve it."

The rest of the trip continued in silence, and Lucian was left wondering what he did, or said. Until he realized that he was dealing with someone with a lot of pain and rejection. Maybe she was upset that he could go where she could not.

At some point, the trail leveled off into a long, narrow gorge. Lucian saw several large caves up in the cliffs, some of which had lights. Mountains towered almost vertically around them, with only a narrow sliver of clouded light shining down from what had to be kilometers above.

"This is where my path ends," she said. "They'll kill me if I take one step more."

She nodded toward a signpost with a symbol Lucian would have recognized anywhere – the Septagon, each point holding one of the Seven Aspects of Magic. It seemed to be a universal sign of mages, the Manifold, and magekind. He almost wanted to ask Serah about it to confirm, but her feet were already pointing up the trail. He didn't understand how she survived without shoes here, but somehow, she made it work. She still had a fair distance to walk back to the cave, and it looked as if she was ready to be off.

"This is where our paths part, Lucian. May the fraying be kept far from you, and sanity close at hand."

She turned to go, taking a few steps before Lucian called. "Hey!"

She half-turned. "What? Were you expecting a goodbye kiss?"

He blinked in surprise. "No. It's just . . . I don't know. Never mind."

She gave a small, sad smile. "Well, don't be too sad. We'll always have the wyverns. If for some reason they don't let you in, the valley here is generally safe from predators. There's probably some bush you can hide in until daylight."

"I hope it doesn't come to that."

"Quit your dallying. Don't tell them you met me. And when they ask how you killed the wyverns, don't mention how much you wrecked the pass. That'll lead to questions."

Again, he got the feeling she knew more than she let on. But he didn't want to explore that possibility.

"Goodbye, Serah. And thanks."

She nodded, then walked up the trail into the gathering gloom.

5

LUCIAN FOLLOWED the trail toward the light radiating from the massive cavern entrance. It was as Serah had said. A wooden wall, about five meters tall, together with a gate closed off the entire entrance. Two wooden outposts rose from beside the gate, each containing a guard wearing leather armor, each armed with a spear and bow. Lucian felt their eyes boring into him as he approached. He tried not to think about what a pathetic figure he cut in his prison jumpsuit, scraggly hair, and unkempt beard. Even for this world, he probably looked rough.

"Who goes there?" one of the guards called, who had a trim goatee. "What brings you to the gates of Kiro?"

Lucian held up a hand in what he hoped was a sign of peace. The guards stood straighter, each keeping a hand on the bow mounted to their backs. Seeing that, it took great effort for Lucian to not reach for his Focus. If they were mages, and anything like Serah, they might be able to detect it. It was basically the same thing as throwing up his fists.

"My name is Lucian," he said. "Lucian Abrantes. Yesterday, my pod crashed in the Upper Reaches. I followed the trail down here."

The guards exchanged a glance. The original one turned back to him. "And what do you want with Kiro?"

"Shelter," Lucian said. "It's getting dark, and I don't want to die to wyverns tonight."

"The wyverns don't hunt this low," the guard scoffed. "The thick air slows their flight too much."

"I didn't know that."

"It's lucky that you found us without the benefit of a guide. We've had reports of several pods falling in the Upper Reaches, but you would be the first to arrive at our gates."

The guard's tone said he was suspicious of Lucian's story. Serah had warned him not to say she had led him here, but Lucian had the feeling that this guard would accept nothing but the truth.

"I had help," he said. "I won't say who, though."

"We're not letting you in unless you *say* who, Off-Worlder."

"I told them I wouldn't say who they were. I'm just trying to honor my word."

The two guards looked at each other a moment before the first guard turned back to him. "Was her name Serah?"

Lucian remained silent.

"That answers my question. We know of her. It is forbidden to speak or deal with frays, Off-Worlder."

"I didn't know that," Lucian said. "She led me as far as the valley, stopping at the sign. She pointed me the rest of the way."

The first guard watched him for a long moment. That guard held his fate in his hands. With just a word, he could give him life or death. He was tempted to argue his case, but it was better to hold his tongue. He'd learned from the Transcends that sometimes the best thing you could do was keep your mouth shut.

After a painstaking half minute or so, the guard licked his lips again. "Well, at least you're being honest. Our scouts reported a new arrival farther up the rift, along with who he was traveling with."

Lucian wondered what else they knew. Could they know about the wyverns, or how he'd killed them? He didn't see how it was possible.

Lucian retrieved the wyvern fang tied behind his waist, which was almost long enough to drag along the ground. He held it up high and hoped the guards could see it well enough in the gathering darkness.

"I was attacked by two wyverns near the Snake Pass. A nearby landslide roused them. I fought them off and harvested one of the fangs, on the advice of the fray." It felt wrong to call her that, but it seemed the guard expected it of him. "She said such a thing would be of value to you."

Again, the two guards stared down at him. They stared so long that Lucian feared that they wouldn't answer him. Had all this been for nothing? His heart pounded in his chest. It was getting cold. Even if this valley was safer than higher altitudes, he did not want to pass the night in the open.

Keeping his mouth shut was difficult, but he reached for his Focus without touching his ether. He needed calm, and decided the risk was worth it. He watched the guards carefully, to see if there was any reaction. Their faces remained stoic. Lucian didn't think they could detect him doing this. In fact, they didn't seem like mages at all. Certainly, not everyone on this world would be one.

"Wait here," the guard finally said.

He disappeared behind the wall, while the other stood watch, wary of any move.

Lucian waited a good ten minutes before the wooden gate creaked open, revealing a delegation of four men, all dressed in leathers and wielding shockspears. They walked forward as a single unit, though one of them hung back a few paces, older and prouder than the rest. He had long, shaggy hair the color of ash, and in addition to his leathers, he wore thick necklaces of bone and had earrings crafted of what appeared to be wyvern talons, at least a quarter of a meter long. In a higher gravity, those talons would have been unbearable to wear. His sharp nose reminded Lucian of a hawk, and his eyes were similarly shrewd, like a bird of prey.

He took quick note of the other men surrounding him, strong warriors all, well-muscled and having the look of discipline. But one of those guards stood closer to the leader, stronger and taller than the rest, with skin of onyx and a square jaw that seemed to be cut from granite. The eyes that peered at Lucian were not friendly.

"Hands where we can see them," the man said, the command brooking no argument.

Lucian held up his hands. "I have no weapons. They took my spear on the barge."

They patted him down all the same, making quick work of it. The dark-skinned man was rougher than the rest, even pushing him away lightly. Lucian almost stumbled. His eyes were cutting. What was this guy's deal?

"Don't try anything," the guard said. "We'll counter you faster than a sand shrike."

"Didn't plan on it."

The guard grunted and motioned the others to stand back. At this moment, the long-haired leader stepped forward, arms crossed below his broad, hairy chest. Age hadn't done much to take his musculature away. His face was stoic, appraising, and weather-beaten.

"Let me see the fang, young man."

Lucian held it out, but the old man made no move to take it. He extended his palm, which became wrapped in an aura of blue light. Lucian's eyes widened at the unexpected streaming of magic, but the man was not attacking him. He was drawing the fang toward him – slowly and carefully, so that it landed bottom-side down. Once he grasped it, he inspected it all around, before giving a curt nod.

"Unspoiled," he said, approvingly. "They often bite themselves before the moment of death. It's as if they know why we hunt them."

He nodded at one of the guards, who took the fang and ran back toward the gate.

"Hey," Lucian said. "That was mine."

"Are you saying you wish to have your gift back?"

Gift? Now, Lucian was in an awkward position. It would look bad if he asked for it back. And what would he do with it, anyway?

"It's yours," Lucian said. "Now, I need—"

The man held up a hand, cutting him off. "Talk less, son. You'll dig less holes that way."

He nodded to his guards, who seemed to relax a bit. The only one who didn't was the tall, lead guard, who stood closer.

"The gate guard told me you killed two wyverns," the long-haired man said.

Lucian nodded. "Yes, sir."

"But I only counted one fang."

"I left the rest for the one who helped me."

The old man seemed to stiffen at that, and his face became strangely sad. "Serah, you mean."

"Yes."

He gave a chuckle. "She made out like a bandit, then. She probably followed you to see how the fight would go, expecting you to fall and take your things. She must have been very desperate to do that."

"I had nothing to take. I think she was just trying to help."

"She would do that, too. If she felt the inclination." The old man scrutinized him. "Your story will be verified, of course. Our scouts have already reported the landslide at the Snake Pass.

Now, you didn't happen upon these dead wyverns on the way down here, did you?"

"Of course not," Lucian said, hotly. "I killed them myself."

"Not an easy thing to do, that. Our greatest warriors have trouble with even one wyvern, though you rarely find one on its own. The husband and wife always hunt together."

"So I've heard."

"I'll tell you what," the old man said. "The truth will be known in time. Until then, I have a cot and a hut for you. And yes, three square meals a day." He held up a finger. "On one condition."

Lucian arched an eyebrow. "What's that?"

"Two conditions, actually. That your worth is tested by becoming one of my watchmen."

The men around him stared at their leader in shock, the big guard even shooting Lucian a scowl. The old man carried on, regardless.

"And the other condition is that you take a bath and shave that *god-awful* beard."

Lucian couldn't help but smile. "Done. And done."

"Very well. Then welcome to Kiro Village. There is one last thing: our Elder of Medicine needs to check you for signs of fraying. But you don't have the look of a fray to me."

"Elder," the black guard said. "Is it really wise to give one so young so much responsibility as a watchman, especially given the dubious nature of his story?"

"If he's lying, then that will become obvious quite soon, and in an embarrassing way, I imagine. Any man who can take down *two* wyverns and live to tell the tale should wipe the floor with any of my warriors." The leader shot a glance at the guard. "Even you, Captain Fergus."

Fergus's face became a mask of anger, while his meaty hand tightened on his shockspear. No, Lucian did not like that. Not at all. But he didn't want to correct the Elder.

"Come," the Elder said. "My name is Ytrib, the High Elder of Kiro." He turned to Fergus. "See that he's fed and kept separate for now. In two hours, he can give his Accounting."

Accounting? Lucian didn't like the sound of that. But it wasn't as if he had a choice.

Fergus clenched his jaw, but in the end, nodded his head regally. "Of course, Elder Ytrib."

When Elder Ytrib turned back for the gate and the other guards followed, Fergus held back for a moment, staring daggers at Lucian. "I've got my eye on you, Off-Worlder. Perhaps he believes your story, but I'm not so easily swayed."

"You can verify my story yourself. Go to the Snake Pass and you'll find the wyvern bodies on the rocks."

"I need not do that," Fergus said, with a dangerous smile. "As captain of the Kiro Watch, I'll be personally responsible for your training. I doubt you could last five minutes against even the least of my warriors." He eyed Lucian disdainfully. "You have the look of softness about you. And soft men don't survive Psyche long."

With a smug expression, he turned and marched back toward the gate, where the other guards were waiting to escort Lucian.

Lucian sighed. Things just couldn't get better without getting worse.

6

LUCIAN WALKED through the gates of Kiro Village to find something far from expected.

These were no mere cave-dwellers. There were buildings, several dozen of them straddling two sides of a deep, underground stream. Most of those buildings were of mud-toned brick, but there were also larger tents and pavilions, as well as hollowed spaces and tunnels in the cavern's sides. Fires and torches lent an orangey ambiance, though that light was not enough to completely conquer the gloom. In the cool, damp air wafted the aroma of roasting meat and spices, setting Lucian's stomach to growling. The stream ran the length of the cavern, deeper into the mountain, its source apparently a spring. The village lay on both sides of that stream, on various cliffs and tiers, connected by a bewildering network of platforms, ladders, boardwalks, and rope bridges. A particularly long rope bridge connected both sides of the village that were separated by the stream.

At the very back of the cave was a large brick building, the only one that was two stories. This village had to hold at least a hundred people, if not more.

"This way, Off-Worlder," Captain Fergus said, leading the way and using his spear as a walking stick. Unlike Lucian's old spear on the Isle of Madness, his appeared to be made from bronze, and it almost certainly didn't self-retract.

Lucian hurried after him.

A gaggle of laughing children ran across their path, all looking at Lucian. Two women paused their work drawing water at the stream, watching Lucian go by while speaking in hushed whispers. Two old men sat on the porch of a nearby house on stilts. They were smoking something or other, while following Lucian's passage with their eyes.

"I take it this place doesn't really get off-worlders," Lucian said, trying to break the ice.

Fergus remained silent.

Lucian cleared his throat. "Where are you taking me, Fergus?"

"*Captain* Fergus to you. We have an empty hut in the back of the village. You can stay there. For now."

His tone clearly implied Lucian wouldn't last long. Lucian bit back the sharp remark that wanted to come. He had to be on his best behavior, and he needed this place to survive. After he was settled in, he could figure out his next move.

Their path wound through the left bank of Kiro, a trail of wooden slats buried in dirt forming the main drag. They passed numerous homes and buildings. They also passed several of the town's inhabitants, most of them dressed in well-worn leather clothing. Some also wore clothing that seemed to be made from a material similar to cotton or flax, if more roughly made than what Lucian was used to seeing. All they had here were the resources of this world, along with the ingenuity to make something of them. Lucian was further impressed when his path took them by a water mill, after which was a steep drop ending in a waterfall.

The waterfall tumbled into an underground lake, around

which were a few more buildings, but the torchlight ended there, probably signifying the end of Kiro. The larger, two-story building was on the opposite bank, and it seemed one could reach it by taking the path by the mill, toward the long rope bridge.

They descended a steep set of steps that took them to the cavern floor. They were deep enough in the cave that it would have been pitch black if not for the copious amount of burning torches. Fergus led Lucian to the very last building, what Lucian suspected was the least desirable home in the village, since it was the farthest from everything.

"This is it," Fergus said. "I hope it'll do."

"It beats sleeping outside."

"Humph. Well, you can put your things . . ." Fergus looked him over, before realizing Lucian didn't *have* any things. "You can put *yourself* inside until it's time for you to give your Accounting."

"What's the Accounting, again?"

"It's your chance to address yourself to the community, and the Elder Council decides whether or not you can stay."

"If I stay, will you stop calling me Off-Worlder at least?"

"You've already been accorded more respect than you're due. Off-Worlder."

"What do you have against me, Fergus?"

His expression darkened. "*Captain* Fergus. I will tell you straight up. I don't believe a word of what you've said. What are you, sixteen in standard years?"

"Twenty-one. Maybe twenty-two, I don't know."

"Really?" This news seemed to be a shock to him. "And an Earther by the sound of your accent."

"Have you met many Earthers, Captain?"

"One too many," he said, drolly. "Get yourself cleaned up. When using your chamber pot, make sure you're well downstream of where folks draw their water. Once done, come to the bonfire outside the meeting hall."

"Is that the big building?"

"Yes, the big building. You have an hour. Don't be late."

Fergus left, and Lucian was glad for it. He hoped he wouldn't have to deal with him much longer.

He went inside the hut and streamed a light sphere, finding the inside to be surprisingly accommodating. There was a small table and chair, carved with able skill and craftsmanship, if not much artistry, and on top of the table stood several candles. The cot along the wall looked quite tempting, and Lucian had to stop himself from lying down. If he did that, he wasn't going to be waking up for a long time.

What did Elder Ytrib expect of him? Apparently, the fang wasn't enough of a ticket of admittance. His stomach churned at the thought of talking in front of the entire village, but he had certainly been through worse. Alone in this hut, his false bravado meant nothing. Soon enough, they'd find out the fraud he was. Captain Fergus had mentioned pitting him against some of his warriors. Surely *that* couldn't be happening tonight. If it did, then he would be out on his ass within a couple of hours.

Even if he didn't have to prove himself in battle, he was expected to speak in front of everyone. He'd never been one for speeches, and his throat was raw from all the talking he had done with Serah. After not using his voice for so long, his speech was a bit rough. First impressions were everything, and it was important that this community accept him . . . at least for now. The alternative was starvation and death. That was, if he wasn't killed by a fray or wyvern first.

He pushed these thoughts from his mind as he streamed a small bit of heat into the candle wick, allowing the sphere to wink out. He used that candle to light the others, finding a leather tunic, pants, and boots waiting for him by the hammock. How had they had time to prepare all this? Things seemed to work fast around here. He just hoped the clothing fit him. On the table was a bowl and a straight razor, seemingly made from flint. There was a bowl of . . . *something* . . . next to the razor. It looked like lard. It seemed Elder Ytrib had been quite serious about the beard coming off tonight.

Lucian shaved using the paltry light of the candles. He had applied the animal fat and got the idea to use the surface of the lake outside to see his reflection. The water was smooth enough to somewhat see what he was doing, though he had to stream a light sphere again to do it. He had to go slowly, to ensure he didn't cut himself. He tried to ignore some women drawing water near the waterfall who seemed to be looking his way. Well, he was downstream, so his hair wouldn't float toward them. He had already lost most of it to the dark void of the cave.

Once done, he was surprised at how clean-shaven he was. The stone blade was sharp and well-made. The face staring back from the lake's surface shocked him. He was rail-thin, with new lines that made him look five years older. How had Fergus ever thought he was sixteen? He looked thirty. The man staring back was no longer the boy who had left Earth. He'd come a long way, but he still had so much farther to go.

That was, of course, only if he could survive the Mad Moon.

The two women by the waterfall had left, leaving the lake-front empty. He retrieved his clean clothes from inside the hut and placed them on the shore, letting his light sphere wink out. Then, in the darkness, he stripped off his clothes and slipped into the lake. The water was colder than anything he had ever felt since Volsung, but he needed a bath. He washed himself as best as he could without the aid of soap. Once done, he went to the shore and stood naked and shivering, wondering how he would dry himself. He settled for swiping with his hands. He couldn't stand the cold air any longer, so he stepped into his new clothes. They were rough and itchy, but infinitely better than the disgusting prison jumpsuit he had been wearing. He wasn't sure what to do with his old clothes. They needed to be burned, but he set them on the chair in the hut. Maybe someone could find a use for them.

Lucian donned a pair of socks along with his new leather boots. The rough, flaxen shirt felt scratchy on his skin, but he supposed he'd have to get used to that. The outfit was colorless, looking like something out of medieval times. There was no auto-tailoring here with nanotech, no changing colors. It would have to do.

He judged about half an hour had passed since Fergus left, but it would be wise to be early. He was no longer cold from his dip, and was actually feeling refreshed, if exhausted. As he walked up the shoreline toward the main village, he couldn't help but feel as if he were in a dream.

He ascended the stairs leading to the main part of the village, brushing past people on his way. No one talked to him. He was still an off-worlder, and apparently unwelcome. Even if people didn't talk *to* him, he could see they were talking *about* him – from porches, from inside homes, from narrow alleys. There were even people pointing from across the stream on the opposite end of the village. It seemed all of Kiro knew he was here.

He headed to the rope bridge spanning the stream. It swung back and forth as he walked across carefully, trying to ignore the frothing white water beneath. He heaved a sigh of relief once he reached the other side.

He wasn't the only one heading toward the meeting hall. There were young people about his age, middle-aged laborers, and older folks as well. There was an entire community here, probably one of many taking up residence in Psyche's rifts. And in a tight-knit community like this, Lucian knew it was hard to be accepted. They had likely known each other all their lives.

And yet, this was what was expected of him. And he needed

to stay alive. He knew he should try to be more friendly, but he was just too exhausted. When he looked directly at the towns-folk, it seemed as if they were focusing on anything else. And yet when his eyes went forward, he could feel their eyes return to *him*. The only exception were two girls about his age, who giggled when they saw him. They walked on ahead, laughing the entire time. Well, it seemed no matter where he went, girls would be girls. It was a strange thing to find comfort in.

A hand clapped on his shoulder, causing him to jump. He turned to see a balding, bearded man in his middle years, with a swarthy gut and hairy forearms. How a man of his heft could sneak up on him, Lucian could never guess.

"Were you looking at my daughter?"

Lucian sputtered. "Err, no sir. They were just laughing at me, so it drew my attention."

The man gave him a deadened glare, and then suddenly broke into a laugh. "I'm just messing with you, son." He nodded ahead. "Bonfire's that way. Need me to show you there?"

Lucian nodded, still reeling. "Yeah, sure."

"Keep your head forward, and your eyes focused on those flames," the man counseled. "And stop making eyes at the girls here."

Making eyes? He wanted to protest but he knew it was useless to argue.

"Name's Kieron Wardley. I'm the village smith."

Lucian almost said he could tell from his burly appearance and hairy forearms, but he refrained. He was getting too tired for his own good. Unfortunately, he would have to speak at length soon while not sticking his foot in his mouth.

Lucian and Kieron passed some of the nicer buildings of Kiro, including the smithy Kieron must have owned. He could feel the heat emanating from the open-air forge. Lucian wondered just what kind of things he made here. He hadn't seen much in the way of metals in this place, outside the guards' bronze shockspears. And why bronze, anyway? Maybe this world was iron-poor, or maybe they didn't have the capacity to get their fires hot enough.

They had now arrived at the bonfire, the flames about twice Lucian's height. There were around twenty people gathered so far, and all conversation went silent at Lucian's approach. He stood still for a moment. Should he wave or something?

"Your seat's over there," Kieron said in his deep voice, pointing a meaty hand at the opposite end of the flame. There was a wooden chair, separated from the rest of the assembly, while the rest of the seating was arranged on the other side.

He watched in silence as the village filled the chairs up, including the two girls he had seen earlier. He kept his eyes far away from them. Captain Fergus, along with some of his guards, stood right outside the meeting hall entrance just a few meters away. From within that building, Lucian could smell spiced meat and the aroma of freshly baked bread. His stomach rumbled. He hadn't eaten since Serah had shared some of her breakfast, and that hadn't been much at all. He was so hungry that he was feeling somewhat lightheaded and nauseated. Hopefully, this was over and done with quickly.

His eyes flicked back to the pretty, dark-haired girl, who he guessed to be Kieron's daughter. *Why* was he looking at her again? Exhaustion and nervousness were a poor combination.

At last, the murmuring of the crowd died at the sound of approaching footsteps. It took every ounce of will for Lucian not to turn. He wondered whether he should stand, but decided to remain seated. There were still five empty chairs, placed slightly in front of the rest. Elder Ytrib and another elderly man with a long, gray beard sat down, along with three women. All the women wore their hair long, their bone jewelry clanking on their necks and from their ears. Lucian noticed what looked like the tip of the wyvern fang he'd given to Ytrib was now part of the Elder's necklace. That might be a point in Lucian's favor.

The following silence was thick, and the only thing that could be heard was the crackle of flames and the rush of the stream. Lucian wiped a bead of sweat trailing down his brow. The heat of the flames was almost unbearable. Or was that only his nerves?

At once, Elder Ytrib withdrew his spear, which made Lucian go stiff in his seat. But he only rapped it three times on the rocky ground beneath.

"Rise, Outsider. Your Accounting has begun."

Lucian swallowed the lump in his throat and rose. He hoped he hadn't missed a spot shaving. Is that why the blacksmith's daughter was smiling with the mischievous eyes? He needed to stop looking at her.

"You may begin your address."

Instantly, a hundred pairs of eyes went on him. Lucian cleared his throat, hoping that whatever he said, he didn't sound stupid. He wasn't good at being judged, as his fatal audience with the Transcends had clearly shown.

"First, my name is Lucian. Lucian Abrantes. In case you didn't already know. I'd like to thank you and your people for your hospitality. I landed two days ago way up in the Upper Reaches. Um, I crashed, to be more accurate. Hopefully, all of you will allow me to stay here until I get my bearings." He gave a nervous laugh. Everyone remained silent. "Well, I'm honored to be here, and would be happy to answer any questions you might have."

"The Elders will be asking the questions," one of the female Elders said, primly. Her long gray hair and hawkish gaze reminded him too much of Transcend White, and of course, Vera. Like those two, he got the sense that she was a powerful mage indeed. "I will begin. Are you frayed, Outsider?"

"No," he said. Why were they staring as if he were lying? "At least, not to my knowledge. I've been told it's hard for a fray to know they are fraying until the signs are obvious."

"And *are* they very obvious?"

"Err . . . no. Not by my estimation. There's no rot, and I can still think straight."

"We shall soon see about that."

An icy silence followed this statement. Lucian tried to ignore all the eyes on him.

Elder Ytrib was next to speak. "Give your Accounting, Outsider. That was only an introduction. Choose your words well."

As if he wasn't already trying his best to do that. "I will, Elder." He licked his lips. "As I said before, my pod crashed two days ago in the Upper Reaches. It took me a couple of days before I could find my way down—"

"How did you find Kiro?" one of the other female Elders interrupted. Of the three women, she had the most bone jewelry around her thin neck, adorning her hair, piercing her nose, ears, and mouth.

"A fray led me here. A girl."

Elder Ytrib held up a gnarled hand, and Lucian stopped speaking at once. "You need not name her. We know the details."

Some in the crowd started whispering at that. There was something he was missing. Serah was known here, which made sense, considering she used to live here. That meant these very people had exiled her once upon a time, and associating with her might be a point against him.

The other male Elder, who had a long, narrow face and dark skin, broke his silence. "Why don't you tell us some of your history, Outsider. Who you are, where are you from, and what brings you here?"

"Yes, I should have done that at the start. My name is Lucian, as I said before. I'm from Earth."

That made the crowd whisper even more, as if Earth were some mythical place that people only heard rumors about. In this backwater of a backwater, he might as well have said he had come down from heaven itself. If only these people knew that Florida was closer to a drowned, watery hell than heaven, they might change their opinion.

He gave them the basics – how the League had identified him as a mage and forced him to go to Volsung. How the Transcends there had exiled him for failing the Trials. That was a bit of a lie, but he didn't want to get into specifics. He told them a bit of the Isle of Madness, as well as his choice to come to Psyche rather than remain there. All watched him with rapt attention, none so much as the Elders. Captain Fergus from beside the Elders' chairs didn't bother hiding his scowl.

"You know the rest. I came down here, killing two wyverns on the way. And now I stand here before you."

Lucian waited an inordinately long time. The fire crackled, the stream ran, and everyone just watched him, as if waiting for him to break under the pressure. At last, Elder Ytrib broke the silence.

"All that's very well. Now, how do you think you might best serve the village?"

Now was the chance to make his case. "I'm a hard worker. I won't complain. I'll do any task that's given to me. I'm used to that type of thing, especially from my time as a Novice in the Volsung Academy."

"And yet the Transcends exiled you."

"That's true," Lucian said. "I made some mistakes. But I believe I've learned from them."

Elder Ytrib held up a hand. "All right, all right. Well, I think you've said enough, unless you have anything further to say?"

Lucian felt the tension go out of his shoulders, at least somewhat. His part was done. Now, all he had to do was wait. "I think I've said what I wanted to say."

"Well," said the heavily pierced woman, "he seems harmless. In need of a hot meal, and it's not like us to turn someone away, especially when they've already given a gift of immense value."

Lucian assumed she was referring to the wyvern fang Serah had sawn off for him. "I can fight, too. If it comes down to it."

The Elders stared hard at him, and Lucian knew he had made a mistake by opening his mouth. He had to treat these Elders as if they were Transcends. Do not speak unless spoken to. Of course, he could only hope these Elders didn't treat him the same way the Spectrum had.

"I concur," the first woman said, who looked like Vera. "We should give him a chance. See if his story holds up."

"I also agree," the youngest of the three women Elders said. She had more black in her hair than gray, along with a plump figure.

That left the two men, who exchanged a glance before one of them broke the silence.

The tall, mournful one with dark skin stroked his beard. "Not an easy thing, to take on someone when things have been so hard. But supposing what he contributes is greater than what he takes, I'm for it."

"It's settled, then." Elder Ytrib stood, and broke into a wide, gap-toothed smile while holding out a hand. "If you'll join us, Lucian, then welcome to Kiro."

Lucian approached and took it, feeling a relief such as he had never known. "Thank you, Elder Ytrib. Thank you, Elders."

"Save your fawning," the hawkish woman said. "I'm Elder Jalisa. I guess you might call me the village Seer. My gifting is prophecy and Psionics."

The other Elders introduced themselves. The thin woman with the bone jewelry approached. "And I'm Elder Sina. I'm something of an herbalist. If you're sick, I'm the one who will treat you."

Lucian nodded respectfully to both.

The sorrowful-looking man approached. "I'm Elder Erymmo. It's nice to have a fellow Earther among us."

"There is no nationality or planetary affiliation among us," the quiet, portly female Elder said, approaching. "We are one community here and one blood. Now and forevermore." She favored Lucian with a welcoming smile. "I'm Elder Gia. Elder Ytrib is my husband."

Elder Ytrib wrapped an arm around her.

The Elders turned, as if of one unit, to include the rest of the assembly. "Come. Let's feast, and make our new brother, Lucian, welcome."

Lucian was swarmed. First by the children, who jumped around him like jackrabbits, and then the adults, who gave more sedate introductions.

Once that was done, there was nothing but to join the stream of people entering the meeting hall.

7

INSIDE, a veritable feast had been spread on a large mat on the floor. It seemed that Lucian had nothing to be afraid of at all. His acceptance had probably been a foregone conclusion. The interior of the meeting hall was spacious and well-lit, containing a large lower floor and a small upper loft made from wood. People took up spots around the food right there on the floor, all laughing and talking.

Kieron grabbed Lucian's arm. "Come. Sit with us."

Lucian followed him in a daze. Being around so many people like this was so foreign to his recent experience that he didn't know how to process it. People were shouting his name, especially the children. It was more noise than he'd dealt with in a long time. More *life* than he had experienced since . . . well, *ever*. This would not be one of the more reserved meals at the Volsung Academy, that was for sure.

Lucian sat next to Kieron and tried to ignore the dark-haired daughter that had been eyeing him earlier, who sat next to another young woman, the one she had been walking with toward the bonfire. Next to Kieron sat a pretty middle-aged woman, long and willowy, who watched him with hooded eyes.

"Lucian," Kieron said. "This is my wife, Julia."

Lucian wasn't sure of the mannerisms here, so he nodded his head and smiled. "Pleased to meet you."

Kieron's daughter and her friend giggled at that, and Lucian's cheeks flushed.

"Girls, be kind to our guest," Julia said, shooting them a look of warning. Her voice was melodic and calming to listen to. "Why don't you introduce yourselves?"

Kieron's daughter stifled her giggles long enough to give an answer. Her dark eyes were mischievous. "Morgana."

"I'm Myra," the other girl said, shyly. Her eyes were wide and blue, and her hair copper-red.

"Nice to meet you both," Lucian said.

Morgana only watched with a slight smile. There was something strange about her eyes, but Lucian couldn't tell what it was. He wished she would stop looking at him like that. If she kept it up, it was going to be an awkward meal.

Thankfully, neither of her parents seemed to notice the behavior.

"Why don't you serve our guest, girls?" Kieron asked. "He's had a rough couple of days, I'd imagine."

The girls didn't snicker this time, instead doing exactly as Kieron asked.

While the girls were away, Kieron leaned closer. "As you can see, we don't often have guests in the village. The excitement can last for weeks."

"I see," Lucian said. "Are most of you natives of Psyche?"

Kieron nodded. "We've a couple of mages from other worlds. Elder Erymmo is an Earther like you. Captain Fergus is from Irion, and Elder Jalisa from Hephaestus Station. All three were sent here by prison barge, albeit years ago. But the rest of us are Psyche born and raised."

"Even Elder Ytrib?"

"Aye," Kieron said, with a nod. "Elders Ytrib, Gia, and Sina are descendants of the first colony, settled over a century ago. It'll be nice to have another mage among us. Of course, the Elders are all mages, and some of the watchmen can stream, too. We have ten mages in all."

"Really? I thought there would be more."

Kieron had a laugh at that. "Oh, nothing like that. I'd say mages are about half-in-half from other Worlds or born here. Of course, anyone, mage or not, must give an Accounting before the village can accept them. There have been . . . *mistakes* . . . in the past."

"I see."

Julia smiled. "As long as your words are true, you have no need to worry."

At that moment, Morgana and Myra returned, setting down clay plates in the middle of the group. There was a haunch of meat from *some* animal Lucian couldn't begin to guess, though it looked like mutton. Could it be they had Terran livestock here, perhaps descended from the original colony? Whatever the case, the meat was covered with some sort of red sauce and was served next to a large bowl of mixed vegetables, some recognizable and some not. Another plate contained puff pastries, along with a green dipping sauce. There were kebabs of creatures that looked like shrimp, or whatever the local equivalent was.

He noticed there was no silverware, either, though there were bowls of warm water spread at regular intervals. He assumed it was for washing before and after eating.

At this point, Lucian didn't care *what* or how the people of Psyche ate. He had never felt so ravenous in his life.

He let them take the lead and watched as they washed their hands and filled his plate, with hands as he had suspected. When Julia gave it to him, he thanked her, and it took all his self-control to wait for everyone to get their own food. When he finally started eating, every eye was on him, watching for his reaction. When he took a bite of the spicy meat, an explosion of flavor, he had never tasted anything as good in his life.

"That's incredible."

Julia's cheeks colored. "I'm glad you like it. It's an old family recipe."

"My wife is the best cook in the village," Kieron said. "She organized the feast tonight."

"I never tasted anything half as good in my life, and that's the truth."

"You flatter me."

Morgana shifted in a bid to get his attention. "Is it really true you killed *two* wyverns?"

Everyone watched him expectantly. Even people in other groups overheard the question and went quiet to listen.

"I did," Lucian said, though he thought it wise not to add more details.

"How'd you do it?" Morgana asked.

Lucian had to be careful here. Of course, with the Orb, he had access to an incredible amount of magic. He couldn't reveal the truth of how he'd brought those monsters down. He didn't want anyone to suspect him in the least. "It all happened fast, so it's hard to remember. I'm lucky to have survived."

"No doubt," Julia said. "We live in fear of those monsters. They are the main reason we can't ascend the Upper Reaches."

"That's it?" Morgana asked, her face disappointed. "No details?"

Lucian saw he wasn't getting out of this. Even as they were watching him, he noticed Captain Fergus had sidled closer, though he made it look as if he was talking to one of his guards. Lucian had the feeling that every word he said would be judged.

"Well, I crashed high in the mountains and started heading down to the valley. The Deeprift, I guess you would call it. As it started getting dark, I saw this cave with a light. I went inside, thinking there were people. Well, I did find people, but they were two frays."

Morgana gasped at the revelation. For a world known for its maddened mages, she seemed unduly shocked that he had come across a couple of them. Lucian found that curious. Perhaps the life they lived down here in the rift was sheltered.

"Anyway, one of them was far gone. A Burner, I guess is what you would call him. He streamed some Thermal Magic at me, and I barely held up. I had no choice but to run, despite the fact it was night." He had gathered quite the audience by now. He didn't want to be the center of attention, but it was impossible *not* to be. He tried to ignore Fergus, who was openly glaring. "It was full-on dark by now, so I had to stream myself a light sphere to see. That's when I heard them coming. Screeches you could hear from klicks away."

"Curious," Fergus said, taking a few steps closer. "Wyverns are known for utter silence when hunting their prey. That is what makes them so dangerous. You never truly see them coming."

All went quiet as they looked at Lucian for an explanation. He turned to Fergus and tried to answer as calmly as he could. "These two weren't. I could hear their shrieks for a long time before they ever showed up."

"Then they've hunted like no wyverns *I've* ever heard of," Fergus said. "And I've hunted quite a few myself."

"Yes, with help," Morgana said, fervently. "Lucian did it all by himself!"

Why couldn't she keep her mouth shut? Lucian kept his face neutral, but he could tell some were doubting him. It was the last thing he needed. Fergus was a respected man in the village while Lucian was an outsider, and Morgana was defending him for her own reasons. And if it *was* true that wyverns were silent when hunting, why hadn't they been when attacking Lucian?

"Did he do it all by himself?" Fergus asked. "I wonder. Perhaps he happened upon a dead one in the rockslide of Snake Pass, I don't know. It doesn't matter. We will learn of this young mage's skill soon enough. The truth has a way of coming out eventually."

With that Fergus left, engaging in conversation with Elder Gia as if nothing had happened.

"I'm not lying," Lucian said, turning back to Kieron and his family.

"We know that," Kieron said. "Fergus is top mage here, but we all saw that fang you brought Elder Ytrib. A wyvern like that wouldn't have been careless enough to die in a rockslide."

Lucian was glad at least he could see the truth.

"That said," Kieron went on, "even if the fang was quite large, it was still not the biggest we've ever seen. Fergus hunted a wyvern several months back that was quite a bit bigger."

"Did he, now?" Lucian wondered why Kieron was bringing this up.

"That's true," Julia said. "*That* one was probably the largest we've seen. Enough venom for the village's arrows to last us months. If what I've heard is true, Lucian's fang didn't have half the venom, despite its size."

"Better than no venom," Lucian said.

The two girls giggled again, as if there were some joke he wasn't getting.

"It's no matter," Kieron said. "You might make a fine hunter yet, if you learn from a man as experienced as Fergus. It's one thing to kill a wyvern with magic. Quite another to do so without that benefit. Sometimes, we men go wyvern hunting in the Upper Reaches. Some of the women, too. Sometimes, we succeed. Sometimes not. But most of us only have spear, long-bow, or javelins to kill with. If you want to truly test your mettle, hunt *without* magic."

Lucian finally understood what they were trying to do: keep

him humble. They didn't think him some sort of god for doing what few had ever done. It was all a test, to see if he would be a good fit for the community, whether he would try to prop himself above the rest.

"You're right. I'm no hunter. If it hadn't been for the noise, I wouldn't have had time to prepare my defenses."

"Perhaps they were fledglings," Julia offered, taking a bite of a pastry. "That could explain why they announced themselves, lacking the experience of older hunters."

"Or perhaps they were gloombats from the Darkrift, and not wyverns at all," Kieron added, with a cheeky smile.

"You saw that fang," Morgana said. "That's no gloombat!"

"I don't know what those are," Lucian said.

"I've never heard of one so high up," Kieron said, "But gloombat venom is something we can use, though theirs is not as potent as the wyverns'. If you happened across a large gloombat, their fangs can grow almost as large."

"They sound like terrifying creatures," Lucian said.

Morgana giggled. "They can be kind of cute. They're fuzzy, have large eyes, and some people even keep them as pets once they're defanged. The feral ones are dangerous, especially when you disturb their colony."

Again, she was staring at him. Julia watched, bemused, though Kieron seemed oblivious. Lucian was thankful for that much, at least.

Before Lucian could respond, everyone's attention switched to Elder Ytrib, who stood in the center of the meeting hall. The light of torches and sconces lent his skin an orangey luster.

"I hope you've enjoyed the feast. I'd like to thank Julia and the people who put this together on such short notice."

There was general applause and several shouts of "hear, hear."

"Today, we welcome a new mage into our ranks. Lucian, would you please stand?"

It was the last thing Lucian wanted to do, but it wasn't like he had a choice.

"Lucian, we hope that you bring much to our little community here. And we hope to give much in return. Tomorrow, you will learn all about life here. There are dangers, yes. *Great* dangers. But we all must do our part to make life worth living. The villages of the Deeprift have learned to work together according to the Code, for the good of all."

Several applauded at this, but Elder Ytrib raised his hand, staying the noise. He leaned on his bronze spear, making it nothing more than a walking staff.

"Tomorrow is gathering day. We'll be going to the river, which we all know can be dangerous. But I trust having another mage with us will afford additional protection." He broke into a smile. "Besides, we have to replace all this food we just ate."

Most laughed at that. At this point, Lucian noticed some of the women filling clay cups with some sort of liquid. Judging by the amber hue, it was alcoholic. One of the women came toward him, offering the cup. Once every person of age had a drink, Elder Ytrib continued.

"A toast. Toward the bright future of our village. May Kiro stand strong, stay safe, and prosper!"

He raised his glass, and the assembly drank. Lucian nearly coughed at the amber-hued drink, such was the kick. It was cloyingly sweet, which didn't do much to take the bite of the alcohol off. He wiped his mouth and did his best to keep the liquor down.

Kieron clapped him on the shoulder. "Not bad for your first shot of mystika."

Lucian cleared his throat. "What's it made from?"

Kieron looked at him, deadpan. "Wyvern testicles. It's the venom that gives it that kick."

THE RIFTS OF PSYCHE

Lucian nearly heaved right there on the spot, as everyone laughed uproariously.

"It's made from fermented glow shrooms and caro pepper," Kieron said. "Not as exciting, I'm afraid."

Lucian noticed some of the people filtering out, though many hung around to talk. When Kieron and his family had left, Lucian was about to leave himself to get some much-needed sleep before Elder Ytrib waved him over. Fergus stood next to the Elder, gripping his spear tightly as Lucian approached.

"I know you're weary," the Elder said, "but I want to go over tomorrow with the both of you."

Fergus stood straighter, while Lucian wondered just what the Elder was going to say.

"It is well that another mage has joined us," Ytrib continued. "There are few enough in the village as it stands."

"He has yet to be proven," Fergus said. "But I intend to discover the extent of his abilities. Of that, you can be sure."

"Yes," Elder Ytrib said. "That was what I intended. Fergus, I would like you to take Lucian under your wing tomorrow. Teach him about the rift, teach him our customs, and fill any gaps in his knowledge. Though he defeated two wyverns, he is still too young to know as much as you in the ways of magic."

Fergus looked at Lucian. "What kind of mage are you?"

"I'm not sure what you mean."

Fergus stared in disbelief. "What do you mean, you don't know? What magic did you use to kill the wyverns?"

"Binding."

"So, Binding is your primary?"

"I'm not sure, yet. It might be."

Fergus looked at Elder Ytrib, incredulous. "You expect me to believe that a child of such limited knowledge killed those wyverns, Elder?"

"Until we have evidence otherwise, then yes. I do believe it."

Fergus shook his head, and Lucian got the sense that he didn't often disagree with Ytrib.

"That said," Elder Ytrib continued, "it is a bit strange. What did that academy of his teach him?"

"I'm willing to learn more," Lucian said. "They saved most of the advanced instruction for the Talents."

"You weren't even a *Talent*?" Fergus asked.

Lucian ignored the question. He was done trying to explain himself.

"Your primary is the Aspect with which you are most gifted," Ytrib explained. "If you used Binding to kill those wyverns, that would make *you* a Binder. And that would make Psionics and Radiance your secondaries, and Gravitonics and Dynamism your tertiaries."

"I was taught that such beliefs were limiting."

"Then your academy doesn't know its ass from its tits," Ytrib said. "It's inconceivable that you could have killed creatures as powerful as wyverns with anything *but* your primary. That makes you a Binder, plain and simple. The adjoining Aspects on the Septagon are Radiance and Psionics, your secondaries. They are things you should not be as proficient in, but you can still do basic streamings. And finally, your tertiaries. Many mages must stream quite a bit of their magic to even do basic things. And finally, your quaternaries you can just forget about. They are possible to stream, but with a great deal of effort and inefficiency. For you, those would be Atomicism and Thermalism."

"I'm pretty good at Thermalism, though," Lucian said. "At least, I think I am."

This was met with silence, until Fergus shook his head. "Impossible."

Ytrib held up a hand. "Now, let's not jump to conclusions, Fergus. If that's true, Lucian, then what you've said is an incredible thing. Of course, it's possible for a gifted mage to stream their quaternaries, but not without a great deal of practice. Since Thermalism and Atomicism are on the other end of the Septagon, they are as far from Binding as you can get. But if you really are good at Thermalism . . ."

Fergus called out to one of the women. "Dalia! Might you bring us a pail of water for the young mage?"

Not for the first time in the past few days, Lucian found himself under the gun. When the pail was brought, the two older men waited eagerly as Lucian reached for his Focus. He found the Septagon image easily enough, despite the pressure, and noticed for the first time that lines interconnected bordering Aspects and Aspects two places apart. He could also see the blue orb shone more brightly than the others, almost so bright as to be blinding. But shining quite brightly next to it was the violet orb, Psionics, while the green orb bordering the blue one was not as bright as the violet one. If Binding *were* his primary, as these two were saying, wouldn't the purple orb, the one representing Psionics, and the green one, representing Radiance, be of *equal* brightness? But it was not so.

Lucian realized the truth, then. Binding was *not* his primary. At least, it hadn't been before finding the Orb of Binding. *Psionics* had been. For the Gravitonics orb was brighter than the Radiance orb. And the blue one would have been *just* as bright as Gravitonics, if not for the Orb of Binding in his possession. That Orb had made his secondary even more powerful than his primary. Far more powerful, from the looks of it.

"I'm not a Binder," he said. "I'm a Psionic."

Ytrib's eyes widened at that. "So, you are saying you defeated the wyverns with your *secondary*?"

Fergus growled. "Why are you lying to us? Do you take us for fools?"

"I'm not lying, Captain." But he could not explain himself further. He could not tell them about the Orb of Binding. Not ever. And he had almost given it away, so maybe he should have just pretended that Binding was his primary. At this point, for all intents and purposes, it *was*. If they somehow, against all odds, figured out the truth, they might kill him for it. The Oracle had told him as much, that the Builders had turned on each other for the right to bear even one Orb and become a Vigilant.

"Then if you are a Psionic, you must be even more powerful with Psionics than with Binding," Fergus said. "Rest assured, you will be tested on this."

What Lucian knew for sure was that he always felt Psionics had been his strong suit, while Binding and Gravitonic Magic had come somewhat easier for him. Even if he had failed his Gravitonics Trial, he was able to wing it after watching Rhea perform. According to this theory, his *actual* tertiaries would be Radiance and Thermalism. He could perform Radiance readily enough, though he hadn't tried anything more complicated than light spheres, not counting the Radiance Trial where he'd isolated radio waves. Nor with Thermalism had he tried anything harder than heating or freezing water, though he had streamed an impromptu Thermal shield last night to defend himself from Ramore. But then again, it had used his ether quickly, and he would have been burned to a crisp without Serah's help.

Neither had asked him to test his Thermalism on the pail of water sitting beside them, so Lucian ignored it.

That left Dynamism and Atomicism. Dynamism was no doubt his weakest Aspect. It had been the most difficult to learn, and it exhausted him much more quickly than the others. That he had done so well on the Trial was something of a miracle, and probably had more to do with the fact he had worked to conserve his ether as much as possible. The final Aspect, Atomicism, was impossible for Lucian to learn at the Academy. He had never streamed it before, but perhaps such magic wasn't forbidden on Psyche.

"Tch," Fergus said. "Fine. I'll test your mettle tomorrow, newcomer. Of that you can be sure."

Fergus turned around to leave, while Ytrib and Lucian watched him go.

"Why does he have it out for me?"

"He doesn't," Elder Ytrib said. "At least, not in the way you think. Fergus is loyal to a fault. That's why he's Captain of the Kiro Watch. He's just trying to protect me. In his own way."

Fergus paused by the exit, not leaving as Lucian supposed he would. The man was *still* keeping an eye on him.

"I hope I can prove myself."

"I hope so, too. It would be a shame for another mage to not work out."

Lucian frowned. "What do you mean?"

Ytrib shrugged. "It seems we can't keep our mages. The last one frayed. I think the strain was too much for him. Another led a party into the Darkrift, chasing some rumor of treasure. She never returned. And of course . . ." Ytrib trailed off, electing not to continue. "The point is, don't expect this to be easy, Lucian. You have made extraordinary claims, backed up with that fang you brought us. Soon enough, we will know how it was earned."

So, the Elder didn't totally believe him, either. At least he wasn't being an ass about it, like Fergus. "That's fair, Elder."

Lucian stifled a yawn. It was long past time he went to bed.

"Go get some sleep. I'll send someone to wake you since you are not used to the darkness yet. Be at the cave entrance tomorrow morning. And for breakfast, meet here."

Lucian took his leave, trying to ignore the hard stare Fergus gave as he left. There would be no winning that one over, and Lucian had to get used to the fact.

The town was mostly empty as he wove his way back. He was swaying, either from the residual effect of the mystika or sheer exhaustion. He almost stumbled down the stairs leading to the lake. The sounds of the waterfall became distant as he walked down the shoreline. Some of the houses had lights on within, though Lucian couldn't imagine staying up another minute.

He was about to reach his door when he noticed someone standing out front. "Who's there?"

Lucian streamed a light sphere to find Morgana standing at his door.

8

"LUCIAN. I'm sorry, but there's something you should know.'"

Her dark eyes were sincere with no sign of her former mischief. Something had happened.

"What's that?"

"It's Captain Fergus," she said. "I overheard him talking to some of the guards. They are going to humiliate you in front of everyone tomorrow."

"What do you mean by that?"

"Well, I heard him talking to Gabriel. They are going to do their best to make you look incompetent. Like you don't belong here."

Again, Lucian didn't know what that meant. "Are they going to set me up somehow, or . . .?"

"I don't know," Morgana said. "I only came here to tell you to watch your back. Elder Ytrib told my family to take you under our wing, so to speak. I'm just doing my part."

"I see. Well, I appreciate the warning." Why did he get the feeling that this was just an excuse for her to come out and see him? He already knew Fergus was up to no good.

"I'm sure you'll be able to handle him. You killed two

wyverns, after all. But Fergus is a proud man and doesn't like being shown up."

"Thanks for the warning."

"Take care."

When she left, she brushed by him closely enough to make him wonder whether she had done it on purpose. There was something strange about her, but again, he just couldn't place his finger on it.

He entered the hut, took off his boots, and went straight to sleep.

———

HE SAW a golden city at the foot of an impossibly tall mountain range. Those mountains reached into the clouds like daggers, the bottoms of their steep slopes holding towers and palaces. Between two peaks was a wide tunnel at least a hundred meters across and just as tall, situated high above the city but nowhere near the mountains' peaks. That city was a sprawling mass, buildings crowding around stone roads zigzagging up slopes and terraces. Green farms were carved into the mountains, until that greenery was lost to the stone above.

Even with the grandiosity of the city, what he longed to know was what lay beyond that tunnel, that pass through the mountains the city was guarding.

Lucian flew closer, passing over the city's high stone walls, outfitted with towers that held cannons. He zoomed above the winding cobbled streets, all empty of people, though there were hundreds of carts and stalls in the plazas and alleys as if it were a market day. His trajectory seemed to be taking him ahead, toward the slopes of the mountain flanking the city's right, where above its sprawl rose the largest palace of all. Its walls were high, shining golden with a hundred towers, all connected by bridges and halls and wings. Who needed such a place? He had no doubt that this palace was real, only he didn't know what, or where, it was.

That was when the sky darkened. The golden light became hidden as the sun sunk on the opposite side of the mountains. As he drew even closer to the palace, all its windows were dark. All save one. A light shone in a single window of the highest and grandest tower, a beacon in the gathering gloom.

And standing in the center of that light, a shadow. And the shadow was watching him.

Panic seized him. This was a dream. He had to wake up from it, before . . . before what? What could be done to him in a dream?

Come closer, a female voice said. *I've waited for this moment for so long. The Manifold has brought you here. The Manifold has brought the Chosen!*

The Chosen? Was the voice another Oracle? But what would an Oracle be doing in this place, an obviously human-made palace?

Come, Chosen. Tell me about your long journey here. I can help you find what you're looking for.

He didn't know who this was, but he did know he needed to get out of here. As much as he tried to force himself awake, the dream kept its hold over him. What kind of power was this? He was trapped, pulling ever closer to the shadow in the tower, the source of the voice.

Lucian reached for his Focus but couldn't access his magic. Was he being blocked, or was it simply impossible to stream in a dream? He drew closer to the shadow in the tower window, powerless to resist, until he was near enough to see the outlines of a feminine form.

The last thing he wanted was to see her, speak to her, or tell her about himself.

He reached for his Focus again, this time pushing with all

his might to access his ether. Even if he could get a trickle of magic flowing, enough to break him free . . .

You don't wish to fight me, Chosen. I'm far too powerful. Wouldn't you rather have me as an ally? Why do you fear me so?

Because, Lucian responded, *you won't let me leave.*

Not because I wish you harm. The stakes are too high. Though distance separates us, the Manifold desires this meeting.

Lucian didn't understand how she – whoever *she* was – was speaking to him like this. A Psionic link wasn't supposed to work unless two people had met face-to-face and had already shared a link. Which meant one of two things – he had met this person before, or she was doing something with magic that should have been impossible. Then again, perhaps dreams worked differently. After all, the Oracle of Binding had spoken to him in his dreams, and he had certainly never met her. And there was that mysterious Voice that had told him to find the Orbs, the Voice he hadn't heard from in months. The Voice the Oracle of Binding had said was the former Immortal Emperor of Starsea. Lucian couldn't believe that. How could such a thing be possible?

He was just meters from her now, her form still hidden by shadow. He could see the faint outline of her face, along with dark violet eyes that pulled him in with hypnotic gravity.

We were meant to meet, Chosen. The stars have spoken of it. The Manifold has wished for it. Our fates are intertwined, whether you will it or not.

At that moment, visions danced in his head. Though he could not see her face, he saw that she was a woman of surpassing beauty. He saw himself standing at her side. Together, they could rule this moon with justice and power. They would bring the disparate factions of this world together, make them into a force that would bring the League to its knees. Together, they would make the League pay for what it had done to the mages. The mages would have their revenge, would rule the billions of humanity in an unassailable aristocracy.

Was that his dream, or hers? It was hard to tell the difference. All he knew was that with him, the Chosen, and her, the Queen of Psyche, they could not fail. He, with the Orb of Binding along with the Orb of Psionics . . .

The Orb of Psionics? Where had that thought come from?

Yes, she said. *I know where it is, Chosen. And it can be yours, if only you work with me and dream big things. I have seen your thoughts, and I know it is your fate to find the Aspects of the Manifold. You with the Orbs, and with me training you, it would be a simple thing to take revenge on those who sent you here. And that would only be the beginning. It is your fate to find all the Orbs, not a mere two. And it is my fate to help you in this endeavor. You are the Chosen. You are the Worlds' only hope. Together, we can do great things. Things Xara Mallis could scarcely dream of.*

For all she'd said, Lucian could only focus on one part. *The Orb of Psionics is here?*

Yes, she said. *The Ancient Shantozar built his shrine here and hid his treasure in the Burning Sands at the close of the Age of Madness. Yes, I know of that. And more. Shantozar has spoken to me the secrets of Starsea. But he will not show me where his Orb lies until the Chosen has come. And he prophesied that I would feel the Chosen falling on this moon with thunder and power.* She paused, as if gathering her thoughts. *That happened two days ago. I sensed a great uproar in the ethereal field, as something drew an incredible amount of ether into itself. An Orb-wielder had come. The Chosen had come! Lacking a true Psionic link, I could only home in on that power through my dreams, where a part of the mind of all mages goes during sleep. That is how I found you.*

So, she knew everything he did. Or nearly everything. Using the Orb *did* have a cost. It would seem other mages could detect it if they were sensitive to the ethereal field. He would have to be careful with it in the future, and only use it if he had to.

The Orb of Psionics is yours, she said. *But you need me to find it, as I need you to fulfill my own goals. I daresay our goals align very much. Come to the Golden Palace in Dara. We can speak more in person, and you will see how our plans are one and the same.*

The Golden Palace of Dara. That had to be where this was. And if this woman were speaking to him from there, then there was only one person she could be.

Everything I do, I do for the betterment of magekind, the Sorceress-Queen said. *My plans will be apparent once we meet in person. I'm unwilling to say more in a dream, Chosen. With the power of the Orbs, we can bend the galaxy to our will. Mages will be free of the fraying, and we can stand at the fore of a new golden age for humanity.*

How could this possibly be real? *This is insane. I just want off this world!*

You wish to leave this moon. I understand. That wish will be granted . . . in time. Control of Psyche and the greatest population of mages in the Worlds is only a small part of the plan. But first, we must find the Orb of Psionics. With its power, we can take command of the defense platforms and League fleet stationed above us. While you may be the one to wield it, you will need me to teach you the properties of Psionic Magic. And there is none more accomplished in the Worlds at that than me.

Lucian was at a complete loss for words. How could he ever agree to anything so outlandish? And yet, it seemed she was completely serious. One thing he did know was that he could never work with her, not with Serah's warnings about the Queen so fresh in his mind. How did he know she wouldn't try to take control of *him* with her magic? Mind control was one of the powers of the Psionic Aspect, and if the Sorceress-Queen were truly one of the most powerful Psionics in the Worlds, then what was to stop her from doing it?

She seemed to anticipate this rejection, or perhaps, to read his mind about it. *Even if I meant to control you, that is not my goal. You are a Vigilant of Starsea, the Chosen, and a powerful mage at that. I would require a weaker vessel, a weaker mind.*

That didn't do much for Lucian's assurances.

Come to Dara. We will speak more, Lucian.

The Sorceress-Queen was already turning away from the window, and the dream faded.

9

LUCIAN AWOKE TO DEEP DARKNESS, the images of his dream swimming before his eyes. The only light came from outside the window, from the torches along the lakefront.

As much as he didn't want to admit it, he knew the dream to be real. The Sorceress-Queen had somehow visited him, and more than that, they needed each other to find the Orb of Psionics. At least, according to her. And she had left more questions than answers.

Only one thing was sure. He didn't believe for one moment that she had his best interests at heart, especially after what Serah had told him. Why would *she* want him to rule by her side without even knowing him?

But still, she knew things she shouldn't have known about Starsea and the Orbs. And for that reason alone, she *might* be telling the truth, or at least part of the truth. If she really knew how to find the Orb of Psionics, then he needed to visit her. But how to do so and guarantee his safety? The fact that she knew he had an Orb himself was dangerous. She could kill him and take the Orb for herself.

But what if she *were* telling the truth? That was frightening in its own way. It seemed she wanted to use him to find the Orb of Psionics and use the Orb of Psionics to "take control" of the League Fleet above them. Was such a thing really possible, even with an Orb? If it was, then that was terrifying. He wasn't interested in her vision of fighting back against the League. All he wanted was to get off this moon, hopefully with the Orb of Psionics in his possession without starting a new Mage War.

But if that wasn't possible, what then? Lucian couldn't say. All he knew was, as it stood, he would have to work with her, or at least gain more information. But the Sorceress-Queen wouldn't give him anything freely, and he would have to help her with her plans. Even if he was stronger than her in Binding, she was stronger than him in everything else.

Lucian thought about it for a while and was unable to go back to sleep. So, he got up, got dressed, and left the hut. It was impossible to say what time it was, but it felt as if four or five hours had passed since he went to bed. He was still exhausted, but there was nothing to be done about that.

He was walking toward the main part of the village when he noticed an old man sitting by the light of one of the lakeside torches. As Lucian got closer, he recognized Elder Erymmo. Lucian wondered what he was doing down here.

Erymmo turned from where he had been staring at the lake and stood at Lucian's approach. His long gray hair, beard, wrinkled skin, and thin form made him look quintessentially wizard-like, what Lucian thought *every* mage looked like before he learned he was one himself.

"Lucian," he said. "Walk with me. There are things we must discuss."

It was as if Erymmo had been waiting for him. He remembered something Elder Ytrib had said about Lucian being tested for signs of fraying, so maybe that was happening.

Lucian fell in beside the elderly man, and they made their way back toward Lucian's hut. Neither said a word, though Lucian's curiosity was stoked when they walked beyond the hut, and the Elder streamed a light sphere by which to see.

The trail grew rougher as the path descended deeper into the cavern, following the fast-moving stream. Elder Erymmo set a fast pace, and Lucian was hard-pressed to keep up.

"Where are we going, Elder?"

Lucian's only answer was silence.

The trail branched off, and they found themselves in a grove of rocks and underground growing plants, mostly glowing mushrooms growing in damp corners. Water ran down the walls in small rivulets, the tiny streams joining a tributary that trickled toward the main flow of water.

Erymmo nodded toward a small, fist-sized rock at the center of the grove. "Lift that rock using Binding."

Lucian reached out his hand and reached for the Binding Aspect. He anchored the rock and set a focal point on the stalactite-encrusted ceiling. The rock lifted, following a thin tether. About halfway up, Lucian slowed the stream, where the pull of the focal point equaled that of gravity pulling the rock downward. The rock levitated, remaining perfectly still.

"That's a beautiful tether," Erymmo commented. "Steady. Sure. And you didn't stream more than necessary. You may release your stream; I don't wish to exhaust you."

In fact, Lucian was nowhere near exhausting himself. He could feel the Binding Aspect pulsing with power, but he wasn't even tapping into the Orb of Binding now. The ether flowed as steady and clean as the stream in this cavern. He cut the stream, and the rock fell to the ground, seemingly in slow motion due to the lower gravity.

"Now," Erymmo said, "do the same thing, but with a Psionic stream. You need not hold it steady."

Lucian reached for the Psionic Aspect, streaming a burst of

magic, focusing it on the underside of the rock. It shot into the air, bouncing of the ceiling before falling back down.

"Good. A light sphere?"

Lucian took a deep breath. He'd never had to switch between Aspects this quickly, but he found it good practice. He streamed the sphere, weaker than Erymmo's. Once he'd held it about five seconds, Erymmo nodded.

"That's all your primaries and secondaries," he said. "Your streams of your secondaries are fairly clean. But the purity of your Binding stream is like nothing I've ever seen. Not in all my years." Erymmo's bushy gray eyebrows shot up, as if demanding an explanation.

"How are you able to follow my streams so closely?" Lucian asked. "I was never taught to do that."

"That's quite elementary," he said. "So long as you aren't being blocked, you can reach your Focus to another mage's stream and follow it. You can even allow the other mage to control your Focus as well."

"Why would I ever do that?"

"Two streaming as one can be more powerful, and it can allow a more experienced mage to take the lead. But it also requires a great deal of trust. Joining streams is called *confluence*."

"Of course," Lucian said. "I think I've locked onto another mage's stream before without realizing what I was doing, but I didn't know it was possible to *add* to another's stream. What about blocking, though? Others have been able to cut off my magic before, but I don't know how they did it."

"That is advanced, a subset of a technique called *branding*," Erymmo said. "It's quite simple to stream a Psionic ward to counter that. I'd be happy to show you if time allows it. But for now, it's more important that you learn about wards. You must understand those before you can learn brands."

Lucian hadn't expected this impromptu lesson, but he

welcomed it. He would have had to wait for years at the Academy to get access to this knowledge. "What's a ward, then?"

"A ward is what we call a passive stream. It exists without your active engagement for a certain amount of time – from hours, to days, or even longer for more powerful ones. Wards require a portion of your total ether supply. It's a trade-off. You'll have less ether overall to use for active streams, but you will also be defended from attacks of the Aspect the ward is designed to protect you from."

"I see," Lucian said, wondering if a Psionic ward could have kept the Queen from paying him a visit in his dreams. "So, how do I do it?"

"Wards require two streams at a minimum. A Psionic ward, for example, needs to be set with a Gravitonic or Binding shell, each coherent to the other. The coherence allows the streams to *push each other along*, so to speak, allowing them to last in the world without actively streaming it. Think of wards as insurance to make sure another mage doesn't catch you unawares. Of course, it requires judiciousness. If you know another mage's strengths, you can create wards that counteract that strength ahead of time, since most enemy mages will choose to attack you with their primaries, or if they're strong enough in them, their secondaries."

"What is Fergus's primary?"

Erymmo chuckled. "Worried about our dear captain?"

"A little."

"Fergus is a gifted Radiant, and the most powerful mage in our village. His wards are second-to-none, and he can do them well in almost every Aspect. Like most Radiants, he's also greatly sensitive to any abnormal deviations in the ethereal field. Don't think you can defend yourself against him with just one lesson from me."

"Could you teach me to stream a ward, anyway?"

"Certainly," Erymmo said. "Especially since I do not believe you are close to fraying. But I'm interested in how you've developed your Binding stream so . . . cleanly. I daresay it is near one hundred percent purity, with hardly any trace of Manifoldic toxin . . . *if* any. Of course, that cannot be possible."

Lucian tried to play it off with a shrug. If other mages learned how "pure" his Binding streams were, it might make them suspicious.

"I don't know," he said. "I had a good teacher at the Academy."

"I see," Erymmo said, his tone suggesting he knew Lucian was hiding something. "First, back to wards. As I said before, a ward can only defend against a specific Aspect. A Radiant ward, for example, can only defend against Radiant Magic. So, if you are in a duel with a Radiant, you better have a strong ward prepared. Now, to *stream* the ward, you must open a dual-stream, with the warding stream as the primary, and a cohered stream as the secondary. That second stream is called the *shell*. Its only purpose is to hold the primary stream in place."

"I think I understand. So, how do I stream one?"

"Patience, young mage," Erymmo said. "You must imagine the primary stream diffusing around your entire person. If hostile magic is streamed *at* you, your ward will focus on the point of attack and counteract it. Of course, a ward can be broken with a powerful enough stream, but it will take much more magic to undo a ward than to form one. That is part of their advantage. Then again, if you waste your ether on a ward and another mage comes at you with a differing Aspect, then *you* will be at a disadvantage."

"So, how is warding different from shielding? Like a Thermal shield or a Dynamistic shield."

"Shields require only one Aspect and are *active* streams.

That means they burn ether as you use them. Wards require a subset of your pool in advance and remain active for hours or longer, depending on the total ether a mage dedicates to the ward, and they unravel on their own after a certain amount of time, and must be restreamed. A shield can be advantageous, as upfront the ether investment is less, but over time, will be greater than that of a ward. And of course, active streams cannot be maintained during sleep, while wards can. That makes wards useful if you're out in the wilds and want to be protected from frays, for example. Radiant wards can detect deviations in the ethereal field, allowing a mage to wake up in time to defend themselves. As said before, wards require *at least* two Aspects to set, while shields require only one."

"Wait. You said *at least*. You can add more than one Aspect to a ward?"

"You can. You still need a shell Aspect, and coherence between all three. But obviously, it requires a greater supply of ether, and you can only stream one ward at a time, and a ward as strong as the total supply of your ether pool. That is something that can only be guessed at; a ward will collapse if there is not enough ether to supply it. If you decide to ward against two Aspects, the Aspects still need to be complementary – that is, within two spaces of each other on the Septagon. And obviously, a dual ward in effect is a tristream, only streamable by the most powerful of mages with large pools of ether. Anything above that is theoretical. As I'm sure you know from your training, a dualstream uses four times as much ether as a single stream, and a tristream uses nine times as much. Of course, a quadrastream would use sixteen times as much. So on and so forth. So yes, you *could* make a Dynamistic and Radiant ward with an Atomic shell, for example, which would defend you from Dynamistic and Radiant Magic. Or alternately, you could create a Dynamistic ward with an Atomic and Radiant shell, which would last for an exceptionally long time before needing to be refreshed. The more streams in the shell, the longer the ward will last. In theory, six Aspects could be used to shell just one, leading to a ward that would, in theory, last an infinite amount of time."

Lucian was learning far more than he had ever bargained for. These lessons were no doubt reserved for the Talents in the Volsung Academy. "Could multiple mages join streams and create a ward like that?"

"In theory, yes. If they worked together closely, with intense concentration and no mistakes by anyone. And it would require a great many powerful mages. I don't know the *purpose* of such a ward, which is why it has likely never been done. But assuming you got enough powerful mages – no doubt *dozens* at the least, and you had a leader whose Focus was trained and powerful enough to *direct* all that magic, to the point where the leader didn't pass out or fray from it, then yes, it is possible. Or you could do any variation thereof – six Aspects, five, or four, so on and so forth. But if any one of those mages loses their Focus, then that Focus will slip out of the lead mage's control, making creating such a theoretical ward extremely problematic. And it's likely having access to that amount of magic will fray the mind of anyone controlling the stream."

"So, how about when a mage *completely* cuts you off from magic? How is that done?"

"By using a brand. I won't show you how to do that, but essentially, a brand is a ward that you place on another mage, or in the world itself. It requires more magic than a ward – the farther you stream the brand, the more ether required. You can create a branded light sphere, for example, that will remain in place for hours and specify it to remain a certain distance from you."

Lucian had always thought light spheres were active streams. "*That* would be useful."

Erymmo nodded. "Indeed. Advantageous if you're traveling

at night, and it uses less magic than an active Radiant stream. And to answer your original question about being blocked, that would be a Psionic brand formed around a target mage's Focus. You would have to contend with their own defenses, be they wards or shields, and it takes at least a few seconds for even the most accomplished of mages to lock the brand in place. Basically, once you're experienced enough, you can feel it happening and hurry to defend against it."

"So, how do I defend against it?"

"A Psionic ward is usually sufficient, and you can get one up faster than it takes a rival mage to block you, assuming a fast reaction time. But as discussed before, a ward itself can be overpowered, especially if you're caught by surprise."

"Okay. I think I'm ready to learn how to ward, now."

"I should first say, I have not had a Psion in many years, young mage. As with Elder Jalisa, my role is that of healer and prophet for Kiro."

"A prophet? Does that mean you interpret dreams?"

"I do. Depending on the dream. Why do you ask?"

If Lucian told him his dream, he would have to reveal his knowledge about the Orb of Binding and the Orb of Psionics. Perhaps he could only tell part of it, but of course that risked Erymmo figuring out the rest on his own.

"Have you ever heard of Shantozar?"

Erymmo went stiff at the mention of that name. It clearly meant something to him. "What do you know of that? Where did you hear that name?"

"It was mentioned in my dream. Who was he?"

"*Who* mentioned him?"

Lucian hadn't expected that question. But Erymmo's steely gaze could not be denied.

"Someone calling herself the Sorceress-Queen."

Erymmo's expression went ashen under the light of his light sphere. Whatever answer he had been expecting, it clearly hadn't been that. Lucian had made a mistake in saying that much.

"We must return to the village," Elder Erymmo said. "It's safe to say our lesson on wards must come at another time, but certainly before you go to sleep tonight. Elder Ytrib must hear of this."

10

APPARENTLY, Elder Erymmo judged Lucian's dream important enough to even gather the other Elders, despite the early hour. Elders Jalisa and Sina joined Lucian and Elder Erymmo in Elder Ytrib's hut. Elder Gia set before them a meal of flatbread, rice, and fish, and they ate as Lucian explained his dream. He left out plenty of crucial details, essentially only telling them that the Sorceress-Queen wanted him to find the Orb of Psionics, saying he was something called "Chosen."

As soon as he finished, Elder Sina scoffed, her bone jewelry rattling as she shook her head.

"Why do you lie, boy? What would the Sorceress-Queen want with a young whelp like you?"

"I agree that it *doesn't* make sense," Elder Ytrib said, eyeing Lucian anew. "It would seem that you are far from what any of us expected, though in what way, it's hard to decide."

"He has great potential," Elder Erymmo said. "Never in all of my life have I felt a Binding stream so pure. Even the Masters of the Mako Academy never approached this level of purity."

"Might we see for ourselves?" Elder Gia asked gently.

Lucian realized he had no choice. How soon before they

guessed the truth? Or was the truth so unbelievable that they would never consider it in a million years?

He had to hope it was the second one. He focused on a nearby empty cookpot, tethering it to the ceiling above. It floated in midair, and Lucian's skin prickled. That feeling was every single Elder following his stream.

"That will suffice," Elder Ytrib said. "Rotting fish guts. You weren't kidding, Erymmo."

Elder Sina gave him a hardened stare, as if suspecting some trick. Elder Gia's face was ashen, as if what he was doing was impossible. Elder Jalisa watched curiously, her dark eyes shrewd.

"You must explain," Elder Jalisa said, her voice reedy. "If my estimation is correct, then you can stream that Aspect indefinitely, almost without limit. That is *not* something even the greatest Binders can do."

Lucian cleared his throat. "I don't know how I can. Binding has always been my strongest Aspect."

"You said last night your primary was Psionics," Elder Ytrib said. "Why are you changing your story?"

"What you are doing is impossible," Elder Sina added. "I've seen nearly eighty percent purity before, and never thought I'd see anything exceeding that. Your stream, Lucian . . . unless I miss my guess, is one hundred percent pure magic. Manifoldic toxin is absent from your stream entirely."

"What of the other Aspects, Elder Erymmo?" Elder Ytrib asked.

"What I've tested so far is all polluted, as might be expected. His Psionic stream is quite pure for a mage of his ability level, while his Radiant stream is of middling purity. I suspect his tertiaries will be even more inefficient and didn't deign to test them."

"I see." Ytrib's brow furrowed in thought. "Since all this is so highly irregular, it might behoove us to test all his Aspects. Even the quaternaries."

"If I'm expected to stream later today in the valley," Lucian said, "that might exhaust me."

"Maybe so," Ytrib said. "But if your Binding is truly this pure, then you will at least have access to that Aspect. I don't see how you can possibly mask the purity of your stream." He nodded, stroking his beard. "Go ahead, Lucian. Let's test the other Aspects."

The Elders watched carefully as he streamed each Aspect, except for Atomicism. As with Elder Erymmo, he performed the same basic tests – lifting the pot with Psionics and streaming a light sphere. Next, they had him lift the pot with a Gravitonic stream, which Lucian did with a bit more difficulty. He was starting to feel drained, and it would only be harder to stream as he drifted further from his primary.

"His Radiance is nowhere near as pure as his Psionics," Elder Jalisa said. "Which is not what we should expect if both are secondaries. And his Radiance is less pure than Gravitonics. Most curious."

He next streamed Dynamism, a simple shielding that he couldn't hold for more than five seconds.

"Quite weak," Elder Sina said. "Now for Thermalism."

He was able to boil a pot of water quite easily, though he was pushing his limits. The taste on his tongue became acrid, enough for him to cough.

"Stop," Elder Gia said. "You are close to overdrawing."

Lucian cut off his stream.

"Given these results," Elder Gia continued, "we can expect Atomicism and Dynamism to be his weakest Aspects."

"But that's not consistent with Binding being his primary," Elder Ytrib said. "His weakest should be Thermalism and Atomicism."

"We can't be entirely sure unless we ask him to stream

THE RIFTS OF PSYCHE

Atomic Magic," Elder Ytrib said. "And I would not have him do that. At least, not here."

The Elders settled into silence. He was a puzzle to be figured out, and it was a puzzle that could only be solved if he opened his mouth and told the truth. But the risk was too great. If any of them knew what he had, they might kill him for it. The Oracle had said that friends and family turned on each other for the mere chance to hold an Orb.

For that reason alone, Lucian couldn't trust *anyone* with what he had.

"Well, friends," Elder Ytrib said, after a long silence. "I believe we have exhausted every other possibility."

At once, their gazes fixated on him. Those eyes were knowing, judging, seeming to see to the marrow of his bones.

"Lucian," Elder Jalisa said, "I don't believe you are tricking us in any way, nor do I believe you were simply born this way. Nor do my fellow Elders here. There is only one explanation that makes sense."

She paused, as if to give him an opportunity to confess. But Lucian wasn't going to say anything.

If they wanted to say it, then they would say it.

"It would seem legends have come to life," Elder Gia said. "We know the truth, Lucian, for there is only one explanation for why your Binding stream would be of perfect purity. Our only question is, where in the Worlds did you find the Orb of Binding?"

———

THERE WAS no use denying it. If they really wanted the Orb, then they would kill him for it. But despite this fear, it didn't seem as if any one of them had that in mind.

The least he could do now was tell his story, hopefully to convince them that killing him was a bad idea. With some prodding, he told the full story, leaving nothing out this time. He even told them about his dream with the Sorceress-Queen, at which all their expressions darkened.

Once done, Elder Erymmo cleared his throat. "When he mentioned Shantozar, I suspected the truth. But I didn't believe it until now, until I saw that the purity of his stream was not *my* madness."

"How do you even know about the Orbs?" Lucian asked. "Where I come from, few know about them."

"It's no story," Elder Gia said, her expression one of reverence. "It's *history*. I don't know how it is outside Psyche, but here, most believe in the Orbs. Not everyone, but most."

"I didn't," Elder Jalisa said, faintly. "I once studied Arian's *Prophecy of the Seven* from a scholarly perspective as a Talent of the Irion Academy, long ago. I sought to disprove it. But when I was sent to Psyche, I took my memories of the prophecy with me. I wrote out everything I remembered, and discovered things in those lines that were closed to others. I supposed you could say it was . . . a *revelation*."

"What revelation, Elder?"

Elder Jalisa watched him closely. It seemed the other Elders were deferring to her. This was clearly her area of expertise.

"There were Seven Orbs, keys to the Manifold and called the Jewels of Starsea. Starsea was the ancient empire of the Builders. Of course, their existence was prophesied by Arian in the days when magic was new to the galaxy. Well, new to us humans. Magic has always existed, but was somehow lost during the days of Starsea. None can say just how much time has passed since then, but certainly over a million Earth years. The Builders, sometimes called the Ancients, used it to create their gates, but that is the only remnant of magic that has remained. When magic returned, Arian had his prophecy about the Seven Orbs. But his revelation from the Manifold was . . . garbled. It was impossible for mages to understand his words, or at best, they might understand a small fraction of it. Even so, many mages took these fractions of truth and used them to seek the Orbs, though none were ever found. At least, not that we know of."

Lucian wondered how she could have even memorized Arian, especially if what he had written was garbled. The words of his prophecy were indecipherable. The times he *had* read it, nothing made sense outside one passage, which had described the Orbs and their existence. But apparently, Jalisa had gleaned enough information to know what he knew – and perhaps more.

"Where did you find the Orb, Lucian?" Elder Sina asked. "You haven't told us yet."

"Volsung. There is an island far to the north, near the ice cap. I'm not sure where it is on a map, but it's where the Academy sends their exiles. I sort of . . . stumbled upon it without realizing what it was."

"Of all the places in all the Worlds," Jalisa said, not believing. "The odds are insurmountable."

"Unless the Manifold *meant* him to find it," Elder Gia said. She turned her attention to Lucian. "I believe you were meant to go to that island, to find that cave, and finally, to hold that Orb. And likewise, you were meant to come here to Psyche to find the Orb of Psionics."

"The Queen-Mage means to use him to locate it," Elder Erymmo said. "But we can never allow that."

"Tell me about her," Lucian said. "Why is she so bad?"

All stared at him in wide-eyed disbelief, before Elder Ytrib held up his hands placatingly. "He is new to this world, friends. He knows nothing." That only seemed to mollify them a little bit. Ytrib continued. "The Sorceress-Queen is an evil woman. And a powerful Psionic, quite possibly the most powerful there has ever been. She has a rare gift that is a curse for the rest of us. Her magic is so advanced that she can create brands that last for years. These brands allow her to keep track of her subjects, even to directly control them, if need be."

"Elder Erymmo told me a bit about brands, but what does that mean in terms of the Queen?"

"It means that she can keep tabs on her subjects without needing to be present," Elder Sina said. "Of course, she can't directly possess *all* her subjects, but certainly she can do so at need with one or even a few people. The brands allow her to sense the mental state, and even the thoughts, of those who carry them. If ever you were to meet her face-to-face, no doubt branding you would be her first action."

"Could she do that to me in a dream?"

"No," Elder Sina said. "She must physically see you. And if it happened, it's something you would certainly be able to feel. Whether the unarcane would feel the same thing, I can't say."

Unarcane. That must be the term that mages used to describe non-mages.

"The brands lose power over time and need to be refreshed," Elder Gia said. "It's not known how long it takes, exactly. But once it weakens, the Sorceress-Queen can simply renew the brand with a new infusion of magic and it's as good as new. That is how she lays claim over Dara, how none can stand against her. She streams little active magic – every one of her brands drains her total ether supply, but she need not be physically powerful when her branded Mage-Lords and Mage-Knights can do the fighting for her. She trains her Psionic Mage-Knights to brand their own minions. She's like a spider, trying to weave a web large enough to ensnare all of Psyche. She's the reason that we, long ago, were driven from the Golden Vale and into the deep Riftlands, the only place on Psyche we can hide from her patrols. Rarely do they pass through here, but sometimes, her slavers come and take who they may, labor to fuel her growing empire. They are destined for the fields, the mines, her armies, or even for sport in the Blood Arena." Her eyes looked at him intensely. "If she *ever* found you, Lucian, everything would be lost. Psyche would be as good as hers if she had your Orb."

So, it was safe to say that her desire to work together with him was all a lie. She most likely wanted him to find the Orb of Psionics, though Lucian didn't understand why she needed him for that. It made him wonder why she ever thought she could fool him in the first place.

"She thought I'd be lost and alone," he realized. "She thought I'd be happy to have her help."

Lucian realized that the Elders might want his Orb, too. Was there any reason he should trust them? Maybe he should be reaching for his Focus right now.

"We will have to discuss this among ourselves," Elder Ytrib said. "Suffice it to say, Lucian, you are under our protection. If it's the Orb the Sorceress-Queen is after, then she must never learn that you're here. You have an artifact of great power, and I suspect you don't have the faintest idea how to use it."

"I used it to kill the wyverns."

"Yes," Elder Jalisa said. "And almost killed yourself in the process by bringing down the Snake Pass."

"And there's no doubt that the Sorceress-Queen will learn of that destruction," Elder Sina said. "And you already mentioned she detected you from the fluctuation in the ethereal field."

The prospect was terrifying. Kiro was just a day's walk from the Snake Pass. She or her agents could easily track Lucian to Kiro.

"We've gotten ahead of ourselves," Elder Ytrib said. "Go to the meeting hall and get Captain Fergus. Tell him to come here."

"Am I still going down to the valley today?"

"Yes," Elder Ytrib said. "We need you now more than ever, Lucian. You must train as you've never trained before. There is no room for failure. You must make up for the shortcomings that caused you to be exiled from the Volsung Academy. You hold one of the Orbs now, and if it falls into the Sorceress-Queen's hands, she will be able to bend all of Psyche to her will. With the Orb of Psionics, none could stand against her."

"So, she's one hundred percent lying that she wants *me* to keep the Orb?"

"I suppose it's possible she has some other plan we're not aware of," Elder Jalisa said. "However, she would not allow you to keep it unless she knew some way to control you."

"She hinted that the Orb of Psionics could take control of the defenses above Psyche, somehow," Lucian said. "How would that even be possible?"

"I'm not sure," Elder Erymmo said. "All we do know is that the Sorceress-Queen has been a constant presence on Psyche since the end of the Mage War. If the fraying has not worked on her body, then it has surely warped her mind, especially since she is not known to restrict her use of magic. Then again, her strength with Psionics is such that her stream is highly pure, which has made it possible for her to hold out this long. That said, she would love nothing more than to escape this world with two Orbs in hand, and an army of fiercely loyal Mage-Knights and Mage-Lords at her back."

It was a terrifying thought. All Lucian knew was that he had a dangerous enemy.

"I'll go find Fergus."

He left Elder Ytrib's hut and headed for the meeting hall.

11

LUCIAN FOUND Fergus eating breakfast alone. He watched
Lucian disdainfully as he approached.

"Captain, the Elders wish to see you."

Fergus arched a questioning eyebrow. "To speak with *me*?"

"Yes," Lucian said. "I'm just the messenger."

Fergus grunted, setting his food down and washing his
hands in a nearby bowl. "Stay here, then. And find something
to eat. The farming party will set out soon."

Fergus left, bronze shockspear in hand. Lucian took a bowl
of soup, filled with vegetables and some sort of meat. He was
too hungry to question what exactly was in it.

By the time Fergus returned half an hour later, Lucian had
finished his soup and the meeting hall was almost full. Lucian
supposed that this crew of fifty was to be the farming party. The
watchmen stood separately, dressed in leather armor while
holding their own spears of bronze. Some of them cast surreptitious glances Lucian's way. Lucian wondered if he would be
getting his own spear. It would feel good to have some sort of
weapon he was familiar with.

Fergus stood at the entrance to the meeting hall. He rapped

his spear three times on the stone floor, and all conversations stilled at the sound.

"All right," he boomed. "Time to move. Let's get this over with before evening."

Everyone stood, some grumbling, and began to filter out of the hall.

Lucian approached Fergus after noticing the other watchmen doing the same. The warning Morgana had given him yesterday was still fresh in his mind. "What do I do, Captain?"

"Remain silent unless I call upon you," he said. "If I need something, I'll tell you. You have my word on that."

Lucian swallowed his pride. "As you say, Captain."

Fergus let out a sigh, as if Lucian's case were hopeless. When the last of the gathering party had exited the hall, Fergus motioned for his guards to follow. Most of them looked to be about Lucian's age or older. Lucian wondered if any were mages like him.

As they walked through the village, Lucian couldn't help but wonder how Fergus might make an example of him. He wondered who among these watchmen were part of that scheme. Perhaps all of them. Was there anything he could do to prepare for it? The Elders had already exhausted him with their tests, so he was in no position to defend himself. Of course, he always had his Binding Magic. But if other mages were like the Elders, they would notice the purity of his stream. And that might lead to questions. Of course, it was possible Fergus had been apprised of the situation.

Whatever the case, it was clear Fergus despised him.

Once they had reached the gate of the village, Lucian was surprised at how bright it was outside. Not that it was "bright" by any means, but it certainly was compared to the gloom of the cave. Lucian had to squint as he emerged into the cool, misty air, golden with sunlight diffusing from above. The sun here had to have been bright to shine through all this atmosphere. Perhaps it was a good thing Psyche was a cloudy world.

"Off-worlder."

The guards pulled to a stop as Captain Fergus thrust a spear, point down, in Lucian's direction.

"What?" Fergus scoffed. "Don't tell me you've never used one of these before."

Lucian took the spear, giving a few twirls of a basic ceremonial sequence he'd learned at the Academy. Several people stopped to watch the movements, flashier than they were practical. This spear didn't retract like the one he once owned, but it would suit his purposes. "I know little enough, Captain, but I'm eager to learn more."

Lucian hadn't meant that to sound sarcastic, but a few of the other watchmen snickered. Their laughs were stifled with one venomous glare from Fergus.

"You will learn, Off-Worlder. Of that I assure you." Fergus faced the rest of the watchmen. "Keep an eye out. I know we are still in the Deeprift, but that is no guarantee of safety. Eyes sharp."

The group moved quickly down the narrow trail at a jogging pace to catch up with the rest of the gathering party, which had gone on ahead. After thirty minutes of skirting the right side of the rift, the trail forked. The left path followed the rift deeper down, while the right path turned into a long set of stairs descending into a tunnel. To Lucian's surprise, they went into the tunnel, down the stairs that took them deep underground. There was a light at the end of that tunnel, but it was far in the distance. The villagers lit the path with torches, making streaming light spheres unnecessary.

After about ten minutes, they emerged on the other side to find themselves standing hundreds of meters above a narrow valley, with slopes so steep it could almost be called a canyon.

Craning his neck, Lucian could see golden light filtering through the thick atmosphere above. The tops of the mountains were lost to that radiant light, making it seem as if the world were nothing more than this valley, this rift, delving deep into the heart of Psyche.

"Is this still the Deeprift?" he asked.

The watchmen proceeded ahead, seemingly ignoring him. All but one, who paused beside him. He had pale skin, flaming red hair, and brilliant green eyes.

"This is the Greenrift," the guard said, with an easy drawl. "So-called because . . . well, it's *green*."

Lucian saw that he was right. The rift's lower reaches were green with vegetation. And at the bottom ran a swift river that plunged deeper into the fissure. Lucian wondered if all the rifts were like this – carved with swift running water from who knew where, until it collected in some place of darkness deep beneath the surface. For all he knew, that water might fall to the center of the moon itself. The thought seemed ridiculous, but perhaps this world was small enough for that to happen.

Each side of the rift was lined with multiple rows of terraces, each filled with green vegetation. This was where they had to be going. The terraces ended about a hundred meters above the level of the water, where the steep slopes became bare and brown. Even higher, far above all their heads, the terrain was rough and rocky, and Lucian could see even more caves. They would need to watch above as much as below. Wyverns could be lurking in those shadowy entrances. If some were to come out, there would only be a short amount of time to seek shelter.

Lucian and the red-haired watchman brought up the rear.

"Quite the sight, isn't it?" the watchman asked.

Lucian nodded his agreement. "I've never seen anything like it."

The guard laughed. "Neither had I. Not until I came here."

Lucian put out a hand. "I'm Lucian."

"I know," the guard said, taking his hand. "My name's Cleon. I'm a Thermalist."

Lucian took the hand. "I guess you could say I'm a Binder."

Cleon nodded toward the group making its way down below. "It's just you, me, and Fergus that can stream out of this bunch. Aside from our Elders and another three old ones back at the village, that makes for all the mages of Kiro."

"Not many," Lucian said.

"No. We mages are a rarity, even on Psyche. Though in Dara, there are many more. A lot of opportunity there for a mage."

Lucian wondered why Cleon was telling him this. Like him, though, it seemed he wasn't from this world, or at least not from the Riftlands, so that gave them one thing in common.

It took another half hour before they'd reached the terraces below. Lucian stood next to Fergus and Cleon as the villagers labored at the harvest. It was hard not to feel like they were forcing the villagers to the hard task, at least at first. But the guards spent all their attention facing outward from the harvesters, scanning the rift for signs of trouble. That told Lucian it was a team effort, each person playing their part according to their skills.

It was important to do well. If Lucian didn't prove himself today, he might find himself harvesting with the laborers. He was sure Fergus would like nothing better than that.

"You need to be looking up as much as down," Fergus instructed them as he walked by on one of his rounds. "Wyverns from above, humans from below."

"Yes, sir," Cleon said, saluting.

Lucian copied the salute, and at an arched eyebrow from Captain Fergus, added his own, "Yes, sir."

When Fergus strolled away, Cleon leaned closer to Lucian. "You watch below, I'll take the sky."

"Sounds good to me. Where are you from, Cleon?"

"I'm a slum rat from Dara, originally."

"Dara? I thought you were an off-worlder, too."

He shook his head. "Most Psycheans are natives. Because I was a mage, I rose to be one of the Queen's Mage-Knights." He gave a bitter laugh. "How proud I was of that. It worked for me, for a time."

"What do you mean by that?"

His expression darkened. "Long story. I won't bore you."

The story probably wasn't boring, but Lucian knew better than to pry.

"That's why I'm here. Hoping for the day all the tribes of the Rifts are strong enough to take down Dara and the Sorceress-Queen. Who knows? It might happen. Or she may crush us all. She's taken all the Golden Vale by now, and even most of the Westlands beyond the Mountains of Madness. Her empire covers most of the moon, all the way to the Burning Sands on Planetside. All that's left really are the Riftlands."

"Stop your yakking, Cleon!" Fergus called.

Cleon shut his mouth. Lucian only knew one thing about the Sorceress-Queen. He did not wish to ever see her in his dreams again. But that would likely not be the case. His fate was intertwined with hers, if only because he held the Orb of Binding. The thought made him sick.

Things seemed quiet in the Greenrift. The day grew brighter, but the mist hanging in the air didn't seem to dissipate. Even so, Lucian could feel the sun burning through it.

When Fergus was far away, Lucian asked Cleon another question. "How far is Dara from here?"

Cleon cast a glance in Fergus's direction before answering. "Hard to say. If you follow the roads through the Rifts, several months. I went by a faster and more dangerous route. I followed the Darkrift, paying a guide, and ended up somewhere in Snake Rift. After that, I found my way to the surface.

THE RIFTS OF PSYCHE

That took me about a month, give or take a few days. After the Elders of Kiro heard my story, they let me in. They said anyone who could survive the Darkrift was a welcome addition to their community. Truth be told, though, if you have magic and a working brain, they will let you in easily."

"I thought I told you two to can it!"

When had Fergus come back? Cleon stood straight to attention, while Lucian was slower in obeying. Fergus got in his face and stared him down, hard.

"Step forward, Off-Worlder."

There was nothing for Lucian to do but advance, drawing the eye of every watchman and half of the gathering villagers.

Fergus was now in his face, expression grim. *"Keep. Watch!"*

Instantly, every watchman's attention refocused on their watch points, while the villagers returned to their harvesting with renewed vigor.

Fergus paced back and forth in front of Lucian, his face a storm cloud of anger. His grip on his spear tightened, as if he were itching to use it.

At last, Fergus seemed to reach a breaking point, nodding to the space in front of him. "Stand across from me, Off-Worlder. It's time for your first lesson."

Lucian most certainly didn't want to do that, but he couldn't disobey a direct order. He stood directly across from Fergus, about five meters away.

"All of you, keep your watches. I would test this mage."

———

LUCIAN WONDERED HOW "TESTING" him in front of everyone would help the villagers harvest faster or the guards watch the rift better, but he was just a day one grunt, so who was he to question? If there was any watching to be done, it would be watching *him* have his ass handed to him.

"All right, wyvern-slayer," Fergus said. "Let's see what you're worth."

Lucian hardly had time to react. Fergus reached out his left hand, which unleashed a sudden flash of green brilliance. Lucian stumbled backwards, blinded, fumbling with his spear. When he felt cold metal at his throat, he knew he had been bested – and in less than five seconds.

"Your Radiance defense is non-existent, as expected. Again."

At least Fergus had the grace to allow Lucian to regain his vision, first. Lucian crouched, feeling a fire in his belly as he deftly handled the spear, which felt so light in Psyche's gravity. This round, he wouldn't embarrass himself.

"Hah!" Fergus shouted, in what Lucian supposed was the beginning of a new bout.

Lucian felt himself getting heavier, even as Fergus leaped high into the air, far higher than he should have been able to. Using his Focus, Lucian detected two streams emanating from Fergus – one that made him heavier, and the other making Fergus lighter. As Lucian struggled to remain standing, his legs buckling, he knew he had to counter one or the other.

What would Fergus expect the least? Lucian reached for Gravitonics, and instead of undoing the gravity amplification disc beneath him, he focused on the anti-grav stream that allowed Fergus to leap so high. His stream met resistance, but to Lucian's surprise, the tactic was somewhat effective, because Fergus started dropping faster. Fergus's eyes widened slightly, his only betrayal of surprise, but the captain regained control quickly. He was falling straight toward Lucian, even more quickly than before, which meant Lucian would be "killed" by him even faster. Lucian raised his spear to defend himself, but it was so heavy he could hardly lift it. Fergus landed on Lucian's opposite side, where he placed his spear at his back. Lucian was so heavy that he couldn't turn fast enough to deflect the attack.

"Not a good showing for Gravitonics, either."

The pressure of Fergus's Gravitonic Magic eased, allowing Lucian to breathe freely once again. His legs were still shaking from the effort of standing.

"You can yield," Cleon called from the sidelines.

"Not yet," Lucian said. He had to wait for his opportunity. If Fergus was testing him on each of the Aspects, eventually they'd get to Binding. That was when he'd show him.

But it seemed as if Fergus wasn't interested in testing Lucian at his strongest Aspect. Next, Fergus swung his spear, but no lightning flowed from the spear's tip. Instead, a kinetic wave pushed against Lucian, forcing him back to the terrace edge. He responded with his own kinetic wave, but somehow, Fergus was able to shield it. It went back and forth like that for a while, until Fergus started pelting Lucian with rocks. Lucian streamed a Psionic shield, which slowed most of the rocks down, but some still made it through his defenses. While under that barrage, Fergus pounced. Lucian could hardly defend against Fergus's spear as it found an opening near his abdomen.

In the next bout, Fergus made Lucian's spear so cold he couldn't even hold it. By the time the stream was underway, Lucian couldn't figure out how to reverse it. He tried to do the same thing to Fergus's spear, but he felt his stream being countered, making it an exercise in futility.

He knew he should just give up. He was already bloody and bruised, and his ether nearly depleted. When Fergus's spear became shrouded in lightning, Lucian immediately threw up a Dynamistic shield. To his surprise, that shield held at the first streak of lightning from Fergus's spear tip. They danced around each other, energy shields up and spears wreathed with electricity. Lucian felt his ether fast depleting.

It was then that Lucian remembered Transcend Yellow's axiom: the mage who ran out of ether first, lost. He didn't know whose pool was larger, his or Fergus's, but he knew it was the only way he could possibly beat the more experienced captain. Lucian weakened his shield. Fergus took the bait, his spear becoming awash with electricity. But just before he slammed the tip into Lucian's shield, Lucian drew even *more* ether, strengthening the shield not only to match, but overpower. By the time Fergus struck, it was too late. The captain cried out at the nasty shock he got, almost dropping his spear as he was pushed back.

Lucian went on the offensive, collecting the residual energy of his shield into a lightning bolt that streaked from the tip of his spear. Fergus easily countered, somehow absorbing that magic with his own spear, then shooting it right back.

Lucian raised his shield, but he was already so weak. The shield shattered with a thunderous crack, and Lucian was knocked back a few meters. Fergus didn't even bother delivering the killing blow this time.

"You've done him good enough, Captain," one of the older villagers said, stepping forward. "One would think this isn't training, but a personal vendetta on your part."

"This isn't over until he yields," Fergus said.

Lucian seethed. When he spat, blood came out. He'd taken a rock right to the face during the Psionic bout. No longer filled with the pain-reducing effect of ether, the pain of it was visceral. Perhaps it *was* time to give up.

"We have yet to test my Binding, Captain Fergus. Would you care to go another round?"

Fergus watched him, seeming to consider. Lucian then saw his strategy. Tire him out with all his other Aspects before testing him on what he was good at. Perhaps he *did* somewhat believe him about the wyverns, but the captain couldn't go back on his disparaging remarks. Perhaps the Elders had even told him about the Orb this morning.

But Lucian knew he couldn't let pride get in the way. Using the Orb was like lighting a beacon, one that would attract the attention of the Sorceress-Queen. But surely, she couldn't detect it if he opted to use only a little magic?

"Aye, one more round," Fergus said. "Now, we will see if you were lying about those wyverns."

They both faced off again. By this point, no one was making a pretense of gathering or watching the rift. All eyes were on the captain and the recruit. Lucian hadn't made a good showing, but he could show them all with his best Aspect powered by the Orb. It was a chance to undo all his losses and prove himself.

Captain Fergus and Lucian just watched as a cool wind blew through the rift. When this had gone on about half a minute, Lucian wondered whether Fergus was waiting for *him* to make the first move this time. He seemed more guarded this round. That took great discipline, to not underestimate an opponent he had already defeated five times handily.

When Lucian reached for his Focus, a woman screamed. Shortly after that, one of the watchman was shouting.

"Slavers! Slavers in the Rift!"

Lucian followed his line of sight to see a contingent of men emerging from a cave at the bottom of the rift, just a few hundred meters down the trail.

12

FERGUS TOOK COMMAND INSTANTLY.

"Retreat! Everyone back to Kiro, now!"

Somehow, his voice boomed far louder than it should have, perhaps enhanced by some magic Lucian didn't understand. Whatever the case, the Kiro villagers got the message instantly, taking their gathering bags and running up the trail in a coordinated maneuver that had clearly been rehearsed. Meanwhile, all the watchmen converged on Fergus, who now stood on the trail to guard the villagers' retreat.

Lucian went to stand in line with them, with Cleon on his left and Fergus at the vanguard. He felt for his ether, finding that there was only a small reserve left. Having it out with Fergus had been the height of stupidity, but there was no way to come back from that now.

He would probably have to use the Orb, especially considering as many as *fifty* bronze-clad soldiers were marching out of that cave, their armor and spears glinting in the sun. At their head was a violet-caped man with a purple plume at the top of his bronze helmet, carrying a silvery shockspear that was already streaming electricity. Even from distance, Lucian could

dove behind the boulder. A peek around the side revealed the hoplites were even *closer*. Lucian had about thirty seconds to make something work.

Lucian wasted no time. He deepened his Focus and created a focal point on the trail itself, about twenty meters away, while setting the anchor point at the base of a high cliff above the trail. Lucian let ether rip through him, all of it drawn by the power of the Orb. More and more magic streamed out of him, until the Binding tether radiated with blinding blue light.

"Take cover!"

Lucian released the stream, and instantly, the ground shook from the sheer amount of energy Lucian had streamed into the tether. The tether collapsed the cliff in a torrent of rock and dirt, burying the trail in a flood of earth. Men screamed and died as tons of rocks made the trail completely impassable. The dust hadn't even settled, but Lucian could *still* hear men approaching, clanging spears and shields in a blood frenzy. At least a few had slipped past the landslide and were mere meters away.

Fergus nodded. "We can take these."

Lucian's stomach seemed to do a flip. All of this was happening too fast. He had likely already killed with the rockslide, but now he might have to kill in person, and didn't know if he'd be able to do it.

But there was no time to think about it or amp himself up. Fergus was already charging with a roar, with Cleon right behind. And Lucian couldn't let them fight alone. As soon as he stepped out from the boulder, the air was choked with dust. Two bronze-clad soldiers charged from the grit-filled air, spears out and shields raised. Taking the lead, Fergus sidestepped the first while ramming his spear into the guts of the second. Cleon's hands became wrapped in red light, and he streamed a small fireball at the first one. The soldiers raised his rounded bronze shield in time, eating the impact of the fireball with ease, even as three more advanced from the dust.

One broke free of the pack and charged right at Lucian. Still holding the Binding Aspect, he streamed a tether to the hoplite's shield, pulling it toward the mountain side. Unknown to Lucian, the soldier's arm was fastened to the shield, causing the entire *man* to fly up and away toward the mountain.

But despite seeing full well what had happened to him, the other soldiers charged forward, fanatical in their devotion and their eyes glowing with violet light. These men were possessed by a force outside themselves, for anyone else would have been fleeing by now. But Fergus and Cleon stood ready.

"Cover your eyes!" Fergus shouted.

Lucian did so without waiting for an explanation. Even closing and covering his eyes with his arms, a flash went off. He lowered his arm to see the three hoplites stumbling forward blindly. Fergus and Cleon dealt with what was left quite easily, making quick work of it. Lucian's stomach churned a bit at the efficient butchery and was glad he didn't have to do that dirty work.

"Let's move," Fergus said, after cleaning the blood from his spear. "If they have Binders or Psionics with them, they'll be able to force a path through those rocks."

They didn't waste any time, running up the trail toward the tunnel. As soon as they had left the dust behind, a bend in the trail took them out of sight of the mages and their henchmen.

"Those are the Queen's men?" Lucian asked.

"No doubt," Cleon said. "And that purple-caped one I would recognize anywhere."

"Who?"

"Mage-Lord Kiani. My former commander, and someone I swore to kill."

"We're *not* turning back," Fergus said. "You'll have to save your quarrel for another day. Lucian needs to stay alive. It's *him* they're after."

Cleon gave no response to this, either because he had nothing to say, or they were getting quite winded running up the trail. When the tunnel entrance came in sight, Lucian couldn't have felt more relieved.

"You'll have to bury it," Fergus said. "You have the ether for that?"

"He *can't*," Cleon said. "He must have overdrawn like crazy with that rockslide."

Neither had a clear picture of how the Orb worked. "I can do it."

Once they had gone a good distance up the tunnel, Lucian streamed the tether. Holding it, he ran with the rest of them up the stairs, releasing only when they had gained a good distance. It would not do to have the *entire* tunnel collapse on them, a possibility since magic could have unforeseen consequences.

With a thunderous boom, the entrance to the Greenrift collapsed, and the three men continued to run toward the Deeprift and freedom.

13

BY THE TIME LUCIAN, Cleon, and Fergus stood before the gates of Kiro, they collapsed such was their exhaustion. It wasn't just the constant running uphill. It was the extreme fatigue from streaming more magic than he ever had in his life. Even if all that magic had come from the Orb of Binding, there seemed to be a mental limit he had surpassed.

He was in over his head, and he knew he was incredibly lucky to have not passed out or even outright killed himself. He needed more advanced training, but who in all the Worlds could teach him how to handle the insane amount of magic he had just streamed?

As uncomfortable as the thought was, his mind went to the Sorceress-Queen. The Sorceress-Queen, who was apparently sending her soldiers after him. How had they gotten into the Greenrift in the first place? If they were truly coming after him, and Dara was weeks or even months away, then how could the Queen have responded to his presence so quickly? It didn't add up, but Lucian was too tired to reason out the possibilities.

"Inside, men," Fergus said. "The Elders must hear of this!"

Despite these words, Lucian felt himself fading. His vision

darkened, while sounds seemed to come from far away. He heard Cleon saying something, but it seemed like another language from another world.

———

WHAT FOLLOWED WAS A LONG DARKNESS, a darkness so deep that there weren't even dreams. It was as if Lucian were dead. When he did wake up, he was inside a hut with a fire burning at its center, over which hung a steaming pot of soup. Lucian blinked, supporting himself with his arm. He was lying on a bed of some sort of woven grass which emitted a sweet fragrance. There were two hammocks across the hut, but both were unoccupied. The periphery was filled with various articles – pottery, roughly made stools next to a small table, tools such as a pickaxe, scythe, and fishing rod, along with amphoras filled with some sort of liquid, probably water or cooking oil. There were bronze spears and shields hanging from the wall, but one spear in particular caught Lucian's eye, which seemed to be made from dark gray graphene. That was a genuine, retractable shockspear, the kind only forged by Academy Atomicists. Such a spear would have had to be *brought* here, somehow, as Lucian doubted anyone had the capacity to create one of its kind with this world's primitive technology.

Lucian hadn't been awake more than five minutes when Elder Erymmo stooped into the hut, his solemn face watching Lucian from the doorway. This must have been the Elder's home.

"Elder Erymmo? What happened?"

The elderly man considered him for a moment. "You overexerted yourself. It can happen if you stream too much magic, too quickly. Streaming burns the body's physical energy as much as it does ethereal." Elder Erymmo was already ladling some of the soup into a wooden bowl. "Can you sit up?"

Lucian thought he could manage that much. It took some time to sit up, and he felt a moment of vertigo as his vision darkened. After a few steadying breaths, his sight returned. Elder Erymmo was holding the bowl before him.

"Eat slowly," he said. "We have much to talk about."

Lucian took a bite of the soup, which was filled with greens, potatoes, and prawns.

Elder Erymmo took up the stool nearest Lucian, watching him for a moment. "Things can change in such a short amount of time. It isn't often we have the Queen's soldiers in the Greenrift. Led by a Mage-Lord, no less. That they have infiltrated this deeply into the Riftlands is a cause for great worry. Captain Fergus reported heavy armament and at least fifty hoplites, with no less than six Mage-Knights. That is no ordinary slave train. It's a war party. And they were sent here for one purpose."

Lucian already knew the truth, but hearing it stated so boldly only cemented it in his mind. "They were looking for me."

Elder Erymmo gave a slow nod. "They *still* are. You buried the entrance to the Greenrift, but we must collapse the entire tunnel and give up the terraces. At least, we must for now. We have stores to last a few months, which hopefully is enough to see us through. But soon, food will be the least of our worries."

"What do you mean?"

"That Mage-Lord and his men are headed here, Lucian. The Deepfork is a three days' march north of the terraces, and it's another four-day march down the Deeprift to reach Kiro. And if they are hardy and run much of the way, they might be here even sooner."

"So we get our defenses ready," Lucian said. "We have mages and soldiers too, right?"

Elder Erymmo's face was grave. "We do. But the Sorceress-Queen may have more men scouring the rifts than even that group. If two or more groups of them were to join up, I'm afraid we wouldn't last long. Best case, we defend ourselves at a grievous loss we could never recover from."

"But I don't understand," Lucian said. "How do they know that I'm in *this* village?"

"They might not know you're in this one, but it wouldn't take long before they found the right community. There are about a dozen villages like ours in the Deeprift, and we mostly get along. And it may be there's time to cobble together a decent defense. But we cannot depend on that."

"There's one thing that's still confusing me," Lucian said. "How in the Worlds did she get her soldiers this far without us knowing about it? Isn't Dara a couple of months away at least over land?"

"It is," Elder Erymmo confirmed. "I see two possibilities. The Sorceress-Queen's brands make it possible for her to instantly communicate with anyone who has one, and that would include all her Mage-Lords. It's unlikely someone of such a high rank would be directly controlled, but the Sorceress-Queen would be able to give and receive information from them, despite distance. In this possibility, she would have had some men already in place in the rifts, in secret. Which I find unlikely. The other possibility, which to me is the more probable one, is that they were carried from Dara by the Queen's airship, *Zephyr*."

Airship? If they had that, then they could be in the Deeprift faster than Erymmo had suggested. In fact, they could be here at any *moment*.

"I see what you're thinking," Elder Erymmo said. "The Riftlands are treacherous for an airship's passage. The mountains bordering the Deeprift are so tall that it will still take a few days to find a pass low enough for the ship to get through without its crew suffocating. The *Zephyr* has never been sighted this deep in the Riftlands for that very reason, besides the fact that traveling the rifts with its wyverns and strange wind patterns is practically a death wish. Yet even so, we must allow for the possibility, given how much the Queen wishes to find you."

Those words only reminded Lucian of his dream. He suppressed a shudder.

"What do we do then, Elder? How do we fight them off?"

Elder Erymmo watched him grimly, his expression ashen. Lucian had a similar feeling when the Transcends of the Volsung Academy exiled him. Surely, these people wouldn't do the same thing, but he wouldn't be surprised. He had experienced betrayal before, and he already felt the anger building up.

"As for what we do," Elder Erymmo said, "that is a matter still to be decided. You must accompany me at once to the Elder Council."

"You aren't going to send me away, are you?"

On that point, the Elder remained silent. He stood and gestured for Lucian to follow. "Perhaps it is better if we waited until everyone's in the same place."

There it was, then. "No need. I can be out of here in thirty minutes."

Elder Erymmo's eyes widened. "Don't be foolish. Come with me."

Lucian stood on shaky legs and allowed himself to be led out of the hut.

14

LUCIAN TRIED TO IGNORE THE VILLAGERS' stares as he followed Elder Erymmo through the dirt streets of Kiro, but he couldn't help but look up at the ringing of a hammer at Kieron's forge. The blacksmith paused his work at his bench to look up. His expression was grave before returning to his labor.

The path turned from the main drag which led to the meeting hall, instead sloping upward into a tunnel entrance. It wove up a set of stairs until it broke into the open air, a chamber of a cavern with large openings at the top. But at the very center of this chamber was a stream fed by small water-falls tumbling over the cavern's sides, and in the center of that stream was an island. A rope bridge led there, and in the middle were a dozen wooden chairs arranged in a circle.

Six of those seats were occupied; four with the other Elders, and the other two by Captain Fergus and Cleon. Lucian didn't even have the mind to take in the beauty of the grove. Every one of those eyes were staring at him, and the feeling that this was *just* like the Transcends wouldn't go away.

It was his bad luck to be the holder of one of the Orbs of the

Manifold. All too soon, he and Elder Erymmo had crossed the bridge.

"Be seated," Elder Ytrib said. "And stop looking like you think we're going to push you into the river."

Lucian sat, deciding it would be best to keep his mouth shut. Every time he said something, he only made things worse.

Elder Gia's plump face was friendly, but Lucian didn't trust that expression. It could easily be a mask for something else. "I trust Elder Erymmo has briefed you?"

"Regarding the Sorceress-Queen coming after me? Yeah, sure." Lucian eyed each Elder in turn. If it was going to be a fight, then it would be a fight. Fergus only stared at him disapprovingly, as if not remembering the fact they had fought side-by-side in the Greenrift. Cleon only stared at the ground, his face paler than usual. Like Lucian, it seemed he would rather be anywhere but here. That said, Lucian wondered what exactly Cleon and Fergus *were* doing here.

"What we have to say isn't easy," Elder Ytrib began, "but it's necessary. It is a brute fact that the Queen's Mage-Knights and her minions will be here in a week, or even less. We have less than that amount of time to decide what to do. Ideally, we will reach that decision by tonight."

Fergus shifted in his seat. "Elder. I mean no disrespect, but why have we not summoned the most responsible citizens and soldiers to this meeting? It hardly seems fitting that this off-worlder and former Mage-Knight would have a seat on this esteemed council."

"They are here, Captain Fergus," Elder Gia said softly, "because we are the only ones on this moon who know about the Orb of Binding, along with the Sorceress-Queen herself."

Lucian looked at Cleon, whose face went even *more* ghostly. Fergus *had* mentioned it in the Greenrift, which explained Cleon's presence.

"We cannot risk anyone here letting that information out," Elder Gia finished.

"As I said before," Cleon said, "I won't breathe a word of it. I promise you that on the grave of my parents."

Fergus scoffed. "There is more honor among rift adders than a Mage-Knight of Dara."

"*Former* Mage-Knight," Cleon corrected. "If you hold my former station against me so much, then why did you let me join the watchmen in the first place?"

Fergus sighed. "Desperation."

"Enough," Elder Jalisa said, her voice crackling like a whip. "This bickering avails nothing. We must decide what to do about the off-worlder and his Orb."

"Simple," Captain Fergus said. "Give me twenty good men and every mage in this village, and I can escort him to the Darkrift blindfolded and bid him good luck."

"Fergus," Elder Sina said, coming out of her silence with a soft voice. "I would not expect such cruelty out of you."

"It's not cruel," Fergus said. "It's for the safety of Kiro. The Queen is after him, so let her follow him into the Darkrift. Kill two gloombats with one javelin, so to speak."

"That is the *worst* possible thing we can do for the safety of Kiro," Elder Erymmo said. "If ever Lucian falls into the hands of the Sorceress-Queen, she will have a tool so powerful that none can withstand her. We all know what she is capable of with purely her *own* Psionic magic. Just *imagine* what horrors she can unleash if she were to get her hands on the Orb of Binding."

"Then hand the Orb over," Fergus said, reaching out a hand to Lucian. "I shall make quick work of it. Nothing can stand up to my shockspear."

"Fool," Elder Jalisa muttered. "The Orb *cannot* be destroyed. *The Prophecy of the Seven* states as much."

Of all of them here, Elder Jalisa knew the most about

Arian's work. He wondered what she knew that he didn't, and whether she would share that information.

"Of course," she went on, "the work is an incomprehensible babble, but under the influence of the Manifold, it is possible to discern *some* of the reason behind the madness."

"And what, pray tell, is this reason?" Fergus asked. "I mean no disrespect, Elder Jalisa, but the Orbs are a child's fable. No one believes they *truly* exist."

"Then how do you explain the magic Lucian streamed?" Cleon asked, his voice somewhat shaky. "*No one* should be able to do what he did, pulling down the mountainside like that! Even *you* have to believe he killed those wyverns up in the Snake Pass by now."

Fergus looked from Cleon, and then back to the Elders. From the relaxation of his features, Lucian could see that he was at last starting to accept Lucian's abilities with Binding.

"It's true I've never seen magic of the like," he said. "If any other Binder streamed to that degree, it would have either killed or frayed them."

"I'm glad you see that much sense," Elder Jalisa said. "If you sensed the purity of his stream, then you would know the truth, Fergus. No poison taints his Binding. He can stream as much as he wishes without ill-effect. That is in accordance with the prophecies of Arian, with the powers accorded to the Orbs of the Manifold."

"Not exactly," Lucian said, his face reddening. He knew he shouldn't interrupt an Elder, or contradict one, but honesty was important. "Using that much magic still exhausted me, even if the amount of ether was still unlimited."

"Mental load," Elder Ytrib said. "Yes, that takes training, strengthening your Focus to handle multiple streams of varying strength. That only comes with experience."

"So, I will always be limited in that way," Lucian said. "Unless someone can teach me to stream more efficiently."

"Maybe so," Fergus admitted. "I could feel the strength of your Binding Magic. Imagine what you could do if you had a modicum of expertise."

Even if it had been Fergus's aim to insult him, Lucian found himself agreeing. "I need to learn more. I don't deny that. I'm the last person who should be holding the Orb of Binding."

"Then why not relinquish it to one of your betters?" Fergus asked.

At this, there was a stark silence. Lucian would have thought that any of them would jump at the chance to have it, just like all those Ancients back in the days of Starsea. Indeed, he did see greed in the Elders' eyes. And fear. Which would win out, he couldn't say.

"I will not give up the Orb," Lucian said. "First of all, I don't know *how* to do it. The Orb isn't a physical object. It's something that fuses inside you. Getting rid of it might kill me, for all I know. Besides, I can't be sure of anyone else's plans for it."

"And what are *your* plans for it, Off-Worlder?"

"My name is Lucian, Captain Fergus. Please learn my name and treat me with respect. We fought side-by-side today."

"Why, you little . . ." Fergus clenched his jaw, but under the scrutiny of the Elders, he relented. "Well, is it *not* an important question? What does this young man plan to do with such a powerful artifact? What does the Orb of Binding even *do*? Where did it come from?"

Lucian saw that he would not only have to catch Fergus up, but Cleon, too. It wasn't something he *wanted* to do, but when Elder Ytrib nodded his assent, Lucian saw that it was necessary. Even Elder Jalisa would have gaps in her knowledge, because he hadn't mentioned every detail about his meeting with the Oracle of Binding. Not even Arian's words would speak to everything she had said.

"I still don't see what this has to do with me," Cleon said. "I came to Kiro to escape trouble, not find it."

"This concerns you," Elder Sina said. "Remain seated."

Cleon crossed his arms. It looked like he might bolt, even with Elder Sina's warning.

"I guess I'll start at the beginning," Lucian said.

"Let's hear it," Elder Jalisa said. Her dark eyes seemed hungry for knowledge.

So, Lucian started at the very beginning, with the day he found out he was a mage at the League Health Authority. He didn't understand why he started there, but they didn't stop him, even as he related details he believed to be extraneous. They seemed surprised that he had met Vera, when he told her about how she was the teacher of Xara Mallis, though none of them made any comment about it. He told them of his short tenure at the Volsung Academy, his quick progress, and how the Transcends had stabbed him in the back, leading to his exile on the Isle of Madness. And there, he told them of his dreams, how he had come across the Orb of Binding, as well as his meeting with the Oracle.

And he told them everything the Oracle had said – about the rise and fall of Starsea. He talked about how the Orbs were there from the beginning, and how wars were fought for them. And that if all of them were held by a single being, it would stop the fraying from rotting the minds and bodies of mages, while making the being that held them immortal.

It was only here that he was interrupted by Fergus. "Impossible."

Lucian swallowed his anger. He had to be prepared for dealing with objections, because others might be thinking the same thing. "I thought so too, at first. But then she gave the Orb to me, and everything I've been able to do since then confirms that I have it. If I *didn't* have it, then how is my Binding stream so pure? How can I do these things that would otherwise be impossible? And why would the Sorceress-Queen be so set on finding me?"

Fergus didn't have an answer for all that, though Lucian wished he did.

Lucian continued his story. He told them about the Vigilants and their ambitions to hold all Seven Orbs, to become the Immortal Emperor, to rebuild Starsea after it had been destroyed by the Swarmers – called by them the *Alkasen*. There were only two options to stop the fraying and the *Alkasen*, the cycle of destruction foretold by Arian. The first way was to gather all the Orbs and hold them, becoming the new Immortal Emperor. Or, to take the Orbs to the Heart of Creation, from where they had originated. The Heart of Creation was only reachable through the First Gate deep in Dark Space, the abode of the *Alkasen*. Only there could the Immortal destroy the Orbs, ending magic and the Starsea Cycle once and for all.

Once Lucian was done, it was hours later. Night had fallen, and no one made a move to adjourn the meeting. Everyone was quiet and solemn, even Fergus, who seemed at a loss for words for once. There had been so much information that Lucian was afraid he'd left something out, or even worse, said something incorrectly. Even saying it out loud sounded like pure madness, and he was half-expecting any one of them, or perhaps all, to throw him out of Kiro once and for all.

But none of them laughed. All just watched him with what seemed to be pity.

Elder Ytrib was the one to break the silence. "Thank you, Lucian. I would call an end to this council, were this not a matter of such gravity. But as it stands, we cannot disperse until we decide what we are going to do about the Orb. Every second that passes, the Sorceress-Queen's agents draw nearer." He paused to look at him, and Lucian got the feeling a hammer was about to fall. "You can't remain in Kiro, Lucian. The Sorceress-Queen would just find you here. But there is nowhere on all of Psyche for you to go. This world is a prison, and wherever you run, the Sorceress-Queen will hunt you down. Be it days, weeks, months, or years, she will one day find you."

Everyone nodded at that, and it sent peals of dread down Lucian's spine.

"There is only one clear answer," Elder Jalisa said, her eyes sad as she watched him. "As crazy as it sounds, it's the only thing that makes sense." Everyone watched her, looking for some shred of hope in the situation. Elder Erymmo was already nodding, as if he had guessed where she was going.

"It's said that the Orb of Psionics is somewhere on this moon. Arian mentioned an Ancient named Shantozar who came here, one of the seven Oracles of Starsea. Or at least, he came to a world that matches the description of this one. The pertinent part he wrote reads thus:

> *"Under the White World with red-whorl eye,*
> *Upon a moon of violet, violent sky;*
> *Peers beneath Burning Sands and wind,*
> *Lies the Amethyst of Starsea within."*

She paused, to let the words sink in. "Or so such a line might be translated from his mad garble. Ever since the end of the Mage War, many mages on Psyche have heard those words and have sought the Orb of Psionics, to no avail. But the prophecy clearly speaks of Psyche. The White World with red-whorl eye must be Cupid. Psyche is the moon with violet and violent sky. The Burning Sands lie under Cupid's gaze, and they even derive the name from those lines. And the Amethyst of Starsea is clear enough. Each of the Orbs was called by its attendant jewel. Psionics is violet in its manifestation. There-fore, the Orb of Psionics, the Amethyst of Starsea, lies buried somewhere in the Burning Sands, under the Great Gaze of Cupid's Eye."

Cleon suddenly stood. "All right. *Enough.* I *know* I don't belong here. I don't understand a word of what anyone is saying. I'm leaving. I'll never breathe a word of this to anyone, you have my promise."

"You're in too deep now, Mage-Knight," Fergus said. "Keep your seat."

Lucian thought Cleon would really leave this time, but to his surprise, Cleon sat back down, sinking into a sullen silence.

"The Sorceress-Queen said the Orb is on Psyche as well," Lucian said. "At least, she said as much in my dream. I don't think she wants to kill me. At least, not immediately. I think her plan is to use me to find the Orb of Psionics, somehow."

He left out the part about her invitation to work with her. All the Elders knew that by now, but to say so out loud in front of Fergus might only flare his suspicions and make things more difficult going ahead.

"I wish you well in your quest, Off-Worlder," Fergus said. "You can find the Burning Sands far beyond the Pass of Madness. Perhaps with your Binding powers, you will find a way where others have not."

At those words, Lucian felt a despondence such as he had never known. Was that truly to be his fate, to be sent on a mad quest with almost no possibility of success?

Well, that was what he signed up for the moment he gave himself up to the prison barge.

"Getting to Dara itself is a nearly impossible journey," Elder Sina said. "Much more the Burning Sands beyond. They say those who enter that place lose their way and never come back. Lucian can't ever hope to uncover the Orb of Psionics alone. It is only with the power of that Orb that he can hope to defeat the Sorceress-Queen and her Psionic Magic."

"Then there's no hope," Cleon said.

"No," Ytrib said. "There is no use saying something is impossible until you've tried."

133

"Many *have* tried to find it," Fergus reminded him. "All have failed."

"But that doesn't mean it is impossible," Ytrib said, stubbornly. "I know. It's easy for me to say, sitting here."

None of them seemed to consider the obvious: what if Lucian didn't *want* to do this? He knew he had no real choice. The Sorceress-Queen would hunt him wherever he went, of that he had no doubt. And there was the even *more* impossible goal of getting off Psyche altogether. The Orb of Psionics could apparently help with that as well, though he didn't know how.

"I have no choice," Lucian said. "I will leave tomorrow if that's what it takes."

"You cannot do this alone, Lucian," Elder Ytrib said. "You will need help. If we were sending you off to die, we would send you alone. But you dying will not solve our problems, but only exacerbate them. As we mentioned before, the worst thing possible would be for the Sorceress-Queen to take the Orb you already have. So, we must do whatever we can to prevent that."

"Elder," Fergus said, nervously. "What are you suggesting?"

Elder Ytrib leveled his gaze at the captain, his bushy eyebrows rising. "You know *exactly* what I'm suggesting. I called you and Cleon here not only because you know the truth about the Orb. I've called you because *the both of you* will be helping Lucian find the Orb of Psionics."

15

FERGUS'S EXPRESSION BECAME GRIM, while Cleon's jaw hung open. Even Lucian couldn't help but stare at the Elders in disbelief.

"Wherever Lucian goes, the Sorceress-Queen will follow," Elder Ytrib explained. "With the Sorceress-Queen's men in the Riftlands, and possibly the *Zephyr* too, we need our most powerful Radiant to go with him. That Radiant is you, Captain Fergus Madigan."

At these words, Fergus nodded, though his eyes still seemed shocked. "Of course, I will do whatever you ask of me, Elder Ytrib. But if you send me away, I won't be able to defend the village."

"Kiro will be lost if Lucian fails," Elder Ytrib said. "And the Queen will eventually be drawn here if he were to stay. Lucian and the Orb he carries are our salvation, along with the Orb of Psionics. We *must* believe that it's there and can be found."

From Cleon's pale face, it looked as if he might heave at any minute. Lucian felt much the same.

"If that's true, then I will take every guard in the village,"

Fergus decided. "Whatever gives us the greatest chance of success and keeps the Queen's men away from here."

"On the contrary," Elder Gia said, softly. "There can be no more than four of you. The last thing we want is to attract attention, and the more people who go, the more likely it draws the Sorceress-Queen's eyes."

"Why can't Lucian ward himself?" Fergus asked.

"You know the answer to that," Elder Gia said. "He is young in the ways of magic, despite the power of the Orb of Binding. You will teach him not only to ward himself, but to stream magic. You are well-versed, even in the Aspects that are not your strengths. There is no better guardian to appoint to Lucian."

Guardian? Lucian found the word distasteful. It made it sound as if Fergus were adopting him.

"They shouldn't have to come if they don't want to," Lucian said. "I can find my own way."

"Fool," Fergus said. "This isn't about *any* of us, or what we want. The fate of Psyche is at stake, and if *your* story is to be believed, the fate of humanity itself. *Everything* depends on finding the Orb and defeating the Sorceress-Queen before she finds you."

Slowly, everyone's gaze shifted to Cleon, who groaned.

"Is he okay?" Elder Sina asked.

"Doesn't look like it," Elder Erymmo said.

"Watchman Cleon?" Elder Ytrib asked.

Cleon only groaned louder.

"Why is he being forced to go, anyway?" Lucian asked. "I understand Fergus, with his wards and all. But why Cleon?"

"Cleon must go for three reasons," Elder Ytrib said, holding up a finger. "One, he knows about the Orb of Binding." He held up another finger. "Two, Cleon is an accomplished Thermalist, and his strongest Aspects complement Fergus's weaknesses, meaning they can ward against almost anything." Ytrib held up a third finger. "And last of all, your path will take you through Dara and the Pass of Madness, the only way into the Burning Sands. Cleon has lived much of his life in Dara and will know how to navigate the streets."

At this, Cleon actually *did* heave, but nothing came out but water.

"Get a hold of yourself, man!" Fergus said. "Anyone *this* lily-livered will run at the first sign of trouble!"

"He didn't run in the Greenrift," Lucian said.

"Not Dara," Cleon said. "I'm not ready for that."

"You're going back, whether you're ready or not," Fergus said. "The Elders have spoken."

"This isn't my fight. My life is *here* now. I have a girlfriend. I'm . . . starting to put the past behind. And now, you would make me face it again?"

The past? What in the Worlds was he talking about? Cleon had run from something in Dara, that much was clear. Lucian couldn't help but be curious.

"Our time spent in Dara will be minimal," Fergus said. "We have one mission and one mission only: to find the Orb of Psionics and use it to end the Sorceress-Queen's reign of terror. Dara will be one of the most dangerous parts of the journey, but with you, our chances of success are all the greater."

Cleon shook his head. "I'm going to be recognized. I was a Mage-Knight. People know me there, even if it has been five years."

"So, you won't go?" Lucian asked.

He heaved a sigh. "Seems I have no choice, do I? If I refuse, I'll be exiled for my troubles, or at least reviled."

"Why are you being so difficult?" Fergus asked.

"Difficult? You realize we're going to die? And probably *long* before we reach Dara and the Golden Vale!"

"If that is our fate, then that is our fate," Fergus said. "*We* are the only ones who can find the Orb of Psionics. We are the Riftlands' only hope. The Worlds' only hope!"

"That's rotting madness," Cleon said. "Even *if* we somehow made it to Dara and through the Pass of Madness, we'd still have *two thousand* kilometers more just to get to the Burning Sands, if not more. It's so hot there it'll melt the skin off your very bones and there isn't a drop of water to drink. Add to that dust storms, moonquakes, and constant lava flows from Cupid's gravity, and you're only *guaranteeing* what is already a foregone conclusion. *Our* deaths."

"*That* is our path," Fergus said, easily. Lucian had to wonder if he was faking that confidence. "Either be exiled, Mage-Knight, or help us. Your choice."

"I already said I *would* help," Cleon said. "Doesn't mean I won't complain every rotting step of the way."

Fergus shook his head and sighed. "*These* are the men I'm to lead into the Burning Sands, Elder Ytrib? Can I not choose some others?"

"Four is already too many," Elder Jalisa said, her voice rattling. Her expression seemed weary, which might have explained her recent reticence in the conversation.

"Who's the fourth?" Fergus asked, his expression not holding out much hope.

"It would be one of us, but we are too old for such a long, dangerous journey," Elder Erymmo said. "And we will need capable mages to defend Kiro, for the Queen's agents will no doubt come here anyway. As it stands, we might even die before you do."

"Then we must evacuate the village at once!" Fergus said.

"We will certainly do what we can," Elder Sina said. "However, it will be impossible to hide this village. We will have to band with the other communities to give you three a head start. And hope with all of you gone, the Queen's focus will turn away from the Deeprift."

"If our fourth is not anyone from the village, then who is it?" Fergus asked.

Every eye then went to Elder Ytrib, whose face was a mask of sorrow. Lucian wondered why they were looking at him like that. *He* wasn't going.

"There are two paths to Dara," Elder Ytrib said. "One is through the Riftlands, which will take months to cross. And the other is through the Darkrift, which is fastest, but also the most dangerous."

Lucian was wondering where Elder Ytrib was going with all this.

"If it were any other circumstance, I would urge the first option," Elder Ytrib continued. "But the Sorceress-Queen has a greater chance of finding you if you travel in the open. Especially if she is roving the rifts with the *Zephyr*."

Elder Jalisa scoffed. "Even if she *is* looking for Lucian with it, they have a better chance of survival traveling the Rifts."

Elder Erymmo nodded at that, apparently agreeing. Lucian had to admit the Darkrift sounded ominous.

"I took the Darkrift once," Cleon said. "I would never go that way again. I only made it here through sheer luck. Anyone who goes down there is bound to lose their way."

"That is where your fourth comes in," Elder Ytrib said, who was now looking at Lucian. "I believe you've met my daughter, Serah."

Lucian's eyes widened at that. Serah was his *daughter*? He fumbled for words at this revelation.

"No one knows the Darkrift like her. That is no guarantee of safety, but she's been all over the Riftlands and knows more secret paths than anyone. Though she was exiled by my word, she is still my blood. I . . . love her dearly, and even now wish she were home, and not out there." He shook his head. "But that cannot be."

"It can be if you just give the order," Lucian said. He

wondered how the Elder could have exiled her, especially if she was his daughter. It was hard to imagine *anyone* doing such a terrible thing.

Fergus looked as if he wanted to punch Lucian. "*No* fray can live in Kiro, Lucian. Not even the daughter of an Elder. The law applies to everyone, great or small."

Fergus was just the type of person Lucian didn't like. The goody-two-shoes type, always following the rules to the letter, no matter the consequences, and no matter who got hurt. He didn't have the strength to argue with him.

"I met Serah on my way down here. If not for her, I'd be dead from the wyverns and would have never found this place. She is nowhere near frayed, even if she's showing some physical signs. Her mind seems fine."

Elder Ytrib's face paled, along with Gia's, and Lucian got the feeling he had gone too far. Ytrib at last spoke, choosing to ignore Lucian's point. "I know if you three find Serah, she will lead you as far as Dara. If anyone has mapped out Slave's Run and the Darkrift, it's my daughter."

"I thought Slave's Run was just a story," Fergus said. "Something the Daran slaves believe because it gives them hope."

"My daughter has told me it exists," Elder Ytrib said. "I've spoken with her. Quite recently."

Now, every eye went to him. Fergus's expression seemed the most shocked. It meant Elder Ytrib had broken the law that all Rifters were supposed to follow.

"Yes, I've broken the law. Many times. But you don't understand the pain I feel."

"It was at my insisting," Elder Gia said.

"No," Elder Ytrib said. "It's my fault alone."

"I don't understand," Lucian said. "Why *can't* you talk to Serah? Why have these laws in the first place? They seem . . . well, stupid."

Elder Jalisa's face was stony. "The Code is necessary for the safety of the Deeprift. In the past, frays have banded together and laid waste to what little farmland we have, even killing. *Any* fray can turn into a Burner at any moment. We have our laws for a reason. It's how we have survived this long."

"I admit my fault," Elder Ytrib said. "And I'm ready to abdicate my seat on this council if others here call for it. I only said this much to let you know, beyond a doubt, that my daughter has explored the Darkrift substantially. More than that, she has located a passage she believes to be Slave's Run."

"*Believes* to be," Elder Jalisa said. "It's still safer to go through the Riftlands to reach the Golden Vale. It's tenuous, yes, but my vote is for the more traditional path. That said, it might be most prudent to let Fergus decide as need dictates."

"I will do my best," Fergus said.

"The fate of the Worlds stands upon this tower of slender reeds," Elder Jalisa said. "The merest breeze will displace them."

At this sobering reminder, all went quiet.

"So, when do we begin?" Lucian asked.

Everyone looked at him, as if *he* should know the answer. As if *he* were the one to give the rest moral guidance. Surely that couldn't be the case. Surely, things were not already this desperate.

"Cleon," Lucian said. "I'm sorry you're a part of this."

Cleon didn't respond. The words sounded hollow, even if Lucian hadn't meant them that way.

Lucian turned to Fergus. "I know we don't see eye to eye on things. But we'll have to work together from here on out. I'm willing to listen to you, and even to let you lead, but only if you are willing to not discount me for my age or call me *Off-Worlder*."

Fergus ground his teeth, as if this were too much to ask. In the end, however, he let out a sigh. "Done."

"It should be said that none of us are doing this because we have a choice," Lucian said. "I think we're all aware of the stakes, so I won't go over that again." He looked at the others. From their long faces, his speech wasn't doing much to inspire. "We have a wild card, though. We have the Orb of Binding. With that, we might make it farther than we ever thought possible."

"How?" Cleon asked.

Lucian shook his head. "I don't know. If I had any choice, I wouldn't be here right now. And since you guys are roped in with me, we have to try. Focus on the small goals first. Finding Serah should be easy enough, right? She's not a day's walk up the rift from here, just beyond the Snake Pass. If we walk fast, I bet we can be at her cave by tomorrow."

Her companion, Ramore, was another problem entirely, but Lucian wouldn't mention that yet. He wanted to make this seem easy. He'd warn them about Ramore once they were on the trail.

"Simple enough, I guess," Cleon said. "So, when *do* we begin this mad, rotting quest?"

"Tomorrow morning," Lucian said. "Before the break of dawn."

Cleon whistled. "You're a cruel bastard, aren't you?"

"He's right," Fergus said. "Even now, that Mage-Lord, his Mage-Knights, and those hoplites are marching up the Green-rift for the Deepfork. If the *Zephyr* is giving them a lift, then they'll be here even sooner. If it were me, we'd leave tonight. But I understand if you both need to recuperate from this morning."

Lucian shook his head. As if Fergus didn't need the rest as well. If Fergus were going to be this insufferable the whole journey, finding the Orb of Psionics would be the easy part.

"I can arrange for your supplies," Elder Gia said. "Food, water, cookware, packs, tools. You must travel light, but you will need sufficient provisions to see you to Dara and beyond."

"Assuming we make it that far," Cleon grumbled.

"We *will*," Fergus said. "We *will*, because *I* said so."

"That's nice." Cleon stood. "Well, I have to take a leak. And make love to my girlfriend one last time before I head off on a suicide mission." He looked at Fergus, to Lucian. "I'll see you gents tomorrow, bright and early."

This time when Cleon left, no one stopped him.

"I should begin preparations," Fergus said.

Things were happening so fast. As soon as Lucian had found safety, it was being snatched from him. He would have to head back out into the wilds of this hostile moon, and not only that, survive the Sorceress-Queen, who was many times more powerful than him, who had hundreds if not thousands of mages and hoplites at her command.

Lucian doubted even the Orb of Binding could stand up to all that, but he had no choice, as he saw it.

It was his fate to find the Orb of Psionics or die trying.

16

ALL LUCIAN WANTED to do was head back to his hut and sleep. But it seemed he wouldn't get his wish. Both Elder Erymmo and Fergus approached him before he could make his escape.

"One thing, and I'll leave you be," Fergus said. "You shouldn't be staying on your own by the lake anymore. I don't doubt the loyalty of every man and woman in Kiro, but the Sorceress-Queen is a dangerous foe whom we shouldn't underestimate. As unlikely as it is, there may be a spy in the village. We shouldn't take the chance."

"Where do I stay, then?"

"Kieron is an honorable man, and his house is one of the largest in the village. I'm on my way there now to let him and Julia know. Go straight there after Elder Erymmo is done speaking with you."

"Are you sure, Fergus?"

"You're a hero, Off-Worlder." He cleared his throat awkwardly. "I mean, Lucian. It'll be fine. Julia sets the finest table in the village. It'll be the perfect place for you to rest tonight."

"What if they ask questions?"

"I'll tell them we're going wyvern hunting. You've already killed two, so they won't think anything is amiss. We already have a custom of having each family host a newcomer, so that they can get to know everyone."

If that was the case, then Lucian had to wonder why Fergus had made him stay by himself at the lake. Pure dislike, probably.

"Be on your best behavior," Fergus added. "They must not sense anything wrong. By the time they realize the truth, we should be long gone. Try to eat a lot and get a long night's rest. You'll most certainly need it."

With that, Fergus left Lucian behind with Elder Erymmo.

"And now, I must say my piece," the Elder said, solemnly. "And I'm afraid it will be more than a piece. There is something you must be careful of going forward, Lucian."

"What's that, Elder?"

"The Sorceress-Queen will not only be looking for you physically, but mentally. She is the most powerful Psionic in all the Worlds. Or at least, if there *is* one more powerful, I haven't heard of it."

"There's Vera. The mage I met on the *Burung*."

"Yes, there is her," Elder Erymmo said. "But it's hard to imagine there being a Psionic more powerful than the Sorceress-Queen. She has been a constant presence here on Psyche since the end of the Mage War."

"The war ended fifty years ago," Lucian said. "But in my dream, I got the sense the Sorceress-Queen was quite young. How could that be when she's been here over fifty years?"

"I don't know about that. Though few outside her own nobility have seen her, she is known to be quite old. However, her powers are those of the mind. She can, and does, use mind tricks to appear a certain way. When she must. Perhaps she thinks she can better influence you if she appears in the guise of a young and beautiful woman. One of the basic tenets of thought manipulation is that it's better to inflame a positive emotion than a negative one. Your subject will be far more likely to do your bidding willingly."

"So what are you saying? That she's trying to make me fall in love with her or something?"

"In love?" Elder Erymmo looked aghast. "Almost certainly not. Seduce you, perhaps. You must be on guard of that, Lucian. If she can get a toehold, whatever the means, it won't be long before the entire mind falls prey."

The mere idea that an eighty-plus-year-old woman was trying to seduce him in the guise of a young woman made him sick, so much so that he didn't have words.

"We are delving into the unethical," Elder Erymmo said. "We won't debate the morality of mind control. Suffice it to say, it *is* possible, and it's a powerful tool for those who use it, for good or for evil. The Sorceress-Queen can outright control the minds of her subjects with her brands. With all that said, most obey the Sorceress-Queen willingly, without the need for outright possession – the technical term for any sort of mind control. It's easy to manipulate others without active magic when you can read intentions, if not their thoughts. She can enter the dreams of other mages, and implant ideas that the mage will act on in the waking world."

"How is that possible? My mind is my own, so I don't see how she can influence it."

"A mind is far more moldable than you realize. That is why you must always guard it. If people can be influenced by ideologies, propaganda, fears, and misinformation *without* the aid of magic, enough to start wars, revolutions, and abandon all sense and reason, how much *more* can the human mind be manipulated *with* the aid of magic? If you take that idea, and multiply it a thousandfold across many minds in an empire, for example, then you'll come close to what the Sorceress-Queen is capable

THE RIFTS OF PSYCHE

of. Add to that an artifact as powerful as the Orb of Psionics, then it might be the end of the Worlds as we know them, especially if she finds a way off Psyche. Worse, mages have a particular vulnerability – a mage's mind, or at least a part of it, is connected to the Manifold. She can reach you through there. Not easily, mind you. It takes far more magic for her to break your defenses than it does for you to defend against them. That is why it's so important for you to learn to stream wards. It's during sleep that you are most vulnerable, especially when you've reached a point of incredible exhaustion. That is when you, or any mage really, becomes vulnerable to dream implantation."

"And you can teach me to defend myself from that?"

Elder Erymmo nodded. "That's why I've come to speak with you. Fortunately, a Psionic ward is usually enough to keep other mages from interfering with your dreams, and you won't need the ether while you're asleep, anyway. Forming a Psionic ward before bed should become a daily habit of yours. Normally a dualstream is sufficient, however, the ward can be strengthened by making it a tristream."

"How long will it last?"

"That depends on how long the streams in the ward cohere. Usually that's eight hours before the ward unravels, or even longer if the warder is particularly skilled. To create a Psionic ward, either Binding or Gravitonics will form the shell. As stated before, the shell's purpose is to keep the Psionic Magic in place through stream coherence. Through coherence, the two streams act in tandem to keep the ward active. It's paramount you learn to do this before you sleep tonight. Now, expand your Focus to me and follow along . . ."

Lucian did as instructed. Elder Erymmo began with a Binding stream, with which he surrounded himself. Lucian saw why he called it a shell. The blue aura surrounding him had the appearance of a shell, or perhaps an egg. That layer of magic was thin, almost nonexistent. Lucian followed along and felt the stream was simple to perform, the magic circulating around at the same steady rate.

Then, Elder Erymmo opened a new stream, this one Psionic. The way the magic streamed felt . . . different from the kinetic manifestation Lucian was accustomed to. It was slower, more like an eddying creek that filled every groove and crack than a sudden burst. Elder Erymmo's Psionic magic spread, filling the empty space within the Binding shell. It didn't fill *all* the space. Lucian wondered why, until he realized that the shell was leaving room for more potential streams. Theoretically, there was enough space for the rest of the Aspects to be streamed within the shell, though the amount of magic necessary to do that would no doubt kill whoever attempted it.

Once done streaming, Elder Erymmo closed his eyes and combined the two streams – or rather, "cohered" them. The bubble was now indigo from the fusion of Psionic and Binding Magic. Lucian realized he had unwittingly done the same thing when he'd escaped the snow-filled valley on the Isle of Madness, only in that instance, he had cohered Binding and Gravitonic Magic.

Lucian felt Elder Erymmo's stream cut off, leaving the indigo ward visible for a few seconds before it faded. Lucian followed the same steps, his own ward fading. Though the ward was no longer visible, inside Lucian felt that something was . . . different. As if his potential were weaker. The ward was fed from his base supply of ether, so if he ever needed to stream, he would have less ether to do it with. How that worked in conjunction with the Orb of Binding, Lucian couldn't begin to guess.

"Good," Elder Erymmo said, with an approving nod. "You're a natural."

"Where did the ward go?" Lucian asked. "I can still feel it. I think."

"It's there," Erymmo confirmed. "Even if you can't see it. Now, for the sake of teaching, if I were to do the opposite and make Psionic Magic the shell and Binding Magic the ward, then you would have a decent defense against Binding Magic. You might do this in case you were worried about someone tethering you or Binding your body parts together."

"That sounds . . . awful."

"A hard thing to do, that. Thankfully, as you gain experience, you can learn to sense what other mages are gifted at before it comes to blows by feeling their Focus. That will give you a clue about what to ward against. And if they attack you with an Aspect they are weak with, they will burn more ether to do so, and it will be easier for you to defend."

"I see. Makes sense."

"The advantage of wards is that they take little magic compared to the opponent who wants to break them. Remember: shields are active streams, and are typically more powerful, but are temporary and burn more ether in the long run. A ward stays in effect for much longer and is a passive stream. The disadvantage is that they are weaker than active shields and take up a portion of your ether pool. The amount depends on the strength of the ward."

"I think I understand."

"Now, let's test your ward and make sure it's set right."

Before Lucian even had a chance to feel nervous about it, there was a curious tickling at his mind. It was the strangest feeling, like an itch he couldn't quite scratch.

"Your ward is well-made," Erymmo said. "Even I can't puncture it. Your ward should keep you safe from dream implantation."

"And it will go away on its own?"

"It will weaken over time, but usually a ward doesn't lose effectiveness until after eight hours or so," Erymmo said. "After that, they dissolve quite quickly. As you get a feel for things, you'll learn when a ward is active and when it is not. While a ward is active, for example, it will be more difficult to open new streams. Upon dissolution of the ward, that ether will be gone until it is naturally replaced or drawn from the ethereal field. Another disadvantage of wards if you wish to think of it that way."

Lucian wondered what would have happened if he'd had a Gravitonic ward in place on his first day on Psyche. If Serah had been an enemy, it could have easily been his death. He not only had to learn to stream wards effectively. He also had to learn to detect the strengths of other mages, to size them up in a flash, in case the worst happened.

"I'll keep that in mind," Lucian said.

"That's all I had to show you. If you wish to learn more about wards, and their uses, I suggest talking to Fergus about it. As a Radiant, he is an expert in wards."

"Why are Radiants better at wards than other mages?"

"Most of their magic depends on wards and brands. Light spheres, for example, work better as brands than active streams, as we discussed this morning. Seeking and conceal-ment wards are also Radiant talents. So, of course, is the detec-tion of light across all its spectrums."

Lucian clearly had a lot to learn, but this new knowledge should serve well enough for now. "I should probably get going."

"I wish you well, Lucian," Elder Erymmo said. "Come by tomorrow morning, and my shockspear is yours."

Lucian's eyes widened at that. "The graphene one you have hanging on the wall?"

The Elder nodded. "You'll need it more than me."

Lucian almost refused, but he knew the Elder had a point.

"The road ahead will be difficult," Elder Erymmo said, "but Fergus is a good man, and the best mage in the village. With him, you won't have to worry about the Sorceress-Queen or her agents finding you. Go, Lucian. Get some rest. You are most certainly going to need it."

With that, Elder Erymmo went to join the other Elders at their deliberations.

———

LUCIAN FOLLOWED the trail back to the village. He was grateful for the empty streets, though he felt lonely walking in the darkness, the only light coming from inside homes. Conversations and laughter filtered out from doors and windows, which only reminded him of everyone he had lost. The sound was doubly sad, because those people didn't know the threat they were under because of him.

He wanted to go back to his hut by the lake. He wasn't in the mood for conversation. But Fergus did have a point that it was better to be safe. He tentatively approached the door of Kireon's cabin and knocked three times on the wooden door. When it opened, it revealed Kieron's ruddy, bearded face beaming a wide smile. His mood seemed to be the complete antithesis to Lucian's.

"Welcome!" he boomed. "Julia and I were wondering if you'd gotten lost. Come inside!"

Lucian stepped into the light of the home, finding a well-swept floor covered with a mat of rushes. A fire burned low in a mud-brick fireplace, lending a warm ambiance. Over that fire simmered a pot of stew, its aroma savory. Julia was leaning over that pot, giving it a stir.

"Julia, Lucian is here."

"I know, honey, but I doubt he wants his stew burned." Once done to her satisfaction, she stood and smiled. "Welcome to our home, Lucian. Please, have a seat. It's warm by the fire."

Lucian nodded. "Thank you."

Lucian went forward, where a couple of wooden rockers

were placed before the hearth. Toward the left was a dining table with six chairs, all simple but well-crafted. Two pitchers of drink sat in the center, beaded with condensation. Above his head, Lucian noted a loft accessible by a short ladder, and another room leading off from the main family area. Fergus was right that this was one of the larger homes in Kiro.

Once Lucian was seated, Julia looked at her husband. "Kieron, dear, please see to setting the table. Lucian, it'll only be a moment until dinner is ready."

"I'm looking forward to it."

Julia's cheeks colored as she looked upward toward the loft. "Morgana! Where are your manners? We have a guest. Come keep him company while I finish up dinner."

"Yes, Mother. I'm still getting ready."

Lucian shifted in his seat, hoping the encounter with Morgana would not be as awkward as it was last night. He heard the floor creaking from the loft above, and then Morgana climbed down the ladder, wearing a pink skirt and red blouse with a large red ribbon in her dark hair. She skipped the last few rungs, landing neatly on the floor. Lucian stood, not sure of the mannerisms of this place, but it was better to be safe.

When she turned, her face was made-up, and her eyes smoky and holding a curious gleam that caught his attention. She strode toward him confidently, offering a hand. Lucian took it, wondering if he were supposed to kiss it or something.

"My stars, Morgana," Julia said. "You look so lovely!"

"Well, you said to get ready, Mother, so I did." She looked at Lucian. "Hello, Lucian."

"Morgana. It's . . . nice to see you."

Her eyes sparkled even more as she took her hand away. "Well, I don't want anyone to say our hospitality is . . . wanting."

Julia looked from Morgana to Lucian for a moment. "I . . . think I'll see to the bread. You two catch up."

Lucian almost told her to stay, but she was gone before he

THE RIFTS OF PSYCHE

could get a word out. But by this time, Kieron was done readying the table and came to stand by Lucian. Maybe he could rein Morgana in, but Lucian wasn't holding out much hope.

"I have to say," Kieron said, jovially, "Captain Fergus has warmed up to you a lot! And I can see why, after your heroics today. I'm glad you're on our side, especially with what folks are saying."

"What do you mean, *what folks are saying*?" Morgana asked, her expression at once becoming pouty. "You *know* I don't like being in the dark, Father."

At this moment, Julia returned from outside with the dinner rolls. Lucian supposed that was where the oven was.

"Morgana, behave yourself," she said.

Lucian wondered how she knew her daughter was being unruly with just one look. But perhaps unruliness was Morgana's default. "Lucian, why don't you have a seat at the table? Kieron, take his boots. Morgana, get the washing bowl."

Morgana sighed. "Yes, Mother."

As she stalked off into the back room, Julia shook her head.

"Something has gotten into her lately," Julia said. "She's usually much more agreeable. Please, Lucian, have a seat. Dinner is ready."

Lucian sat at the table and tried to ignore the following awkwardness. If he could have had his way, he'd be eating alone in his hut, but for now, he'd have to survive this.

Morgana returned and offered the wash bowl, steeped with some small white flowers, a mischievous glint in her brown eyes which had a tingle of violet. Had her eyes *always* been that color? Lucian was too flummoxed to remember.

He washed his hands quickly while Morgana smirked. She turned just as her parents were heading back. After they had laid the pot on the table, Morgana offered the wash bowl to them both, her face a mask of innocence.

"Thank you, Morgana," Julia said. "That's much better."

"Forgive my earlier rudeness," she said, including Lucian in the apology. "I know I can be a menace, but I mean well."

"That she can be," Kieron said, with a chuckle. "Let's eat!"

"You spoil her," Julia said. "Morgana, please fill the cups. But not the mystika, that is for your father to serve." She looked at Lucian. "It's his own brew."

Morgana served Lucian first, standing almost directly behind him as she reached over and filled his cup. She brushed his shin with her foot as she walked around the table, so lightly that it *might* have been an accident. She was growing bolder.

She next filled her parents' cups with tea before filling her own. Kieron served Lucian some stew, which was filled with meat and root vegetables. When Morgana took her seat, she scooted her chair closer to Lucian and gave him a warm smile. He wondered how soon he might get out of here. He was already starting to think of excuses.

"Before we begin," Kieron said, reaching for the other pitcher, "some of my mystika, in recognition of Lucian's bravery today." He poured out four shots of the drink. "You bring honor to our family and our table by being here."

Lucian cleared his throat. "The honor is mine, Kieron."

They drank, and the sweet drink burned Lucian's throat and settled warm in his stomach.

It was quiet again as they all took their first bites of stew. The meat was tough and stringy, though the stew had done some work to soften it, while the flavor was good and savory. The vegetables were mostly familiar – potatoes, chopped-up beets, leeks, onions, with a few other things he didn't recognize.

"It's delicious," Lucian said.

Julia smiled, pleased. "It isn't much, but thank you, Lucian."

"They are already rationing the community larders," Kieron put in. "They say a slave party will be making its way up the Deeprift in just a few days."

"Good thing we'll have Lucian to protect us," Morgana said, lightly touching his knee. Lucian jerked his leg away, doing his best to keep his face neutral.

"Didn't you hear, dear?" Julia asked. "Lucian will be gone for the next few days, hunting wyverns with Fergus and Cleon. It's important we have enough venom on hand to make those slavers think twice about stepping foot in the Deeprift!"

"Oh," she said, sadly. "That's much too bad."

Lucian almost spit out his stew when Morgana's foot rubbed his shin. It was hard not to betray the surprise on his face. He shifted his feet away, but that did nothing to curb Morgana's determination. She just reached farther, and Lucian was helpless to escape. What in the Worlds was this girl doing?

"Is everything all right?" Julia asked, concerned. "I didn't put too much caro pepper in the stew, did I? It can be rather hot for the foreign palate."

"No, you didn't," Lucian said, hastily.

"You poor thing, your cheeks are burning so. It's like you swallowed a coal."

"The stew is perfectly fine," Lucian gasped. Morgana's foot was trailing up dangerously. He had to put an end to this. "I'm sorry. Where's the bathroom?"

"We have an outhouse out back. Morgana, why don't you show him?"

"No need," he said, getting up. "I can find it."

Before any of them could say another word, he was out the door.

17

LUCIAN MADE his way behind the home, where he found the outhouse. All he needed was a moment to think about what to do – to cut his losses and head to his own hut or follow Fergus's orders and stay.

He had to think of some excuse to get out of this, but what? He wasn't sure even *that* would solve the problem. She had shown up at his hut last night, so he wouldn't put it past her to do the same thing again.

All he had to do was survive dinner. After that, her parents would surely be a curb on her behavior.

His thoughts were broken with the sound of footsteps approaching from outside.

"Lucian?" Morgana called. "I hope everything is all right?"

"Rotting hell," he muttered. He wasn't sure how to respond. "I'm fine. You can go back inside."

She did not go back inside. Instead, she took a few steps closer to the outhouse door. "I guess things got a little . . . *heated* . . . in there."

Well, at least she was admitting it. "What's gotten into you? You're making things really awkward."

It was quiet for a while, almost long enough for Lucian to think she had gone. Then she stepped closer, and the door moved, as if she had placed her hand on it. One move, and she could push it open. "I've never seen anyone like you before. Handsome. Brave. And . . . you've seen things. I want you to tell me stories of what it's like out there. Off Psyche."

"Maybe later. If you control yourself. Just don't open the door."

"Don't worry. I wouldn't do anything you don't want me to do, Lucian."

Lucian nearly choked. He had to be careful with his answer. The last thing he needed was for her to become angry or cry. But at the same time, she was pulling no punches. He couldn't let her manipulate him. For some reason, he was reminded of what Elder Erymmo had said, how people could easily be influenced to act a certain way even without the aid of magic.

Well, he couldn't let her do that to him.

"All that stuff at the dinner table," he said. "You need to cut it out. All you're doing is making me angry. You don't want that, do you?"

She laughed. "Angry? That was just a bit of fun."

"For you, maybe. I don't like it."

"What's *that* supposed to mean?"

"Do you really want to know?"

At that point, she began pushing on the door, which Lucian kept shut with his foot. The time for words was over.

He streamed a small bit of Psionic Magic, enough to push the door wide open. Morgana sprawled backward with a startled cry, tripping over her skirts and falling into the dirt, her eyes wide as saucers. When she got up in a huff, her cheeks were red and her eyes had narrowed dangerously.

"Lucian! How . . . how *dare* you! You've dirtied my clothes."

Lucian had to say, it was satisfying to have the upper hand

for once. "Now, let's get through dinner peacefully. *No* more games."

She watched him for a moment, as if sizing him up again. There was something dangerous in her eyes, something that made her seem much older. He knew that was crazy because she was just an impulsive young woman.

"Very well," she said, icily.

She headed back toward the house. Lucian waited a couple more minutes before he followed.

Hopefully, things went better when he returned.

———

FOR THE REST OF DINNER, Morgana was the picture of perfect propriety. Lucian was even beginning to enjoy himself, especially when the mystika loosened tongues. Kieron told crazy stories about his hunting trips.

"You have to come upon the wyverns from above," he said. "Not easy, that. They nest high in the mountains, and it's rotting hard to breathe up there."

"Kieron . . ." Julia said, warningly. "No cursing at the dinner table."

"Forgive me, dear." He refocused on Lucian. "And the stalking is most certainly not easy when wyverns are so good at smelling. But granted you *can* get above them, the rotting bastards never think to look up."

"Kieron, language!" Julia chided.

"Interesting expletive," Lucian said. "I haven't heard it outside of Psyche."

"Really, now?" Kieron said. "I wouldn't know. Anyway, the only way you can hunt wyverns is with spears and harpoons."

"And magic," Lucian said.

"Aye, that too, though only mages have that benefit."

"A pity they can't be trained to carry people," Morgana said. "They are certainly large enough."

Kieron had a laugh at that. "They are wild beasts, Morgana. They would never consent to be flown by the likes of a human."

"They say the Queen's Mage-Knights fly them."

Kieron dismissed her with a wave of his hand. "Stories. If the Mage-Knights flew them, the Riftlands would be under the Queen's full control by now."

"Cleon has told me as much."

Kieron blew a raspberry. "He tells tales if he thinks it might earn him a pretty girl's favor."

Morgana was about to contest that, but Julia cut her off. "What are you doing, passing time with Cleon? I don't want you anywhere near a man from Dara."

"I saw him in the store, and besides, *he* was the one who talked to me." She blinked her eyes innocently. "Anyway, we got to talking. He mentioned the hunt, and said the wyverns aren't much to worry about, that the people of the Golden Vale hardly paid them any mind. The Queen's magic is enough to tame them. And the Mage-Knights' valor, of course."

"That Cleon spins some wild tales," Kieron grumbled. "You shouldn't believe every word that comes out of his mouth. You should know better."

Morgana's face hardened. "I *do* know better, Father. I'm thirteen, a grown woman."

Lucian almost spit out his mystika, until he remembered the years were longer here. That was probably eighteen or nineteen in Earth years.

Kieron waved a warning finger at her. "The fact you're sniffing around the likes of Cleon and not speaking to this perfectly suitable young man right here tells me you are *not* grown."

Lucian coughed. From the corner of his eye, he could see

Morgana smirk. Was Kieron hoping to set him up with his daughter? Like rotting hell that was going to happen.

"Kieron," Julia said. "I think you've had enough tonight."

"Cleon and I were only *talking*, Father," Morgana said. "That is not a crime in Kiro, is it?"

Kieron, with some effort, took his hand off his cup of mystika, not seeming to have a response.

It was getting late, and Lucian could no longer hide his fatigue. He tried to stifle a yawn.

"It's time you got to bed, Lucian," Julia said. "You've a long day tomorrow, and no doubt had an exhausting one today."

"What about our parlor games?" Morgana asked. "I wanted to be partnered with Lucian."

Kieron looked up at that. "Well, if Lucian isn't opposed . . ."

"I'm afraid I can't," Lucian said. "I can't keep my eyes open a minute longer."

"He's tired," Julia said, her tone brooking no argument. "Morgana, could you show him to bed?"

"I'd be delighted," she said, her voice far too cheery. Before he could protest, she took his hand and guided him toward the ladder. There had to be more than one room up there, because that seemed to be where Morgana's quarters were, and surely, they wouldn't put him, a stranger, in the same room as her. She went up the ladder, and he waited until she was at the top before he followed.

What he found was a cozy space, with a small bed in the corner, a chest, and then another cot which had been made up on the opposite side. Well, it did look as if he'd be sharing the space with Morgana, but it seemed flirtation was far from her thoughts for the moment.

"This is your bed," she said, her voice somewhat cold as she led him to the cot. "I hope it's comfortable enough." Lucian just stared, wondering how he was going to survive the night.

Morgana watched him, arching an eyebrow. "What? Are you waiting for me to tuck you in? Or do you want a story?"

"Morgana, are you mad about earlier?"

"Of course," she said. "That was uncalled for!"

Lucian wanted to argue, but it would be better to just agree with her and apologize. He would be out of here tomorrow, and the last thing he needed was drama. "You're right. I went a bit too far."

"Save it," she said, crossing her arms.

"Look, I'm sorry it had to come to that earlier, but you were crossing the line. I dealt with it as I saw fit."

She was already heading down the ladder, completely ignoring him. Lucian shook his head. It was useless, but at least he had the space to himself for now.

He pulled back his own blanket, opting to keep his clothes on, given the circumstances. The sooner he got some shuteye, the better.

It was quiet, and Lucian was so tired that he had almost completely nodded off, safe in the knowledge that his Psionic ward was still active. Reaching for his Focus, he could feel its presence, as well as his depleted supply of ether. The ward should last him the rest of the night.

Within moments, Lucian was asleep.

18

LUCIAN AWOKE to someone grasping him from above. He was about to shout, but felt a hand over his mouth.

"Hush, now," Morgana said. "You'll wake everyone. This is important."

Though her voice was calm, there was something in it that seemed off. He didn't trust it. Lucian writhed away, but she stood before his cot, blocking his escape. In the darkness, her eyes held a curious violet glow.

"Morgana, what are you doing?"

"Please, listen. There isn't much time. I can't be here long."

Can't be here long? What in the Worlds was she talking about?

"You must tell me where you're going, Lucian. More is at stake than you know. We are allies, not enemies, as others would have you believe."

"Morgana, what in the Worlds . . .?"

At once, he realized the truth: those violet eyes were a sign of Psionic control. And he remembered where he had heard that same tone of voice.

The person possessing Morgana was none other than the Sorceress-Queen herself.

"How is this possible?"

"Never mind that. You are Chosen, Lucian. And we must work together for the good of all. I have a plan, but it requires your help. Get to the Deepfork, and I can explain more."

"What's your plan?"

"There isn't time, Lucian. It's hard to reach you from this far. If you try to get the Orb on your own, you will never make it."

"I can't trust you," he said, hardly believing he was talking to the Sorceress-Queen. "Your men tried to kill me in the Greenrift."

"Kill? No they didn't. They were trying to find you. More is at stake than you know. Remember the Deepfork, Lucian. Meet me there."

Morgana cried out and tumbled forward, the violet in her eyes fading. Lucian ran forward to catch her.

Footsteps ran up from the floor below, toward the ladder.

"What's going on?" Kieron shouted from below.

In a moment, he was in the loft, his eyes wide and expression fearful, with Julia not far behind.

Lucian knew the scene didn't look good. Morgana had screamed and was in his arms, her chest heaving and expression terrified. Lucian stood facing her, looking like a predator on the attack.

Kieron's face reddened. "You step away from her right now."

Julia was already pulling her daughter away, covering her protectively.

"Where am I?" Morgana asked. "What's happening?"

Julia looked at Lucian, her eyes seething. "What did you do to her?"

Lucian's heart was stabbed with horror. He tried to respond, but didn't know how to convince them of what had really happened. Or whether they would even believe him.

"Get out of my house," Kieron said, stepping forward. Lucian backed into the corner. He didn't want to have to stream, but Kieron seemed ready to use those big muscles to snap his neck.

"I know it's hard to believe," Lucian said, "but Morgana was somehow possessed by the Sorceress-Queen. The Queen was trying to get a message to me. She should be herself now."

Kieron paused, if only for a moment. Whatever he had been expecting Lucian to say, that wasn't that. "What are you going on about, boy?"

"It's true," Lucian said. "If we can bring one of the Elders here, they will back me up."

Julia looked at her daughter, unsure. "She *has* been acting rather moonstruck lately. Ever since Lucian got here. It goes beyond Lucian being a handsome young off-worlder. She's also been more . . . mouthy than usual. Not herself in the least."

"Morgana has always been like that," Kieron said. "We can't let him get away with this! I let him into our home! We fed him, drank with him, shared our table with him!"

"Kieron, calm down before you do something stupid. Have you *really* not been paying attention to your own daughter? Something strange is going on. There's something in her eyes. I know our daughter, Kieron, and her eyes have always been brown. But these past couple days they have almost looked . . . *purple.*"

For the first time, doubt entered Kieron's features. "Are you saying you *believe* him?"

"It doesn't seem he's lying, Kieron."

Lucian was grateful that Julia's cooler head had prevailed. "As far as I understand, violet eyes seem to be a sign of possession."

"Possession?" Kieron asked, his eyes widening. "How can the Queen do that all the way from Dara?" He pointed an accusing finger at Lucian. "Maybe *you're* the one controlling her mind! And maybe my wife's mind, too! The Elders will hear of this!"

The burly blacksmith's voice was shaking. With a start, Lucian realized the strong man was *afraid* of him. Muscles could do nothing against magic, but even so, his fists were balled up, as if he were ready to fight to the death for his family.

"Kieron, he's not controlling me," Julia said. "Do you see my eyes?" Julia took his hands, holding him steadily. "It's *me*. You've looked into these eyes a thousand times by now. More than that. Now tell me. Who is staring back?"

Kieron's lip quivered for a moment. "It's you, Julia. It's you."

"Kieron is right about one thing," Lucian said. "We should get Elder Erymmo here. He knows about these things."

"That's the best idea we've had so far," Julia said. "He's the best Psionic in the village."

Morgana gave a stifled cry, and Julia rubbed her back. "It's all right, dear. Things will be cleared up soon."

Morgana's eyes went to Lucian, seeming to see him for the first time. "Lucian? What are you doing here?"

"She doesn't seem to remember a thing," Julia said. "What's the last thing you remember, darling?"

"I . . . remember going to bed. And after that . . . *this*."

"What about dinner?" Kieron asked. "Do you remember that?"

"Of course," she said. "The Accounting Feast in the meeting hall."

"No, dear," Julia said. "That was the day before yesterday. Are you saying the last thing you remember was going to bed *after* that?"

Morgana nodded, wiping tears from her eyes. "What's *happened* to me?"

"It must have happened last night after she had gone to bed," Lucian said. "Like I said, Elder Erymmo will probably clear up any confusion about how it might have happened."

"Kieron, please get Elder Erymmo. We haven't a moment to lose."

Kieron looked at Julia for a moment, as if questioning that, but in the end he nodded. He was out of the house within the moment.

The following silence was heavy. No one spoke, though Julia held her daughter as she cried, and moved her to her bed. Considering the possession, Lucian felt bad for the way he had treated Morgana. Her strange behavior made sense now. He didn't understand *exactly* how possession worked, or how the Sorceress-Queen had been able to do it, but all he could remember was what Elder Erymmo had told him. Mind control worked by inflaming emotions, so she was probably inflaming whatever feelings Morgana had for Lucian into an inferno. But what could have been her purpose with that? Probably to get his guard down, to get him to tell her things that would help her find him. If that was true, then the Sorceress-Queen already knew far more than she should have.

Lucian wanted to apologize for his behavior, until he realized that Morgana probably didn't remember *anything* of what had happened. The entire time he had spoken to her tonight, he had been speaking to the Sorceress-Queen. The thought made his skin crawl, and he had trouble believing it was real.

But he couldn't get past how the Sorceress-Queen could control her in the first place. It had to have been through Morgana's dreams – especially given that the last thing she remembered was going to sleep.

Of course, if that were true, it meant Morgana was a mage.

"Can you use magic, Morgana?"

Her eyes widened at that. "Why would you bring that up?"

"That's only known to the family," Julia said. "But yes. She has Emerged recently."

"It's the only way the Sorceress-Queen could have reached you," Lucian said.

The door opened and two pairs of footsteps entered the house. Within a moment, both Kieron and Elder Erymmo were in the loft. The Elder looked very tired, his eyes hooded with exhaustion. But upon seeing Morgana sitting on her bed, crying, he became very alert.

He went to her. "Morgana? Would you look me in the eyes, please?"

Her eyes were still tear-filled, but to Lucian they seemed brown rather than violet.

Elder Erymmo nodded. "You seem to be fully yourself. But the time has come for your training, Morgana. We Elders have respected the wishes of your parents for some time, but now Kiro needs you more than ever."

Morgana watched him for a moment and then nodded. "Okay. Whatever you need me to do."

"Please, give Lucian and me a moment," he said. "Will the rest of you wait here?"

"By all means," Julia said.

Lucian followed the Elder outside to the stream. It was only once they stood by the running water that Elder Erymmo broke the silence. "Kieron told me what you said. Now, I need to know what Morgana heard while under possession. For whatever you told her, the Sorceress-Queen would have also heard."

"Yeah, I figured that much."

"I grossly underestimated the Queen. I supposed she would try to dream implant you, but I never thought she would do it to *others*. And to use Morgana, a mage who has barely manifested her powers, was a stroke of genius. What exactly did you tell her?"

"Only what was discussed at dinner last night. She knows that Fergus, Cleon, and I are leaving Kiro tomorrow to go wyvern hunting. The Sorceress-Queen also told me to meet her at the Deepfork, after she revealed herself to me."

Erymmo frowned as he took in this news. "The Deepfork is

a few days downrift from here. It seems she still believes she might convince you with her words."

"Don't worry," Lucian said. "After everything, there's no way I'm going to ever trust her."

"While that's good, she might not need your outright cooperation. If she believes you are going wyvern hunting, which I doubt, that would still lead you to the Snake Pass. It's likely that she's sending her men from the Greenrift straight there, in pursuit of you."

"Where else could I possibly go? She thinks I'm the Chosen. And according to her, the Chosen's fate is to seek all the Orbs and stop the fraying. And she says I need *her* to do that. I don't want to admit it, but what if she's right?"

Elder Erymmo whistled. "That's a problem. If the Sorceress-Queen wants anything with the Orb of Psionics, it isn't good. Of course, she would want you to think you need her. But it would be far better to find the Orb on your own, without her assistance. With Fergus, Cleon, and soon, Serah, I believe your chances are better than you realize."

"There's still the problem of how to outrun her if she really does have her airship." Lucian sighed. "This is hopeless, isn't it?"

"In truth? It might very well be. But do we have a choice but to try?"

Lucian laughed bitterly. "I should've never gotten on that shuttle."

"If you hadn't," Erymmo said, "then who would be the one to find the Orbs?"

So, did Erymmo think he was the Chosen, too? The thought was enough to make him sick. He had never asked for this. But he could have stayed on Volsung. He had only himself to blame. The only thing under his control were the decisions here and now.

Tomorrow, he would be setting off on a quest across the face of Psyche. There was no other way to put it. He had to resign himself to that fact, as certainly as Fergus had done.

Erymmo watched him solemnly. "As it stands, the Sorceress-Queen knows you're here."

Lucian didn't have to ask what that meant. They had to leave Kiro now.

19

WITHIN THE HOUR, Fergus was knocking on Elder Erymmo's door, packed up and ready to go. It annoyed Lucian that Fergus seemed so fresh after getting no more than four hours of sleep.

Lucian was about to head out the door when he felt a hand on his shoulder.

"Wait a moment," Erymmo said. "Or have you forgotten?"

The Elder went to the wall and grabbed the graphene shockspear. He held it reverently for a moment, before giving it to Lucian.

"It's yours," he said. "This was made by an old friend of mine, an accomplished Atomicist. He forged it directly from a carbon deposit on this world."

Lucian assumed from Erymmo's manner that his friend was long dead. "Are you sure?"

"Of course I am. He would have been glad for you to have it. Bronze or steel works fine, but graphene is best. Light. Strong. And it will never lose its sharpness. Kiro, for whom this village is named, was among the best. He learned Atomicism at the feet of Mallis herself."

Lucian's eyes widened at that. He had so many questions, but Fergus had already cleared his throat.

"Go," Elder Erymmo said. "Remember everything I've taught you. And continue to train, to be the best you can be. Do that, and you will find your way."

"Good luck here, Elder. Be safe."

As he left, Lucian wished Elder Erymmo had been one of the Transcends at the Volsung Academy.

Shockspear in hand, he followed Fergus to the meeting hall. It was still too early for anyone else to be up. Once inside, Cleon was already there, heating a pot of stew. He stuck his finger inside and licked it.

"I hope you won't do that on the trail," Fergus grumbled. "It's revolting."

"Believe me," Cleon said, "I've stuck it in much worse places."

Fergus's mouth twisted with disgust. "You are truly vile. Only you among my watchmen can speak to his captain without even a modicum of respect."

"That's the thing, Captain," Cleon said. "You need me for this, so you have no choice but to put up with me *and* my vile ways." He licked his lips. "Stew is done. Can I pour you a bowl, Captain?"

He sat down at the bench. "Yes. And be quick about it."

As they ate, Lucian noticed three packs of gear lined up against the wall. He had no idea which was his, but he was glad Fergus had taken care of the details. He didn't have the first clue about what was needed to survive on this world.

All too soon, they finished their meals. Lucian tried to blink away his weariness. He would have fallen asleep, if not for Fergus standing, causing his bronze armor to clank.

"It's time we left, men. I'd like to find Serah before the sun sets."

"Sure thing, Boss." Cleon stood with the aid of his bronze

171

shockspear. For the first time, he seemed to notice Lucian's weapon. "Hey. The old man gave you that?"

Fergus shook his head. "No respect."

"Elder Erymmo did, yes," Lucian said.

"Maybe you should let me or the captain have it. Until you learn the ropes, that is."

Lucian gripped the spear tighter. "He gave it to me. It's mine."

Cleon shrugged. "Suit yourself."

"We're burning daylight," Fergus said.

Cleon nodded. "My girl should be waiting for me at the gate. That is, if I didn't tire her out too much last night."

"We get it," Fergus said. "You have sex. Congratulations."

Cleon was about to get his own retort in when Lucian cut him off. "No more bickering or we'll end up killing each other before the Queen can. Let's not make the Elders regret their decision of putting us together."

That made Fergus's back straighten, while Cleon just rolled his eyes. "Please. They *don't* trust us. We're just their only chance."

"We leave," Fergus commanded, puffing out his chest. "Cleon, I would suggest donning your armor. The bronze, not the leathers."

"Nah," Cleon said, examining his fingernails. "That'll only weigh me down."

"Weak," Fergus muttered. "Well, have it your way then, but a good set of armor can be the difference between life and death." He turned to Lucian. "And you, Lucian?"

"I'm not used to wearing armor like that."

"It'll go light on you," he said. "Being an Earther and all. And it'll keep your strength up."

"The clothes on my back will work well enough."

Fergus shook his head. "Very well. Just know that I can't

protect you from every stray arrow or javelin. They fly faster and farther on this world."

"Like bronze armor would stop a javelin," Cleon scoffed. "It's better to stand out of the way. Or use magic."

"Magic will only be used at direst need. If the Sorceress-Queen or her Radiants are near, they can detect any fluctuation in the ethereal field. You will stream nothing more than wards unless *I* give the command. *I* am in charge here, and the chain of command will be adhered to."

This time, no one raised any protest. They went to their packs, and Lucian waited for the other two to pick their packs before he took the remaining one. It was so *heavy*. The lessened gravity only meant it had to be stuffed densely. It might be they could make the entire journey to Dara without the need to resupply.

With a grim expression, Fergus took the lead, using the butt of his spear as a walking staff. Lucian looked at Cleon, who shrugged, before following him.

———

WHEN THEY REACHED the village gate, a small gathering was there to see them off. It was still dark outside, almost pitch black. Fergus streamed a weak light sphere to float about a meter above his head, one just bright enough to see by.

"Stay within five meters of me at all times," he said. "Otherwise, I can't guarantee my ethereal concealment ward will cover you. And of course, it won't fully protect against active magic streams. That's why you don't stream unless you're told. At night, I'll increase the strength of the ward, and you can stream safely then."

"Aye-aye, Captain," Cleon said, with a sarcastic salute.

At that moment, a beautiful woman with raven black hair approached Cleon, embracing him fully.

"Lydia, darling," he said.

"I want to *punch* you right now." She held him tighter, her eyes closed.

Cleon held her close as he stroked her hair. "Now, now, Lydia. If I could have it any other way, I would."

"You rotting fool. You're going to die out there and leave me all alone!"

When the woman pulled back, it seemed she *did* have a mind to punch him. And Cleon seemed ready to take it.

"I deserve that," he said. "Lydia, I will move Cupid itself to get back to you."

She shook her head. "You've made your choice." When she turned her green eyes on Lucian, they were filled with pure loathing. As if she blamed *him* entirely for what was happening. What had Cleon told her? Probably things he shouldn't have been saying.

"Just go," she said.

Once she was gone, Fergus sidled up to Cleon. "You told her the truth?"

"She pulled it out of me, Fergus. Women's intuition and all that."

"Take five minutes to finish your goodbyes," Fergus said. "Then, we leave for good."

With that, the three men separated. Lucian found himself standing alone because he had no one to say goodbye to. He pretended to be busy checking the contents of his pack when a familiar face came up to him.

"Morgana." Some of his fear from last night lingered. But when she looked at him, her brown eyes were lucid.

"I couldn't sleep, so I thought I'd see you off. I . . . just wanted to apologize for everything. Even if I don't remember it."

"It wasn't your fault."

She reached for his hand, and Lucian allowed her to take it.

"Elder Erymmo explained everything to me. Now, I'm to be the village's newest mage." She smiled weakly. "That's not something my parents wanted. Still, I suppose it's how I might best serve Kiro."

"I'm sure you'll make a good mage."

She laughed. "Then you don't know me at all. I will make a terrible watchman." She watched him, sadly. "When you come back, maybe we can speak more."

He knew he was expected to say something similar. But he just couldn't lie to her.

"That probably won't be happening, Morgana. Where we're going is dangerous, and it might be a long time before we return."

She came forward and kissed him lightly on the cheek. His eyes widened, but he didn't stop her. She headed back to the village and was soon lost to the darkness.

"Well, look at you," Cleon said, looking after Morgana. "You landed the prize fish, and now you're leaving. Fate can play cruel tricks with us, eh?"

Lucian just ignored him and was grateful when Fergus joined them both.

"We're wasting time." He turned to the watchtower, cupping his hands. "Open the gates!"

Instantly, the gates opened inwardly, revealing the valley outside. Without even a backward glance, Fergus strode forward, where the Deeprift was already gray with the first hints of dawn. Lucian and Cleon followed the Captain, taking the first steps of a long journey.

20

FERGUS SET A FAST PACE. His legs were long, and his bronze armor and pack did nothing to weigh him down. Lucian was almost jogging to keep up.

Worse, the entire way was uphill. If the gravity were anything close to Volsung, Lucian would have been long dead. His pack was heavy even in the lower gravity.

As the sky brightened, Lucian could see Psyche's rugged beauty. The sides of the Deeprift were like walls rising into infinity. Trails and clefts branched off from the main rift, while silvery cascades fell over the sides. That water, Lucian saw, created a thick mist, through which golden light filtered to create multiple arcing rainbows.

Lucian couldn't help but marvel, but to Fergus and Cleon, it was just another day.

Cleon started whistling. Fergus grunted, increasing the group's pace.

Cleon called out. "You're going to wear us all down when the air gets thinner!"

"I would have us beyond the Snake Pass by lunchtime."

"Are you insane? We need to pace ourselves. What happens

if we run into trouble on the way up? We'll be too tired to lift our spears!"

At this warning, Fergus slowed down. "All right. A five-minute break."

When Lucian looked down the rift toward the valley below, its caves and settlements were completely out of sight. They had been walking for several hours without so much as a pause. He took a deep pull from his canteen. He was grateful he hadn't taken the armor. Fergus was breathing heavily, though it seemed he was good to go for a while longer.

"What're you trying to prove, Captain?" Cleon asked. "We know you're a big, strong man."

"Serah may have moved on by now, and it seems that I'm the only one who cares," Fergus said. "Frays rarely stay in one place for long, and it's been two days since Lucian's seen her."

Two days? It felt like two *weeks*. As hard as it was to believe, he had only landed here three days ago.

Going up rather than down, Lucian found he didn't recognize anything. The light was brighter today, perhaps because the mist was thinner than a few days back. Even if it was thinner, it was still impossible to see the top of the Deeprift. It had to be kilometers above them.

"All right," Fergus said. "Let's move."

They didn't make the Snake Pass by lunch. It was more like late afternoon, and Lucian was exhausted. He was worried Fergus might want to check out the pass itself, to see if Lucian's story held up. But Fergus made no comment as they walked by the collapsed pass.

"Keep an eye out, men," Fergus said. "If what Lucian said is any indication, they expect us to come this way."

Lucian scanned the rift on both sides, but so far, it seemed they were the only ones here.

It was getting noticeably harder to breathe. It wasn't just the hard trek. The air *was* getting thinner, and much cooler and drier. There were also fewer waterfalls, and the greenery clinging to the rift's sides was all but gone. The wind blew harder, chilling him to the bone. While the cold weather was nothing compared to the Isle of Madness, Lucian hadn't felt that cold for months. He suppressed a shiver.

"Can't be much farther, can it?" Lucian asked. "I could swear her cave wasn't far beyond the pass."

It was another half hour before the trail branched off to the right. This landscape gave Lucian the creeps. It only reminded him of the wyverns he'd fought off, and it seemed they could be lurking in every crevice and cave they passed.

"This path leads to the Upper Reaches," Cleon said, fearfully.

"It's where we need to go," Fergus said. "Lead on, Lucian. And be quick about it. We can't be caught out here in the darkness, and we need to get a fire going."

Lucian led them up the trail, which was rougher than he remembered. In fact, there were *multiple* trails, leading to varying heights in the rift. It was impossible to tell which one he had followed to get to the Snake Pass.

When Lucian paused at a fork, he frowned.

"Lost your way?" Cleon asked.

"I don't remember this. It was dark, so I guess that shouldn't be surprising."

"I'm not sensing anyone near," Fergus said. "No mage, anyway. Of course, they might be warding themselves."

"The cave has to be close," Lucian said.

"Take the path that looks most correct," Fergus said. "And don't take too long about it."

Lucian fought to remember that night. He had been blinded by fear, and the darkness had made it impossible to know where he was going. He considered the two paths before him. One went straight, not changing in elevation, while the other snaked its way up the righthand side of the rift. Surely, if the trail had been *that* steep, he would have remembered going down all those switchbacks.

"It's straight," he said.

"You sure about that?" Cleon said, his fiery red hair whipped by the wind. "I'm not ready to die yet."

"We'll know if I'm wrong after ten minutes."

Cleon shook his head, and they took the trail.

Lucian remembered then that he had failed to tell them about Ramore. "She's living with another fray, too. A Burner named Ramore. He almost killed me with Thermal Magic."

"And you're just telling us *now*?" Cleon asked.

"A Thermalist," Fergus said. "Cleon, you must make sure we're warded before we go in there."

"Sure thing, Cap."

A few minutes later, they rounded a bend to see the entrance of the cave, on a ledge about a hundred meters above them across a narrow gulley.

"That's it," Lucian said.

"As forlorn as forlorn can be," Cleon said. "This land has the feel of wyverns. See all those caves up there? What was Serah *doing* here?"

"Escaping notice," Fergus said. "Some of the Deeprift villages make a practice of hunting frays. It's safer for frays to live in the Upper Reaches or even in the Darkrift."

"That's a sad life."

"Indeed."

Without another word, Fergus started forward. Now that he knew where the group was going, he wanted to take the lead again.

Within minutes, they were fifty paces from the cave mouth. Fergus held up a hand.

"I sense no mage in there," he said. "But she may just be a good warder. Be cautious and spears ready. And keep an eye out for the Burner."

"Maybe I can go first," Lucian said. "She knows me."

"She knows me, too, though it has been a few years," Fergus said. "We go together. It might take all three of us to bring the Burner down if it comes to it."

"If you kill Ramore, she will kill you."

Fergus laughed bitterly. "She has reason to already. It was *I* who led her out of the valley when Kiro exiled her. That wasn't easy on anyone, but least of all Elder Ytrib."

By now, they were close to the cave entrance. Close enough for Lucian to notice that something was amiss. It was a sight that made his heart drop.

He pointed at the entrance, where a body lay sprawled on the ground, almost completely lost to the darkness.

"Rot it," Fergus said. "How did I miss that?"

"Too busy running your mouth, Captain," Cleon said. "Should we investigate?"

Lucian had a bad feeling about this, but what else was there to do?

"Looks dead to me." Fergus said.

The only question was whether the body belonged to Serah, Ramore, or someone else entirely. There was only one way to find out.

Since the other two weren't moving, Lucian took the lead. He reached for his Focus. If this were some sort of trap, it would be better to be prepared for it. Remembering Serah bragging about her Gravitonic Magic, he streamed a Gravitonic ward around himself, using Psionic Magic as his shell. To his surprise, the ward set fine. It seemed Elder Erymmo's lesson had stuck.

"You streaming?" Fergus asked. "I thought I told you—"

"—Serah is an accomplished Gravitist. We need to be defended against that."

"Yes, do that," Fergus said, somewhat testily. He seemed annoyed he hadn't thought of the idea first. "Can you extend your ward radius?"

"How do I do that?"

"Reach your Focus farther and commit more ether." His eyes watched him, appraising. "That is, if you can handle it."

Lucian nodded, and expanded his ward about five meters, which should be enough to cover everyone. His ether pool constricted, making him feel momentarily lightheaded. It was hard to say, but he probably only had half of his pool left to stream. That made him uneasy, but they weren't here to fight. They were here to talk.

Lucian watched as Cleon set a Thermal ward, while Fergus's concealment ward was still active. With each of their wards, protecting them from Gravitonic, Thermal, and Radiant magic, they were as well-protected as they could be. Lucian's heart pounded at the thought that Ramore could be lurking within, ready to strike.

"I'll take point," Fergus said. "If the Burner is in there, Lucian, Bind him and let me take care of it. I don't want to leave anything to chance."

"And Serah?"

Fergus paused for a moment to think. "Cleon will deal with her."

That settled, the three men strode toward the dark entrance of the cave.

———

WHAT HIT Lucian first was the smell. Burned flesh had to be the most disgusting stench in all the Worlds. It took holding his Focus for Lucian not to heave the contents of his lunch.

The sight of it was almost as bad. The body was a charred husk, to the point where it was impossible to tell who it was. Size alone wasn't enough of an indicator, since so much had burned away. Bone showed through the blackened skin of the arms.

Whether this death had been self-inflicted, or the result of a fight, Lucian couldn't say.

"Search the cave," Fergus said. "She might still be around."

Lucian's stomach churned at the thought that Serah might have met the same grisly end. He refused to believe it. As a frayed Thermalist, Ramore could have done this to himself out of his own madness. It seemed the most likely explanation.

Little could be found in the cave. Either Serah had packed up and left, or the cave had been looted by somebody. Or *somebodies*.

The three stood near the cave entrance again. The sky was darkening. It would be night in just a couple of hours.

"Cleon, thoughts?" Fergus asked.

Cleon was poring over the cave entrance. "Plenty of footprints here. Fresh. No more than two days old. Most point to and from the Upper Reaches." He pointed in the direction Lucian had wandered from three days ago.

"Can you pinpoint a set of footprints that might be smaller than the others?" Fergus asked. "Belonging to a woman, perhaps?"

"Hard to say," Cleon said. "Plenty of larger footprints, though, made by boots from the look of it. The tracks tell a story. Could be that Serah and her unlucky friend here were ambushed in the dead of night, and all their stuff looted. The one here was burned to a crisp while the other was taken prisoner. We already know the Queen is interested in the Snake Pass. And only mages would have the ability to take another mage hostage. That tells me there's a level of organization here that few but the Sorceress-Queen have. The prisoner would have to be Serah since the Queen would want nothing to do with a Burner. And since Serah's companion was a Thermalist,

182

it makes sense he met that end. Perhaps with a misdirected stream."

"Is there another option?" Lucian asked.

"Pretty much the same thing as the first, except Serah got away and the Darans are chasing after her."

"You don't think this could have been one of the Rift villages?" Fergus asked.

Cleon shook his head. "No. This cave is far outside the bounds of the lower Deeprift, and they wouldn't risk coming this high unless they had a score to settle. And we already know the Queen is out in force. Maybe these men came seeking information. But it's hard to imagine it being the same men from the Greenrift. It's too far. So this has to be another group."

"Seems far-fetched," Fergus said.

"I'm working with incomplete information here," Cleon said. "If we want to find out what really happened, we need to follow those footprints."

"That's the strangest part," Fergus said. "Why would they go *up* rather than to the Snake Pass if they were trying to find us?"

"At the time, they didn't know I was down in the Deeprift," Lucian said. "They do now."

"So that means they might be headed back this way."

Everyone looked back outside, but so far, there was no sign of hostiles.

"If they were trying to get to Snake Rift, then they couldn't use the pass," Lucian said. "It's buried."

"Even so," Fergus said. "The Upper Reaches are a death trap, especially for outlanders. It seems strange."

"It's a puzzle to be sure," Cleon agreed. "And it tells me that Serah most likely got away rather than being taken prisoner."

"How do you figure that?" Fergus asked.

Cleon shrugged. "If she wanted to lose those men, she would have gone *up* rather than *down*. As you said, they are outlanders. They don't know the Upper Reaches like she does, and being from the Golden Vale, they don't have the lungs for it. And she would know all the hidden caves to shelter in. All she'd have to do is outlast them."

"Well, if she can hide from them, she can probably hide from us, too," Fergus said. He sat on a nearby rock, next to the ashes of the fire Lucian had sat around not three nights before. It was a surreal feeling.

"One other thing," Lucian said. "She would have never left Ramore unburied. That means she was forced to leave, or she was taken by force."

"That too," Cleon said. "I didn't say as much because the point was obvious."

"Thanks," Lucian said, sarcastically.

"The question is," Fergus said, "what do we do with the information we have?"

"Other than hope I'm a better tracker than the Queen's men?" Cleon shrugged. "I've got nothing."

"Assuming it's the Queen's soldiers," Lucian said, "then how is it possible that they came from above? You said there's nothing up there of interest."

"The final piece of the puzzle," Cleon said. "The *Zephyr*."

"Of course," Lucian said. "If the confrontation in this cave took place two days ago, then the *Zephyr* must have dropped those men off somewhere close to this cave." It suddenly came to him. "They were placed by my drop pod! Of course, that's where they'd want to start looking. From there, the men tracked me to this cave, where they found Serah and Ramore. There was a fight. Ramore died while Serah escaped. They decided to chase Serah, figuring she probably knew something about me. This was before the Sorceress-Queen learned my true location from Morgana." He nodded. This had to be the complete picture. "Serah *must* have escaped, otherwise she probably would have told them where I am by now, and that group of soldiers would be at Kiro's gates."

"Bingo," Cleon said. "Couldn't have put it better myself."

"The only thing I don't understand is this airship," Lucian said. "How big is it? What is it capable of?"

"Her airship is guided by mages," Fergus explained. "Binders can pull it every which way across the face of Psyche. It floats through the efforts of her court Atomicist, Nostra. She creates the helium that makes it float. The ship itself is rather large if reports are to be believed."

Cleon nodded. "The *Zephyr* is a doozy. And Mage-Lord Nostra is largely responsible for building Dara itself, creating material that simply wouldn't exist on this planet otherwise. The *Zephyr* is her crowning achievement, though. Granted, the ship is of limited use in the Riftlands. It can only go so high before the air becomes too thin, and the rifts themselves are difficult to navigate. Still, it can move faster than people on foot."

"It's hard to believe such a thing exists," Lucian said.

"Well," Cleon said, "it does. I've seen it, for rot's sake. But try convincing Rifters it exists when Dara is over a thousand kilometers away and most haven't seen the Golden Vale. There are many here who don't believe *anything* exists above the sky. They think things like the Hundred Worlds and the Mage War are only stories told to children. Another fifty years of isolation, and not even the old ones will be around to keep things straight."

"This is beside the point," Fergus said. "If she does have the *Zephyr*, and she *is* using it, then it would go a long way to explain how her men can be everywhere at once."

"I think so, too," Cleon said. "That ship can crew up to two hundred men. And you can bet a good portion of them are mages, if only to have enough firepower to keep the wyverns away."

"The air is too thin up high," Fergus said. "The *Zephyr* still has to fly within the rifts for the air to be breathable. She must be very desperate to find Lucian if she's willing to risk the crown jewel of her military in the Riftlands, especially by flying into the Upper Reaches."

And neither of them had mentioned the most obvious thing. The Queen herself was probably on board, but Lucian didn't have the heart to mention that. "There's still the question of what we do about Serah."

"I say we move on," Cleon said. "Even *if* she's alive, it's like trying to find a jewel bug in the Darkrift. We're likely to kill ourselves in the Upper Reaches. No food, little water, and the wyverns can catch us in the evenings."

"I'm inclined to agree," Fergus said.

The very idea of leaving Serah revolted him. "Seriously? She's in trouble, and you would just leave her behind without even *trying* to find her? What would Elder Ytrib say?"

At least Fergus had the grace to look ashamed. Cleon, on the other hand, seemed ambivalent.

"She saved my life," Lucian said. "Without her, I would have never found Kiro. We're going after her."

"What, is she your girlfriend or something? Might not want to tell Morgana."

"Be serious," Lucian said. "We need her pathfinding skills. And she's a good Gravitist. You have to admit that's damn useful."

Cleon gave a noncommittal shrug.

"Enough," Fergus said. "Lucian's entanglements are none of our concern. I have a choice to make. Whatever is more likely to get us to Dara and beyond is what I will decide."

"That's easy then, Captain," Cleon said. "Huff it through the pass and into Snake Rift. After that, there's the Blue Rift."

"As I said, the choice is mine."

"Maybe we should camp here for the night," Cleon said. "After we give that one a proper burial."

"What if those men are coming back, though?" Lucian asked.

"I'll sense them long before they're here," Fergus said. "They can't hide that many mages from me."

They buried Ramore, the work going fast with Binding Magic and a heavy stone to dig with. It was hard to feel anything for a man who would have killed him. But Ramore had once been sane, and not all that long ago. It made Lucian feel hollow, but he hardened himself to it. It was Serah's grief, not his. Assuming she was still alive.

Once Ramore was underground, Cleon started a fire with a Thermal stream, using firewood Serah had left behind. It seemed strange to eat dinner after such grisly work. Lucian tried to ignore the sickly-sweet smell of rot lingering in the air.

They ate quickly, keeping the fire roaring near the mouth of the cave. That light would make them visible to hostile humans, but it was necessary to keep away the wyverns. As the fire burned bright and hot, the three watched outside the cave uneasily.

"Well, who has first watch?" Cleon asked.

"I'll take watch," Fergus said. "And you, Cleon, have second watch. Lucian needs rest the most."

Cleon mumbled something under his breath that sounded like rotting hell and some other expletive. "Fine. As if my girl didn't keep me up all night."

"Sleep with your spear in hand, Lucian," Fergus said. "You may need it before too long."

Lucian lay with his back to the fire and closed his eyes, the exhaustion of the day hitting him in full. But he wasn't quite done yet. He reached for his Focus and refreshed his Psionic ward, making its range large enough to cover all of them. Once that was done, he was out like a light.

21

LUCIAN WAS the first to wake. Across the fire, Fergus snored loudly, while Cleon was nodding off on his perch next to the cave mouth. So much for keeping watch.

Lucian walked over to him. "You alive?"

He jerked awake. "Still breathing." He looked at Lucian appraisingly. "Well, you want me to cook you breakfast, or what?"

Lucian got his meaning. He dug into his pack until he found some food, not recognizing half of the ingredients. Well, Cleon wanted him to cook breakfast, so that was what he would do. He filled the cookpot with some water and enough vegetables and meat for three people and set it over the fire. Half an hour later, it smelled all right enough.

Fergus stirred, and woke, sleepy-eyed. The three gathered around the fire to eat, which had burned to embers by now.

"You let the fire get too low, Cleon," Fergus said, taking a bite of the soup. His eyes widened as he sputtered. "Dear God. How much caro pepper did you *put* in that?"

"Enough to give *you* a fire," Cleon said. "Lucian, how'd you know I liked my food spicy?"

Lucian shrugged. "Just a hunch."

When Lucian took his first bite it felt as if he'd been kicked in the mouth. Cleon laughed uproariously.

"All right," Fergus said, mouth hanging open. "*I'm* responsible for the cooking from now on."

Lucian still felt the heat an hour later, when they were following the trail to the Upper Reaches. The tracks were so evident that even Lucian could have followed them. It seemed the Sorceress-Queen's war party wasn't concerned about being followed. That made Lucian uneasy. It reminded him of what Kieron had said about the wyverns, that they didn't look up because they had no fear of being hunted.

When they crested a final rise, the land flattened considerably, though it still sloped upward. There was no life up here, and the surface was bare and gray, with the distant slopes lost to violet mist. The air blew cold, making Lucian shiver. Compared to the bottom of the Deeprift, this was a different world entirely.

"The Upper Reaches," Fergus said, throwing a fur mantle over his armor. "Things are about to get more dangerous."

"The tracks go this way," Cleon said. "Straight into the fog."

"Quiet," Fergus said. "We might be getting close."

Cleon blew a raspberry, but didn't offer a rebuttal.

For the first time since arriving on Psyche, Lucian was out of the Deeprift. Even though he was breathing heavily, he just couldn't get enough air.

"Can we stop for a second? I'm getting lightheaded."

To his surprise, they slowed down. He breathed deeply.

"Stay hydrated," Fergus said.

Lucian drank from his canteen, though it didn't do much for his altitude sickness. And it would only get worse as they climbed higher.

"Your friend has a good set of lungs on her," Cleon said. "I feel a bit winded myself."

"Can you keep it down, man?" Fergus asked. "You would make us food for the wyverns."

"They aren't awake, anyway. But as you will."

"They *will* be awake if you keep it up."

"It's hard to imagine *anything* surviving up here," Lucian said. With luck, they would be distracted from arguing with each other.

"Nothing but wyverns," Fergus said. "They shelter here in the Upper Reaches. We will need to be especially wary when the land rises again. There's still a few thousand meters before there are any peaks."

"You'll suffocate, first," Cleon said. "They can't be far ahead, and not much higher."

"So, there's nothing up here," Lucian said. "Just a cold, barren wasteland."

"That about sums it up," Cleon said. "Shall we?"

They continued. The land began to slope even higher, until they were climbing at an almost forty-five-degree angle. How long they climbed, Lucian couldn't say. They paused for breath numerous times, until the sun had lowered dangerously. He didn't want to ask what the plan was for nightfall. Any cave up here could be the lair of a wyvern. The sooner darkness fell, the sooner they would come out.

They climbed yet another ledge, this one leading into a cave. Lucian almost called for a stop to shelter for the night, until Cleon wandered along the precipice, seemingly finding something.

"Wait!" Fergus said. "What are you doing?"

Cleon held up a hand. He seemed to be on the scent like a bloodhound. He kept walking, faster and faster around the mountainside, until he came to a sudden stop at a cliff.

Once Lucian had caught up, he looked over the edge only to see a layer of thick gray clouds.

"The trail ends here," Cleon said.

Fergus looked around in disbelief. "That can't be, unless you're saying they *jumped* off here."

"No," Cleon said, his eyes cunning. "I think they may have been picked up. It's a bit high for the *Zephyr*, but it's the only real possibility."

"You mean, they were *airlifted* out of here?"

"Yes," Cleon said. "And likely, our friend was with them. Unless her trail branches off somewhere in the last few kilometers, without *me* picking up on it."

"Wait," Lucian said. He pointed downward. "She went over." He broke into a smile. "She led them here, to a dead end."

"I don't understand," Fergus said.

"She's a Gravitist. She bragged to me how she was so good she might as well fly. Well, what if she *did* fly, right over the edge?"

"Clever, if true," Cleon said. "Though no Gravitist is good enough to fly. The sheer amount of ether to pull off a stunt like that is too much. But perhaps she's good enough to break her fall, even from such a height. If so, that leaves one question. How do we pick up a trail where there *is* none?"

"You don't," came a female voice from behind them.

At once, all three men turned to the sight of Serah, one eyebrow arched quizzically and shockspear in hand. Unlike before, she had boots on now, though her leather clothing seemed far too light for the cold weather. And yet, she showed no sign of being cold. Her blonde hair blew in the wind while a slight smile tugged at her lips.

"Serah," Fergus said. "We've been looking for you. We have things to discuss."

She looked around, taking in the cold, howling wind. "*Must* we?"

"Circumstances have changed," Fergus said. "Do you have a place you're staying around here?"

"If I did, why would I invite you?" Her eyes went to Cleon. "Who is this?"

"Cleon Coley, at your service."

She rolled her eyes. "I very much doubt that." Last of all, she noted Lucian. "And how did you get mixed up in this? Don't tell me Kiro wanted to hunt me down after my act of charity."

"This isn't a hunt," Lucian said. Serah's blue eyes went to him, and were mistrustful. "Fergus is right. We do need to talk. It's important."

She watched him for a moment and gave a small laugh. "Well, normally I'd say *no*, but I can't leave you three out for the wyverns." She looked up. "I'm staying up there, and we'd better get moving before the *Zephyr* comes trawling back. I can give you a boost." As she approached, she gave Lucian a sly wink. "Couldn't stay away from me, could you?"

"Something like that."

"All right, enough yapping," Cleon said. "Where are you boosting us to?"

"That ledge over there," she said, pointing about ten meters above them. "Wind's down a bit, so should be safe. Who's going first? Lucian? Fergie?"

"Don't call me that," Fergus said, expression darkening. "You can send me first."

"Ah, you're the brave, esteemed leader, no doubt. Well, it makes sense to do the heaviest first. It'll take more ether."

Before anyone could say anything, Fergus suddenly glowed with silvery light.

"Aim for that ledge up there," she said. "There's a cave entrance you can't really see from here. And *try* not to get off course. I really don't want to waste my ether pulling you over there."

"What do you take me for?"

"Never change, Fergie."

With a growl, Fergus knelt and gave a mighty leap. Lucian's

eyes widened as he sailed upward, far above the cliff they were standing on, and onto the ledge above.

"I can tether everyone else up," Lucian said.

"That's sweet," Serah said. "I've got this, though."

"I guess I'm next," Cleon said.

She streamed, wrapping him in an aura of silvery light. Cleon leaped, slightly overshooting the ledge. Lucian almost had to tether him to keep him from falling, but Serah did something to adjust the gravity pulling him, making him fall more quickly once he was over the edge.

"A little too eager, that one," Serah said. She turned to Lucian and smiled. "Alone at last. Miss me?"

Lucian blinked. "Maybe now's not the time."

She sighed. "I should've expected that. Well, you ready for the leap of faith?"

"Is there any trick to it?"

"Yeah," she said. "Just keep your eye on the goal."

"Sounds simple enough."

Instead of standing at a distance to stream, she touched his arm. He was surprised at how warm her hand was. It was well below freezing out here.

"We'll go together. It'll keep you from killing yourself."

"I can handle it," Lucian said.

"I know, big, strong man and all. Maybe I just need *your* help as a weak, defenseless woman."

"*Hey.*" Cleon was shouting over the edge. "Stop flirting and hurry it up!"

She shook her head. "Damn fool. He'll call the *Zephyr* down over us." She streamed Gravitonic Magic around them both, until they were wrapped in a bubble of gray light. "Let's move."

They made the jump together, and Lucian couldn't help but gasp as the ground fell away. Maybe it wasn't really flying, but it was close. The boosted jump took just a few seconds. Serah landed neatly in front of him while he landed behind. The four of them stood before a small cave entrance. They would have to crawl to fit in there.

"Ladies first," Cleon said.

"I think not. I'll bring up the rear. Just keep going straight until you reach the chamber."

Cleon shrugged, and went into the cave first, followed closely by Fergus. The large, armored captain could barely squeeze inside.

"All right, I'm freezing now," she said. "Let's get inside."

Lucian went in first, followed by Serah.

22

THE TUNNEL WENT on for a while, or at least, it felt so to Lucian crawling on his hands and knees. When he stood, he found himself in a small chamber. He couldn't stand without stooping. With the four of them crowding in, there was barely any space. Fergus closed his eyes, as if pretending to be anywhere but here.

Lucian didn't blame him.

"Couldn't you have picked a better cave?" Cleon's voice was loud and booming in the chamber's confines. Lucian winced from the ringing in his ears.

"Oh, I apologize," Serah said. "Next time when I'm picking out a place to stay for me, and me alone, I'll make sure it's as fine as any manse in Dara."

"That's where I *should* be," Cleon said. "If I hadn't run off to the Riftlands like some rotting fool, I might be Mage-Lord by now."

Fergus opened his eyes. "This is our situation, and we must make the best of it."

"There's little enough air up here as it is," Cleon said.

"Maybe a couple of us should sleep outside. I nominate Fergus and Lucian."

"Is that a joke?" Serah asked. "We still have things to discuss. For one, why are the three of you following me?"

Cleon was about to respond, but thankfully, Fergus cut him off. "We wanted to ask something of you. We were sent here by your father."

Her expression darkened. "I figured. What's the old man up to these days?"

"Busy preparing Kiro's defenses against the Queen's soldiers. By now, they will have reached the Deepfork and are well on their way up the Deeprift."

Her face paled at that news. "Soldiers? They were chasing me, too, but I lost them last night. Thankfully for me, they didn't think to look up."

"Is the *Zephyr* about?" Fergus asked.

"It came by to pick them up last night. And I'm hoping It doesn't come back."

"I already figured that out," Cleon said. "I'm basically the brains of this group. I'm the one who tracked you here."

"First of all, someone with earwax for brains could have followed that stampede. There were at least twenty soldiers, with four or five of them being Mage-Knights. And at least one had the purple plume of a Mage-Lord."

"You're sure about that?" Fergus asked.

"I'm not blind. I led them here, right to the cliff. I thought they would lose their way up here, but then the *Zephyr* showed up."

"And was the Queen on it?" Fergus asked.

"That, I don't know. I wouldn't be surprised. If seems like a full-scale invasion of the Riftlands is happening. If there's another group at the Deepfork, there may be more yet."

"You're right," Fergus said. "For all we know, there may be."

Serah's face fell. "Well, we all knew this would happen

someday. I guess I thought we had more time." She met Fergus's eyes. "So, you want my help to defend the village my father exiled me from, all because I'm the only Gravitist of any skill you know. My answer to that is *no*."

"That's not why we're here," Lucian said.

Her eyes turned on him. "What is this, then? Why else would you be here?"

"We need to get to Dara. Your father told me you know your way around the Darkrift. And the way to a passage known as Slave's Run."

Her eyes widened. "You can't be serious. You've been on-world, what, four or five days? And *you* want to go into the rotting Darkrift?"

"We are very serious," Fergus said. "And we know that *you* know where it is."

"I don't."

"Your father told us you did."

Her expression darkened. "Rotting hell. So rather than exile *me*, he wants to kill me off? I've had it with him. I owe him nothing. I'll point you the right direction, but don't expect any further assistance."

"Aren't you the least bit curious about *why* we want to find it?" Cleon asked.

"It's not my business. You can stay here for one night since it's too dark to survive out there. Come morning, though, I want all of you out of here. And out of my life, too, if you please."

"Just listen," Lucian said. "This might be our only chance to defeat the Sorceress-Queen. If you don't help us find Slave's Run, then we'll have to travel across the Riftlands all the way to Dara. If we do that, the *Zephyr* will surely catch us."

Serah sniffed. "Sounds like a personal problem to me."

Fergus huffed. "Let's be reasonable, Serah."

"Reasonable? I'll tell you about reasonable. What has the Riftlands ever done for me besides give me grief? I don't like the Queen either, but I can survive her just as well as I can survive Rifters. Probably even better, since Rifters make a sport of hunting frays."

Cleon shrugged. "She has something of a point."

"Why must my father always meddle? Why can't I live the rest of my miserable life in peace?"

"What about Ramore?" Lucian asked.

She looked at him, her brows lowering over her blue eyes. "What *about* Ramore? He's dead. I supposed you saw that on your way here." She shook her head. "He turned himself into a human torch to help me escape." Her eyes filled with tears. "Just the thought of his body back there, pickings for the wyverns . . ."

"The body was undisturbed when we found it," Fergus said, solemnly. "We gave him a proper burial."

She blinked. "You did? Well, it's more than I expected of you. No offense."

"We only ask that you hear us out," Fergus said. "Nothing more."

She looked from Fergus, to Cleon, and finally, her eyes met Lucian's and seemed to hang there. Curiosity burned. She had to be wondering why they wanted to go to Dara, and how they planned to defeat the Sorceress-Queen. Despite Serah's words, Lucian knew she didn't like her from their previous conversations.

"Okay. I must admit, you've piqued my interest. It's not every day you meet people who are so dead set on being . . . well, dead. All right, I'm all ears." She looked at Fergus's pack. "As long as you share some of your food."

"Deal."

The cave was too small for a fire, and there was no real ventilation, so they ate cold jerky, bread, and crimson fruit, a berry that must have been native to Psyche. Lucian watched the others wrapping the fruit and meat in the bread, eating it like that, so he followed their example.

Once done, Serah licked her fingers. "That's good eating. Now, you have ten minutes to explain yourselves. Unless you bore me."

"This might take more than ten minutes to explain," Lucian said.

"Ten minutes."

"Okay," Lucian said. "You want to know how I could defeat those two wyverns on my own?"

"How?" she asked, arching an eyebrow.

Lucian was about to tell his story when Cleon interrupted him. "He has the Orb of Binding. There. You asked for ten minutes, and we gave you ten seconds. Does that settle it?"

She looked from Cleon to Lucian skeptically. "You're joking. The Orbs are just a story. My dad used to tell me that one when I was little."

"They're very real," Fergus said. "I saw its power two days ago in the Greenrift. Lucian was able to do things I've never seen *any* mage do. He created an avalanche and saved our entire harvesting party from the Queen's soldiers."

"You mean, he saved *you*, Fergus?" Cleon asked.

"I will admit as much. The way he handled his Binding stream was blunt and childish, but yes, he saved me."

"Thanks," Lucian said.

"It's true," Fergus said. "You are a child when it comes to magic. You're an exile of your academy and barely old enough to have Emerged."

"I'm twenty-one, thanks." At least, he *thought* that was his age.

Serah's eyes were wide and her face pale. She didn't answer for a moment, as if she were still processing the information. "The Orb of Binding. That means the others are real, too. That means . . ." She looked at each of them. "Wait. You're going after the Orb of Psionics, aren't you?"

"She's quick," Cleon said.

She ignored him. "It's said to be *under a White World with red-whorl eye and a moon of violet, violent sky.* It's part of *The Prophecy of the Seven.*"

"Yes, that's what Elder Jalisa said," Fergus said. "We believe the Orb of Psionics is somewhere under the Eye of Cupid."

"That would take you to the Burning Sands," she mused. Her eyes went to Lucian and almost seemed to pity him. "That means you have to go through the Golden Vale and Dara, through the Pass of Madness, the Westlands, and finally, the Burning Sands."

"Unless there's another way," Lucian said.

She shook her head. "The Pass of Madness is the only way from the Golden Vale to Psyche's Planetside. The Mountains of Madness surround the entire moon north-to-south, bisecting it completely. And those mountains reach tens of kilometers high. Their surfaces are too sheer to climb. Such is the reason for Dara's existence. It straddles both sides of the moon, Planetside and Voidside."

"So, we *have* to go through Dara," Lucian said. "That can't be avoided."

"I'm afraid not," Serah said. "If you really want to find the Orb of Psionics."

"We do," Fergus said, puffing out his chest. "At the behest of your father and the Elder Council, we've been sent on a quest for the good of all Psyche."

"A quest?" Serah asked, with a chuckle. "You've been *dreaming* of this moment, haven't you? And when and if you do find the Orb of Psionics, you intend to use it against Queen Ansaldra, no?"

Ansaldra. So, that was her name.

"She's no queen of mine," Cleon growled.

"That sounds quite personal to you, Cleon."

"It is. My reasons are my own."

"No worries. I didn't plan to ask."

"So, will you help us find Slave's Run or not?" Fergus asked. "You need not actually go with us *to* Dara. We only need to know the entrance."

She gave a dark chuckle. "That's rich. First, you don't even know what you're asking. And second, if you guys *really* want to use the Darkrift, you'll lose your way the minute I show you the entrance."

"What do you mean?" Lucian asked.

"Slave's Run is hard to reach," she explained. "It goes *deep* underground, as deep as the Moon Sea."

Lucian frowned. "The Moon Sea? I don't understand. There's a sea *under* the Darkrift?"

Fergus nodded. "It's not confirmed, but it's said most water settles deep underground on Psyche before filtering up through the surface again."

"It *is* confirmed, because I've seen it," Serah said. "The water glows with some form of microscopic life, and Slave's Run follows it. On one end of the Moon Sea you can climb up and reach the Blue Rift, from which comes most of the Riftlands' water. The surface of this moon is quite porous. An effect of the low gravity and the tidal forces of Cupid."

"Leave it to a Gravitist to explain the workings of gravity," Cleon said.

"I digress. Basically, you can use Slave's Run to reach the Mountains of Madness and enter the Golden Vale."

"Why's it called Slave's Run?" Lucian asked.

"The answer is in the name," Serah said. "Escaped slaves use it to run from Dara to the Riftlands. Less so in recent years since the Sorceress-Queen has firmed her grip over the Golden Vale and beyond. The name has stuck, though."

"I took the longer path, but went through the Darkrift for

most of it," Cleon said. "It was not easy in the least, and it would take several months to make it to the Golden Vale. And that's not counting any scuffles we get into on the way."

"So, Slave's Run would be faster?" Lucian asked.

Serah nodded. "Much faster. Assuming you can get there, it'll cut weeks off your journey." She smiled bitterly. "The catch is you have to go through the Darkrift to reach it. And the Darkrift is a labyrinth. Even I haven't fully explored its depths. Besides the risk of losing your way, there's gloombat colonies, Burners, and of course the danger of falling down a hole you can never get out of."

"All right, that settles it," Cleon said. "We're going the long way."

"Maybe so," Fergus said. "But if we ever need to go the other way, the question is, can *you* lead us to Slaves' Run or not?"

"I can. However, you should go the long way. In this case, your friend Cleon is right."

"We are not friends," Fergus said. "He is my subordinate, and I am his captain."

"That's harsh, Boss," Cleon said. "Well, we'll have plenty of weeks to bond yet."

The Captain's face remained stony. It was clear he had given up instilling any semblance of discipline into the former Mage-Knight long ago.

"The trip aboveground would take months," Lucian said. "And that's *if* everything goes smoothly."

"Better to take your time and be alive than look for a shortcut and be dead," Cleon said.

"What about the *Zephyr*?" Fergus asked. "The Queen and her troops are actively hunting for Lucian. Doesn't that change the equation a bit?"

From Serah's silence, it seemed it might have.

"I don't want to go into any bloody, rotten, stinking Darkrift," Cleon said.

"You must, if that is what we decide," Fergus said. "You're a part of this group, whether you like it or not."

"Not by choice," Cleon muttered.

"What about you, Lucian?" Fergus asked.

Every pair of eyes went to him. Fergus, his face serious and steely. Cleon, whose blue eyes betrayed fear. Serah, who just looked tired and wanted this conversation to be over.

"We should sleep on it," he said. "Maybe the morning will bring answers."

"That's the best idea I've heard all night," Serah said. "I'm still confused about a lot. Like how you found this rotting Orb to begin with. But I just can't focus on anything right now."

"Before you rest," Fergus said, "be sure to stay near us. I'm warding Radiance, which will keep anyone from detecting our streams, while Lucian is warding Psionics, which will stop the Queen from interfering with our dreams."

Her face paled when she looked at Lucian. "She really *is* after you, then."

"This isn't a game. I wouldn't be doing this unless I absolutely had to. I know you don't have all the information yet, Serah, but I will answer any questions you have. It would be great if you could come with us. At least part of the way."

"I'll think about it," she said. "For now, I need some shuteye."

The four of them ended up sleeping side by side, nearly touching. The cave was still cold despite the close quarters, and the cold was only accentuated by the howling wind outside. Water dripped on Lucian's face from the condensation of everyone's breaths. He covered his face with his jacket. But before he allowed himself to fall asleep, he set his Psionic ward, making sure it was strong enough to cover all four of them.

Once done, he closed his eyes.

23

WHEN LUCIAN AWOKE, his skin was burning. Or rather, the fire was coming from directly *below* his skin, like insects stinging him all over.

He tried to keep himself from screaming, but he could only hold out so long. Everyone was up in the instant, with Fergus streaming a light sphere.

"What in the rotting hell is going on?" Cleon asked.

Serah was soon rubbing something on Lucian's skin that spread instant coolness and relief. The pain didn't completely ebb, but at least he wasn't screaming anymore. Fergus looked on worriedly while Serah continued rubbing in the balm.

"What is that?" Lucian asked.

"Karealas sap," she said. "Good for all manner of pain. No fray's kit is complete without it. There's nothing better for immolations."

"Immolations?"

"A side-effect of overdrawing," Fergus said. "Not uncommon a day or three after the incident in question."

"Overdrawing? I've barely . . ." Then Lucian remembered the fight with the wyverns. Overdrawing had been necessary to stream his kinetic wave. And he may have overdrawn during the fight in the Greenrift, too. Things had happened so fast that it was hard to remember.

Whatever the case, he had streamed more in the past few days than he had in months. And that was bound to have some effect.

"I get immolations, too," Serah said. "It's just part of being a mage."

"Then how come I've never heard of it before?"

"It's likely your Academy shielded you from such information, at least to begin with," Fergus said. "At Irion, we didn't teach our Initiates about them. And it's not something often spoken of, because . . ."

As Fergus trailed off, Cleon picked up the slack. "Well, we might as well be straight with him." Lucian had a feeling he wouldn't like what he was about to hear. "It's a sign of fraying, Lucian. It happens when you overdraw."

"I see."

Lucian sat up. The pain was all but gone, and he put his shirt back on. "Well, I'll have to be careful."

"See that you do," Fergus said. "Sometimes, overdrawing can't be avoided. You need ether to get out of a hard situation, we've all been there. Just know that it can lead to some particularly bad immolations down the line."

"You mean I'm not done with this yet?"

"Hard to say," Fergus said. "Duration, intensity, and overall number of immolations can vary. One thing is for sure. You don't want to overdraw too much, or you'll have a nasty surprise down the road."

"It's unavoidable sometimes," Serah said. "You empty your pool and you need to draw more, drinking the poison all the while. Do that too many times, too fast, and your body starts to reject it. Leads to passing out. You don't want to get to that point, because then you really *are* dead."

The rest of that morning was Lucian catching Serah up on everything. He did the best he could with that, knowing it was too much information. But she had a sharp mind and asked all the right questions. Within an hour, she knew as much as Fergus and Cleon.

Now, he would have to wait on her answer.

"It's too much," she said. "But I'll tell you what. I was going to Snake Rift anyway, and there's safety in numbers. Let's get there first."

"Sounds fair," Lucian said.

"It pains me to say this," Fergus said, "but we need you, Serah."

"Your persuasion skills are second to none, Fergie. Let me translate. You need my Gravitonic Magic. I'm a busy woman, and I don't help people just because they are on a *quest* to do something as foolhardy as it is utterly impossible."

"Is there anything we can do to convince you?" Lucian asked.

"There's nothing that you can give me. Just don't push me on this. For now, this is something for me to do, nothing more, nothing less. I'll probably change my mind later."

"This *isn't* a vacation," Fergus said.

"It is whatever I want it to be," Serah said. "Until I decide it isn't that anymore."

Fergus's expression was a mask of frustration. "You can't just . . . look at the world how you want to see it!"

"I think you just summed up my entire philosophy, actually."

"We're wasting time," Lucian said. "We're glad for your help, Serah. Welcome aboard, as long as you want to stay."

"Thanks. It's nice to be appreciated."

Once they had eaten and packed up, Lucian's mind became preoccupied with his immolation. He felt fine now, but how many more of these would it take to fray? He couldn't help but look at Serah's left arm, where the fraying rot had already taken hold. That gray, scaly skin looked almost reptilian. How much longer until *his* skin looked like that?

He brushed away these thoughts as they ate a quick breakfast. Serah seemed to be making point of not looking his way. Had she caught him staring at her arm? He felt doubly bad, because he hadn't even thanked her for the balm, and now, she was even risking her life for him. He wanted to make things right, but he didn't want to say anything with Fergus and Cleon right there.

Once packed up, they crawled out of the cave. Lucian thought it would be a relief to get out of the Cave of Claustrophobia, but with one gust of the bitingly cold wind, he was ready to go back in.

They stood on the ledge for a moment, Cleon standing in the lee of the rock face and shivering.

"How do we get down there?" he asked.

Serah turned back, her blonde hair blown sideways. "That would depend on how much you trust your friend here." She nodded toward Lucian.

"Trust *me*?" Lucian asked.

"And if I don't trust him?"

"Then you'd better hope you're a good climber."

Fergus frowned. "You're not going to create an anti-grav aura around us?"

"No. That would be suicidal with this wind, not to mention too much ether to cover four people."

Cleon's scoffed. "As if *Lucian* tethering us down there is any safer."

Serah ignored him. "Beyond this ledge is a much flatter slope that leads to the Snake Rift. There's a stand of rocks down there. You'll need Radiant Magic to see through these clouds, but once you do, you'll see those rocks clear as day."

"I catch your meaning," Fergus said. "You want me to light it up so Lucian can tether us down there?"

"Precisely. If that Orb is as strong as everyone's saying, this would make the perfect test."

Lucian had a bad feeling about this. "What did you mean by light it up, Fergus?"

"Radiants are the best for seeing the unseeable," Fergus said. "Watch, my boy, and learn."

At that moment, Fergus became wreathed in an aura of green light. His eyes, normally brown, now shone green, taking on new intensity. He peered into the mists for a moment.

"Found it."

Not a moment later, something glimmered in the distance. The rock, invisible before because of the fog, now shone like a miniature sun.

"Can you reach your Focus that far, Lucian?" Fergus asked. "Most Binders would burn themselves out in seconds trying to move a *pebble* that far."

Lucian thought about it for a moment. He wasn't sure what the Orb of Binding was truly capable of, but it had done things he would have deemed impossible. But now, others' lives were in his hands. It made his stomach drop.

"Is there another option?" Lucian asked.

"With this wind, my Gravitonics will be no help getting us down," Serah said. "We'd have to climb, but there's a crevice that's impossible to traverse without magic."

"So, the only other option is backtracking to the Snake Pass."

"And that'll be a slog," Serah said. "If the *Zephyr* comes on us there, we'll have no hope of escaping."

Lucian sighed. The fact that everyone's lives would be in his hands made him sick. Everyone was watching him. Why couldn't they just give him space?

"Do all of you trust me to do this?" Lucian asked.

"Hell no," Cleon said. "But I'm not going back to the Snake Pass, either."

Fergus watched Lucian, stepping forward and placing a hand on his shoulder.

"I'll go first," Fergus said. "It'll be far easier for me to stream if I can get closer to that rock." He looked at Lucian. "My life is in your hands, Binder. Make it go as quickly as you can."

"Without smashing your body into a bloody pulp, of course," Serah said.

"Yes," Fergus said. "There is that."

Lucian ignored the joke. It was not what he needed right now. "Okay, so get Fergus down there first, then Cleon I assume. Serah after. And then . . ." Lucian frowned. "I just realized I've never tried to Bind *myself* to something before."

"It's no different from Binding another person or object," Fergus said. "Only the stakes are higher."

"Can't we hurry this up?" Cleon asked. "I'm freezing my ass off here."

"And I'm burning ether," Fergus said. "Get me down there, Lucian. Fast."

Serah nodded. "Go ahead, Lucian."

He had to get moving quickly. He didn't know how long Fergus could keep the stream going. Lucian reached for his Focus, creating a tether from Fergus to the distant rock. It was hard to say how far away it was. A couple of klicks at least. Lucian drew ether from the Orb, streaming more and more magic into the tether.

Fergus was lifted into the air and sailed downward toward the rock, following the blue line into the mist.

"Geez," Cleon said. "Hope you're not going to make *me* fly like that."

Lucian ignored him. He needed his full concentration to keep his Focus strong and sure. It he lost it, even for a moment, the tether would dissipate and Fergus would fall to his death.

It took about a minute for Fergus to travel the entire distance. When Lucian felt the Captain was getting close, he slowed the stream to allow for a gentle landing. The rock continued to glow steadily.

"All right, Cleon," Lucian said. "You're up."

"I've got no choice, do I?"

He stepped up to the precipice and closed his eyes. He was shaking, either from nerves or the cold. Perhaps both.

"Don't piss yourself," Serah said.

"Are you sure you want those to be your last words to me?"

Before she could get in her own retort, Lucian attached a new anchor point to Cleon, who shot off the cliff with a yelp. Serah laughed as Cleon screamed for his life, his voice lost to the wind. Once Cleon had made it safely, Lucian let go of the stream.

"Now what?" he asked.

"We're done," she said. "With them out of the way, we can waltz off into the sunset."

"Come on, be serious."

At that moment, the light from the rock began to sputter. Was Fergus running low on ether?

"We may not have much time," Serah said. "You think you could stream us both down there at the same time?"

"I don't know. Maybe. Getting those two down took less effort than I thought. There seems to be no limits to the Orb."

Her eyes marveled. "Amazing. That's what we'll do, then."

The rock shone again, and Lucian reformed the tether. This time, he created two anchor points, one for both he and Serah. The Orb of Binding thrummed, feeding Lucian more and more ether, all of which went into building up the strength of the tethers.

"I can't believe you're doing this," Serah said. "This amount of magic is unreal!"

As soon as the tethers reached the right tension, Lucian and

Serah were pulled away from the cliff with surprising speed, so fast that Lucian was afraid he might lose his pack. His Focus felt more slippery this time, as if it couldn't handle this amount of magic as efficiently. It was a hard limitation on just how much magic he could stream. The ground below rushed up to meet them, but they could at least see through the mist now.

"I hope you know what you're doing," Serah shouted.

Lucian didn't want to tell her he was hoping for the same. Maintaining his Focus was difficult under the strain. His concentration almost slipped a couple of times, forcing him to refocus his efforts.

"We're almost there!" Serah said.

They were close enough to see a large boulder and two figures beside it standing on a flat expanse. Lucian slowed the flow from the Orb, and within moments, he and Serah touched down a few meters away from Fergus and Cleon. Fergus stopped streaming his Radiant Magic on the rock, and it faded to its usual gray color. His face was paler than usual. Lucian hoped he hadn't had to overdraw.

"We're here," Fergus said. "Now, which way is Snake Rift?"

"West," Serah said, pointing. "We'll have another choice to make there. Cross the rift and try to shoot across the Upper Reaches on the other side, or travel the rift itself and make for the Blue Crossing."

"Let me guess," Lucian said. "That connects to the Blue Rift?"

"You catch on fast," Serah said. "That will take longer, but it's safer. In the Upper Reaches, you're trading humans for wyverns and exposure to cold, and wyverns and exposure to cold are undoubtedly more dangerous." She peered into the gray, cloudy sky. "Speaking of, we should really get moving."

"I thought wyverns only hunted at night," Lucian said.

"They do," Serah said. "However, our smell and body heat might be too much of a temptation to resist. And I don't know how long it'll take to cross the Reaches here. I've never been this way before."

"Doesn't look like there are any caves or mountains around these parts," Cleon said. "Should be safe."

"You might be surprised," Serah said. "We've dallied enough. Let's move."

She took point without waiting for anyone else. Fergus opened his mouth, before Cleon clapped him on the shoulder.

"Looks like the Captain has been usurped."

"Why, you little—"

"Hurry!" Serah called.

The three men brought up the rear, plodding across the gray landscape.

24

THE GOING BECAME EASIER, even with the thin air. The land was flat, sloping slightly downward. The problem would come later when it was time to descend into the Snake Rift.

By early afternoon, the slope was steeper and rockier. They had to weave around fallen boulders, lower themselves down sheer cliffs, and have Lucian tether everyone across crevices. Even if the ether from the Orb of Binding was infinite, Lucian's mental capacity to stream it wasn't. He wasn't only physically tired, but mentally. Exhaustion was written on Serah's features as well, but even so, she took the lead and found a path through what seemed like a trackless waste.

They wove through a narrow ravine carved from a swift-moving stream tumbling down the rocks. Serah walked quickly, jumping from rock to rock and setting a brutal pace. At times, she'd stream an antigrav disc or two to bridge the wider gaps, holding them long enough for everyone to cross. Even Fergus was starting to get winded.

"Surely, we can break here for lunch and refill our canteens," he said.

When his deep voice echoed off the ravine's side, she placed a finger to her lips. "No. We can do that later. We still have ten kilometers of this to cover."

"Ten *kilometers*?" Cleon asked. "Seriously?"

"We've already done that, and it'll take another couple of hours with this pace."

"I'm pretty beat," Lucian said. "Maybe just a *short* break?"

"No."

Fergus watched her suspiciously. "What are you hiding?"

Her only answer was to keep moving.

"That's not a good sign," Cleon muttered.

"Serah?" Fergus called.

Serah stopped, her face whipping around. "Quiet!"

When Fergus spoke again, he was quieter, if only marginally. "If you would just explain—"

"Guys . . ." Cleon said, pointing up.

Lucian didn't know how he had missed it before. In a cleft of rocks right above them, below a stunted tree, lay a pile of eggs, each about the size of a human head.

He hoped it wasn't what he thought it was.

They practically ran the rest of the way. No one complained. They couldn't put those eggs behind them fast enough.

They went around a final bend with about a kilometer left that seemed to end at a steep drop-off. The fading light meant they had an hour or less to get out of this canyon and seek shelter.

Lucian kept looking over his shoulder, expecting to see or hear wyverns following. But the canyon remained silent save for their footfalls. They dashed from rock to rock and forded the stream multiple times. It was a race against time to get out of here before it got too dark.

Once they arrived at the precipice, Snake Rift stretched before them. True to its name, it zigged and zagged every which way. It was smaller than the Deeprift, at least half of its width. Even so, the rift's walls rose hundreds of meters above and below. There didn't seem to be a clear way down, though Lucian spied a trail on the opposite side of the rift.

The question was, how to get there?

"Can you tether us again, Lucian?" Fergus asked.

The mere idea made him want to groan. "I'm starting to feel tapped out."

"We *all* are," Serah said. "We need to get out of here fast."

"What about your anti-grav aura?" Cleon asked. "Too far to leap?"

Serah nodded. "I don't have the ether for that, even for one person."

Lucian saw there was no choice. "I can tether everyone over one by one, like last time."

"I don't see any other way," Serah said. "It's getting dark, so we need to be . . ."

At that moment, a great *whoosh* rushed over the ravine. Lucian looked up to see not a wyvern, but the passing of a long, wooden hull. It was there and gone in less than ten seconds.

Lucian could only stare, his mouth agape. Had he *really* just seen that? Judging from the others' expressions, they were similarly shocked.

But before anyone could say anything, shrieks filled the evening air.

The *Zephyr* had just kicked a hornet's nest.

———

"WE'VE GOT TO MOVE!" Fergus shouted.

There was no time to consider options. In seconds, wyverns would be upon them, and not even the Orb of Binding would be able to save them if there were anywhere as many as Lucian was expecting.

The only option was escape. Once again, Lucian would

have to reach for the Orb, despite his exhaustion. Everyone's lives depended on it.

Lucian reached for his Focus, setting anchor points on all four of them. There simply wasn't time to do things safely by streaming them across one at a time; it was either this, or death. He streamed a single focal point across the rift, at the largest boulder he could find next to the trail. He began streaming, magic burning through him in a nonstop torrent, building up the power of each of the tethers. Far more magic was needed than he had expected. His vision started to fade, replaced with a world of blue and white lines. He didn't have time to question it, nor to even feel fear. He had to make this work.

"Hurry it up, Lucian," Cleon said.

His voice seemed to come from another world. And still, the four tethers needed more magic, more tension. The world fell away, until all that was left was the Orb burning in his consciousness like a shining blue sun. And beyond that sun was something else. A familiar fear he never wanted to feel again.

That presence reached out for him. *You would kill yourself for them? Save yourself. I can show you that which you seek.*

Lucian ignored the voice, siphoning the surrounding ether emanating from that sun. He couldn't question what this place was or what exactly he was seeing. He got the feeling it might be the ethereal field itself manifesting before him.

He screamed as the surrounding energy infused inside him. He redirected it all into the tethers. Surely it should not take *this* much magic, but for the first time in his life, Lucian was creating four separate streams. Each additional stream, he knew, became more expensive to create and maintain. A quadrastream took sixteen as much magic as a single stream. He was doing something that the Transcends of the Academy would deem impossible for almost any mage, and he was doing it without experience.

But he also had no choice. Time seemed to slow as the blue reality faded. Lucian felt his body return to the Shadow World, his reality. His mind snapped fully back to the ravine. No more than a few seconds must have passed, but now every part of him was shining with blue radiance. And the tethers were ready.

When Lucian let go of the tension, at once, all of them sailed away at breakneck speed across Snake Rift. Cleon lost his pack, but still brimming with ether, Lucian opened a *fifth* stream, anchoring the pack to Cleon. Ether burned through him even faster, shockingly fast, but only for a moment. Cleon grabbed the pack, allowing Lucian to close off the stream. Lucian only slowed down once they were meters from the trail, setting them down near the focal point. He let go of the stream entirely with a gasp.

As more wyvern shrieks filled the air, Lucian's vision blackened for a moment before returning. He looked back at the entrance to the ravine across from them. There were a dozen of those things coming for them, all as large or larger than the ones he had fought alone.

Fergus stood with his spear, along with a shield that seemed to be made from light itself, with a brightness to counter the wyverns. Cleon's hands were wrapped with fire. Serah knelt, shockspear at the ready with a silvery aura of Gravitonic Magic surrounding her.

The shrieking wyverns poured over the ravine exit across the rift. In the skies above, there was no sign of the *Zephyr*.

Despite his exhaustion, Lucian opened a new Binding stream, focusing the magic at the point of his spear. Until now, he hadn't realized magic other than Dynamism could be streamed along a shockspear, but somehow, he was doing it. More and more magic collected in the growing blue sphere, which shone brighter and brighter. Again, the world faded, as the Shadow World receded and was replaced by the Manifold and the ethereal field it generated.

Remembering the voice he'd heard before, he didn't want to delve too deeply.

With a roar, Lucian thrust his spear skyward, releasing a blinding burst of blue magic from the spear tip. A fork of blue lightning shot outward, connecting with the forerunner of the wyverns. It shrieked as the lightning split into multiple paths that bound even *more* wyverns. It was the same thing that had happened at the Snake Pass, except instead of the lightning grabbing boulders, it was grabbing wyverns. The air emanated with pained screeches. His consciousness was beginning to fade as his Binding stream petered out . . .

"Stop!" Serah said. "You're going to kill yourself!"

Lucian let go and would have collapsed had not Serah caught him. Forcing his eyes open, he could see that the wyverns were leashed to each other by tethers, all pulling them toward each other.

"Cover your eyes and grab onto each other!" Fergus said. "I'll lead us to safety. Just trust me!"

"What are you on about?" Cleon shouted. He shot a few ineffectual fireballs in the direction of the wyverns. Lucian's Binding lightning was beginning to fade as the wyverns fought against their restraints.

"Do as I say!"

Lucian covered his eyes, and not a moment later, a nova-like burst of light penetrated his eyelids. The wyverns screeched their dismay.

"Follow!" Fergus said. "And don't open your eyes!"

Lucian felt himself pulled along by Serah, judging by the size of the hands. The ground rocked, causing Lucian to almost lose his feet, shortly followed by a rain of rock.

"What in the rotting hell was that?" Cleon shouted.

"Stop panicking," Serah said. "You're making things worse!"

"The *Zephyr* is back," Fergus said. "Their mages are attacking us."

"Why aren't they attacking the wyverns?" Lucian asked.

"Don't know," Fergus said. "There's a cave up ahead."

"Get in there!" Serah shouted. "We'll figure out the rest later."

The light was dimming outside his vision. He risked opening his eyes. It was no longer bright. In fact, it was quite dim, and it appeared they were now inside the cave. From behind came the sound of screeching wyverns. Looking back, Lucian could see the *Zephyr* floating down the rift. Hopefully, the ship and the wyverns would keep each other busy long enough for them to escape.

"Deeper," Fergus said. "This cave goes quite some distance, it seems."

"Better not be a dead end," Cleon grumbled.

"That's not likely," Serah said. "Most cave systems on Psyche connect with others. If we go deep enough, we can find our way out later."

"Unless we get lost."

"Way to stay positive, Cleon," Serah said.

"It isn't like we have a choice," Lucian said. "Unless you want to take your chances with a dozen wyverns and the *Zephyr*."

At that moment, Lucian felt something . . . *pushing* against his mind. He placed a hand on his forehead, a high-pitched ring throbbing in his ears.

Serah placed a hand on his arm. "Lucian. You okay?"

The sound became louder, until he was on his knees. He shut his eyes in a vain attempt to ignore the sound, but it only grew more dominant, until it was *all* he could think about.

Fergus said something, though Lucian didn't know what. His vision went black and he knew no more.

25

WHEN LUCIAN WOKE UP, all was dark. All except for a single light, floating in the distance. Two pairs of hands were carrying him along. *And* he had a splitting headache.

"He's awake," Cleon said. "Should we set him down?"

"Here's fine," Serah replied.

Lucian groaned. "Where are we?"

"Somewhere under Snake Rift," Serah said. "Other than that, we're lost as lost can be."

"But no one's chasing us anymore, thanks to me," Fergus said.

"You mean, no one's chasing us *yet*," Cleon said.

"Cheery as ever." Serah knelt and looked at Lucian, her eyes concerned. "How are you feeling? Did you . . . *see* her?"

See who? Then, he remembered the Psionic attack and being knocked out. Had that really been the Sorceress-Queen attacking him?

"No. All I felt was . . . darkness."

"Our ward must have worked, then," Fergus said.

"That's great, but here's the situation," Cleon said. "We're deep underground who knows where, and we can't go back the way we came. As far as we know, soldiers are hot on our trail. It will be much faster for them to follow us than for us to find the right direction."

No one could argue with his assessment of the situation. The sooner they got moving, the better.

"Get him some water," Fergus said.

"Can you hold it?" she asked, handing him his canteen.

"I've got it." He drank deeply.

"Now, we need to figure out how to get out," Serah said. "I've been in the tunnels of Snake Rift plenty of times, but none of this is recognizable. There's a chance if we keep going down, we might run into something that looks familiar. From there, I might be able to find Slave's Run."

"That's too many *mights*," Cleon said. "You're going to need to do better than that."

"Cleon, quiet," Fergus said. "I know you're anxious, but we need to work together if we're going to get out of this alive."

"Alive? You're optimistic."

"I know it looks bad," Lucian said. "But we have to keep moving. You're here, after all."

"I never asked to be here. And yet here I am, all because of that rotting Orb."

He kicked a rock and yowled when he stubbed his toe in the process. No one had the heart to laugh. It was more pathetic than anything.

"Lucian is right," Fergus said. "Do I need to remind you of the stakes, Cleon? Where is your sense of honor and duty?"

"Both of those dried up five years ago, when I realized what honor and duty get you. Absolutely nothing except those who would take advantage of both for their own selfish ends." He went silent, as if he had said too much. "If we have a death wish already, then we might as well see it through. I say let's go to the Darkrift instead of the surface, like before. With our fearless

Serah leading the way, I'm sure we'll be up to our necks in gloombats or worse before long."

"Better than getting killed by the Queen's mages, in my view," Lucian said.

"Death is death either way," Cleon said.

"Every minute we stand here arguing is a minute for the Darans to catch up," Fergus said.

"You're good to walk, right?" Serah asked Lucian.

"Should be."

"So, the plan is to keep moving and hope Serah finds something she recognizes," Cleon said. "Lovely."

"If you have a better plan, I'm all ears," she said.

"Can't say that I do. Lead on."

The next few hours passed in silence. The caverns of Psyche seemed truly endless. There was nothing but Fergus's light sphere to lead the way, which needed to be refreshed every few hours. Lucian only hoped that with the light sphere and the concealment ward Fergus wouldn't be overstretched. And he didn't just have to do it in the near term. If they were really going into the Darkrift, he'd have to maintain that light for days, or even weeks, on end. Lucian couldn't imagine the toll that would take.

And the thought of being down here that long was terrifying. They had enough food for a few weeks, but after that, they would have to supplement their diets with something underground. Lucian would have to trust Serah knew what was safe to eat. For as long as she decided to stay with them.

Most of the life Lucian saw seemed to be fungus, various mushrooms, and bugs. Lots and lots of bugs, and not small ones, either. He hoped there were better things to eat than that down here, but so far, it wasn't looking like it.

"So, how long will it take to get to Dara once we find Slave's Run?" Fergus asked.

"Well, finding the Run itself should take a few days at least, if not longer," Serah said. "And after that, assuming we make good progress and don't get lost, about another two to three weeks."

"Math isn't my strong suit," Cleon said, "but doesn't that work out to something like fifty kilometers a *day*?"

"That's if you're traveling above ground," Serah said. "It's about half that when taking Slave's Run because you're not weaving back and forth through the Riftlands. Slave's Run is a straight shot so you can move as fast as your feet can carry you."

"Three weeks to Dara is fine," Fergus said.

"That's only *if* we find the entrance to Slave's Run," Serah said. "I'll do what I can to find it, but it might mean having to surface to reorient ourselves."

"Whatever needs to be done," Fergus said. "So, which way is the surface?"

"Up," Cleon said, pointing his finger.

Serah shrugged. "He's right. If we go up, we'll pop out somewhere." She nodded down the passage. "Let's move."

———

THEY HAD BEEN WALKING upslope for hours before feeling the cool, night air of the surface. It was so dark that Lucian could hardly tell they were outside. Only the fresh, open air was a clue that they were outdoors.

"We should head back into the cave and set up camp for the night," Serah said. "With daylight, we can orient ourselves a little bit. Pray we're somewhere I've been before."

"And if we're being followed?" Cleon asked.

"Cleon's right," Fergus said, his eyes hooded with exhaustion. "We must press on."

"Fergus, you won't be able to hold that light much longer. And wyverns are always a threat, even this low in Snake Rift."

"Serah's right," Lucian said. "You look like you're going to keel over any minute, Fergus."

He opened his mouth to protest, but in the end, sat on a nearby rock. Within moments, he was asleep sitting up and his light sphere had winked out, leaving the rest in darkness.

"Well, there goes our light." A moment later, Cleon was using a floating fireball to provide light. "Let's find some fuel for a fire. I'm burning ether here."

"Will they be able to track us?" Lucian asked.

Cleon sniffed. "They'd have to be idiots to not pick up our trail. It just depends how that fight with the wyverns turned out."

"It's hard to imagine them winning that," Lucian said. "There were so many."

"Well, you can't take anything for granted. But if we *are* to die, we might as well die well-rested and with a fire to warm our arses."

They went a few meters inside the cave to gather some scrubby vegetation for a fire. It didn't burn too well, but it provided enough warmth to cook dinner. They ate quickly, and once done, gathered enough scrub to keep the fire going all night. The risk of wyverns was simply too high, even if the fire drew attention. Lucian wondered from how far away it could be seen, even inside the cave as they were.

"Who's keeping watch?" Cleon asked. "It's not Fergus for sure, and it's not me because I did it yesterday."

"I can take first watch," Lucian said. "Serah will have second."

"Or we could all just get enough sleep because we're exhausted," Serah said.

"Bad idea," Cleon said.

"Fine, we'll do it Lucian's way. Wake me in a few hours."

With that, she settled down to sleep.

Lucian streamed the group's Psionic ward, something that

was fast becoming a habit. After that, there was nothing but the darkness to occupy him. Darkness that made it impossible not to nod off.

He stood up, but he was simply so overcome that trying to stay awake was an exercise in futility.

He lay on the ground, not even having the energy to get out his bedroll.

———

LUCIAN AWOKE VERY MUCH ALIVE, which was enough to tell him that they hadn't been tracked. Fergus was already up and preparing breakfast, and the others were soon roused by the noise.

He immediately felt guilty for falling asleep, but Fergus made no mention of it.

"Lucian, go check inside the cave with Serah and see what you can see."

Together, they walked deeper into the cave. The tunnel was almost perfectly round, as if it had been artificially made.

"Looks like a well-traveled path," Serah said. "It'd be best to get out of here as quickly as possible. Either way, doesn't seem like we were followed."

When they returned outside, the morning light revealed a deep, narrow fissure. Over the cliff was a few hundred meters drop to a dark, still lake running the fissure's length.

"Looks like we've hit bottom," Serah said. "Almost." She took a good look around. "It's still Snake Rift, though we've come down a bit in elevation."

"How do you know we're still in Snake?"

"I don't think we walked far enough to cross over into Blue Rift. Blue Rift is mostly water and wider. I'm ninety percent sure this is Snake, and in the Lower Reaches."

"So, what does that mean?"

"We'll talk about it over breakfast."

Around the fire, Fergus was passing around breakfast bowls.

Cleon still looked half-asleep, blinking drearily. "Please tell me it's good news."

"No signs of us being followed." Serah took a bowl of porridge. "What's more, that's Snake Rift out there."

"So, what's our next move?" Fergus asked.

"Two options as I see it. Go back the way we came and try to find the Darkrift from there. Or, we can head down the Snake Rift and look for this tunnel I know. I *think* I can find Slave's Run from here, but I'll be surer of finding it from the other cave. But it'll probably be a day or two of travel on the surface. Depends how fast we go."

"The *Zephyr* could still be out," Fergus said. "Probably is, actually."

"If we're staying above ground, then we need to head west, toward the Blue Rift," Serah said. "I vote for that. Looks quiet out here. Plus, we can keep watch for the *Zephyr* and find a hiding spot if we see anything. If Fergus's concealment ward isn't spotty, our magic shouldn't be detected."

"My ward won't be spotty, I assure you."

"You're saying you can't find the Darkrift from this tunnel?" Lucian asked.

"I *probably* can, but if I can't, it could mean backtracking. Or worst case, we lose our way entirely. Most of the shallower paths have markings to keep you on track, but once you get deeper, you have nothing but your wits to keep you alive."

"Staying on the surface is the only thing that makes sense," Cleon said. "Better to find the Darkrift from a place you know."

"Surfacing will also give us the choice to continue on to Blue Rift if we want. Just one of dozens of rifts we'd need to cross to reach the Golden Vale, and then, Dara."

"I will make that decision when it comes to it," Fergus said.

"If things are as quiet as you say, then I might be inclined to stay above ground. Especially if it seems like the Sorceress-Queen is confining her search to the Deeprift."

"The *Zephyr* spotted us in Snake Rift," Lucian said. "And the *Zephyr* probably knows we went underground. If they didn't pursue us on foot, then they are surely searching the rift for us now."

"A fair point," Serah said. "However, Snake Rift is so-named because of its length and how it twists. There are *thousands* of caves leading in and out of it. It's the worst place to try and look for someone."

"But the Sorceress-Queen might be on board," Cleon countered. "Lucian's Psionic ward fell quickly."

If not the Sorceress-Queen, then *someone* had been testing his ward yesterday. "I hadn't set it since the night before, so it was weak already."

"It's a risk we'll have to take," Fergus said, deciding. "These caves are unsettling, and all the more so if they are unrecognizable to Serah." He looked at her. "So, it'll take one or two days to reach this other cave entrance?"

"Hard to say. Once we're on the trail, things should start looking recognizable. The path will branch two different ways. Down will lead to the Darkrift, and up will lead to the Blue Pass."

Fergus heaved a sigh. "Well, I don't like being out here. But I believe the risk of wandering these dark tunnels and hoping for the best is more dangerous."

"I agree," Cleon said.

"Same," Serah said.

All eyes went to Lucian. He certainly didn't like the idea of going above, but Fergus was right. These tunnels *were* unsettling, and if he were forced to be in them, it would be best for Serah to recognize which one it was.

"I'm for it," he said. "But we have to make sure our wards

are set well. The Sorceress-Queen is probably out there hunting us."

"I'll strengthen my ward today, committing most of my ether," Fergus said. "Just stay close and it will keep anyone from sensing us. That, I guarantee."

"Will you be okay doing that?" Serah asked.

"I'll be fine," Fergus said. "It isn't like we have a choice, anyway."

Lucian didn't like the sound of that, but he realized Fergus was right. This was as good as it was going to get.

Lucian could only hope it was good enough.

26

EVEN IF THE surface was more dangerous, being in the light again was worth it. The only sounds were their footsteps and the wind. Snake Rift was rougher than the Deeprift, with less vegetation and more rocky outcrops and rockslides. Lucian got the feeling there were few, if any, people who lived here. There was no sign of another human being, or even an animal.

It just needed to stay that way.

After half an hour, it was clear they were in some tributary of the rift rather than the main rift itself. The fissure was so narrow that it would be difficult for the *Zephyr* to maneuver. However, the entrance to the Darkrift could only be accessed from the main part of Snake Rift, which would be much wider. Lucian could only hope that the earthen tones of their clothing would blend with the gray rocks and brown dirt. They stayed as close as possible to the rock face, which would make them harder to pick out.

By noon, they had reached the main rift. As Lucian had suspected, it was tall and wide enough for the *Zephyr* to maneuver easily, though the many twists and turns might prove a barrier.

Serah looked each way, her eyes following the line of the trail leading westward. "This way."

She went left, which led down toward the water. Everyone followed.

After an hour of walking, Cleon broke the silence. "It's too quiet."

Serah rolled her eyes. "Don't tell me you're going to complain that things are *too* boring now."

Cleon cracked a smile. "Beat me to the punch."

"Let's pray it *stays* boring," Fergus said. "I would very much like to return to Kiro alive."

"Same," Cleon said. "Though at this point, I would settle for mere survival."

They walked for hours, the narrow sliver of sky above only growing marginally brighter. True to its name, Snake Rift swerved back and forth, delving deeper into Psyche's surface. The light from above became a thin crack, and their surroundings were so dim that it was almost as if they were underground again. The water had become a fast-moving stream, tumbling over rocks, and frothing white. Lucian imagined that stream didn't end until the Moon Sea tens of kilometers below them.

"I think we've made it," Serah said, stopping near a boulder with a Septagon carved into it. "This marks the boundary of Snake Rift and the beginning of the Darkrift."

Lucian looked above, only to see a small sliver of light. Rock arches covered the space above just as often as open air, creating faded sunbeams that illumined dancing motes of dust. Little by little, the surface had transformed into an underground cavern, though Lucian couldn't have said exactly *when* the transition had occurred.

"Well, at least we can't be followed here by the *Zephyr*," Fergus said. "But it seems the option to go on to Blue Rift has been taken away."

"There's still a branch that will lead us there," Serah said. "If I can find it."

"Lead on," Fergus said. "And stay alert. They probably suspect we are heading this way, especially if they check the Blue Pass and find it empty."

Lucian clasped his shockspear tighter, looking back over his shoulder and half-expecting to see pursuers, Mage-Knights in their colored robes and bronze-clad hoplites. And the purple-caped, purple-plumed man Cleon had called Mage-Lord Kiani. Going underground again didn't feel right, but there was no choice but to keep moving. Anyone could be behind them, and Lucian didn't want to meet potential enemies.

———

IT WAS ONLY a few hours more before the skylights disappeared altogether and the Darkrift began living up to its name. Fergus had a light sphere always following the group, along with his strengthened concealment ward. He showed no signs of fatigue, but Lucian knew if there was ever a fight, it would be up to the rest of them to pick up the slack.

They were still following the stream, which ran by the trail. It had narrowed significantly in the last few hours, but now it ran even faster. The stream and the echo of its flowing water were the only sounds. If the rest of the trip were this peaceful, Lucian would be a happy man.

Serah led at the fore, and turned her head while walking. "Once we go away from this stream, we will have to be quieter. Things down here are not keen on sight, but you will not *believe* how they can hear or smell."

"What's down here besides gloombats?" Lucian asked.

"Nothing you really want to meet," Cleon said.

"Burners, mostly," Fergus said. "Frays with minds so rotten

they are more animal than man. They'll attack anything that's *not* them. It's the last stage of a frayed mage's life."

"So, they just stay like that until something kills them?"

Fergus nodded. "Or until they kill themselves. They lie inert in dark places, mostly. Places like the Darkrift are perfect for them, and one of the reasons this place is so feared."

"Can we get moving?" Cleon asked. "I'd like to make Slave's Run as soon as possible, and not think about what might be lying in the dark."

"I second that," Serah said.

They continued. Lucian tried not to think about the threats that could be lurking around every bend. This was made worse once *he* had to take over the light. Even Fergus couldn't maintain two wards for hours on end, so he let Lucian take over the light sphere at least. Radiance was not Lucian's strength, but Fergus needed the break. By this point, Lucian's Psionic ward had dissolved, meaning he had the ether to spare for a Radiance ward.

Now, the tunnel was completely black. It was hard for Lucian to tell the time, but by now, it must have been dark outside. They had been walking for hours with not so much as a break.

"When do we set up camp?" Lucian asked. His voice was louder than he thought, even with the rush of the stream.

"Keep moving," Fergus said. "We only camp once we've found a good spot."

"What's a good spot?"

"That," Serah said, pointing. "Can you brighten your sphere, Lucian?"

Lucian did so, increasing the amount of ether. Across the stream rose a steep ledge that looked climbable. But it wasn't the ledge Serah was pointing out. There was a fissure entering the rock face, shadowed in darkness, that the sphere light couldn't quite reach.

"That looks promising," she said. "We can get some shuteye. Even as bright as Lucian's sphere is, it won't reach in there."

"Sounds good to me," Cleon said. "Will there be room for everyone?"

"I can go check it out," Lucian said. "The rest of you can wait here."

"I can boost you," Serah said. "Wouldn't want you getting yourself killed this early."

Together, they crossed the stream. Lucian was surprised at how much force the water exerted. Though the water only went up to his knees, he kept slipping. It was easier to be pushed around in this low gravity. A waist-high stream might be enough to carry him off.

"Careful," Serah said.

The stream emptied in a small, dark pool that looked deep, and it seemed that the pool joined another fast-moving stream, where the trail picked up again. Lucian only had eyes for the cliff, though. He dropped his pack and instantly felt much lighter on his feet. He scaled it easily, only a few flecks of rock crumbling away from his efforts. There was no need for Serah to give him a lift with her magic.

Once he'd reached the top, he found the ledge was quite narrow. He headed for the fissure running into the wall, his sphere light revealing an empty chasm about two meters deep. It was tall enough to cover even Fergus's head. It was about twenty meters long and a quarter of that wide. It would be the perfect place to hole up. Assuming they slept as far from the pool as possible, no one could see them from the trail. All they had to do was clear their tracks.

Lucian returned to the cliff and waved up the others.

The packs were easily moved to the top with antigrav auras streamed by Serah. She tossed them up one by one. Then, the rest climbed hand over hand, finding the ascent as easy as Lucian.

They could only hope that this ledge didn't attract attention. It didn't look out of place from the trail, but would an enemy pursuer take note of the fissure and want to investigate it? Then again, they had to sleep *somewhere*, and this was the best spot they'd found.

Serah was the last one up, after she had erased whatever tracks led here. Lucian only lowered the brightness of his sphere once she was on top of the ledge. Together, they walked to the fissure, where Fergus and Cleon were already setting up camp.

"No one will ever know we're here," she said. "Especially once that sphere goes off."

Dinner that night was dried meat, pickles, and crimson fruit. There was no fire. They had brought no fuel with them, so they were limited to what they could find or whatever Cleon could stream.

"My concealment ward is as strong as any I've ever made," Fergus said. "If another Radiant is trying to sniff us out, he'll be sorely disappointed, I assure you of that."

"I got rid of the tracks heading here, too," Serah added. "Not that there's much on this rock, anyway. There's a fording up ahead, so they'll just assume we crossed that."

"Let's hope so," Cleon said.

Fergus nodded at Lucian, his signal to dissolve the light sphere. When it winked out, the darkness was absolute, seeming solid enough to press up against him. His heart raced a bit. It only reminded him of being at the bottom of the Ocean of Storms.

He reached for his Focus, using it to insulate him from the panic. When his heartrate slowed, he closed his eyes. He longed for someone to be close to him, just so he could be reminded he wasn't alone. He thought back to his first night on Psyche, where he and Serah had slept under the rubble. Now, though, there was no rubble to be the excuse that pushed them together.

In time, Lucian fell asleep after streaming his Psionic ward for the night.

27

WHEN LUCIAN OPENED HIS EYES, he could see a light floating in the distance. Then another. And another. A long line of light spheres drifted across his vision. At first, it seemed like a dream. But as he opened his eyes more fully, he could make out shapes moving among those lights. *Human* shapes.

They had been found.

No one else seemed to be awake, though he could hear someone snoring nearby, who he thought to be Cleon. When Lucian touched a hairy leg, the wiry man seized up as if electrocuted.

"Quiet," Lucian whispered.

Since Cleon actually did remain quiet, he must have seen the lights, too.

"Wake Fergus," Lucian whispered. "I'll get Serah."

Lucian crouched and snuck over to Serah, who was breathing softly on the other side of the fissure. Thankfully, she already seemed to be awake.

"I see it," she whispered.

The lights were getting farther, meaning they had been fooled by Serah's misdirection. How long before they realized something was wrong? Before too long, they would head back here.

Once the lights had completely disappeared down some passage or another, someone heaved a sigh of relief.

"We're not out of this yet," Serah said. "They'll double back once they realize the trail's gone cold."

"What do we do, then?" Cleon asked.

"Two options, as I see it. Stay up here and hope they don't find us. Or run like hell."

Lucian didn't like either of those options. "Well, if they realize the trail ends around here, they'll find us easily. And judging from those lights, we're severely outnumbered."

"I agree," Serah said. "Only problem is, they went the direction *we* were supposed to go. And they are really pushing themselves."

"So, we just go back the way we came and take one of the other passages," Lucian said. "Or we might even surface and make our way back to Blue Rift."

"There's the *Zephyr*," Serah said. "It's likely this is the same group of soldiers that was chasing *me*, or maybe the forces chasing you and I combined. That means the *Zephyr* dropped them off near the entrance of the Darkrift. That ship will be parked out there, waiting for them to return with Lucian in tow."

"Perhaps we could take it on," Lucian said. "If most of the soldiers and mages are down here, then it might be a good opportunity to strike."

"Are you fraying?" Fergus said.

"Rot that," Cleon said. "No way in hell I'm fighting the *Zephyr* if there's even a *chance* the Sorceress-Queen herself is on board. Which she probably is since someone was attacking your ward last night."

"We need to act fast," Serah said. "They'll be coming back any time."

"There were several other paths back the way we came," Lucian said. "I say we run, skip a few of them, and pick one at random."

"Sounds like a great way to fall down a hole," Cleon said.

"Well, we're running out of options, so unless you have an idea..."

Fergus held up a hand, quieting everyone.

"We must put distance between us and them. That's the number one priority." He looked at Serah. "What do we need to do?"

"More or less what Lucian said," Serah said. "Find a path and hope they don't follow it. Lucian, stream a dim sphere. Something that might be mistaken for a ghost eel. We're going to travel upstream from where we came, at least for a bit. We can't make fresh tracks."

"That'll be cold," Cleon said.

"Better than being dead," Serah said. "We should get moving. I'll try to find another tunnel we can use, but no promises."

Lucian streamed the sphere, so dimly that he could see nothing beyond a meter in every direction. In less than two minutes, everyone was packed and ready. Not half a kilometer away, his enemies were hunting for him, and the only thing that kept them from being detected was Fergus. Fergus, who was fast tiring from maintaining the concealment ward nonstop.

They lowered themselves from the cliff and into the cold stream. Lucian was grateful the water didn't go above his knees, but the going was still slippery and miserable. It didn't take long for his boots to soak through and his feet to go numb. There was nothing to be done about that. Lucian brightened his sphere because they were just slipping too much. If they were being followed, they'd have no way of knowing. The pitch blackness, combined with the light of the sphere, made it impossible to see into the darkness behind. They wouldn't know they were being pursued until the lights were on them.

Serah led them up a tributary of the stream, where another tunnel branched off from the main one. With luck, they wouldn't be followed this way.

A few more minutes of walking, and Serah found another trail running alongside the new stream. This one would be rougher going. They had to crouch multiple times just to fit under the ceiling, and also to climb over various cave-ins. Lucian's greatest fear was reaching a dead end and having to go back, and then running into the Queen's men.

He was relieved when the trail opened again, at what appeared to be a large underground lake, far bigger than the one they had camped beside. Lucian couldn't say *how* he knew they were in a massive space. It was something he felt.

"Put the sphere out," Serah whispered.

He did so instantly. At first, he couldn't see anything. But once his eyes had adjusted, the lights were back, only far in the distance. How far was that? A kilometer? Half that? However far, it was too close.

"You think they saw us?" Cleon asked.

"I don't know," Serah said. "It's clear they're on the other side of this lake."

"Head back?" Fergus asked.

"Let's sit still for a while," she said. "How's your ward, Fergus?"

"Weakening," Fergus said. "We need to go in the opposite direction, even if we backtrack. I can probably keep the ward this strong for another few hours. It's either that or weaken it, which makes detection more likely."

"I remember this lake," Serah said. "They're following the exact path we need to be on."

"Well, how are we supposed to get past them?" Lucian asked.

239

"We don't," Fergus said. "Our best move is to gain some distance and camp out a few days. Let them continue their mad chase."

Lucian had to say it made sense. Sometimes, the hardest thing to do was nothing at all.

"That means finding a safe place to hole up," Serah said. "We can't go back to where we were before. After missing us the first time, they might investigate the fissure more closely."

The lights were getting closer. Shouldn't they have been going the *opposite* way?

"I think they might have seen us," Cleon whispered.

"Time to move," Fergus said.

They backed into the tunnel from which they'd emerged, but not before an explosion of rock fountained from the ground beneath. Someone stumbled in front of Lucian, causing him to trip up.

"Run!" Serah said.

Fergus streamed a light sphere, illumining the entrance of the tunnel. One fireball, and then two, shot across the still surface of the lake. Cleon raised a Thermal shield, which absorbed the missiles. More fireballs flew their way.

Lucian ran after the others right into the tunnel. He reached for the Binding Aspect, not accessing the Orb so as not to draw too much ether. Even with Fergus's ward, it might draw too much attention. Lucian tethered the floor and ceiling by the entrance and unleashed a heavy stream of magic. When the tension was too much, a resounding crack echoed through the tunnel. The ceiling started to collapse. Hopefully, that would block the entrance of the tunnel rather than collapsing the entire thing. Whatever the case, Lucian was running.

The others were already far away, with Fergus's light sphere quite distant. Lucian streamed his own sphere and ran, his head swimming with fatigue. Rocks and dust fell behind him, and pebbles pelted his back.

By the time he reached the stream again, the others were waiting.

"They'll have to double back the way they came," Serah said. "Which will put them here in about an hour or two if they go at an all-out run."

"I'm no longer maintaining my ward," Fergus said. "There's no point until we get some distance. Our only choice is to keep ahead of them."

"Rot it," Serah said. "Let's go."

She led them at a run, weaving through the tunnels of the Darkrift in seemingly random directions. Lucian noticed the general slope, however, led downward. He gasped for breath. The others were far fitter than he was.

"I . . . can't breathe . . ."

"You'll *really* not be breathing if you're dead," Serah shot back.

Lucian stumbled on. The trail ended in a cliff, seemingly a dead end. There was nothing below them but dark water with no way out.

"What now?" Cleon asked. "If we backtrack, we'll run into them for sure."

"Only one answer to that," Serah said. She walked toward the cliff. Surely, she wasn't going to *jump* down there.

"Are you out of your *mind*?" Cleon asked.

But it was too late. In the next moment, she was jumping over the edge without so much as a scream. It took a long time before there was a splash, at least ten seconds.

"It seems our options have been taken from us," Fergus said, stripping himself from his bronze armor. "It's a sad day to leave this behind."

"There could be no way out of there!" Cleon said. "We could drown! What about our packs?"

"I know," Fergus said, pushing the armor over the edge so that it wouldn't be found. "But we just have to hope there *is* a way. And hope they aren't desperate enough to follow us. As for your pack, I hope you're a strong swimmer."

Cleon sighed. "Fine. I already knew I was dead, anyway. But does it *really* have to be drowning? That's such a bad way to go."

"Oh, stop the theatrics," Fergus said.

"Hurry!" Serah's voice echoed up. "I see a way out."

"That's all I need to know." With that, Fergus hopped off the cliff with a decidedly bigger splash than Serah.

That left Lucian and Cleon. Cleon stared at him with wide eyes.

"This cliff must be thirty meters high," he said. "It'll hurt like hell when we land."

"Can't swim?"

"Of course I can swim."

"All I needed to know."

Without warning, Lucian streamed a kinetic wave at Cleon, instantly knocking him back. He flew into the air a little farther than Lucian had intended, unleashing a stream of curses. The only words Lucian could discern were "rotting son-of-a-whore."

Before Lucian could second-guess himself, he jumped, not daring to look down.

28

WHEN HE HIT the cold water, the shock was unreal. He reached for his Focus to calm his nerves as he plunged deeper into the darkness. This was not the night on Volsung he had almost died. Here, the water was still. There were no waves. The surface was above, just a few meters away.

He clawed upward and took a deep intake of breath.

The others were already swimming, so Lucian joined them. They swam for a good fifteen minutes, enough time for the cold to settle into Lucian's bones. He saw Fergus's sphere shining ahead, the only light in this darkness. At any moment, he expected the Sorceress-Queen's soldiers to be right behind them. But every time he looked over his shoulder, there was only darkness.

Lucian was the last to pull himself onto the shoreline. The sand gleamed white, soft beneath his boots with shiny crystals mixed within.

"I'll stream us a fire," Cleon said.

"Not yet," Fergus said. "Let's find a better spot."

Serah was jumping up and down to generate body heat. "There must be *some* tunnel to follow here."

"I thought you said you saw a way out," Cleon said.

"This is it."

They followed her up the shoreline, and Fergus increased the intensity of his sphere, revealing stalactites, stalagmites, and an endless labyrinth of rock formations.

"Rotting hell. We'll get lost in there for *days*," Cleon said.

"We're deep in it now," Fergus said. "The only way out is through."

"It's the perfect place for *them* to get lost in, too," Lucian said. "We have food for weeks. There may even be good fishing in this lake, for all we know."

"Forgot my rod," Cleon said.

"Don't need a rod," Lucian said. "We're mages, remember? A good shock and we'll eat like kings for weeks."

"Pipe down," Fergus said. "Sound carries far here, and it's not just people we have to be wary of."

There was silence for a moment, but only for a moment.

"I'll eat my boots if we ever find this mythical Slaves' Run," Cleon said.

"It's *not* mythical," Serah said. "I've seen it before." She looked back toward the shore. "This lake must be the same one we saw earlier. Just a different spot."

"Is this the Moon Sea?" Lucian asked.

She shook her head. "We haven't gone far enough under-ground to reach that. If we were there, you'd know it." She peered into the darkness. "Let's get farther into these rocks, then we can see about a fire to warm up."

Shivering, they followed Serah deeper beneath the surface of Psyche.

They crunched over rock formations that had not been disturbed in eons. They passed bony skeletons of what appeared to be ancient, alien fish. Or more like alien monsters. Some were up to ten meters long. They even walked through one of them, tail to mouth. The lake they had swum in was already deep, but clearly it had been deeper long ago. The thought that Lucian had been *swimming* in that dark water was enough to give him chills. These things, or at least their evolutionary descendants, likely lurked the dark, fathomless deeps.

"This is no place for people to tread," Cleon whispered.

For once, everyone seemed to agree with him.

After half an hour of walking, they came to a stop and let Cleon stream a fire, which he locked with a Gravitonic shell. It was eerie to see fire floating like that, as it would in outer space in the absence of gravity. Yet it was fire, just like any other. They could use it to cook and warm themselves, and lend some semblance of life to this dark, cold underworld.

Fergus got out the cookpot and started warming up a soup.

"I don't know about you guys," Cleon said, after they had finished their meal. "But I'm tired of this running shit."

Heads nodded all around. Everyone stared into the floating orb of flame.

"We should think about continuing on," Fergus said. "I know everyone's tired, but they could be right behind us."

"Rot that," Cleon said. "I'm going to sleep."

"It's best we keep our strength up," Serah agreed. "Even you, Fergus. You can't push yourself too hard."

For a moment, he looked as if he were about to argue. Then, he let out a mournful sigh. "I know."

Lucian was already nodding off.

"It's best we put out this fire," Cleon said. "Get what warmth you can, wrap yourselves up. Might get a bit chilly."

Lucian did that, even if all he wanted to do was fall asleep. His clothes were still damp and would remain so for the foreseeable feature. To completely dry them, Cleon would have to create a bigger fire, which would not only use up his ether but attract unwanted attention. Then again, perhaps the things that lurked down here would stay away from fire, like the wyverns.

When the fire went out, complete darkness returned. It was

a heavy feeling, just knowing there were kilometers of rock and dirt above him. Save for random drops of water, it was dead quiet. If any of them so much as snored, it might be heard for hundreds of meters. Then again, it would make it that much easier to detect someone's approach.

"Ward is set," Fergus said.

That reminded Lucian to set the group's Psionic ward. Even if he was gaining more distance from the Queen, or whoever had been attacking him, he didn't want to take unnecessary risks.

As soon as he shut his eyes, he was out.

———

HE WAS SHAKEN awake by someone.

"Time to move," Serah said.

A light came on, so bright that it hurt his eyes. Once his eyes adjusted, he realized the light sphere wasn't bright at all. It was simply so dark that even a match would have been blinding. Fergus lowered the intensity of the sphere and allowed Serah to lead the way into the darkness. Lucian got the feeling that she was guessing the direction as much as any of them. Everything looked the same down here.

Cleon apparently had the same thought. "Do you know where we're going?"

"Down," she said.

"And how do you know this way is down?"

Serah stopped, causing the rest of them to pause. "You hear that?"

Lucian strained his ears. He didn't hear anything at first, but then he heard something like static. No, not static. Running water.

"Where you can hear water, it's heading down," Serah said. "Almost all streams eventually reach the Moon Sea."

"The Moon Sea must be what, tens of kilometers below us?"

"Thereabouts. But that's where Slave's Run is. The place you asked me to lead you to in case you need reminding."

"*I* didn't ask. If it were up to me, we'd be out of the Blue Rift by now."

"Quiet," Fergus said. "I've had it up to here with the both of you."

It was another couple of minutes before anyone spoke.

"Lucian's been quiet," Cleon said. "How're you holding up back there, pal?"

"Just ready to get out of here."

Cleon had a laugh at that. "It'll be a while, my friend. Get used to the darkness. Might be you never see the sun again."

"It won't be dark forever," Serah said. "The Moon Sea is the most beautiful site on Psyche, and few have ever seen it."

"Few *live* to see it," Cleon corrected. "And nothing's more beautiful than the sight of home after a long journey, and nothing shines as bright as the smile of your girl."

At those words, Lucian thought of Emma. He knew he shouldn't think of her as his girl in any way. They had never been together. And yet he couldn't *help* but think of her. Even if it wasn't possible to see her again, it was nice to dream.

They at last reached the stream. As good as Serah's word, it led steadily downward into the darkness. Whether it got them to where they wanted to go was another question entirely.

Serah broke the silence. "My hope is this stream will reconnect with another lake at a lower elevation. From there, we should be able to pick up the trail again. Hopefully with those men far behind us."

What followed was hours of mindless walking. Even if there was an entire underworld around them, it might as well have not existed because of the darkness. The only world was the one revealed by Fergus's sphere. And Lucian had to say the Captain was not looking his usual, healthy self. His face was coated with sweat, and he breathed heavily despite the downs-lope walk.

"Let's take a break," Lucian said. "Maybe I can light the way for a while."

"Maybe you can relax the ward a bit, Fergus," Serah suggested. "I doubt we're anywhere near them now."

"I won't risk it," Fergus said, sitting on a nearby rock and wiping his brow. "A bit of water and food and I'll be good to go."

They stopped to eat, but even after the rest, Fergus wasn't doing much better.

"You're pushing yourself too hard," Lucian said. "I know you're a Radiant, but you can't stream that ward nonstop."

"That is why we must get moving now, Lucian," he said. "It's my job to get you to the Orb of Psionics safely. And yes, that might require sacrifice on my end." His gaze took in the rest of them. "Just as it will take sacrifice for all of us."

The other two were quiet at that. Serah looked off into the darkness, while Cleon kicked a rock.

"Another thing," Fergus said. "It's a miracle we've made it this far with all this conflict and bickering among us. That's something I've been meaning to say for quite a while. We must work together as a team or we'll never make it to the Burning Sands, much less Dara or even Slave's Run. We have strength together. We cover each other's weaknesses well. But if we each have our own goals and ambitions, then this mission has already failed."

It probably wasn't what anyone wanted to hear, but it had the ring of truth. Lucian felt the others' eyes going to him, as if *he* needed to say something. He supposed that made sense. It was because of him that anyone was here at all.

"I know coming down here is not anything you guys had in mind," Lucian began, somewhat awkwardly. "It's definitely not what I had in mind. None of us asked to be mages. It's just . . . something we're stuck with, I guess." To his surprise, they seemed to be listening to him. "As for me, I have no choice but to keep going. There's no home for me to go to. I have no friends or family left. This stupid mission is the only thing I've got. I could refuse to do it. I've thought about that countless times. But if I do, where does that leave everyone else? Or even me? If I had another choice, I'd have taken it already. I guess what I'm trying to say is, I'm sorry all of you are caught up in this. You're victims just as much as I am." He lowered his head. "I hope none of you have to die for this. That . . . wouldn't be fair."

There was a long silence following that. He had overshared. Why would they care about his own misgivings, or even accept his apology? It was too late for that now.

Fergus broke the silence. "I underestimated you, Lucian. I apologize for that. You carry an incredible burden. A burden that will be impossible for you to see through without help."

Everything wanted to spill out of Lucian. Here in the darkness, what he said didn't seem to matter. All of them were probably going to die, anyway. What was the harm in being honest?

"That's my problem," Lucian said. "Accepting help. Always has been. I was a problem child. Grew up without a dad. My mom was always off fighting some war or another. I had to raise myself, mostly. I'm sure my life was easier than everyone else's here, so I probably have no excuse. But I had no one to help me, so I had to help myself. I still work that way. Even now, it hurts to ever need help. I'd do this on my own if I could. Take on the whole world if it meant no one else had to suffer." He sighed. "I can't, though. I tried to do it all on my own at the Academy, and they exiled me. Maybe I should just stop fighting the tide."

He looked up at the others, who were all watching and listening. He wanted to stop talking, but he might as well complete his thoughts since he'd come this far.

"It's not fair to ask you for anything. But you're already here, voluntarily or not. The truth is, I need your help. We need to get to Dara, first. And after Dara, we need to reach the Burning Sands and the Orb of Psionics. I don't know how that's going to happen, but we're out of options. For some reason, I'm the one the Oracle entrusted with the Orb of Binding. If I die, one of you will have to finish what I started. I've already told you everything I know about it."

"I wouldn't take that thing if my life depended on it," Cleon said.

"If you were there, listening to the Oracle as I did, you might change your mind," Lucian said. "Wars were fought over a single one of these back in the times of Starsea. Everyone wants to live forever. Everyone wants the power to change the universe. Right?"

"I don't know what I'd do with an Orb," Cleon said. "Not save the rotting universe, I'll tell you that much."

"I'd run far away," Serah said. "Find a way off this moon somehow. See the Worlds I hear off-worlders talking about. Has to be a way of doing that with an Orb."

"What about you, Fergus?" Cleon asked. "You're awfully quiet."

The Captain's eyes were closed. "I'd use it to make the Rift-lands safe. And I would keep the Queen and her soldiers far away."

"That's a Fergus answer if I ever heard one," Serah said. She frowned in thought. "Speaking of Starsea, there's a city of ruins on an island in the middle of the Moon Sea. I've never been there before, but I've seen it from a distance. I've always known that old city is theirs."

"Wait," Cleon said. "You're saying there's a *city* down there, and you're just now telling us?"

"There hasn't been much time to talk," Serah said. "Besides, there was no point in mentioning the Moon City. I never honestly believed we might make it this far. I only caught a glimpse of it." Her blue eyes found Lucian's. "It was beautiful, but sad. Towers, broken bridges, all rising like ghosts above the still surface of the water. When you told me about Miami, Lucian, I thought of the Moon City."

Lucian knew the two probably couldn't be more different, but didn't bother mentioning it. "I hope we see it soon."

"We should continue," Fergus said. "I have a couple of hours left in me. I think."

"Are you sure, Captain?"

"I wouldn't say I was good if I wasn't, Serah. Lead the way."

"Actually, you *would* say that."

Fergus grunted. "Lucian can stream the sphere."

Lucian took over the lighting and fell in behind Serah while Cleon and Fergus brought up the rear.

They walked far longer than two hours, and every bit of distance put between them and their pursuers made Lucian feel better. The terrain sloped down even more, to the point where sometimes they had to climb hand over hand.

"I can't help but feel we're descending into an abyss," Fergus said.

Some rock broke under Lucian's right foot. It fell into the darkness, and he didn't hear so much as an impact. That wasn't a good sign.

"This is the way we need to go," Serah said. "There's a bottom somewhere."

Soon, the slope was so steep that they couldn't proceed any farther. They found a ledge just large enough to accommodate the four of them.

"This will have to do for now," Fergus said. "We can figure things out when we wake up."

It felt dangerous to sleep so close to the edge, but Lucian saw no other option. After streaming his ward, he slept.

———

THE NEXT DAY, they descended into "the abyss," as Cleon had called it. It took the greater part of the day. At various points, Serah was forced to use her magic. Even with the lower gravity of Psyche, the climb was terribly draining. Lucian and Cleon shared the responsibility of providing light, Lucian with light spheres, and Cleon with fire orbs held together with Gravitonic Magic. The flickering fire made shadows dance in every nook and crevice, making it difficult to find handholds.

"How much longer?" Cleon asked. "Fergus could just focus a light beam and see how much farther we have to go."

"As I said before," Fergus said, between breaths, "doing such a thing would be supremely idiotic. Anyone, or *anything*, down in this abyss would see us coming."

"Which begs the question. Why are we climbing down this rotting thing, anyway?"

"Because," Fergus said, dropping to a lower ledge, "we need to go down."

Lucian peered into the darkness. "I think I see something."

Everyone stared into the dark abyss. A single light shone in the distance, like an eye staring.

"Nope," Cleon said. "Don't like that."

"The way is down," Serah said. "A single light won't bite you."

"Are you sure about that?"

They continued to work their way down until the rock walls of the abyss simply . . . fell away. Below them spread a giant cavern. The abyss was more of a deep hole in the ceiling of this entire cavern below. And what was more, Lucian could see that the single light now had separated into multiple lights.

"Looks like our friends are down there," Lucian said.

"Impossible," Serah said. "How could they get there before us?"

"The lights are static," Fergus said. "Looks like they've set up camp."

"Whatever the case, isn't that good news?" Cleon asked. "It must be a half a kilometer drop to get down there, if not more. No way they could get to us now, even if they could see us."

Lucian allowed his sphere to wink out. It probably wasn't bright enough to be seen, but it was better to be careful.

"Maybe it's not the Queen's men at all," Serah said. "More likely it's a group of frays. An outpost, maybe. In fact, I seem to remember there being one in this huge cavern, where the frays like to forage and fish."

"Will it get us closer to Slave's Run?" Fergus asked.

"For sure," Serah said. "It's a risk, but if this is the place I'm thinking of, it'll only take a couple more days to get to the Moon Sea."

"Are you kidding me?" Cleon asked. "Meeting a group of frays could be worse than Mage-Lord Kiani and his men. What if they're Burners?"

"Burners don't live in communities," Serah said. "Burners survive alone and will attack anyone they don't have a strong personal connection with."

That reminded Lucian of Ramore. From Serah's stoic expression, it was clear she was doing her best to put that out of her mind.

"So, it's either the Queen or frays," Fergus said. "I don't have a mind to climb all this again. What took two days before will take a week or more going up."

"You're right," Serah said. "Once we're down there, I can investigate and see what we're dealing with. Or we can try to go around them."

"I don't understand," Lucian said. "How are we even going to *get* down there?"

"We could do it like the mountain," Serah said. "That's the only way I see happening."

Fergus nodded. "We have no choice but to be seen. Both the light I stream and Lucian's tethers will be highly visible."

"So we're doing the same thing?" Lucian asked.

"Fergus will have to set up a beacon again," Serah said. "I know you're drained, Fergus, but we really have no other choice."

"I'll have to let this ward dissolve to be sure I can do it," Fergus said. "If those men are anywhere close to us, I'm afraid any fluctuations we make in the ethereal field will draw them right to us."

"They are still two days away from this place, if they're heading here at all," Serah said. "I've walked that trail before. Even if they are hoofing it, I don't think they could make it before us."

"I'll have to trust your judgment," Fergus said.

"We need to do this quickly," Serah said.

"Four at the same time would be too draining, even with the Orb of Binding," Lucian said. "It was overwhelming last time, and this distance is much farther than across Snake Rift." He peered down into the darkness. "I can probably tether two at a time safely, if it's about as far as the mountain."

"I admit, I've never seen anyone create a tether like you," Fergus said. "Very well. Let me know when you're ready. Cleon and I can go first, like on the mountain, then you and Serah can follow."

"I'm ready," Lucian said. "Make sure your stuff is secured."

"Here we go again," Cleon said.

Fergus nodded, and almost immediately became wrapped in an aura of green light. Not a moment later, a spot shone in the distance.

"Now," he said.

Lucian streamed, creating the focal point on that shining beacon, what appeared to be a flat rock rising several meters. Binding Magic rushed out of him in a torrent. He streamed two anchor points on Fergus and Cleon.

As soon as the action was done, the magic ripped out of

him so quickly that it took his breath away. It took a few seconds for the tethers to be infused with enough magic, and once the tension was sufficient, both men shot off the ledge with yelps, their screams echoing as they blitzed into the cavern. A corona of blue fire surrounded Lucian, his arms extended.

He could sense Fergus and Cleon now, halfway toward the goal, even if he couldn't see them. His Focus slipped as they gained more distance. The tether flickered a moment before Lucian could reform the Focus, streaming even more magic. The tether burned brighter, illuminating the cavern with a brilliant blue glow. The distance was much farther than he had originally thought, but the Orb only drew more ether, matching exactly what he needed. There seemed to be some strange reticence from the Orb, however, but Lucian was still able to stream without issue.

The stream dissipated as soon as Cleon and Fergus connected with the ground far below.

"You okay?" Serah asked.

Lucian nodded. "I think. The Orb felt a bit . . . strange. It was more draining than I expected."

"Do you have enough to get us both down there?"

Lucian looked at where Fergus's waypoint was still shining. He needed to get them both down there before Fergus's reserves exhausted. "It's just the distance that makes it hard. I can manage it."

He reached for the Orb of Binding again. He could no longer hold his Focus as strongly, but he *had* to. If he didn't, he and Serah would be stuck up here while Fergus and Cleon would have to fend for themselves below.

That thought alone gave Lucian the strength to firm his hold. This time, though, the Orb didn't seem to *want* to supply its magic as willingly. Lucian didn't understand *how* he knew that, but he certainly felt it, as if it were a living thing. Lucian didn't understand why he was thinking of the Orb as a sentient being with its own wants. It wasn't a sentient being; it was a thing, and *he* was its master. And as its master, he had to make it work for him.

Only, nothing would come. His vision swam before him due to his effort to stream Binding Magic.

"Serah . . . I can't. Something's wrong with the Orb."

"Rotting hell," she said. "Fergus is going to run out of magic soon."

At that moment, Fergus's light went out. It flickered a few times, before the cavern went dark for good.

With Fergus and Cleon down there, and he and Serah above, they were as good as stranded.

———

"WHAT NOW?" Lucian asked. The hope had gone out of his voice.

"Hold on to your ass," Serah said. "We can't leave them down there, so it's time for Plan B."

They were surrounded by an aura of Gravitonic Magic. Lucian instantly felt lighter on his feet. Serah pulled him and the two of them drifted into the cavern below.

"Serah, what the hell are you doing?"

"Now, you *have* to stream," she said. "I can't hold this aura long enough, and if you don't tether us to the waypoint, we'll die."

He reached again, but he was so tired. So tired, that he couldn't even be mad at her. Her voice had a dreamlike quality, and his Focus seemed to float in the distance, impossible to latch onto.

"Did you hear me? Lucian. Lucian!"

"Stream," he managed.

"Lucian! Use the Orb!"

He faded. When he came to, they were still falling. So, so slowly, as if sinking underwater.

"I can't hold it anymore, Lucian," she said. "I'm burning up. . ."

He reached for his Focus, knowing all the while he wouldn't find the Orb. But he couldn't let them die. The ground could not have been more than a hundred meters below them. He streamed a light sphere to see how far until the bottom. But there was still nothing visible below them.

At that moment, Serah's Gravitonic aura fizzled out, and instantly, their acceleration increased. Her eyes fluttered closed. He pulled her close and streamed his own Gravitonic Magic. Ether burned through Lucian in a torrent, his pool quickly draining. Maintaining this aura used so much more magic than an antigrav disc. It would only be a few more seconds until his ether had completely burned away.

Lucian let go of the stream. He just couldn't stream Gravitonic Magic efficiently enough. They had one final chance, as he saw it. And if it failed, then they would both come down too hard with fifty or so meters left. Not even Psyche's gentle gravity could save them then.

"Lucian?" Her eyes looked at him, afraid. He had never seen her like that. He realized then that she was young, like him. And like him, she didn't know what she was doing and was caught in a trap.

"This isn't over yet," Lucian said.

If the Orb wouldn't help them, then *he* would. At the final moment, he brightened the light sphere following them, revealing the rocky ground beneath. It was about ten meters below. Then, drawing as much ether by overdrawing as he could, he unleashed a powerful kinetic wave directly toward the ground, blasting it with a force that was double the gravity pulling them down. The force pushed off the ground, breaking the speed of their fall.

Lucian could only hope their speed had slowed enough.

They landed with a hard thud, bouncing off the rocky earth before hitting it again. Both slid against a thick stalagmite. Lucian struck it, chest first, and then more lightly with his head.

All went dark ...

29

"LUCIAN? LUCIAN!"

His eyes opened to see Serah above him, illuminated by a floating orb of fire.

"I was about to slap you. We need to get moving."

"Moving?"

"Did you hit your head or something?"

Lucian touched his forehead, and his fingers came away sticky with blood.

"Rotting hell. Didn't see that in this light." She paused a moment. "Stay here. I'll try to find the others."

She left her pack behind and bounded off into the darkness. Her floating orb of fire was quickly eaten by the pitch black, leaving him blind.

Lucian faded in and out. He reached for his canteen and could barely hold it steady enough to drink. After he drank, he slept some more.

Sometime later, he was awoken by footsteps and a fiery light. Serah knelt beside him.

"Still out? Doesn't look good, I'll say that much. I went to where they landed, and they were *nowhere* in sight."

His head seemed clearer now. "Where are they, you think?"

She shook her head. "I don't know. I was burning too much ether to keep my fire going, so I headed back."

"I don't want you to get lost out there, Serah. We just have to figure out what to do."

"Well, you knocked your head so you're going to have to stay put. If the people in that camp noticed us coming down, they would have found us by now. My guess is they were distracted with Fergus and Cleon. It would explain why they're gone."

"We need to go after them."

Serah nodded. "I agree, but we can't do anything until our ether regenerates. We've been overdrawing too much. Besides, you need to sleep that off."

"We can't just—"

"If those lights are really from frays, then Fergus and Cleon will be fine. They don't kill whoever they happen upon, like Burners would." She paused a moment. "Most of the time."

Lucian would just have to hope that was true. If anyone knew about how frays behaved in this underworld, it was Serah. "Okay, then."

"Try to get some rest. I'm going to let the light go."

He reached out and grabbed her hand. Her eyes widened, as if surprised by the move.

"Sorry," he said. "I hate the dark."

She touched his face. "I know. I'm right here, and I'm not going anywhere. Things will be fine. I'm letting the light go out. I'll make myself sick if I hold it any longer."

Darkness returned. Lucian hated not being able to see anything. But feeling the warmth of Serah's hand in the darkness helped him not feel alone. He tried to not think about what predators might be lurking out there, predators that hunted by smell or sound. It wasn't likely they'd survive the encounter with the Orb of Binding nonresponsive.

Serah didn't just hold his hand. She lay beside him, her shoulder touching his, the only thing of warmth in this dark, cold place.

"Serah . . . thank you."

"It's basic human decency. And you're all right, for a non-fray. I might even call you friend someday."

There was a moment of silence. "Takes you a while to trust people, I take it."

"That's a given."

"Same," Lucian said. "For what it's worth, though, you've saved my hide more than a few times. If that's not a friend, I don't know what is."

She had no response for that. They fell asleep hand-in-hand in the darkness.

———

LUCIAN WAS BACK IN DARA, only this time, he was actually inside the Sorceress-Queen's high tower. At first, he was confused. He *shouldn't* be here.

That was when he remembered that he hadn't warded himself in a while.

He fought to break away from this dream, but it was already too late. He could see her shadowed form sitting on a crystalline throne. Her dress was long, black, and bedecked with gems reflecting nearby floating sphere light. Despite that light, her form was still shrouded, so he could see nothing other than her shape and a blur where her face should have been. He thought he could discern two eyes, like twin amethysts shining in an inferno.

"We meet again," she said, her voice sonorous.

Lucian tried to speak, but there was nothing he could say to someone of such majesty, power, and beauty. He felt himself getting sucked in by those violet eyes.

"I need your help, Lucian," she said, her voice losing its royal edge.

She no longer sounded like a queen, but simply a woman who needed assistance. And *he* was the only one who could render it. He felt a tugging at his heart, a deep need to make her happy. He listened attentively.

"Things have become most difficult for me. Only you can assist me."

Lucian swallowed, and by some miracle, found his voice. It took every effort not to say yes immediately. "Why would I do that?"

The Sorceress-Queen frowned, as if not expecting that answer. "We both want the same thing, Lucian. We want the Orbs to be gathered. We want the fraying to end. And it's only together that we can achieve that aim. You must stop running. The Darkrift is dangerous. Even with the Orb of Binding, you are more likely than not to die." She gave a moment's pause. "I don't say that to scare you, but only to speak sense. Your aim is to keep your Orb far away from me. But you must be reasonable. You will surface at some point, and I will find you. You *need* me, Lucian, whether you're willing to admit it or not. Perhaps you do not trust me; that is understandable. But I hope soon to remedy that lack of trust. To show that we are on the same side."

She at last went quiet, as if to give him an opportunity to ask questions.

"How can I trust you?" he asked. "How do I know you're not playing with my mind right now? How do I know that you're not simply going to kill me and take my Orb the moment you see me? Why won't you show me your face? Why would I ever trust someone who thinks slavery is acceptable, Queen Ansaldra?"

She watched him for a moment, seeming to consider. It was hard not to wilt under that gaze.

"Psyche is a mage prison world, Lucian. If we are ever to be strong, we need a strong ruler. And yes, there is a system of hierarchy on this world. *Order* is needed. I am that order. Without me, this world would devolve into barbarism within weeks."

"You are a despot, then. You rule with fear."

"Out of practicality. My ethos, or even your ethos, has nothing to do with it. What causes a civilization to persist? That's a question I've been dealing with for over five standard decades since the Free Mages were exiled here. And what we've learned is that no civilization lasts where all of its members are equal participants. Human nature precludes that, as humanity discovered in the latter half of the 21st century with the fall of the so-called "Great Democracies" and the start of the Climate Wars. Even as far back as that dark time, we've had the capacity, the technology, and the resources to ensure no human being went without. That no human being had to *work* if they didn't so desire. There was enough food, enough money, enough homes for everyone to live in plenty."

"Is there any point to this?"

Though Lucian could not see her, Lucian could *feel* her smile. "And yet here we are, in the 24th century, and these evils still persist. Unless humanity has somehow solved them since I've been on this world, which I highly doubt. What does that tell you, Lucian?"

Lucian saw where she was going with this. "It doesn't mean you need to have slaves."

"That word is just semantics. I would argue that a so-called citizen of the League is just as much a slave. Trapped in their circumstances, given just enough food, money, and entertainment not to rebel, because their masters could never tolerate a society where the unwashed masses might look the de facto masters eye to eye. A society can only evolve when technology or will allows it. Here on Psyche, our resources have limited us to something that would be the equivalent of the Bronze Age on Earth. How do you build a Bronze Age society *without* slavery?"

"Simple. You choose not to."

"Ah," the Sorceress-Queen said. "But if I hadn't, someone else would have. Is it not better for *me* to do it, the one who is strongest? And even if I wanted to end slavery, how long do you think my society would last if no one wanted to mine or reap the crops? Tens of thousands would starve, and the society would come crashing down, creating a hell far worse than the ones Daran slaves endure every day."

Lucian didn't have an answer for that. It only felt wrong, though he couldn't explain the reason why.

"Even assuming what I've done is wrong, or done purely because I'm an evil woman," she said, "what if by so building this society, I someday give my people the chance to escape this world? For the mages unjustly consigned here to no longer be prisoners?"

"Escape from Psyche is impossible."

She chuckled. "I wouldn't be so sure. Not with the Orb of Psionics. The short answer, Lucian, is that the human mind cannot conceive of a society without hierarchy in some form. And the larger the society, the more impossible it becomes to ensure there isn't an underclass, even when humans develop the technology to eradicate it. We simply can't tolerate the thought of no one being worse off than us. It helps us sleep at night."

"You're wrong," Lucian said. "The Rifters are equals. There are Elders, sure, but everyone has an equal part to play."

"You're speaking of tribes, Lucian. I'm speaking of *civilizations*. Tribal government simply doesn't work at the level of empire and planets. It never will. A strong hand is needed. Class systems are needed. If not materially, then because the human mind simply cannot think differently. The only way humanity will consent to be equals of one another is if you take everything from them. And the only way you can keep a society stable is by nurturing the greed and pride of the elites." She paused. "What's more, I intend to build an empire based on strength. And we *need* to be strong if we are ever to leave this world and have magekind regain its freedom, its power. Imagine an empire encompassing not just Psyche, but a dozen worlds. A *hundred* worlds. A society ruled justly by the mage class. A society without the fraying once all the Orbs are gathered."

Lucian knew that she and him would never see eye-to-eye. "Having a vision like that is dangerous. Are there any limits on how far you would go to enact it? If there are no limits, then I don't see how you can ever see yourself as the good guy."

Though Lucian couldn't see her face, he could sense her displeasure. "You're missing the bigger picture, Lucian. More is at stake than you know. The Unarcane would see us *dead* if it were in their power. So what if a few of them are slaves here on Psyche? They have made *us* slaves, and have done far worse. They would punish us, kill us, simply for how we are born. How is that justice?"

"It's not justice. But what about the average person suffering under your rule who had nothing to do with past wrongs? How is it fair for them?"

"There are always victims in war," the Sorceress-Queen said. "And this is a war of ideology. Not all of them would be slaves. They would not even go by that name. When we reach beyond Psyche, we will no longer need slaves, because we will have the technology again. But the Unarcane can never be as high as the Mages. After all, *we* are the next chapter in the human legacy." She paused. "And I will see it through to my dying breath."

"I want no part in that."

"You have no choice, Lucian. It is your path. If you find the

Orbs, it will prevent the fraying from destroying us. From there, it's only a matter of time before the mages rule the Unarcane, because they can never hope to stand up to us. If not me, then another figure will come along. It will be war all over again, but this time, we cannot lose. And the society we build, whether that's through an autocratic star empire, or through a representative democracy as we saw in the latter part of the last millennium, will be better than the one that now exists. You, Lucian, are the Chosen of the Manifold. My decades of work building up this world, marshaling its people and resources, have been in anticipation of your arrival. My empire was *built* to be your legacy. Maybe you don't see it now, but you will one day."

Lucian fought to keep his face neutral. His *legacy*? The woman was mad. But he could also see her point. If he found all the Orbs and did nothing with them, the fraying would end. Some mage, whether that was Queen Ansaldra or someone else, would start a new Mage War. No longer limited by fraying, the mages would probably be impossible to stop.

What was more, he would be *immortal*, barring accidental death. Lucian wasn't sure what to think about that. Assuming he attained that impossibility, as the Queen believed he was destined to do, he would be more powerful than any mage that had ever existed since the Immortal Emperor of Starsea. There was still a missing piece of the equation. The Oracle of Binding wanted him to *destroy* the Orbs, which would destroy magic forever. Only that could stop the Starsea Cycle, and it would also prevent the Queen's plans from ever coming to fruition.

There were still too many intangibles. Lucian needed to learn more. And yet, the only person he could learn from was her.

He didn't like that part of the equation. Not one bit.

"Once, I thought myself the Chosen," she said. "However, I saw this was not the case as time passed. The Orb of Psionics, after all, never revealed itself to me. As inexperienced as you are, as young, as powerless, as unqualified, *you* are the Chosen. And as such, it's my role to help you. We mages must stand together as a united front. As we once did fifty years ago. Do you think the League will *ever* tolerate our existence? Even if the fraying were to end, do you think they would let us call the shots? They are *terrified* of us. And for good reason."

"You lost at Isis. And because of the mages, that planet was destroyed. That's why they created Psyche."

The Sorceress-Queen laughed. "Is that what you think? No. Xara Mallis was a brave woman. She failed in her own quest to find the Orbs, but I would stand behind *anyone* who had a chance of finding them. Isis was only the pretext for what had already been planned. Psyche would have happened, with or without Isis, with or without the Mage War. In fact, Psyche was the inciting reason for Xara and Vera to abandon the Academy Mages, the spark that set off the Mage War." The Queen watched him, unassailable on her throne. "We were betrayed, Lucian. Stabbed in the back by the League that had promised us a place in its society."

Could such a thing be true? If it were, then everything Lucian thought he knew was wrong.

She seemed to watch him for some sort of reaction. Lucian did his best to not betray any emotion, but against the Sorceress-Queen, such an exercise was one of futility. She could probably read almost anything he was thinking. What did the Sorceress-Queen know about Vera? It was hard not to ask questions.

"Vera had no idea what she had in you," she said. "And now, you have the chance to right the inequities of the past. To become the champion for all magekind. You have a greater part to play in all this, Lucian. Surely, you've felt it. It's not your fate to run and hide. I don't want your Orb. I only want to work with you, to help you. You need training. If you are ever to find all the Orbs, how can you ever hope to do so with barely any education? You *need* me. Who else is there to teach you?"

That was a fair question. The ether the Orb of Binding could draw might be limitless, but at the same time, it had betrayed him almost to his death. And he had no idea why.

"The Orb of Psionics is hidden somewhere in the Burning Sands," she said. "Over the years, I've searched for it many times to no avail. Shantozar will only reveal it when the Chosen comes. If I were Chosen, he would have revealed it by now."

"How do you know all this? How have you spoken with this . . . Shantozar?"

"Shantozar has only given me such information as it pleases him, but I've used my own knowledge of *The Prophecy of the Seven* to put the pieces together. Not all, but enough."

As he thought before, she knew as much or more than him about this. Everything, except for what the Oracle of Binding had told him. She could never find out his true plan for the Orbs.

If she did, then she might kill him.

"I believe I know your reason for wanting the Orb of Psionics."

Lucian's skin went cold. Had she read his thoughts?

She continued. "Or at least, the reason *others* want you to find it."

Lucian felt himself relax, if only a little bit.

"The one called Elder Jalisa was once my student during the early days of Psyche. I'll admit, she was the one to interpret that section of *The Prophecy of the Seven* about the Burning Sands and Cupid's eye. Of course, she went to go find it, believing herself the Chosen since the Manifold had revealed that information to her." The Sorceress-Queen chuckled. "Of course, she was only allowed to see that information so she might one day pass it on to the *true* Chosen. *You.* She hopes you find the Orb and use it to destroy me, and somehow, this would naturally make Psyche a better place."

The light spheres around the Queen burned brighter, as if in reflection to her anger, only barely restrained.

"I'll tell you," the Queen went on, "even if you were to accomplish such an asinine thing, it would be a disaster not only for Psyche, but all magekind. This world would revert to its days of barbarism, and it would be an evil far greater than killing me. You must set aside that foolish notion. We need each other, or all of this will be eaten alive by the Unarcane."

"I think I understand what you're saying," Lucian said. "I just can't . . . trust you. How could I? Your own men attacked me in the Darkrift. If you really want me alive, why would you have ordered that?"

The air in the room seemed to go colder. Or was that only his imagination?

"I must have words with Mage-Lord Kiani," she said. "He can be . . . overzealous. Suffice it to say, Lucian, I can teach you. I don't want to trap you. I don't want your Orb. That is not my place. My place is to help you rise to the mantle. I dare not stand in the way of the Chosen."

"I find that hard to believe. You would go from being the Sorceress-Queen to number two so easily?"

"I was more than number two for years under Xara Mallis. I would . . . advise. For without the Chosen, magekind can never rise to greatness."

All of this was so unimaginable, sending Lucian's mind reeling.

"As hard as it may be to imagine," the Sorceress-Queen said, "if you won't help me, you're only helping the Unarcane, who would see us all dead."

Lucian didn't want to get into an argument with the Sorceress-Queen. That would be pointless. What was important was getting out of this dream. But how?

"I think I understand your viewpoint. At least a little bit."

"Think of my offer, Lucian. You can't run forever, and such running is pointless. You'll only get yourself killed. You are too important to die. If you die, the Orb of Binding could fall into the hands of anyone. There's nothing that says the Chosen can't die. You need protection. And there is none better to do that than me."

"I'm not going to die."

The Sorceress-Queen laughed. "You betray your ignorance. You have much to learn. You need a teacher. Someone powerful and wise to temper your potential. Not since Xara Mallis has there been a mage with as much potential as you, even discounting the Orb of Binding."

Was she trying to flatter him to lower his guard? The light spheres burned brighter, blinding Lucian with their brilliance.

"If you can't learn to handle your Orb, it will reject you as its master."

"I thought I was the Chosen."

Though he could not see her face, the Queen seemed to smile. "Oh, you think that is permanent? No, Lucian. I'm sorry to say, you can't just do whatever you want. Your life now is on a set of tracks toward your eventual goal. Go off those tracks, and I think you'll find that the Orb stops doing what you want it to do. And if you do what you're *meant* to do, as the Chosen of the Manifold . . ." She trailed off. "Well, the Orb will work fine. Doesn't that tell you everything you need to know?"

Lucian clenched his jaw. "You're lying to me."

"Am I? Deny it all you want, Lucian. You are a child in the ways of magic. You need a mentor. How else do you ever expect to leave this world and fulfill your destiny?"

"You're . . ." Lucian had been about to say evil, but he was old enough to know that evil people didn't think themselves as such. Making her angry would do him no favors. At least, not until he knew he had the upper hand.

The Queen shifted in her seat. "Come peacefully to the surface. There is nothing down there in the Darkrift that can save you. The deeper you go, the worse it will be. For both of us."

There was no way Lucian would ever do that. But what she had said about the Orb no longer obeying him was disturbing. And it had the ring of truth.

"I only wished to say this much," the Queen said. "Since you were no longer warded. There's no more need for that since I've said my piece. You are not one I wish to control."

"What about Morgana?"

"The girl?" She chuckled. "I only wanted to get the measure of you. You handled yourself well in that situation. Most men would have behaved . . . quite differently."

"You had no right. That was a violation."

"There is a difference in our philosophies. If such minor mental manipulation might one day save the Worlds, it is a small cost." The light spheres winked out, and all was darkness. "Return to the surface, Lucian. This is not a fight you can win. Find me aboard the *Zephyr* and I will take you to the Golden Palace and introduce you to my court. From there, we can fulfill your destiny in the Burning Sands. If you do not . . ." She snapped her fingers. "You will find yourself as helpless as a ghost eel out of water. One day soon, if you continue in your stubborn ways, the Orb of Binding will sense that you are not going down your prescribed path. And it will betray you without mercy."

She paused, as if giving him a chance to think over her words. They made a deadly sort of sense.

She clapped her hands, and the dream ended.

30

LUCIAN WAS SHOCKED AWAKE, and Serah stirred from beside him. She must have been roused by his heavy breathing and groans.

"What's happened?" she asked. "You all right?"

He reached for his Focus to calm himself. The image of the shadowed queen in her audience chamber had burned itself into his memory.

The darkness was dispelled when Serah streamed a fireball over their heads, providing light.

"Lucian? What's wrong?"

"It was her," he said. "I didn't set my ward."

"What did she say?"

Lucian shuddered. It was the last thing he wanted to talk about. Instead, he stood up and brushed off his pants. "We should get moving. It would take too long to explain, and Fergus and Cleon are in trouble."

"Right." Serah stood with him. "Well, we should head toward the lights. That's the only place they could be."

They set off into the darkness. His head was still pounding, but with the exception of the dream, resting had done wonders.

He wasn't sure how long they had slept, but it felt like a long time. Long enough for Fergus and Cleon to be far away from here, or even dead.

Serah led the way with her fire. Lucian tried not to think about how visible it would make them.

Every few minutes, Serah would extinguish her light, giving their eyes time to adjust. But always, those fires they had seen from above were still hidden.

After an hour of walking, Serah came to a stop. "We should have seen some sign of them by now."

"We need to keep looking. We've barely started."

A quick fluttering of wings from behind caused them to turn. Over their heads flew a large creature, at least two meters wide. It screeched as it shot into the darkness.

"Rotting hell," Serah said.

"What *was* that thing?"

"Gloombat. A whole colony of them could be on us in minutes."

Rotting hell indeed.

"Stream a sphere as bright as you can stand and pray someone cares enough to save us."

Lucian hurried to do as commanded. He reached for Radiance and streamed, though it tore at his mind to do so. A bright sphere of light shone above them.

"It doesn't need to last long," Serah said. "Just a burst to get people's attention."

Lucian streamed until the light above their heads was blinding, a single beacon shining bright enough to reach the cavern ceiling high above them.

"Let go," Serah said. "Save your ether."

The light of Serah's floating fire was nothing compared to the former brilliance of Lucian's sphere, but it would have to suffice. They ran over rough, rocky terrain, weaving in and out of rock formations. When they arrived at a cliff, Serah pushed

Lucian on.

"Jump!"

He didn't have time to doubt. He leapt as far as he could.

And he could see lights floating in the distance.

He sunk in slow motion and fell even slower as he became wrapped with a silvery aura. They were still falling, albeit slowly.

"Light!" Serah called.

Lucian streamed another sphere, revealing a pillar of rock in the distance. Immediately, he saw what he needed to do. As he reached for his Focus, he could hear the collective flutter of wings from behind. He couldn't chance a look back. All he could do was keep his eye on that pillar. He opened another stream, this one Binding, forming a focal point on the column. Ether drew reluctantly from the Orb. He was all too conscious of what the Sorceress-Queen had told him, that the Orb didn't find him worthy.

It had to find him worthy now, or both he and Serah were dead.

He formed two anchor points, one for him and Serah. Deepening his Focus, he streamed.

Nothing happened. They were still falling.

Help me, damn you. I'm about to die!

The magic tore from him in an angry torrent, rocketing he and Serah out of the chasm and toward the pillar. Looking over his shoulder, Lucian could see hundreds of red, beady eyes glimmering in the darkness.

Lucian cut off the stream, but the Orb's power was bursting at the seams, demanding to be used. It was as if it were *challenging* Lucian to handle that power. As if it believed he *couldn't*. With a roar, Lucian reset the anchor point from he and Serah and onto the rock spire, and the focal point on a pair of red eyes in the center of the swarming cloud of bats.

"Get down!" he shouted.

He and Serah barely had time to duck behind a boulder before the rock spire simply . . . *disintegrated* as it shot toward the bats, spreading a scatter of high-speed projectiles. Lucian, streaming by instinct, created a reverse Binding ward around he and Serah, which kept the rocks from tearing them to shreds. Hundreds of screeches echoed throughout the cavern, piercing Lucian's ears. The Orb's power ebbed. Hopefully, that use of magic would satisfy it.

"We've got to keep moving," Serah said. "It won't take the survivors long to regroup."

They ran toward the fires burning in the distance. Several gloombats broke ahead of the cloud. Serah turned, her hands radiating gray magic. She cried out as she sunk the forerunners with a gravity amplification stream. Lucian's stomach churned upon hearing those bodies crunch on the rocky ground beneath. Lucian tried to tether a few of them, but the Orb wasn't responding. Well, rot the damn Orb, then. He reached for the Psionic Aspect instead, streaming a kinetic wave that pushed back against the cloud of bats.

But it was only a stalling move. And Lucian was low on ether. There were still *hundreds* on their tail. Lucian readied his shockspear, knowing it was probably the only real defense he had left.

"We're not going to make it!" Serah said.

Sharp pain lanced Lucian's right shoulder. A small gloombat had latched, its talons piercing his clothes. He let out a yowl, reached for Dynamism, and streamed electricity into the bat's body. The bat screeched as it fell to the ground, the singe of its burnt hair almost making him gag. The pain was hot, but thankfully it didn't sink in deep. It was those long fangs he had to be worried about. They carried venom. One bite, and it would all be over.

Lucian twirled the spear, feeling severely out of practice. He held his Focus, until it was only him and Serah, their spears, and the approaching monsters.

"Go," he told Serah. "I'll hold them off."

"Don't be ridiculous," she said. "Neither of us are making it. Let's just make it a fight to remember."

They stood back-to-back, Serah with her spear of bronze, and Lucian his spear of graphene. He branded a light sphere above them, hoping he was doing it right. If he could give them light while blinding these beasts, it might make a difference. He kept the Dynamistic stream open, channeling the excess electricity into his spear. If he could brand Dynamistic Magic at the point of the spear, he need not stab every bat that neared him – he merely had to shock them dead. But Dynamism was his weakest Aspect, and he knew holding a Dynamistic brand along with a Radiance brand might be well beyond his abilities.

Lucian had no choice but to overdraw. He opened his Focus, pulling fresh ether from the Manifold. His body sizzled with fire, the pain only offset by the euphoria of raw power. Lucian rebranded the light sphere above them, while pooling the rest of his ether into a Dynamistic brand at the point of his sphere. Lightning streamed from his hand, its jagged fingers collecting at the spear point.

From next to him, Serah's spear glowed red with heat. It seemed she had set a Thermal brand that would burn any bat that touched it to a crisp.

They had done everything they *could* do. As Serah had said, all that was left was to make it a fight to remember.

He began by shocking an incoming bat, an ugly thing with wide, leathern wings and buggy red eyes. Lightning sizzled along its furry body, making it go rigid as it crashed past Lucian's feet. The things were slow and clumsy, but there were just so many of them, with hundreds of pairs of eyes glowing in the darkness beyond. Two more gloombats materialized from the inky black. Lucian dealt with one by swinging his spear and unleashing a small fork of lightning, and the other by thrusting his spear outward, impaling it.

A bat pelted him from overhead, the silvery aura surrounding it signifying that it had been brought down by Serah's Gravitonic Magic. Another gloombat flapped madly from the darkness, its fangs trained on Serah's neck. Lucian thrust his spear forward, spearing it right through its furry abdomen. He flicked the beast off his spear, turning to face a new threat – three more bats converging on him from the darkness.

"Stand back!" Serah shouted.

Serah raised her left hand, which became wreathed in fire. Magic collected there for a moment before being released in a vortex of spinning, fiery heat, igniting all three bats in flame. They flapped madly as they spiraled to the ground.

But for all the bats they killed, more appeared. And the rising din of screeches would only draw *more* to their position.

"I'm running low on ether," Serah said. "And I've already overdrawn."

Lucian reached for the Orb again, in vain. It was as if it weren't there at all.

As dozens of gloombats regrouped in the darkness, Lucian knew it was over.

———

THE GLOOMBATS DOVE with reckless abandon. Lucian attempted to stream, but only a paltry amount of ether could be focused, as most of it was tied up in his brands. And with the Orb useless, it would be nowhere near enough to push back the tide.

It seemed unreal that he was about to die in this forsaken darkness. It couldn't be real. But as his eyes met Serah's one last time, he realized that she knew the truth, too. It was over.

Just as Lucian was about to say his final goodbye, Fergus was at his side – bloodied and bruised, but his face fierce and the bronze tip of his spear flecked with blood. It seemed a vision out of some dream.

Lucian gave a crazed laugh. "Where in the rotting hell were you?"

At that moment, Cleon stepped up with his own spear, red-hot at its tip. He pointed it at two diving gloombats, instantly incinerating them both.

"Play with fire, and you get burned," he said.

"Took you two long enough," Serah said.

At that moment, Lucian realized it was not *just* them. At least a dozen other people stood behind them, all ghostly pale and wearing tattered clothing. Most bore old spears, but others held axes and hammers. But almost all of them, if not *all* of them, were using magic. Thermal Magic, Dynamistic Magic, Radiant Magic. It was a storm of magic unleashed at the bat invasion. A particularly crazed-looking man with a halo of white hair and mottled, frayed skin leaped onto a nearby rock. He had no weapon but the magic in his hands, which were wreathed in reddish light.

No, not red. Orange. Lucian's skin went cold.

"Die, you rotting, batty bastards!" he yowled.

He laughed manically as his hands became molten and balled into fists.

"Run!" someone shouted.

There was no time to think. After exchanging a look with Serah, Lucian bounded after the rest of the frays. They leapt over rocks, across crevices, climbed cliffs. Lucian chanced a look back to see the old man wreathed in an aura of orange. And that aura was expanding outward. The screams of dying gloombats sent chills down his spine. They were falling in droves.

The very air seemed to change, warming and . . . *tightening.*

There wasn't a better way to conceive of it. It was as if all energy were being drawn toward that man, being focused into that orange aura, which was glowing brighter and brighter. And then, there was a sudden, blinding flash, followed by a couple of seconds of silence.

And then a rumble and an explosion so loud and fierce that it knocked Lucian flat on his stomach. A wave of heat blasted over him, only alleviated by a Thermal shield someone had hastily thrown up. Lucian didn't know how long that blast lasted, but at least half a minute. By the time it had passed over, the tinge of ozone hung in the air. The caverns were dark once again, and there were no more bat screeches. The following silence was uncanny and unlike anything Lucian had ever experienced.

"He . . . got them all," Serah said.

"What *was* that?" Lucian asked.

She shook her head. "An atomic blast. And a rotting strong one at that."

"I'm glad he's on *our* side," Cleon said.

Fergus approached them. "Is everyone all right?"

"Where did you guys come from?" Lucian asked.

"There'll be time for that later," Fergus said. "We need to clear this area unless you want to deal with radiation poisoning. We need to head to Sanctuary. It's the frays' town. We can explain everything once we're inside."

31

SANCTUARY WAS LOCATED inside a narrow canyon, the top covered thickly with interwoven thatch while a large wooden gate reinforced the entrance. When those gates were pulled back and Lucian entered, it revealed a long, communal space with plenty of burning spherical flames, all floating with Gravitonic Magic. Those fires illumined this island of light in a sea of darkness. Hollow faces stared as they entered. Women, children, old ones.

To Lucian, their mottled skin and pale complexions made them seem half-dead. He felt guilty for thinking that, and he hoped his shock wasn't reflected on his face. He wasn't sure whether to be afraid, revolted, or to feel pity. He kept hold of his Focus, to better ignore those feelings. These people couldn't help who they were, and it felt shameful to be afraid of them.

All were inside the gate in seconds, which was soon shut to the darkness. Lucian held back his sigh of relief.

"Where's the other one?" Cleon asked, his voice booming. "The Atomicist."

The milling frays gave Cleon death glares, as if he had

committed some unforgiveable faux pas. Which made sense – in this place of dark and quiet, sound could attract predators.

"Pipe down, Cleon," Fergus said. "Remember what Elder Osric told us last night?"

"Ah, that was his name," Cleon said, only marginally quieter.

"He'll be back soon," a middle-aged fray said, with brown hair that fell to his broad shoulders. His chest was mottled and gray. "In fact, here he is now."

As good as the man's word, the gate was opened, admitting the balding man who walked with a stooped stature. Only when the gate was hastily shut did Lucian feel at least somewhat safe. As far as he could tell, there was no way into this canyon except through this gate and another gate at the canyon's far end, which was about a hundred meters away.

The old man – who had to be Elder Osric – approached the four of them. His form was thin and haggard, and his pale, cadaverous skin was loose on his bones. His wild, white hair was bald at the top, but fell long and stringy over his eyes.

"*This* is who I almost died for?" he said, his voice rattling.

"Elder Osric, this is Lucian," Fergus said. "He's the one we're taking to find the Orb."

Lucian looked at Fergus in shock. He had *told* him?

"That eel has already been cooked," Osric said, seeing Lucian's reaction. "Your friends told me you could explain everything. It's the only reason I saved your rotting lives."

This Osric already knew they were going after the Orb of Psionics. Did that mean he knew about the Orb of Binding as well? Did he know *everything*?

The brown-haired man was still standing beside them. Lucian could now see a good half of his skin was mottled with the fraying. It made Lucian uneasy, but so far, it didn't seem as if anyone here was mad from it.

"Cyan, my boy," Elder Osric said. "You come with us. We have things to discuss."

Everyone made their way to a floating fire sphere in the center of the camp, around which some large, rounded stones had been gathered. Osric motioned them to sit with him. He and the one he had called Cyan watched Lucian like wyverns eyeing their next meal. Cyan cracked his knuckles. Those thick forearms looked as if they could break bones.

Osric cleared his throat. "Your friends told me some story about how you're after the Orb of Psionics. After hearing that, I was expecting someone a little more impressive than a yellow-bellied, milk-drinking Earther." His gaze took in Serah. "And his girlfriend."

"I'm not his girlfriend."

"Really? Pity for him, then." Osric's light blue eyes noted her arm. "I see you're just starting to fray. We have a home for you here if you want it. You seem handy in a fight."

"I'm good, thanks."

"Suit yourself." His eyes went back to Lucian. "So, what brings you here? Why do *you* think you'll be the one to find the Orb after all these years? My other son died trying to track it down ten years back, like half this rotting moon."

Both frays watched Lucian closely. And he could sense others in the community watching from a distance.

"It's the only way to stop the Sorceress-Queen," he said.

"Bat's shit," he said. "The Sorceress-Queen isn't your war. It's them two's." He nodded at Fergus and Cleon, who shifted in their seats. "I want to know why *you* want to find it. If you don't tell me, then you're on your own to find Slave's Run."

That was the reason Fergus and Cleon had revealed their mission. That, and Osric likely wouldn't have saved he and Serah otherwise.

"Because I have no choice. If I don't find it, along with all the other Orbs, then whatever destroyed the Builders will destroy us, too."

Osric watched him with arched eyebrows. For a moment, he seemed too stunned to speak.

"I have to say," he said, "that's not what I expected to come out of your mouth. But when you get old like me, you learn to separate truth from lies. I don't think you're lying, young man. I just want an explanation."

"You don't have to tell him anything, Lucian," Serah said.

"Yeah, he does, honey," Osric said. "Your friends already told me they want to find Slave's Run. Well, you're not getting there unless I can show you the way, trust me."

"We had no choice, Lucian," Fergus said. "They refused to help unless we told them."

"And they promised to make this worth my while," Osric growled. "That means all four of you are back out on your asses if I don't like your answers, or your general attitude."

"Well," Serah said, "you've got us there, then."

Osric nodded. "As long as we understand each other." He looked at Lucian. "And why are you the hero, the one who wants to find the Orb? Why not Fergus, or Cleon for that matter?"

Telling the full truth would be risky. He was surrounded by frayed mages who could turn hostile at a single word from their leader. If he told them he already had the Orb of Binding, the man could kill him and take it for himself. But something told Lucian he wasn't going to find out where Slave's Run was without telling the truth. Some of it, anyway.

"Serah," Lucian said. "Do you know where we are?"

She let out a frustrated sigh. "No idea."

"You'll die down here without our guidance," Osric said. "Just like the enclaves up above, you have to earn your keep. And you can only do that by regaling me with a good story, and one that makes sense."

"All right, then," Lucian said. "But what I tell you can't go beyond this group. It could ruin everything."

"I'll make that call, young man," Osric said. "Now, out with it."

Lucian heaved a sigh. This man was frustrating to the extreme.

"I hope you're a good man, Osric," Lucian said. "Because I'm about to give you the keys to the universe."

Osric's eyes widened slightly at that, while Fergus, Cleon, and Serah stared at him in shock.

"Well," Osric said, "it's safe to say you have my interest."

Lucian told him about the Orb of Binding – how he'd found it, who had given it to him, and why it was his mission to find all the Orbs – including the Orb of Psionics. To his surprise, no one interrupted his story. Osric listened, completely rapt, along with Cyan.

The telling took so long that Osric had to signal for food to be brought half an hour in. Lucian ate gratefully, some sort of roasted meat that he hoped wasn't gloombat. It was stringy and greasy, and its taste bland. But Lucian wasn't about to refuse Osric's hospitality.

Once he'd finished revealing his intention to find all the Orbs and end the Starsea Cycle, Osric shook his head and whistled.

"I asked for the truth, and what I got is something that's so far-fetched that not even a Burner could have come up with it."

"It *is* the truth," Serah said. "I've seen him use the Orb. Just now, he split this huge pillar of rock as if it were nothing and sent the rock shards flying into the bats."

"I have also seen his magic," Fergus said. "I doubted at first, but he has time and again proven that he can wield an amount of Binding Magic that would fray any other mage."

Cleon nodded his agreement.

"I see," Osric said, stroking his scrabbly chin. "I was going to say I believed him, despite the extreme nature of the story, but I digress. We in Sanctuary believe in the Orbs. Some of our mages have even sought out the Orb of Psionics, like my aforementioned fool son. The words of the Prophecy spread like wildfire here a few decades back. Or like a virus if you prefer. But the Burning Sands are so vast, so dangerous, that finding it is a virtual impossibility. It's not my business, though, if you mean to find it." He eyed Lucian shrewdly. "You did well to tell me the truth. I'll help you. At least, in my own way."

Lucian's eyes widened. "Help us? How?"

"I can lead you to Slave's Run. Personally. It'll take you a couple of weeks to get to the Mountains of Madness, and the monsters on the way will make that gloombat infestation look like nothing."

"That's our road," Serah said. "Unless there's another."

"If there's another way, Osric, you must tell us." Fergus said.

"Oh, I'll lead you down there all right. There's something like a moving floor, that only *I* know the location of. You stand on them, stream a little magic, and they'll go down."

"I've used such a thing," Serah said. "In my own way down to the Moon Sea several years ago."

"There are many in the Darkrift," Osric said. "It's likely you found the one close to Snake Rift. Here, we are beyond the Blue Rift."

"They're called elevators," Lucian said. "Or lifts, if you prefer."

Osric's brows scrunched. "Elevators. I like that name. They are truly magical devices, an invention of this long-dead race that we simply couldn't conceive of until you see them."

Lucian didn't bother to correct him about the history of elevators. "So, one is nearby?"

"Why would there be elevators down here?" Fergus asked. "Who built them?"

"I imagine the same ones who built the City of Ancients,"

Osric said. "What does it matter? This moving floor – err, elevator – is not a waking's walk from here."

Lucian was confused at his wording for a moment, until he realized there was no day and night down here. A "waking" must have been the amount of time one could walk in a day, judged by how long a human naturally stayed awake.

"You must lead us to this elevator," Fergus said.

"Why's it always *must* with you, Captain Fergus?" Elder Osric asked. "I do what I damn well please. Lucky for you, I *will* lead you there. There have been reports of the Queen's soldiers in the Darkrift, too." He arched a bushy eyebrow. "That wouldn't have anything to do with you, would it?"

Everyone looked at each other, but to Lucian, there was no point in lying about it. "She's after the same thing we are."

"There's more to it," Osric said, his eyes shrewd and insightful. "Out with it."

"She also knows I have the Orb of Binding. I don't know how, but she does."

"I see." Osric frowned. "Well, that does make things more dangerous."

"Father," Cyan said, "you cannot risk yourself with these . . . outsiders. Allow me to take them to the moving floor."

He held up a hand. "Peace, Cyan. I know the Darkrift better than anyone. And in case something happens to me, I'll need you to lead the village."

"Father, you're exhausted. After that atomic blast—"

"Exhausted?" Osric laughed. "Boy, I've only just started. You're here to learn, not to rule. Only when I'm dead, and let's pray that doesn't happen soon. I have big plans for the village, and if you don't get ahead of yourself, my boy, you'll live to see them."

Cyan did not seem happy to be silenced, but he didn't argue.

"Now," Osric said, "see that their canteens are filled. We can do at least that much before we set out."

Cyan, glowering, went off without a word and started barking orders at some of the frays of the community.

"Get some sleep," Osric said. "Sleep is necessary to regenerate your magic. Something in my bones tells me we'll need all we can get."

32

LUCIAN COULDN'T SLEEP A WINK. All he could think about was the Queen's soldiers edging closer and closer. And the closer they were, the harder it would be for Fergus to mask their presence. And was there any point to warding themselves when there was an entire community of mages down here? The Radiant hunters would be drawn here like sharks to blood.

Lucian only succeeded in a light doze before being shaken awake by Fergus.

"It's time."

Within minutes, the four of them, plus Elder Osric, were packed up and standing by the opposite gate from where they had come in. When Osric's sharp blue eyes met his, Lucian felt a strange sense of foreboding. It seemed there was something the old man wasn't telling them, but Lucian couldn't have said what. He could only be on his guard. The path forward was going to be more dangerous than even Osric had let on, of that Lucian was sure.

Cyan arrived next, his arms folded with a grim expression on his face.

"Stop with that long face," Osric said. "I'll be back soon. Hear me?"

Despite his harsh demeanor, Cyan embraced his father. "You're stubborn as hell, Pa. I just hope it doesn't get you killed one day."

"This is for our survival," Osric said. "A chance at a better life. Wouldn't you like to see the sun more than once a fortnight? Wouldn't you like to wake up every day to feel its gentle rays on your face? This is the only way that can happen. The moving floor is only a day's walk from here. If I can't survive that, then I don't deserve to be the Elder of Sanctuary."

"Good men have died out there," Cyan said. "Left in search of the Orb and never to return. Don't be one of them."

Osric nodded. "I don't intend on dying. Keep the fires warm and bright for me."

"What do we do if the Darans come? How will we defend against them without you?"

The old man gave a plucky smile. "If they want to fight, lose them in the darkness and let the gloombats have them."

Cyan nodded. "Will do. I don't like the idea of them trashing our community and taking our things . . . but if that's what you want, I'll see it done."

"We can rebuild our larders," Osric said. "But we can't rebuild lives." He turned to Lucian. "You sure you're up to this?"

Lucian wasn't sure in the least, but he made himself nod all the same. "I'm ready."

"All right, then." Osric nodded to the guard by the gate. "Open up."

The gate rolled back. The darkness beyond the small pool of light was absolute. Lucian didn't want to go into that, but there was no choice.

This was the only way forward.

———

As they walked into the darkness, Lucian couldn't get his doubts about the Orb of Binding out of his head. Doubts the Sorceress-Queen had sown.

He had to own it. Didn't he *already* own it? Didn't the Oracle of Binding entrust the Orb to him? And if so, why wasn't it obeying him?

There was only one answer that made sense to Lucian – the Orb was losing faith in him. That thought alone was terrifying. Was the Orb of Binding trying to sabotage him? And if so, how could he stop it?

Lucian had no answers as the path angled deeper underground, crossing streams and snaking down cliffs until there was no path at all, just a rocky landscape cloaked in darkness.

"Nearly there," Osric said. "Just down this canyon, and—"

At that moment, a blinding light flashed at the top of the canyon. Lucian's heart kicked into overdrive as he reached for his Focus.

It was an ambush.

The next moments were chaos. Fergus raised an arm, which became wrapped in intense green light. From his open palm, a single beam shot upward, a blue laser that pierced a man standing at the canyon rim. With a scream, the man toppled over, falling in slow motion. More bronze-armored soldiers appeared, their hands glowing red as fireballs rained from above. Cleon raised a heat shield just in time to eat the impacts.

The old man, Osric, was already scrambling up the cliff, as nimble as a mountain goat. Lucian realized the truth: he had led them to their deaths for some unforeseen payout.

And now, a hulking figure in bronze-armor and a violet cape stood at the canyon's edge. From the shape, he was the very same one from the Greenrift. His voice, thunderous, boomed down, projected by magic.

"Stop at once, in the name of Queen Ansaldra! This canyon

leads to nothing but a dead end. And *your* death should you refuse to comply."

Lucian sought to Bind him, but the Orb was not behaving as it should. He wanted to scream in frustration. There were dozens of soldiers above now, including robed mages bearing shockspears. Against all that, the four of them didn't stand a chance.

If they wanted to escape with their lives, surrender was the only option.

"You led us on a merry chase," the Mage-Lord said. "But it's over. Surrender, and you can keep your lives."

A series of light spheres, blindingly bright, floated over the canyon. If they wanted to resist, they would have to see beyond that brilliance, or Fergus would have to ward the light of an unknown number of Radiant mages. Neither prospect seemed likely.

"Stand down," Lucian said.

"They'll kill us all if we go with them!" Cleon said. "We should go down with a fight."

Lucian shook his head. "I don't want to be responsible for your deaths. They only want me."

Everyone looked at Fergus, whose expression had gone dark. "This is my fault. I trusted that scoundrel."

"You had no choice," Cleon said. "We would have died without his help."

What Lucian didn't understand was why Osric was helping the Queen in the first place. What had she promised him?

They were questions that would have to go unanswered – at least for now.

"What say you?" called down the Mage-Lord. "I haven't the time to bandy words."

"We surrender," Lucian said, "but if you don't agree to spare our lives, we'll fight to the death."

"If we wanted to kill you, we would have done so already," the man said. "The Queen wants you alive, Lucian."

That the man already knew his name was proof that all those dreams were real. It made Lucian's blood go cold.

"I'll only come if you let my friends go. They have nothing to do with this."

"*All* of you shall come," the Mage-Lord said. "That is non-negotiable."

Osric had the audacity to stand next to the man above, like a loyal dog coming to heel.

"I hope you're proud of yourself," Lucian said.

"I do what's best for me and my people," he said. "Soon, my people will be living in the sun."

"Fool," Fergus said. "As if the Queen will honor that promise."

Cleon's face was seething. He stared balefully upward at the Mage-Lord he'd sworn to kill. What had his name been, Kiani? Indeed, it seemed like the same man who had attacked them in the Greenrift from his hulking frame alone.

Serah still seemed to be in a state of shock, the new reality not registering.

"Will you come peacefully?" the Mage-Lord asked.

Everyone turned to Lucian for direction. Why was *he* the leader, now? It was supposed to be Fergus. He sighed. He didn't want this responsibility. And he didn't want this rotting, useless Orb. Now more than ever, he didn't believe the Queen's words about him being the Chosen, about how she wanted to only help him. Likely, as soon as they were face-to-face, she would kill him and take his Orb.

But there was always the chance she was actually telling the truth, however remote. The idea of having her help was distasteful, but at least some of the burden would be off his shoulders. And he would accept that help in a heartbeat if it meant everyone staying alive.

There was only one way to find out if she was telling the truth. But it certainly didn't feel good to rely on the mercy of someone who probably didn't give it often.

"No deaths," Lucian said. "If you so much as slap one of my friends, there will be nothing peaceful about this."

The Mage-Lord above nodded. "I'm not unreasonable. Your fate is for the Queen to decide."

"Sounds promising," Serah said.

"We've got no choice," Fergus said.

Lucian knew he was right. "So, how are we going to do this?"

"First, you must consent to being blocked. And you are to forfeit your weapons."

"Rot that," Cleon breathed.

"These are our terms," the Mage-Lord said. "There is no other way."

"I'll tell you the truth," Cleon said, only loud enough for the four of them to hear. "If we go on that ship, the Queen will get the Orb by hook or by crook. She has her own agenda, and I want no part of it. If it means death right now, then I'm willing to die."

"Don't be foolish," Serah said. "If you die, then you'll be leaving the rest of us to suffer at her whims."

"My point exactly. It's better to go down fighting than to become the Sorceress-Queen's puppet. I lived that life once. Never again."

"I need your decision," the Mage-Lord above said. "My patience wears thin."

Lucian knew there was only one right answer. Fighting to the death only guaranteed the Orb fell out of his hands. The Sorceress-Queen must have been completely sure of Mage-Lord Kiani's effectiveness and loyalty.

Or she simply trusted in the realization of her prophecy.

That she would lead him, the Chosen, to the Orb of Psionics and guide him on his path to find the rest.

"We'll come," Lucian said. "We agree to those terms. But no one gets hurt."

Cleon shot him a look of betrayal, while Serah merely looked disappointed. Fergus hung his head, his shoulders stooped.

"Block them," Mage-Lord Kiani said.

At that moment, Lucian felt a curious prickling at his mind, along with Psionic Magic wrapping around the hands of several of the mages above. Serah recoiled as if slapped, while Cleon let out a frustrated shout. Fergus only ground his teeth, giving a deathlike stare.

And just like that, Lucian no longer detected his ether. A shell of Psionic Magic had formed around his Focus, impossible to penetrate. They were completely at the mages' mercy.

The mages and soldiers climbed down into the canyon. They forced Lucian to hand over everything – his pack, his spear, even his canteen, until nothing was left but the clothes on his back. Even then, he was patted down by two bearded guards wearing conical bronze helmets. Once done, the guards stood back, and nodded at the Mage-Lord, who strode up with a heavy gait.

"They're clean, Mage-Lord Kiani."

Kiani was a sight, at least two meters tall, well-muscled, with a salt and pepper goatee on a late middle-aged face. His beady brown eyes didn't seem to miss a detail.

Cleon growled as the man approached. Mage-Lord Kiani gave a slight smirk. Yes, it seemed he recognized Cleon. Lucian couldn't help but wonder the reason for the bad blood.

"Mage-Knight," Kiani said, jovially. "I pray all is well?"

At this, Cleon gave no acknowledgement.

"That's no way to hail your commander. If you give me a

salute and a heartfelt apology for abandoning your post, I might be merciful at the court-martial."

Cleon only stared up at Kiani, his expression murderous. Lucian had to give it to him; he had a lot of guts to do that.

"Very well," Kiani said, disappointed. "Time to get out of this dark, rotting hellhole." His gaze took in all his men. "Straight back to the *Zephyr*, you lot. Let's move!"

33

NO ONE SPOKE as Mage-Lord Kiani, his Mage-Knights, and hoplites escorted them out of the Darkrift. Not even a week out of Kiro, and their mission had failed.

Lucian replayed the capture repeatedly in his head, wondering how things could have gone differently. Whatever scenario he ran, only one thing was sure. It was a miracle they had managed to get so far to begin with. They had survived the Deeprift, tracked down Serah, and evaded at least a dozen wyverns with the *Zephyr* on their heels. And they would have gone even farther had it not been for Osric.

Yes, they had been wrong to trust him. It was clear that Mage-Lord Kiani had somehow made it to Sanctuary first and worked out a deal with them ahead of time. Osric got what he wanted: a place for his people to settle on the surface, and Kiani got what he wanted: Lucian in chains.

The journey to the surface took three days. During that entire time, the Psionic block around Lucian's Focus did not weaken in the least. There was little talking among the four of them. Indeed, it seemed as if they were marching to their deaths. They were bound and placed in the middle of the party of thirty or so Mage-Knights, with Mage-Lord Kiani leading. Escape was simply impossible.

On the third day, they surfaced. Lucian was glad to see sunlight again. Moored to the ground outside the cave mouth was the mighty airship *Zephyr*, its massive wooden hull at least a hundred meters long. But that hull was dwarfed by the enormous envelope above it, connected to the deck by hundreds of lines. The vessel seemed much too large to float, much more fly at the speeds Lucian had seen it go. But on this world, the low gravity made that possible.

Whatever the case, they were pushed along toward the ship, where the Sorceress-Queen awaited.

Once they stood under the shadow of the *Zephyr's* massive hull, a large basket was lowered from above. The four of them were pushed in, along with Mage-Lord Kiani and the four Psionics he had brought with him, dressed in purple robes with the Septagon emblazoned on the breast. Lucian reached for his Focus, feeling for his ether again. Again, there was nothing. And the Orb of Binding's presence was just as absent.

As the basket was hoisted up, Lucian watched the ground drop away. Once above the railing of the ship, Lucian was greeted to the sight of a wide deck, where about twenty crewmen milled about, busy at their tasks. Dozens of thick wooden masts secured the envelope above. Somewhere on this moon were trees, and big ones, too, to construct a ship of this size.

"This way," Mage-Lord Kiani said. "Her Majesty awaits."

A middle-aged man approached, with slick-backed black hair and a gray uniform with a Septagon emblazoned on the chest. "Mage-Lord Kiani. Your orders?"

"Captain Rawley, set sail for the Golden Palace as soon as my Mage-Knights are assigned to their battle stations. I would not be caught by wyverns, even if it's not evening yet." The Mage-Lord nodded toward Lucian's companions. "And place these three in the brig, their blocks refreshed every hour by the Psionics. And the Sorceress-Queen wants to see this one posthaste."

"No," Lucian said. "You said you wouldn't harm them."

"And I intend to honor my word. It's time that you met her Majesty."

"That's what we get for trusting that rotter," Cleon groused.

Serah didn't have the heart to lambast him for that one. Her head hung low, her eyes on the deck. Maybe they should have gone down fighting, as Cleon had suggested.

"This way," Captain Rawley said to Lucian's companions.

Lucian watched helplessly as his friends were led belowdecks, with all four Psionics following close behind. Once again, he reached for his Focus, but could no more use his magic than before.

"You led us on an impressive chase," Mage-Lord Kiani said, "but in the end, *I'm* the better Radiant than your friend. I knew you were making for Slave's Run, so the trick was intercepting you."

"Well, you missed us on your way down. Passed us right by. So, your Radiance might not be as good as you think."

Lucian didn't know why he'd said that, but the words had the intended effect. The Mage-Lord's face clouded with anger. "You're lying."

Lucian couldn't help but smile smugly. "You can think that." He nodded toward the forecastle, assuming that was where the Queen was. "Lead on. Don't want to keep Ansaldra waiting."

Mage-Lord Kiani's brown eyes were stern, his face a storm of anger. "You had best mind your tongue and your manner with me, boy. And more so with the Sorceress-Queen. *I* am the Mage-Lord of the Golden Mountain. You will address me with the respect I'm due."

Lucian didn't talk back, even if he had a mind to. There was no point trading shots with him.

Mage-Lord Kiani nodded, satisfied. "That's better." He looked at some of his surrounding Mage-Knights, all armed with shockspears and wearing robes the color of their Aspect. That might make it easier for Lucian to defend against them if it came to that.

"Can I get my hands unbound at least?" Lucian asked.

All ignored him.

"We're taking him to the Queen's stateroom," Kiani said. "Let's move!"

The Mage-Knights pushed him along, and Lucian felt sick to his stomach. Within minutes, he could be stripped of his Orb, and much more, his life.

He wondered if these people even knew who he was or what the Queen wanted with him. Not likely. If they knew that, one of them might be stupid enough to try and take the Orb for him or herself.

Kiani led him down a short set of steps into the forecastle. At the bottom, a pair of intricately carved and gilded double doors lay down a short corridor. Two Mage-Knights in violet robes and hoods stood guard outside, bronze shockspears in hand. As Lucian approached, each placed a hand on the handle of each door, opening them in tandem to reveal a luxuriously appointed stateroom filled with rich carpets, tapestries, waxed wooden furniture, and glowing lamps. Lord Kiani nodded him in, while he and his Mage-Knight escort remained outside.

As soon as Lucian passed through the doors, Mage-Lord Kiani right behind him, he noted the pleasing scent of incense. A wide set of windows, set in the ship's stern, looked onto the rift as well as a tumbling waterfall, through which the sunlight refracted a rainbow.

But all of that was nothing compared to the woman standing at that window, her back faced to him. The Sorceress-Queen of Psyche was a young, beautiful, and petite woman, though Lucian couldn't see how that was possible. She rose no higher than Lucian's shoulder, wearing a long-black dress sequined with diamonds and many-colored gems, a dress that left little to the imagination. It seemed his suspicions that she had the appearance of a beautiful young woman were completely true. Her black hair was vibrant, and her creamy skin showed not a single blemish or sign of fraying. An anti-grav brand caused the train of her dress to float behind her several meters, the undulating fabric color-shifting through all the hues of the rainbow. Her hair fell just short of her waist, curling sharply toward the end.

From age alone, Lucian knew this could *not* be the Sorceress-Queen, unless she somehow had access to longevity treatments here. That was unimaginable, given the limited resources of this world. But the extravagance of her dress and the elegantly appointed cabin begged to differ, as well as her general posture, which was straight, regal, and proud. She stood so still that she might have been a statue, and did not seem to be aware of his presence.

Lucian wasn't sure what to do, or what to say. He stopped near the door, not wanting to go any closer to the source of his terrors.

Mage-Lord Kiani cleared his throat. "Your Majesty. I bring before you, bound and blocked, Lucian Abrantes."

He bowed low, as if he were an insect who could not stand her glory.

"Leave us, Mage-Lord," her voice seemed too deep and powerful for a woman her age. "I thank you."

Kiani did not seem to doubt the Queen's safety for a moment. A testament to her power, or a gross oversight?

Lord Kiani slunk away, and the doors closed forebodingly behind. At that sound, the pit that formed in Lucian's stomach had no bottom. Without his magic, his life could end at any second.

At last, she turned. Lucian's breath caught at her beauty. She was young, yes, but there was something in her eyes that was much older and wiser. And those eyes . . . they were violet, as in his dreams, though they were no longer glowing. This short, slight woman, whom he could probably throw ten meters, controlled an entire empire. The face was one of angelic innocence, with wide eyes, an aquiline nose, and full lips. But he knew not to underestimate her or be taken in by her appearance, but such a thing was easier said than done.

She being a powerful Psionic, he knew it could all be a trick of the mind to gain advantage. He needed to treat her the same way he would treat any Burner. How he would treat an *army* of Burners.

She was dangerous. And she most likely wanted his Orb.

"We meet at last," she said. Her voice was clear, confident, and alluring. "I've looked forward to this day for a very long time." She favored him with a small smile. "And you are handsome in person. That's . . . good."

Even if he knew the flattery was designed to disarm him, he felt his cheeks flush and he had to resist the urge to turn his face. He couldn't play the part of a bashful little boy. And yet, her effect made that reaction seem the most natural. Lucian found himself tongue-tied. The Sorceress-Queen might not even *need* to use magic to get her way.

"Are you surprised to see me thus?" she asked. "I'm just a woman. A powerful one, to be sure, and beautiful, I'm also told. But like all women of power, I hope to meet someone who is my equal. Someone I can speak to face-to-face without them cowering as if I were a supernova about to consume them." She gave a small, innocent smile, which did little to soften her. "I believe you might be that man."

"Supernova would be putting it lightly."

Lucian wasn't sure why he'd said that. But she seemed pleased that he had, her smile widening and reaching her violet eyes. It made her seem more . . . human. Was it really her, or was it something calculated to lower his guard?

Lucian reached for his Focus to insulate himself from her effect. His emotions were cloistered, at least for the moment, allowing him to think more clearly. And to his surprise – he could feel his ether. He tried not to betray the shock on his face. If he so wished, he could stream at her and break out of this.

But he knew such a notion was foolish. Not with her right there and dozens of Mage-Knights at her beck and call, and his friends taken belowdecks to some unknown place.

At that moment, he felt his manacles loosened, and they clanked onto the deck below. He blinked in surprise.

"I hope you weren't treated too roughly," she began. "I instructed Kiani to bring you and your companions to me unharmed. What we have to discuss is far too important to leave anything to chance. I hope you will forgive me that."

To Lucian's surprise, he *did* want to forgive her while the sincerity in her soft eyes made him want to instantly agree with anything she said. But he couldn't do that. He had to find his wits and meet her head on. His friends' lives were at stake, and so was the fate of the Orb of Binding.

He cleared his throat. "I'm wondering what you want with me. And to be honest, I expected you to look . . . different."

"Is that so? Well, this is me, body and mind. I've discovered how to do things with magic that most mages would deem impossible. I've had fifty years to practice, after all."

"Is this some illusion designed to trick me?"

"Trick you?" She laughed. "No. This is really me." She extended a hand. "You can touch me, if you wish, and see for yourself. Or, you could ward yourself so you know I'm not tampering with your mind. I promise I'm not doing so, even now. But I understand if you want to for your peace of mind."

Lucian hastily shook his head. "Err . . . no. I'll take your word for it."

She nodded graciously. "Very well. Suffice it to say, this body is mine. Yes, I'm nearly a century old, Lucian, and yet I have used magic to stay young. I *must* be young, for there is much I have yet to accomplish in the Worlds. Indeed, my designs are only beginning."

From the way her eyes focused on him, Lucian knew those designs included *him*.

He streamed a Psionic ward around himself. Her appearance remained the same, only proving she was telling the truth. Her violet eyes remained rooted to his, as if she were already familiar with him.

"Nothing to say?" Her voice seemed somewhat disappointed. "This moment, so pivotal in my dreams . . . and now you stand before me. Exhausted, dirty, and defeated."

Her silence afterward was brutal and cold. Lucian knew she expected him to defend himself, even to defy her.

He could never give her that. He had to somehow divorce himself from his feelings. His friends were depending on him.

"I apologize if I'm not the hero you were expecting. Probably because I'm not."

When she turned, her eyes were angry at first. But then, she smiled, as if Lucian had told a joke.

"You underestimate yourself, Lucian. The raw material is there. But it will take a delicate and practiced touch to refine that into something magnificent. Even without refinement, you managed to find the Sapphire of Starsea." She watched him a moment for a reaction. "Do you really not see it? Why do you think the Manifold has brought you to Psyche, Lucian? Has brought you to *me*?"

The Manifold? *That* didn't bring him to Psyche. The Transcends were responsible for that. He knew he had to answer her, because there was nothing more dangerous than a woman who was ignored or stonewalled. There wasn't only his life to consider.

"I was expelled from the Volsung Academy," he said. "That's why I'm here."

"Wrong," she said. "You are the Chosen of the Manifold, Lucian. *You* are the one fated to bring the Orbs together. *You* are the one Arian prophesied to save magic and magekind from annihilation at the hands of the Starsea Cycle." She gave a small shrug. "Or not. There is nothing in that prophecy that guarantees your success. That is why we must begin our work at once to ensure your survival."

"You have the wrong man," he said. "I'm not the only one with an Orb, after all."

She watched him closely, as if trying to guess what he knew. And Lucian realized he'd slipped up. As far as he knew, *she* didn't know that at least one other Orb had been found. But it was clear from her lack of surprise that this wasn't news to her.

"My own prophecies point to *you* being the Chosen, whatever Orbs have or haven't been uncovered. Do you not hear whispers in the dark, Lucian?"

At once, he was reminded of the strange voice. That voice hadn't spoken to him for months. But that voice had told him to find the Orbs, and to bring them to him. He had almost driven it completely from his memory.

"How do you know about that?"

"I know as much as you do. And more."

His heart started beating faster. "Then who is that voice?"

"You know who it is."

Lucian thought back to his conversation with the Oracle of Binding. She had mentioned that when the Immortal was defeated, he had somehow joined the Manifold. He wasn't sure exactly how *that* worked, but the implications were terrifying.

"The Voice of the Manifold itself is calling to you. It is evidence that you are indeed the Chosen. For it is the Manifold that wants to bring the Orbs together. Such is the natural balance of things. *You* are the agent to make that happen. It has chosen *you*."

"But Arian's prophecy only talked about the Orbs," Lucian said. "He didn't say there would be any Chosen to bring them together."

"You speak in ignorance. No one has deciphered the totality of Arian's *Prophecy of the Seven*. All we have are bits and pieces, as each mage who *can* read it is only allowed to see a small part of the overall masterwork. The part the Manifold wishes to reveal."

Lucian thought back to that night long ago on Volsung when he had read the mad ramblings of that text. All of it had been indecipherable, aside from the one bit that mentioned the Orbs. If there was anything about a "Chosen of the Manifold," then it would have to be from another passage. As much as he hated it, he might have to trust the Queen on that one. At least for now.

"Long story short," the Sorceress-Queen said, "we must work together to find out how to find the rest of the Orbs. And to piece together whatever fragments of *The Prophecy of the Seven* that we can."

"Does *The Prophecy of the Seven* reveal the locations of the Orbs?"

"Yes. Where do you think Shantozar's line comes from?

> *"Under the White World with red-whorl eye,*
> *Upon a moon of violet, violent sky;*
> *Peers beneath Burning Sands and wind,*
> *Lies the Amethyst of Starsea within."*

"Elder Jalisa said as much," Lucian said, without thinking.

"Jalisa." The Sorceress-Queen gave a short laugh. "I exiled her from the borders of Dara. We had something of a . . . disagreement."

"What disagreement?" Lucian asked.

"It was long ago." She seemed ready to move on to more important matters. "Most days, I pore over the lines of Arian's work for additional clues, but so far, my efforts have been fruitless. And of course, I have spoken with the Oracle, whose spirit abides in the Burning Sands. From him, I had the revelation that the Chosen of the Manifold would come to Psyche and point the way to the Orb of Psionics. That he would bear one of the Seven Jewels of Starsea." Her eyes became focused and beady. "I have never *felt* such raw power, Lucian. Such a void you created in the ethereal background. It was as if *all* ether disappeared from a single spot. I have . . . never experienced that before. It was quickly refilled, but for a few seconds, it was as if the foundations of the Manifold itself were shaken."

Lucian tried to ignore the hunger in her eyes. "That wasn't me, but the Orb."

"It was both," the Queen said. "Your Focus is strong, but not just anyone can control the stream of an Orb." Her face became sorrowful. "Alas, the Orb of Binding will not work for you forever. It will only obey one powerful enough to wield it." She watched him with a neutral expression. "And you are most certainly not that yet."

Lucian didn't see any point to denying it. It seemed she already knew everything *he* knew, and more. Even the Oracle had said wielding the Orb of Binding would require competence, that it respected power and the wielder's heart. Lucian was failing on one of those two counts, and perhaps even both.

"The solution isn't what you think," the Queen went on. "That *I* take your Orb. If it were that easy, I would have done so already. The solution is for you to become stronger. That is how I can help."

Lucian couldn't help but be curious. "How?"

"I have delved the Manifold itself," the Queen said. "It's dangerous, but it only kills those who are weak, those who are not devoted to their cause. I am so devoted that I am willing to lay down my power, my crown, my very flesh to help you, Lucian. I've learned much from the Manifold. I can teach you to use the Orbs effectively. Following me is the right path because the Orb *wants* you to work with me."

How could that be true? "I can handle the Orb fine. I don't need your help."

But it seemed the Queen sensed his weakness, his doubt. "Don't you? You know that's not true, so let's not deceive ourselves. The Orb has been testing you. And you have been failing. You are using the Orb like a hammer, like an ace up your sleeve to get out of any trouble you land yourself in. The Orb sees this as a flagrant abuse of its spirit and abilities. It does not exist to serve *you*, Lucian. It has a higher purpose. And unless you are working toward that purpose with tangible results, it *will* betray you. And as a last resort, it will even allow you to die to pass on to one who is more capable. Perhaps then you will not be as Chosen as you think you are."

"What are you talking about?"

"One who is Chosen, can be *un*-Chosen. There's nothing magical that says it *has* to be you. You have a destiny, Lucian. This isn't about you anymore, what you want or need. Just as my empire and my wants and needs pale in comparison to necessity. That necessity is that we work together, for the good of magekind."

Lucian was quiet as he considered her words. He never dreamed he might agree with her, but everything she'd said made a strange sort of sense. He didn't delude himself that she was a good person. But a good Queen and a good person were not necessarily the same thing.

"It's a lot."

"I understand," she said. "But we are on the same side. I would *never* ask you to give up what one of the great Oracles of Starsea deigned to give you. That is an honor not even bestowed on me. *You* are a de facto Vigilant of Starsea, a holder of one of the Orbs. Were we in those days, billions would now be under your command, with sycophants, advisors, and armadas sworn to your name. You would have honors, riches, and titles beyond your wildest imaginings." Her eyes shone brightly, as if those hypothetical things were actually real. "Even if you don't see yourself as such, you *are* a Vigilant. And you will become an even more powerful one once you add the Orb of Psionics to your retinue. But you will never reach those lofty heights without my help. Do you really think I would be speaking to you as an equal if this were not so?"

His mind was reeling. "What are you getting at?"

"You need a mentor, Lucian. Someone who can hold her own. You are young, yes, but you will learn. And you will find no better teacher than me. I will be loyal, dedicated, and teach you magic more effectively than any mage in the galaxy." To his surprise, she reached out and cradled one of his dirty, rough-ened hands in her two own. "And I wish to learn about you more . . . personally. We will have time enough to spend together during the journey to the Golden Palace and the Burning Sands. We need to get to know each other on an equal footing. Learn to trust one another. For trust must be the foundation of what we are trying to achieve."

He took his hand away. Was she serious? Rotting hell.

"I'm not sure where you get the idea that I'd go along with this. You're holding my friends captive."

"Just a few days among the Rifters, and you're starting to believe you are one of them. No wonder you are against me so. As far as your friends, I was hoping you would speak to them. If you can guarantee they won't cause any trouble, they can walk free. Either to stay at your side or go their own separate ways."

Would they ever leave him? Cleon might. He hated the Sorceress-Queen, as well as Mage-Lord Kiani. Cleon would never accept Lucian working with her. And Serah most likely wouldn't, either. Fergus himself hated the Queen, but he was so fiercely loyal to the Elders of Kiro he might stay long enough to try and convince Lucian to use the Orb of Psionics against the Sorceress-Queen.

But if what the Queen said was true, that she could teach him how to use the Orbs, then he needed her. And it wasn't likely he was going to find all of them without learning how to use them.

"I didn't expect you to become convinced immediately," the Queen said. "But you will soon learn this is the most . . . *prudent* course. According to Arian's prophecy, you will uncover the Orb of Psionics. I will teach you how to use it, along with the one you already possess. I am dedicated, as you are, to ending the fraying and the Starsea Cycle."

"And then establishing your new order, where the mages are on top."

She gave a small smile. "It cannot be any other way. The League showed what it honestly thought of the mages during the Mage War. They see us as tools to be controlled, nothing more or less. But end the fraying, and the mages can take their rightful place as the leaders of the human race. Starsea shall be reforged anew, without the Starsea Cycle to hold us back."

"I don't understand. Why not just kill me and take the Orb of Binding for yourself? You said earlier that the Chosen can change."

"It can, but I have no power over that change. The Manifold does. But suffice it to say, if ever the Manifold did change course – which I don't believe likely, especially if you *listen* to me rather than go your own way – then I will do what I deem necessary. You should expect nothing less from me."

"So you are loyal to a vision. Not an individual person."

She watched him, her expression placid. "If you want to think of it as such. But that's as it should be."

"If I am the Chosen, then could I not order you about?"

"You could try, but I would just laugh. You are not ready for that. You are weak and ineffectual. All raw material, no finished product. And despite you being the Chosen, there are foolish ones who would see your Orb and want it for themselves if they were to ever discover you had it. Only I know what you have, Lucian. You are not ready to reveal yourself yet. For the minute you do, you will become a target. The knowledge of the Orbs was one of the major factors leading to the Mage War. Xara Mallis and Vera Desai both set out to find their own Orbs, presumably each with fragments of Arian's prophecy deciphered, or perhaps their own gleanings from the Manifold."

"Xara Mallis is dead," Lucian said. "Vera, though . . ."

Lucian cut himself off, realizing that he had revealed another pertinent fact. But the Queen didn't seem surprised at the revelation.

"Yes, I suspected she was still around. Troublesome woman."

"You knew her during the war?"

The Queen nodded. "I did. Vera was Xara's chief advisor. Xara was also Vera's Psion, until Xara rose to lead the Free Mages."

"Vera had the same idea as you. She wanted to train me, but I refused."

"That certainly would have set you down a different path. But I do not trust Vera. I never did. There is a darkness in her you should be wary of."

Lucian found that rich, but chose not to comment.

"I know you don't understand why I say that. And I know I've done some bad things myself. And I continue to do so with every breath I draw as the Sorceress-Queen of Psyche. But all of this has been for a higher purpose. Together, we can save magekind. Without me, you will flounder and fail. That is a guarantee. And the consequences of that are far too great for us to waste time feeling each other out." She walked toward the window and heaved a frustrated sigh. "What is *taking* them so long? We haven't moved a centimeter."

At that moment, there was a knock at the door.

"Enter," the Queen said, her voice icy.

Mage-Lord Kiani stepped inside, his manner timid and meek. It was strange to see a man of his strength and stature behaving that way.

"What is it?" she snapped. "Why haven't we lifted off?"

"It's the Binders," he said. "They are exhausted."

"Then have them overdraw. We must be back in the Golden Palace within the week."

Mage-Lord Kiani's eyes widened a bit at that, but he nodded. "Of course, your Majesty. It shall be as you say. But these Binders are among the best in the Empire, and it would be a shame to—"

"Did I stutter, Mage-Lord? See that my orders are carried out."

Kiani swallowed, his face paling. "Of course, your Majesty." He withdrew and closed the door behind him.

Once they were alone again, the Sorceress-Queen faced him. "Do you wish to find the Orb of Psionics, Lucian?"

Lucian couldn't deny that he did. "Of course."

"And would you like to learn to control these Orbs, and not have them betray you?"

At this, Lucian remained silent. But the Queen's gaze bored into him, to the point where he couldn't deny her an answer.

"It would be nice."

"Then work with me, at least a little bit. What say you?"

"I will consider it, as soon as you let my friends go."

"It will be done. But first, we must take to the air." She gave a cunning smile. "And as one who holds the Orb of Binding, it will be the perfect opportunity for you to learn."

34

THE SORCERESS-QUEEN LED Lucian to the bow of the *Zephyr*. The crewmen and Mage-Knights she passed bowed so low as to almost be groveling. She didn't pay them any mind, as if they were insects. Several crewmen and even Mage-Knights watched Lucian with widened eyes, as if in disbelief that he could walk beside her as an equal. Even Mage-Lord Kiani kept a respectful distance, his face lowered to the deck. No doubt he was regretting his rough treatment of Lucian earlier.

Her mannerisms signaled not only her power, but that Lucian was an exception to it. Many of the airship's crew were also bowing to Lucian, albeit uncertainly, especially when the Queen rested her hand on his arm, as if to claim him. Lucian wanted to slide away, but there was no way to do that without being too overt about it.

Thankfully, she let her hand fall as she gestured toward the bow, where six blue-robed Binders stood at the ready.

"No doubt you are wondering how a vessel of this size maintains course in the air," the Sorceress-Queen said.

All Lucian wanted to do was remind her of his friends, still imprisoned belowdecks. Fergus had told him the airship used

Binders to move along, but for now it would be best to humor her. "The thought had crossed my mind."

Mage-Lord Kiani's eyes widened, and it took a moment for Lucian to realize why.

"Your Majesty," he added, the honorific sounding unnatural.

She continued, not seeming to notice the blunder. "We have a motor, of course, but fuel requires Atomicism to synthesize, as does the helium we fill the envelope with. Atomicism is not my strength, and my court Atomicist is back in Dara, anyway." She gestured ahead, to the long bowsprit jutting ten meters from the front of the ship carved in the likeness of a wyvern. "Binders provide both direction and speed for the ship. Working in confluence, they can get the *Zephyr* moving very quickly indeed."

The Sorceress-Queen nodded at Captain Rawley, who stood to attention near Mage-Lord Kiani. "Captain Rawley. It's far past time we embarked."

Captain Rawley's face paled as he swallowed the lump in the throat. "Of course, your Majesty." He turned smartly to the Binders. "Binders, ready!"

"Aye, Captain," came the unified response.

He nodded to a nearby crewman. "Raise anchor."

"Aye." The crewman marched sternward, barking some orders to the nearby crew who stood at the ready to turn the capstan. So heavy was *Zephyr*'s anchor that the wheel required six men to raise. Almost as soon as it *was* raised, the ship began lifting off, rising from the ground below.

"Binders," Captain Rawley said. "As soon as we clear that ridge, full ahead. Set course for the Golden Palace." He clenched his jaw a moment. "Overdraw if needed."

The mages gave no response but following the order to overdraw could not have been easy. Lucian watched from the railing as the rift dropped away. Wind buffeted the ship, causing it to drift to starboard toward the rift's steep slopes.

"Cross-bind that breeze," the Captain said. "Keep her on an even keel and in the middle of the rift."

"Aye, Captain." At once, three Binders went to the port side, raising their hands and streaming tethers connecting the bowsprit to a mountain peak on the rift's opposite side. At once, the ship steadied, despite the blast of wind.

"Ahead full," the Captain said.

The other three blue mages joined in, streaming their own tethers on a mountain peak in the distance. The six tethers intensified in brightness, and Lucian felt the ship picking up speed. The wind rushed past his face.

Lucian noticed one of the blue mages stood at the fore, a middle-aged man with a full, graying beard. It seemed the other Binders were taking the lead from him. As the mountain pulled closer, his tether switched to another mountain, more distant. A moment later, so did the others, and the ship was pulled along toward *that* one. Having to keep this up all day must have been exhausting. But Lucian had to admit they were moving quite fast, and were only getting faster.

"We shall make Dara in four days' time, at this speed," the Sorceress-Queen said. "Isn't this far better than braving the Darkrift?"

Lucian had to admit it would be far faster this way. Despite her general disagreeableness, perhaps joining forces with the Queen, at least temporarily, was the best option. It was the only thing that made sense. But what would the others think of it? Lucian did not look forward to that conversation.

The Queen stood next to him at the railing, awaiting his answer. But all he could think about were his friends, imprisoned somewhere on this ship.

"My friends need to be freed still," Lucian said. "Their talents are wasted belowdecks."

"Your friends will be freed in due time," she said. "Just watch for a moment. Learn. Allow yourself to relax. Or are you forgetting your most basic lesson of magic?"

"What basic lesson?"

"From silence, power builds," she said. "You can only be powerful if you are calm and in control."

Why did Lucian get the feeling she was already trying to train him? "I know that. The Focus, right?"

"Yes, the Focus. You think your power comes from the amount of ether you stream?" She shook her head. "That's what most men think. The bigger, the better. They see their magic as the metaphorical extension of . . . well, you get the picture. It can be impressive, but if your magic is all raw bludgeoning, you'll only exhaust yourself and whoever else you're trying to impress."

"Couldn't you have picked a better metaphor?"

She chuckled. "Perhaps. My point is magic takes *finesse*. It comes from the deepness of your Focus, the steadiness of your resolve. Some of the greatest mages I've known had limited pools of ether. Can you imagine what you could do with your Orb if you only learned to Focus properly?"

Despite himself, Lucian found himself intrigued. "So, how do I do that?"

"Hours of introspection and meditation. How else?"

"I was afraid you'd say something like that."

They were silent as one rift passed after another. Rifts that would have taken days, or even weeks, to traverse. They passed them in mere minutes. *This* was the distance they had intended to cross? The Sorceress-Queen was right. They most likely would have died.

"Why are we going to this Golden Palace first?" he asked. "Wouldn't it be faster to go directly to the Burning Sands?"

"We must resupply. The journey to Psyche's Planetside is long, and the land is barren. And my Binders will need a rest. It will also give me the chance to show you my court. Your friends, too."

Lucian watched the Binders pull the massive airship along. They were making good speed, now. "I can't imagine that's easy to keep up."

"It isn't," she confirmed. "But my Binders are the best in the Worlds. No one gets more practice than them, in war or in peace."

"Are you not afraid of them fraying?"

"The fraying finds us all sooner or later."

"What's *your* secret, then?"

"Remember what I told you. Learn to Focus properly, and you can stream more purely. Even if the Academies are wrong about most things, they aren't wrong about that. As misguided as they are, the Transcends are sure of themselves, and take great care when streaming. There must be a good reason for everything you do, whether in magic or in life. What is *your* reason?"

"To find the Orbs."

"And yet, you doubt yourself. I hear it in your voice. You never wanted this burden, and yet, the Manifold has chosen you for it."

She had put it quite succinctly, which was annoying. "That sounds about right."

"No wonder you're having the trouble you are. Until you fully accept your destiny, the Orb will be the one pulling the leash, not you."

Lucian didn't want to believe her, even if this was the millionth time repeating herself. Believing her meant that all this was true. That he had to change. That he could no longer hold the false belief that he could go back to his old life.

But most of all, the Sorceress-Queen was the last person he wanted to rely on as a mentor.

"It seems impossible," he said. "Why would the Manifold have chosen me? It seems beyond belief."

"I have no answer for that, Lucian. But this is the hand we've been dealt, which means we have to try." She placed a hand on his arm. "I'm *here*, Lucian. *You're* here. This is a golden opportunity to discover what has eluded so many mages. Within the week, the Orb of Psionics could be in your hand, and the plans I've laid out can begin in earnest. And after that, only five Orbs would remain. We will study *The Prophecy of the Seven* to unlock the locations of the rest. If you truly are the Chosen, those words will reveal themselves to you."

Lucian had to find a way to get his hands on that prophecy if what she'd said was true. But where to find it? Perhaps the Golden Palace in Dara had a copy.

They both fell into silence. The Sorceress-Queen looked out onto the expanse of the current rift they were in. He couldn't help but watch her from his peripheral vision. All this conversation had done the last thing he wanted. She had been humanized . . . somewhat. What if all this was really true? What if she really *did* want to help him? Maybe she was as evil as everyone was saying. But couldn't there be shades of good in that?

There was a person beneath that royal veneer. A person named Ansaldra, who actually believed she was doing the right thing. And she had a reason for it. She hated the way the mages had been treated after the Mage War and even before it, and thought it was time the mages took the reins – while reining in the fraying. It was an idea Lucian could at least understand, if not get behind fully.

Even if she had been somewhat humanized, he couldn't allow his loyalties to be divided. His first responsibility was to his friends, not her.

No, that wasn't entirely true. His first responsibility was to the Orbs. And who could help him find and use the Orbs most effectively?

He drove that thought from his mind. He didn't like where it was leading him.

"I will permit you to speak to your friends," she said, "but only if you commit to work with me."

"Am I supposed to be your pet or something?"

Her violet eyes gleamed with mischief. "If you wish to think yourself that way, then that's your choice. If you wish to make yourself angry by playing the victim, that's your choice, too. My advice is to stop being the victim. It's only then that you'll experience true freedom. And for that matter, would it really be so horrible to learn from someone who knows what they're talking about?"

Lucian saw she would accept no other answer, nor did he have another choice. This was his reality, and the sooner he faced it, the sooner he could find a way to extricate he and his friends from this situation.

"Maybe not," he said. "I . . . can give it a chance. For now."

The Sorceress-Queen nodded, seeming to accept that answer. For now.

They were passing into a new rift, this one shrouded in fog. Combined with the failing light of evening, it was impossible to see into its depths.

She *honestly* believed this, that he was the Chosen of the Manifold. There was a chance it was all a trick, but if she really wanted to kill him or possess him, wouldn't she have done so already? How could he work with her when she had done so much evil? There were crimes she had committed against her own people. Slaves turned the wheel of her empire, while it was said she used Psionic branding to possess and influence people as she saw the need. He had yet to see evidence of that, but he didn't doubt it was true.

All this would take time to process.

"I'll just be straight with you," Lucian said. "You've oppressed and angered people greatly during your reign. Unlike you, they don't get to see your reasons. It's going to take a lot of time before you can counteract all that."

"On that, I agree, and I wouldn't expect anything less. But everything I've ever done, I've done for the good of magekind. One does not forge an empire on this brutal prison world without spilling blood. To think otherwise is naïve. And unless magekind stands together, then everything I do will be for nothing."

"Part of me wants to believe you. So, how can I know you are to be trusted? That you *really* wish for the good of all?"

"That's the thing about trust," the Queen said. "At some point, a leap must be made."

At some unseen signal, Mage-Lord Kiani approached the Queen, slightly bowing his head.

"Yes, your Majesty?"

"Release his friends and escort them to my stateroom. Unbound and unblocked."

The Mage-Lord's eyes widened. "My Queen. Forgive me, but I would highly suggest—"

"Do it, and you know better than to question me." Queen turned her violet eyes on Lucian, as if in challenge. "If we are to learn to trust one another, then it starts with me. Your friends could bring down this entire ship, causing my death and throwing the Daran Empire into chaos. Now, it's up to you to decide whether indeed we will work together."

Lucian had to admit that she *was* taking a great risk. He was especially worried about what Cleon would do, unfettered and unblocked. He might try to take out Kiani, even if it meant his own death.

Perhaps Mage-Lord Kiani recognized this because his mouth worked for a moment. But in the end, he bowed. "It shall be as you say, my Queen."

Kiani departed, leaving Lucian alone once again with the Queen.

"There is so much more to this," the Sorceress-Queen said. "It's best if I share my vision with all of you at once. If there is to be trust between us, it will begin with me."

35

THE FOUR OF them were reunited once again, albeit under the purview of the Sorceress-Queen. Lucian had never seen such angry expressions. Angry, and shocked. Even Cleon seemed taken aback by her appearance, although it was possible he had never actually seen her in person. Serah kept her eyes pointed directly at the deck, while Fergus's chest heaved, as if at any moment he might explode.

But they stood there free, unbound and unblocked, and no one had died yet.

Fergus's arms became wrapped with green light. Lucian was about to shout for him not to do anything, but all Fergus did was stream a protective ward around the four of them. It was token resistance, unlikely to do much. Certainly, the Queen didn't seem to be concerned about it.

"You have nothing to fear from me," she said, with forced patience. "In fact, I'm trying to decide if it is *you* I should fear. But if we are to take the fight to where it matters, the Daran Empire and the Riftlands must work together. The stakes are too high if we draw out this pointless conflict."

"Rotting lies," Cleon spat. "You brand *any* mage who doesn't agree with you. You are no Queen of mine."

She nodded regally. "I agree that I take extreme and unfortunate measures when a mage revolts against me. Branding is an option of last resort, and I wouldn't expect you to understand, standing where you are. It is an evil, but sometimes, what's foul on the surface is necessary in service to a greater good. A mage who does not agree with my vision is simply too dangerous to be left alone, especially with the fraying to consider."

"Cleon is right," Fergus said. "That's rot."

Serah nodded her agreement.

"With the exception of your temporary imprisonment and your blocks, have I wronged you in any way? All of this could have been avoided had Lucian simply listened to me in the first place and met me at the Deepfork."

Cleon ground his teeth but didn't respond. And neither did the other two.

The Sorceress-Queen continued. "Psyche is a brutal world, and it cannot be held unless my methods match that brutality. Have you ever *tried* to control hundreds of mages, many of whom are frayed to the point of madness? Such cannot be done except by the methods I've devised. An absolute ruler cannot rule except absolutely. My power keeps the Daran Empire from disintegrating. If any of you were alive during the early days of Psyche, what I've built is far more humane than what existed then. If the tribes of the Riftlands had their way, this entire planet would devolve to a barbarous state. *That* is what the League of Worlds wants. They want to keep us small, petty, fighting amongst ourselves, clawing to survive every day. Do you know why they selected Psyche as their prison world, of hundreds of available candidates, despite the fact a sizeable colony already existed here?"

At their silence, Lucian knew that they didn't know, or much less think about it. Just as *he* had never thought about it.

"It's the rifts," she said. "They form natural barriers to the mages ever coming together. And where there are natural barriers, there are social barriers, too. Even now, a mere fifty years after the inception of this prison, cultures have diverged, and even new dialects are forming."

"What's the whole point of this rotting speech?" Cleon asked.

The Sorceress-Queen held up an appeasing hand. "If you think you can intimidate me with a little cursing, I would not be the Queen of Dara. And I've heard much worse among the dockhands and sailors of Hephaestus Station, where I grew up long, long ago."

Such a thing seemed unimaginable, but Lucian couldn't let that fact humanize her further. But it seemed his friends were now listening to her, albeit with skepticism.

"All of this *does* have a point," she said. "The Transcends and the League selected Psyche because they surmised the rifts would keep them disunited, separate, bickering. The last thing they want is for the mages to unite. The whole intent of this moon was for us to fray and die, turning on each other like animals." She smiled bitterly. "Self-appointed genocide, since the Treaty of Chiron forbade outright execution of the mages."

She paused to let that sink in. Lucian had to admit, a lot of what she was saying made sense.

"If not for me, this moon would still be in chaos. The Riftlands are the only area not under my rule – again, because of the inaccessibility of the rifts themselves. And no, not everyone agrees with my methods, and not everyone is treated equally in the Daran Empire. But my aim is to make magekind strong, not to allow a babel of voices to cause confusion. Democracy is messy, and such messiness is the luxury of a society that doesn't live in brutal conditions. We cannot afford luxury. We must be strong. If we are to escape this world, we mages must be united, led by a single leader. We must be everything the League is not – strong, unified, and precise in our attacks."

"I want no part of that," Serah said. "And I don't know why you're telling us all this." Her eyes turned to Lucian. "You don't believe all this rot, do you?"

"No," Lucian said. At least, he didn't *think* he did. "But the Sorceress-Queen will help us find the Orb of Psionics. Or at least, that's what she claims."

"Lies," Cleon hissed. "She wants the rotting thing for herself!"

"I don't," the Sorceress-Queen said. "Lucian is the Chosen of the Manifold. The prophecies of Arian stated that the Chosen would come to the world of Shantozar with a sacred Orb of Starsea in hand. I had dreams of Lucian's arrival, and detected the Orb he held. I am the most powerful Psionic in the Worlds. If I do not believe in the power of my own prophecy, then I am lost. Therefore, I am only fulfilling my end. It is my role to help Lucian, and anyone who helps Lucian is my ally."

"So, you're one of the good guys?" Cleon scoffed. "Fat chance of that."

"There is no good and bad," the Sorceress-Queen said. "The sooner you get that notion out of your head, the better off you'll be. The only good is that which you are willing to fight and die for. If you know that about a person, then you know them to the core. So, I'm going to tell you *my* dream, what I will fight and die for. I fight for a United Empire of Magekind, freed from the fraying in a future where all of Arian's Orbs have been found. I believe Lucian, as Chosen, is our best chance of that happening." She spread her arms. "There it is. That is what I want. You can use it to help me, or to destroy me."

Serah looked at Lucian desperately. "Do *you* believe all this?"

All of them were looking at him for direction. Once again,

Lucian was cognizant of the fact that Fergus was no longer the leader of this expedition. He hated having that burden. Especially because the Queen had him somewhat convinced.

They deserved a straight answer, even if it meant losing trust with them. "I understand your reasons for distrusting her. I do myself. But we have no choice. We would have died in the Darkrift. Even you guys have to see that by now. The Sorceress-Queen is offering to take us to the Burning Sands herself." All of them were looking at him. It was hard to tell what they were thinking. "My point is, regardless of who she is or what she has done, this might be our only chance to get the Orb."

"She's just using you to take it for herself," Cleon said. "She doesn't believe that rot about uniting magekind. If she finds the Orb, then she will take you out. Then she'll have *two* Orbs."

"Once again," the Queen said, icily, "I'm not the Chosen. The Chosen is the only one who can wield the Orbs."

"That's the thing," Cleon said. "It's *your* prophecy. You could've just made all that up."

"I sense that you are especially against me, especially relative to the others," the Sorceress-Queen said. "But you really shouldn't be." Her eyes sharpened as her full attention focused on him. "Cleon, is it?"

"Get out of my head!"

"I'm not in your head," she said. "Mage-Lord Kiani reminded me earlier. You were one of his Mage-Knights who went missing. Cleon Coley. Your parents died during the Westland Rebellion, putting you and your sister under the charge of Mage-Lord Kiani."

"What of it?" he spat.

"That sister married Kiani."

Everyone watched Cleon with shock. Could that be true? If so, what was the story there?

"*I* was there when the Butcher of the Westlands ordered the slaughter of Kalm," Cleon finally said. "Hundreds of men, women, and children, dead. And for what? For standing up to your unjust rule? And you forced my sister to marry him, like that was some kind of reward to me."

"You are missing part of the story, Cleon. Should you tell them, or shall I?"

Everyone looked at him, stunned. Cleon hung his head in shame.

"Cleon is himself responsible," the Sorceress-Queen said. "For if it weren't for him, Mage-Lord Kiani would have never seen his sister as a viable marriage candidate."

"I introduced them, so what? How could I have *ever* known what would happen from that?"

"You are not as innocent as you make yourself seem," the Sorceress-Queen said, her smile triumphant. "You only regret that you didn't get the posting you desired for the arrangement."

"That was *before* the slaughter of Kalm," Cleon said, blue eyes burning. "That was before I knew the kind of man Mage-Lord Kiani was."

The Sorceress-Queen's smile disappeared. "And still, you leave out *another* important part of the story. At the time of the meeting, how old was your sister? And how old General Kiani?"

At this, Cleon was silent.

"He was fifty if you need reminding. And she was seventeen. A man that old doesn't marry a girl that young unless someone is profiting by it."

"I made a mistake," Cleon said. "We were desperate. I . . . thought she would be taken care of. We were poor, orphans . . ."

"Come off it. You thought you would win a nice prize for yourself. Perhaps the title of Mage-Lord, someday?"

He ground his teeth. "Yes, but only to save our family. It was wrong, but I did want her safe and at the time, I thought Lord Kiani was an honorable man. She hated me when I told her, but it was for her protection. But when I learned what he was really like, he exiled me."

"He exiled you for challenging him to a duel," she said. "And he would have given you it, but I forbade him. Mage-Lord Kiani is too . . . useful . . . to waste on one such as you."

The Queen seemed to be egging him on to commit some fatal error.

"We just need to cool off," Lucian said. "You're talking about how we need to work together, but all you are doing is making Cleon angry."

"Stay out of this, Lucian," Cleon said. "Or should I say *lapdog*?"

"I'm no lapdog," Lucian said. "I'm just trying to do the best thing for all of us. There are no easy answers here."

"I trusted her once," Cleon said. "If you do the same thing, then you'll end up like me. Completely lost and broken."

"I don't trust her, and she knows that herself," Lucian said. "I simply said we need her help to get to the Orb of Psionics. Nothing more or less. That's the truth."

Cleon shook his head, not wanting to admit even that. "I made a mistake. The worst mistake of my life. I ran from that mistake. But now, I want to do everything I can to rectify it. I'm done running."

"Poor fool," the Sorceress-Queen said. "Are you so naïve as to think you can come back from this? You've already stepped off the ledge. It is done, and if you still plan to kill Lord Kiani, my loyal vassal, *that* will not sit well with me." Her eyes glinted. "Even a Queen has need of a Butcher. A Queen needs a tool for every occasion, but that's something you would never understand."

"You're enjoying this far too much," Serah said, coming out of her silence. "You want us to work with you, and you're psychologically torturing our friend. Whatever trust you were trying to build with us is gone."

"I'm only trying to show you one thing," the Sorceress-Queen said. "There is no such thing as a good person. Even honorable men, like Cleon, have dark stains. However much they wish to clean them, some stains just don't come off." Her eyes grew cold. "So, let's just drop this charade, right now, that you are good and I am evil. We are merely people, doing the best we can with what we have. We are people who must work together for the mutual benefit of all."

"You're talking about uniting the mages and starting a war against the League," Lucian said. "Chosen or not, I want no part of that."

Her violet eyes turned on him. "Willing or not, that is your fate, Lucian. You can either go into that conflict with a strong position, or a weak one. Much depends on your choices in the next few days."

Fergus shook his head, seeming at a loss. "This has gone so far beyond me. I was only told to find the Orb and give it to Lucian." The large man looked up, though his broad shoulders were still hunched. "I'm with you, Lucian. Whatever you decide."

Cleon cursed under his breath, while Serah just stared daggers at the Queen.

Lucian looked back at the Queen. "I guess we'll see what your words are worth in the next few days. We will work with you. At least for now."

"That's all I ask," she said, with a small, mysterious smile. "For now."

36

IN THE FOLLOWING DAYS, they did not meet with the Sorceress-Queen again together. Rather, Lucian met with her once a day for training. As much as he hated the prospect, he felt he had no choice but to comply.

He stood in her cabin, bathed and dressed in the rich vestments common to the Mage-Lords of her empire; tan breeches and fine, polished boots, a blue vest with silver trim, worn over a puffy white shirt. He felt ridiculous in it, but it was apparently the fashion. And it was her not so subtle way, perhaps, to separate him from his friends, who were not allowed in clothing as fine, though like Lucian, they were given their own cabins.

His first training session, the Queen asked him to stream each of the Aspects for her, sans Atomicism. As she followed each, Lucian's skin crawled at the tingling sensation. She could see absolutely everything he was doing, and it was almost like being naked.

She shook her head. "It's much worse than I thought. The only Aspect that's somewhat pure, with the exception of Binding, is Psionics. You *can* learn to stream your secondaries and tertiaries more effectively, but it will take time, patience, and commitment. You can't be known for being good at one thing, because your enemy will be able to counter it easily. As you get more advanced, you can learn to dualstream almost easily as singularly. And you can even learn tristreams and quadrastreams for the purposes of warding or branding."

Lucian wanted her to elucidate further, but he also didn't want to put himself in her debt.

It seemed, however, that the Queen sensed this reservation. "You should be asking more questions. I can tell when a pupil is lost."

He hated being called that. "I'm not lost."

"Except you are," the Queen said. "You said you would learn, and you agreed that we need to work together."

He repressed a sigh. "What do you wish to teach me today?"

Her gaze was icy, and her expression was forced patience. "If there's any evidence that I think you're the Chosen, it's this. I would have obliterated anyone else by now."

Despite himself, Lucian cracked a smile.

"You think this is a game?"

He was thrown against the wall, held there by a sideways Gravitonic force. He tried to peel himself from the surface, but the pressure only increased. The Queen stood close, an arm's reach away, but Lucian was powerless to even move his finger.

"Let me go," he said. He could feel the blood rushing from his head, his vision darkening.

"Can you extricate yourself?" she asked.

He reached for the Gravitonic Aspect and worked at the Queen's stream with his Focus. At once, he could tell that it wasn't much magic at all. So how was she holding him so strongly? He worked to unravel the stream, but his Focus kept slipping every time he tried. He tried streaming a greater amount of magic, but his Focus slipped even more. It was as if her stream were slicked with grease – a strange image, but it seemed accurate.

"How are you doing that?" he rasped. "I can't cut it off."

The pressure eased. He fell to the deck, gasping for breath. The Queen turned and left him there, flailing like a fish out of water. A few more seconds of that and he might have blacked out, or even had a stroke.

"Remember what I said earlier? You use brute force rather than finesse in your streams. I wasn't using much magic at all, and yet it proved too much for you to handle. You were streaming more than twice as much as me. You should have tried warding yourself first before attempting to directly unravel my stream."

He stood and brushed himself off. "How did you do it?"

"My Focus is stronger. My magic works twice as hard as yours because it's streamed efficiently. Your Focus is what prevents Manifoldic toxin from polluting your stream. It works like a filter. The stronger your Focus, the purer your stream. You can do more with less."

"So, I need to strengthen my Focus."

The Queen nodded. "And that is something that can only come from experience. The Focus is the strength of a mage, not the size of your ethereal pool or the amount of magic you stream. I could feel your fear, Lucian. Some part of you believed you might actually die, especially at the end. Your Focus will insulate you from fear, from elation, from any emotion that distracts you. Emotion is the antithesis to a strong Focus."

Lucian nodded. "Got it."

"No, I don't think you do. You are not diving deeply enough, Lucian. You are being lazy. You must fight that laziness with every breath. There is no short-cut to magic, even for the Chosen."

She watched him for a moment, as if to see whether her point was connecting.

The lessons continued the next day, and each day after that.

Under her watchful gaze, Lucian worked to deepen his Focus rather than stream more magic. At first, it was difficult knowing the Queen was right there, judging every move he made. But he needed to hold his Focus, even under pressure. He showed improvement in the next couple of sessions, but of course, he was far from being where he needed to be.

On the day they were due to arrive at Dara, during the fourth session, he couldn't help but ask a question that had been hounding him.

"Doesn't it bother you that you could be training me to challenge you someday?"

She considered a moment. "I've thought of that myself. But if you are indeed the Chosen, it's in my interest to see you as strong as possible. And by that point, you should see me as an ally rather than an enemy."

Lucian didn't *ever* see that happening. But it did force him to wonder. Why go through the effort of training him if she *didn't* believe him the Chosen? It made little sense to invest her own time and energy if she just planned to kill him later. Which left Lucian in the difficult spot of recognizing that the Sorceress-Queen was actually trying to help him. Just in her own way, where she had control. That was the part he took issue with.

"Are we done for today?" he asked.

"Almost. There is something I wish to talk to you about, first."

Her violet eyes were soft, a rarity for the hardened Queen, though her expression was blank and neutral. "You are clearly a mage of great potential. And I don't want that potential to be wasted."

"It won't be," he said.

"I . . . have something in mind. No doubt you would be averse to it, but it's the only thing that makes sense to me."

Why was she hedging? That made him nervous. A change

was coming. Her mannerisms had gone from cold, regal queen to a woman in need of his help. What could a woman of her power ever need from him?

"What did you have in mind?"

"I hoped that we might speak of things . . . other than your training. I know you don't trust me, but the Manifold dictates that we work together. Even you must recognize a certain level of trust is required for that."

"I could never trust you. There's something you're hiding from me."

"What am I hiding?"

She was going to make him go there. "How you're still young after so long, for one. How exactly you plan to use the Orbs. To use *me*. I'm just a tool to you. Something for you to enact your final vision."

"You're not merely a tool," the Queen said. "That is why I hope to learn about the person behind the prophecy."

"Not until I see you care about something more than vengeance and power."

Her face was like stone. "I care about the salvation of magekind."

"But you're willing to do anything to get there, no matter who gets hurt."

"There is always a price," the Sorceress-Queen said, softly. "I wouldn't expect you to understand. Perhaps I'm foolish enough to hope that one day, you can." She watched him, her eyes intense. "Do you honestly believe innocent lives won't be lost on your account, Lucian? That you won't have to make hard decisions, and harden yourself against them? How will the League react when they learn of you and your power? Even without me at your side, you are fated to tear humanity apart. A new Mage War is coming, whether you will it or not."

"That's not true."

She shook her head sadly. "Stubborn. I'm only offering to

make that transition easier. And yes, it will require some level of compliance and trust on your part. Without me, the goal to which you are committed will become infinitely harder."

"How many times must we rehash this conversation?" he asked. "If I ever trust you, then I would be betraying my friends."

"Perhaps so," the Sorceress-Queen said. "But stay true to them, and you will betray your ultimate mission. Or perhaps they can be brought around to work with me, too. But you would need to be my advocate."

Was she serious? He was at a loss for words. They would never go for that, and as soon as he mentioned it, they would lose all respect for him. Especially Cleon.

"I will say no more about this," the Queen said. "I'll let my actions speak for themselves. I'm taking you to the Burning Sands. I'm training you. I will give you everything you need to accomplish your mission, to rise to the mantle as the Chosen. But I can only do so much. You will not only have to meet me halfway, but rise to the occasion. I trust in something higher than you and me, Lucian. I trust in the Manifold. And the Manifold gets what it wants. Always."

Those words made his skin go cold. Maybe she was right. Was he just being stubborn? Spending time with her was already lowering his guard, making him see things her way, little by little. And the more time he spent with her, the more his guard would lower.

Her eyes watched him, all innocence, but seeming to want something . . . *more* from him. The idea of that was ridiculous, so much so that he immediately wanted to discard it.

But the realization hit him like a thunderbolt. She didn't want to merely be his teacher. Or his mentor.

She wanted a person strong enough to stand beside her. To even *rule* beside her.

She wanted a king.

Her violet eyes watched him, as if suspecting he knew the truth.

"What you want from me," he said, finally. "It'll never, ever happen. That would be the ultimate betrayal to myself."

From her unsurprised reaction, and her small, victorious smile, he saw that he had guessed correctly. "I think you'll find you're capable of things you can scarcely imagine now. After all, look at how far you've come since your youth on Earth. I will say this. Is it *really* such a bad idea? Am I really as awful as you think? Do you think me unattractive or unsuited?"

He imagined that potential future, a future millions of men would have jumped at. He could hold all the Orbs, become the new Immortal of Starsea. And she would be his queen, and together, they could rule all humankind. Armadas, Mage-Lords and Mage-Knights, all under their command. The image was so clear in his mind that it was like a punch in the stomach. Could that vision be true? Was the Manifold pushing him toward that fate, to become molded into someone he couldn't even recognize? Would it happen even if he fought against that destiny with every breath? It seemed a force greater than himself, a river pushing so hard that it was pointless to swim against the current.

Lucian had to decide which way to go. To let that fate carry him to its inevitable end – or to fight against it. He stood on the brink, and the future of billions depended on him. The desire for power, the fight for survival, the hand of a beautiful and capable woman who he might one day match in abilities.

She was willing to fight for that, to even die for it. Was he?

All he needed right now was to breathe.

"I need to go."

He turned his back on her, half-expecting some magic to be streamed against him, to force him down the path he envisioned. But in the end, the door shut behind him, and he escaped unscathed – the decision put off for another day.

———

HOURS LATER, Lucian stood with his friends at the stern, unable to speak as he watched the Riftlands pass below. His mind was a muddled mess, all his motivations and former goals in question. He wasn't sure how to bring this up to everyone, or even whether *to* bring it up. Already, he felt separate from them, and if he shared his fears, they would no longer see him as the same person. They might even see him as the enemy.

All he could do was watch the passing landscape below and stew on it.

It was clear they were not in the Riftlands anymore. The deeper rifts had been replaced by shallower, but wider, canyons, and the mountains between them were not as sheer. And the air was warmer, the sky bluer, the climate gentler. There were even puffs of white cloud that would not have looked terribly out of place on Earth. They even passed small villages in river valleys, with farmland along riverbanks. That told Lucian that wyverns and other predators were not much of a threat here.

"We are getting close to Dara, now," Fergus said. "Perhaps several hours away."

Lucian couldn't bring himself to speak. He had never felt more lost, and every moment that passed, the others seemed more distant. Especially Cleon, but Serah too, in her own way. He didn't blame them, but what else could be done? Their clothing was finer than anything they had ever worn, but it paled in comparison to his. It made him feel even more alone.

Over the following hours, the landscape became more varied. Rivers, lakes, and deep forests filled narrow valleys. Walled settlements rose from high hills and plateaus. Roads crisscrossed the verdant surface. An entire new world spread below them, rugged and wild. But that wildness tamed ever more with each passing hour. The farms became larger, the towns more populous, the roads wider, and the wild forests were replaced with curated woodland. In the more populated areas, a thin veil of smoke hung in the air.

And then, in the distance, Lucian noticed a long line of mountains stretching north to south, the tops of which were lost to white cloud. Those mountains loomed taller and taller as they approached. *Impossibly* tall. Lucian wouldn't have been surprised if they reached tens of kilometers. It didn't look natural. The mountains separating the rifts paled in comparison.

"The Mountains of Madness," Fergus said. "I never thought I'd see them."

Cleon's eyes became strangely reminiscent. "I'm coming home, Lynne. For what little good that'll do you."

Everyone watched him, Serah with pity, and Fergus with curiosity. Cleon hadn't mentioned his sister in the four days since their mutual audience with the Queen. It was for him to talk about if he so chose.

"Keep your head in the game, Cleon," Fergus said. "This isn't over yet."

Cleon shook his head. "She's got us by the balls. Rotting hell, we even have our magic back and there's not a damn thing we can do."

If there were any other way to reach the Orb, Lucian would have taken it. But saying as much wouldn't do any good.

"Do you think she meant any of what she said a few days back?" Serah asked. "There were points where she almost had me convinced."

"Oh, I don't doubt most of it *is* true," Cleon said. "That's the thing about good liars. Ninety percent of what they say is the truth, so finding the lie becomes impossible."

"Where's the lie, then?" Lucian asked. "She needs me to find the Orb, otherwise she wouldn't have me here. She needs you guys because she knows I won't help her otherwise."

"That's comforting," Cleon said.

Serah shook her head. "Well, *clearly* she's smitten with you. Just try to remember there's an old lady behind that fake body of hers."

"Jealous?" Cleon goaded.

"I am in *no* mood," Serah said. "Surely, I'm not the only one who noticed."

"That part doesn't add up," Lucian said. "Not once have I *ever* heard of magic that keeps someone young. The only exception is longevity treatments, but those are fairly recent and haven't spread much farther than Sol and the First Worlds, so it's hard to imagine she would have that here. Maybe that's where the lie is."

"So, you think she has an Orb?" Cleon asked doubtfully. "She claims she's the most powerful Psionic in the Worlds, right? What if that's because she already *has* the Orb of Psionics?"

The others looked at him, confused. It was Fergus who broke the silence. "So, why would she need Lucian, then? And why would she lie about it?"

"I don't know. Maybe she has the Orb of Psionics, and the Orb in the Burning Sands is another one entirely."

Serah shook her head. "That's ridiculous. Lucian said Orbs slow aging. Even with one Orb, she'd probably still look middle-aged."

"We don't know the rate of aging," Lucian said. "It's not like we have a precedent here."

"It's an interesting idea, but I think she might be telling the truth," Serah said. "Just not the *whole* truth."

"There's something I've been meaning to ask you, Cleon," Lucian said. "Has she always looked this young?"

"She doesn't show herself often, but when she does, she likes to play with the light in a way that you can't really see her.

It was pretty common knowledge though that she was some old hag."

"So, this transformation had to have happened recently," Lucian said.

If she didn't hold an Orb, then Lucian was out of ideas. One thing was for sure: someone of her age and heavy magic use would almost certainly show signs of fraying.

None of it added up. Longevity treatments were popular among the League's rich, but it was hard to imagine how she would have the infrastructure and industry here to support that. They weren't going to figure it out now, so he set the thought aside.

Looking toward the bow, Lucian saw the mountains were much closer. From north to south, they stretched far above, almost like a wall rather than a mountain range. He could see why they needed to go through Dara first. There was no way through those mountains except for a large tunnel that wasn't visible at this distance. The Pass of Madness was the only way to the Westlands, after which came the Burning Sands and presumably the Orb.

But now, they were close enough to see a familiar scene from Lucian's dreams.

"Dara," Cleon said.

Serah watched, her eyes wide. "Looks big, even from up here. Is it *supposed* to be that big?"

Below them spread a wide, golden valley, as far as the eye could see north to south, ringed in by mountains on all sides. The Golden Vale of Dara was as beautiful as any landscape he had seen on Earth. Perhaps even more so. This was the heartland of Queen Ansaldra Dara's empire – rolling farmlands, clustered villages, gentle rivers, all flowing south toward some unknown sea.

And in the far distance toward the west was the crown jewel

of the Golden Vale, the Imperial City of Dara itself, situated in the lower slopes of the Mountains of Madness. The buildings basked golden under the light of the morning sun above, the city's size, towers, roads, and many terraces far grander than anything he remembered from his dreams. A high wall, also golden, ringed the half of the city not built against the mountains. Thousands of aureate towers rose above winding streets, streets that stair-stepped up the mountainside. More terraces and roads snaked up the mountain – *dozens* of them – all of which led to the high Pass of Madness above, now close enough to manifest as a shadowy tunnel. With the height of those mountains, the Golden Vale would spend most of its time in shadow, leaving only the morning for it to be true to its namesake. The sun was perhaps an hour from sinking behind the high peaks above.

Lucian got the sense he was being watched. He looked over his shoulder to see the Sorceress-Queen approaching, dressed in a velvet red dress, with the giant Mage-Lord Kiani beside her in his bronze armor, purple cape, and plumed helmet.

"We'll be landing soon," she said, her face betraying no emotion. "The *Zephyr* will resupply overnight. As that happens, I invite all of you to my soiree. Just a small affair, to get you used to the court, and to introduce my most loyal nobles to the wonderful people of the Riftlands."

"What the rot is a soiree?" Serah asked.

"Fancy people party," Cleon said. "Sorry, your Majesty. We'll take your most comfortable room, along with some banquet food sent to our door, with a taster to make sure it's not poisoned." Cleon looked at Mage-Lord Kiani. "Preferably this guy."

"Perhaps I should reword," the Sorceress-Queen said drolly. "I *insist* you attend my soiree. It's important that our association going forth should get off on the right foot. Mage-Lord Kiani shall be in attendance with his wife." She looked at him. "Will you not, Mage-Lord?"

Cleon's expression paled, and for once, he didn't have anything to say.

Mage-Lord Kiani smirked. "Most certainly we will, your Grace. It would be a shame if you didn't get to see my dear wife, Cleon."

"That's enough," the Queen said. "Suffice it to say, your presence is mandatory."

He and the Queen retired to the forecastle.

"My sister," Cleon said, looking as if he had just taken a punch to the gut. "My failure will be staring me in the face."

"What can we do?" Lucian asked.

"Nothing," Fergus said. "Smile, and act as pleased as swine in mud."

"Rot that," Cleon said. "This is my one chance to free Lynne. To right my wrongs." He clenched his fists. "I'm not going to let the opportunity pass."

"That's what she *wants* you to do," Lucian said. "If you off yourself voluntarily, she won't have to do it herself."

"He's right," Serah said. "She's probably trying to isolate Lucian. Pick us off one by one until he's alone and without support."

All of them were solemn as they considered that notion. That only made Lucian feel guilty about what he and the Sorceress-Queen had already talked about. They needed to know her eventual plans for him, but for now, he just couldn't bring himself to say it. After all, even *he* couldn't believe it was true.

"I can't ask you guys to risk yourselves anymore," Lucian said. The next part would be hard to say. "The Queen told me that all of you would be free to leave if you want. So, that's what you will do. Leave. Save yourselves before this gets any worse."

All of them watched him in shock. Even Cleon, to Lucian's surprise.

"Come off it," Fergus said. "I don't intend to break my word.

Not now, not ever. I will help you find the Orb of Psionics or die."

Serah sucked in some air. "That's a bit . . . intense."

Fergus ignored her. "I must admit, I was somewhat doubtful of you to begin with, Lucian. But after everything, how could *any* of us leave you to this conniving, scheming woman?"

Heads nodded all around. How could they be so committed to helping him when defeat was so sure? Would he have done the same for any of them? To his shame, he didn't know the answer to that.

But their commitment only firmed his resolve to see this through. If they were still on board, then he couldn't give up, no matter how bad this got.

"We'll attend the soiree," Lucian said. "Keep a low profile, and don't fall for any of the Queen's traps."

"That means no drama," Serah said, looking at Cleon.

"If my sister is there, I can't promise anything."

"We *know* she will be there," Fergus said. "And if you challenge Lord Kiani, it will mean your death."

"I can't do nothing," Cleon said. "This is the only way I can make things right."

Fergus took him by the arm and drew him close, speaking low. "Doing nothing is *exactly* how you save her. Not with violence that will serve no purpose but to jeopardize this mission. She's saved as soon as Lucian has the Orb of Psionics and can use it to—"

Serah held up a hand, instantly cutting Fergus off. Lucian looked around, but they were still alone. At least for now.

Cleon looked from Fergus to Lucian, then back. "You sure *he* is going to do that, Captain? Seems like every day he's becoming the Queen's man more and more."

"You fool. He's just playing the game. As you should be doing. You need to talk less and use your head more."

Fergus went back to watching the city pass below, his expression baleful.

When the *Zephyr* began to descend, the city of Dara loomed ever larger. They were close enough for Lucian to make out men in the towers of the high wall. Carts drawn by horse-like creatures with long necks rolled over the widely paved highway leading through the city's gates. Swarms of people crowded the busy streets, avenues, and alleys. There were easily thousands in this city. Tens of thousands. The mages could only be a small fraction of the population, an aristocracy of Mage-Knights and Mage-Lords to rule over these masses. Lucian had known that already, but he hadn't expected there to be so *many* non-mages.

"How are there so many people?"

Fergus watched below, as if he himself couldn't believe it.

It was Cleon who ended up answering. "Psyche is where the Worlds send their human trash. Criminals, miscreants, and scum. This is all of them, plus their progeny. Dara is growing all the time. When I left, it was already bursting at the seams." He watched the packed streets. "The Sorceress-Queen, as much as I hate her, is highly effective at keeping the people in line. She took a lot of people with different backgrounds and built an empire with them. And the tool she uses to do that is fear."

As they passed over the streets, the shadow of the *Zephyr* fell upon the roiling crowds. Many stopped what they were doing to look up into the sky. As much as Lucian didn't want to be impressed, he was, even more so since this city had been built with nothing more than human labor and most likely magic when the occasion called for it.

It was clear where they were heading: directly ahead, toward a large palace built into the slopes of the gargantuan mountain, a shimmering palatial complex basking like gold under the sun, with multiple walls, halls, bridges, and high towers. Lucian was awed at the sheer size of it. The scene was all too familiar from his dreams, but in person, it loomed so much larger.

Now, he was here in the flesh. There could be no waking up, no relief at the realization he was thousands of kilometers away from this dreaded place.

The Golden Palace of Dara awaited.

37

WHEN THE *ZEPHYR* TOUCHED DOWN, the ship's deck became a swarm of activity. Men on the ground chained the ship to thick bronze stakes to keep it from floating away. Crewmen and Mage-Knights arranged themselves in two lines, forming a corridor running from the entrance of the forecastle to a large boarding ramp. The crewmen and mages stood ramrod straight, bronze spears and round shields polished and gleaming in the late morning sun.

Lucian and the others had yet to receive instructions, so they waited by the railing.

Mage-Lord Kiani appeared from the forecastle and approached them, inspiring a scowl from Cleon.

"You are in the residence of the Sorceress-Queen Ansaldra Dara. If you threaten anyone within these walls, I have her Majesty's blessing to deal with it as I see fit." He smiled nastily, though that smile seemed to be mostly reserved for Cleon. "I've been tasked to lead you to your rooms personally. The Queen will see you next at the soiree."

"If only it could never be again," Cleon said.

Mage-Lord Kiani ignored the jibe, calling over his shoulder. "Holden! Decker! Get your Mage-Knights here, posthaste."

Within seconds, no less than twelve Mage-Knights stood before them, in a wide array of colored robes – blue, red, green, and more. Lucian realized that if it ever *did* come to a fight, their numbers and specialties would counter just about everything the four of them could throw at them. They were in the Queen's house and home, surrounded by her Mage-lords, Mage-Knights, bodyguards, hoplites, and sycophants. One false move and Lucian knew they would *all* be dead.

All his friends, anyway. She still needed Lucian alive.

There were well over a hundred hoplites in bronze armor, spears, and shields standing ready to receive their ruler on the airstrip below, forming a corridor leading to the palace's side entrance.

"What are we rotting waiting for?" Cleon asked.

"Quiet," Mage-Lord Kiani growled. "Do you really believe you would disembark before her Majesty?"

Cleon was about to respond, but Serah placed a hand on his arm, which was thankfully enough for him to keep his mouth shut.

At that moment, the door to the forecastle opened, revealing the Queen and retinue of Psionic Mage-Knights. Today, she wore a violet dress, with a floating train shimmering with amethysts. Coupled with her pale skin, it gave her an ethereal appearance as she walked between the column of hoplites toward the boarding ramp. Her face watched Lucian impartially as she passed.

Once the Queen made it to the ground, each pair of guards flourished their spears at her passing. By the time she was entering the side entrance to the palace, Mage-Lord Kiani nodded at Lucian.

"It's time."

Lucian stared him down a moment before moving for the

ramp. There was no use in fighting him. All they could do was bide their time and await the right opportunity. The walk to the paving stones below, followed by the long gauntlet through the guards, seemed to take forever. They were like statues, their expressions stonelike. Lucian kept focused on the entrance ahead. Already, the fast-moving shadow of the Mountains of Madness was starting to fall over the palace grounds and the entirety of Dara below. It was amazing how quickly the city went from golden sunlight to faded twilight.

As they passed the threshold, they found themselves in a long arcade lined with gilded marble columns, with a violet carpet extending tens of meters into the distance. Mage-Lord Kiani and his retinue of Mage-Knights led them through corridors, halls, and past massive tapestries and paintings. Lucian wondered how the Sorceress-Queen had managed to find the resources for such luxury.

Lucian looked inside a pair of open doors on the right to see a massive ballroom and an army of liveried servants setting up a long table with dishes and plates.

"Stop your gawking," Cleon said. "She invited you here to impress you. To awe you with her power. And it looks like it's working."

"It *is* impressive," Serah said. "You have to admit."

A couple of more minutes of walking brought them before a simpler door, though it was still intricately carved.

"This will be your room," Mage-Lord Kiani said to Lucian, his manner harsh. Clearly, being the butler was above his calling. "A man named Jarvis should be by soon to tend to your needs."

"Thanks," Cleon said. "If I'm hungry, should I put in an order with you, or Jarvis?"

The Mage-Lord's mouth curled in distaste. "I'll have the last laugh in the end, traitor. All four of you are to wait within for Jarvis's arrival."

The Mage-Lord departed, along with his retinue of Mage-Knights. Not a single person was left behind to watch over them. Either the Queen was confident in her security, or she had made a deadly lapse in judgment.

"Well, now is a golden opportunity to escape if we ever had it," Cleon said.

"Fool," Fergus said. "Can you not feel all the wards around here? Not even my strongest counter-wards will see us escaping this place without tipping her off. We've been hooked."

"Fergus is right about that," Serah said. "The question is, do we go along with this charade?"

"Yes, if we value our lives," Fergus said. "We've no choice but to play along."

"You're right about that, I guess." Cleon shook his head, his expression darkening. "Besides, I couldn't leave my sister behind. I have to fix the past if I'm to ever live with myself."

"Is there anything we can do?" Lucian asked.

"This is my own problem. I got her into this mess, so I have to get her out."

"Cleon," Serah said, "don't do anything stupid. We're here to find the Orb, remember?"

"That's right," Fergus said. "Our mission has not failed yet. But it could if you get us into trouble with the Queen."

"Are you *kidding* me?" Cleon asked. "We already *are* in trouble with the Queen."

"We should get inside the room," Lucian said. "Anyone could be listening out here."

They went inside, and Lucian saw immediately that it was no mere room. It was an entire apartment, and a sizeable one at that. They stood in a marbled entry hall. A set of stairs ascended to the right, leading to some upper rooms, while the lower floor held a parlor with cozy couches and a fireplace. A door at the back led into what looked like a bathroom, while on the right was a richly appointed bedroom with a four-post king size bed. Everything inside was warmly lit by a fire in the hearth and hanging lights, the source of the light seeming to be some sort of oil. Wide windows in the parlor also admitted a small amount of light; it was all the afternoon twilight outside was capable of.

All Lucian could do was wonder whether that bathroom had a shower in it. He ran forward and opened the door, finding a large tub with a copper faucet. When he turned the knob, warm water came out.

"Hot damn! They have hot water here!"

Fergus followed from behind and reached his hand into the water. "I haven't felt hot running water since . . . Irion, I guess. In the hotel the night before they took me to the Academy."

"A Thermal brand, maybe?" Serah said. "Or perhaps a furnace heating it somewhere. Either way, I call dibs."

"Are you crazy?" Cleon asked. "Keep your guard up. This could all be a trap!"

"Well, I haven't had a real bath in months," Serah said. "If I die, at least I'll be clean. You boys have five seconds to get out of here."

"Come on, give her some space," Fergus said.

"Thanks Fergie," she said. "Mind the door, would you?"

Fergus closed the door, leaving the three men standing awkwardly in the parlor. Serah's splashing was the only thing breaking the silence. Well, at least she was enjoying herself.

They went to the couches and sat, since it seemed there was nothing else to do.

"We need to come up with a plan," Cleon said.

"A plan for what?" Fergus asked.

"In case they come to murder us all, obviously." The tone of his voice stated this outcome was natural.

"No one's going to be killing us, Cleon," Lucian said. "At least, not unless we give them a reason to."

"You're on her side now, aren't you? I should've known. The

Witch has gotten into your head. I'm not sure *which* head, but probably the smaller one."

"You can't be serious," Lucian said, indignant. "I'm here for the Orb, and like it or not, we need her help to find it."

"Are you sure she isn't using magic on you? That's the only reason you could be acting as you are."

"Calm down, you two," Fergus said. "Lucian hasn't been branded by her. If she had, I would know it."

"It's the Sorceress-Queen," Cleon said. "We've established that she's strong, so perhaps she has ways of branding that escape our notice. So why *wouldn't* she be able to control Lucian's mind while covering her tracks?"

"Because successful mind control requires *some* complicity. He would have to agree to let her do it, on some level." Fergus looked at Lucian. "Lucian would have never done that. And if she were to force it, it would be too draining on her faculties, leaving her vulnerable to other attacks."

Could that have been why the Queen was trying to make him like her, to make him voluntarily give up control? The prospect almost made him shudder.

Cleon was looking at him in a way that said he doubted his loyalty.

"I'm not on her side," Lucian said. "I don't agree with her or her methods. But I know it's impossible to get the Orb of Psionics without her."

"You didn't think it was impossible before," Cleon said.

"Yeah . . . that was *before* we went into the Darkrift, *before* I saw how rough the terrain is on the way here. And I'm sure once we're beyond the Mountains of Madness, we'll find out how even *more* impossible it would have been."

Cleon crossed his arms and said nothing. The man was nothing if not stubborn.

"Yes, the Sorceress-Queen is powerful," Fergus said. "In the end, though, the only power a Psionic can wield over you is that which you choose to give. Some people do it – either out of surrender, or in exchange for something else. Mind control is not an all or nothing thing. There are degrees of control, from subtle suggestion to outright possession."

Lucian frowned. "What about Morgana back in Kiro? The Queen was able to control her very directly, so does that mean *she* gave up control?"

Apparently, both Fergus and Cleon had been apprised of that, but it was Fergus who answered. "Morgana must have allowed it on some level, even if it was in a dream. Perhaps the Sorceress-Queen promised something that made her give up control. Everyone has mental weak spots, and the Queen is adept at exploiting that."

Lucian wondered what *his* weak spots were. Had the Queen identified them? Was she chipping away at them already?

"Such a thing seems unimaginable," Cleon said. "Who would just give up control of themselves, and why?"

"You should know that better than anyone," Fergus said. "It is the price of power in her empire. All her Mage-Lords are branded in some form or fashion. I could sense it with Mage-Lord Kiani, and several others we passed in the palace. It's her way of maintaining ultimate control."

"So, you're saying Mage-Lord Kiani is mind-controlled?" Lucian asked.

Fergus shook his head. "That's not how possession brands work. She *can* do that, but not to an entire aristocracy of Mage-Lords. What she *can* do is create long-lasting brands with intricate streams – as many as five to ensure they last a long time. Those brands work to keep tabs on people she's interested in – how they're feeling, their physical state, where they are. It's what allows her to keep her power; she doesn't give power unless a person consents to be branded. Of course, every brand takes up some of her ethereal real estate. But that's the Queen's gift. She can stream so efficiently that she can hold dozens of brands on multiple people with almost no effect on her active streams."

Lucian shuddered, remembering how some of the things she'd said made sense. Did they truly make sense, or was she simply influencing his thoughts, despite her own admission that she wasn't? "Are you sure she didn't brand me?"

Fergus shook his head. "You would know if she did. You would . . . *feel* her presence in the back of your mind, as it were. It's likely that if she *did* want to brand you, she would do it with multiple streams that lasted a long time. The streaming of a brand like that would take a lot of effort, but once done, maintaining it would take little effort. It should be noted, branding someone Psionically is not always a *bad* thing. Friends can use it to keep tabs on each other, for example, and anyone you've Psionically linked with already can be spoken to again, although of course distance, stream power, and strength of relationship are all factors."

"Strength of relationship?" Cleon asked.

"Basically, how well you know the person. It would be easier to communicate with a spouse across a few kilometers than someone you've met once just down the street, for example."

"I see," Lucian said. "I'd say good to know, but it just makes me feel sick that she could do it at any time."

"I admit it's possible you're branded, Lucian, in a way too clever for me to detect. But you don't seem possessed to me."

"Thanks for the vote of confidence."

More splashing emanated from the bathroom, along with the sound of water being drained. A moment later, Serah cracked the door, wearing a white bathrobe.

She cleared her throat. "Can one of you gentlemen scrounge up some clothes for me?"

Lucian got up and searched through the wardrobes of the bedroom until he found something that might be her size – a silvery, shimmering dress with a long skirt with frilly patterns. Embarrassed, he also grabbed what appeared to be undergarments, wrapping them in the dress so that they would remain hidden. He avoided the red ones – Serah might get the wrong idea, or worse, roast him mercilessly. He opted for some more innocuous beige ones, the least skimpy pair he could find.

He went to the bathroom and handed the clothing off. "Just grabbed the first thing I found."

She arched an eyebrow. "Interesting qualifier there." She looked at the bundle with a smirk, and then at him. "Something with sleeves?"

His cheeks colored with embarrassment. "Let me see what I can find."

"Thanks."

He returned with another dress, this one green, which had long sleeves. He brought it back to Serah.

"Thanks. Will you let me know how I look after?"

"Um, sure."

She closed the door, and Lucian returned to the couch, bewildered.

"She has her eye on you, Casanova," Cleon said.

"Whatever. That's just Serah being Serah."

"Well, she doesn't talk to *me* like that, and I have a way with the ladyfolk."

Lucian would have countered that, but he didn't see the point.

"You're a fool if you don't see it, is all I'm saying," Cleon said.

"Speaking of fools," Serah said, suddenly emerging from the bathroom in her dress, "didn't I hear someone talking about Lucian being possessed by the Queen earlier?"

Lucian's eyes popped at the transformation. Even if her hair was wet, she wore the dress so well, as if she had been born to it. Her cheeks reddened under their collective gaze.

"Stop staring," she said. "Haven't you boys ever seen a

woman before?"

Those words broke them out of their collective trance.

"Wow," Cleon said. "I almost thought you were a different person, there."

"Shut your rotten mouth."

Cleon chuckled. "*That's* not very ladylike."

Cleon was lifted into the air about a meter, surrounded with an aura of gray magic.

"Hey! Cut that out."

Serah smirked. "Sure thing."

He dropped down onto the couch and rolled off. Just the expression on his face, the look of sheer indignation, sent Lucian and Fergus into fits of laughter.

"I'll get you back for that!" Cleon said. "You'll see."

"Oh, just learn your lesson already," she said. She turned her attention to Lucian. "Well? How do I look?"

"You look uh . . . good," Lucian said.

"Uh, good?" She smiled. "Well, that's better than uh, awful." She plopped onto the couch beside him. "This dress is not comfortable *at all*. Hopefully, they give me something new for this soiree thing."

"Speaking of," Fergus said, "we need a plan for how we're going to get through it."

"We still haven't finished discussing the possibility of Lucian being branded," Cleon said. "I'll admit it's improbable, but none of you know the Sorceress-Queen as I do. I've lived much of my life in Dara, and I've enacted her orders. She is *not* to be trusted in the least."

"Of course she's not," Serah said, now filing her nails. Where had she found *that*? "But that doesn't mean we can't enjoy some comforts in the meantime."

"Where is this Jarvis supposed to be?" Fergus said. "I could do with a rest and a bath myself. In my own chambers, of course."

Fergus was clearly a bit shyer than Serah. Then again, *most* people were shyer than her.

There was a knock at the door, which opened to reveal a short, mustachioed man dressed in fine violet linens laced with gold trim. His nose was turned into the air, and his eyes hooded. Lucian didn't know how the man managed it, but even from his height, he was able to look down upon them.

"Master Lucian, Master Cleon, Master Fergus, and Mistress Serah," he said in a stuffy tone, giving a slight bow. "My name is Jarvis Tian, and I am head butler of the Golden Palace. I'm here personally to inform you that each of your rooms is waiting for you. When the masters are ready, I will lead you to your new accommodations, where you might take refreshment, bathe, and be outfitted for the soiree this evening."

"So soon?" Serah asked. "I thought I might have a bit of a nap first."

"I'm afraid that will not be possible," Jarvis said. "My instructions are from Queen Ansaldra Dara herself, and they *must* be followed to the letter."

"He couldn't disobey her if he tried," Fergus said. "For what it's worth."

Lucian took that to mean that Jarvis had been branded. The mere thought gave Lucian a chill. "I guess I'll see you three later."

Jarvis bowed low and closed the door behind him.

"Snooty man," Serah said. "Lucian, I'll see you at the soiree." At the other two, she arched an eyebrow. "Well, are you coming, or are you going to make me wait all day?"

With a grumble, Cleon stood, and Fergus followed behind. Once all three were out of the door, Lucian was left in silence for the first time in what seemed forever.

He looked around the luxurious space, wondering how in the Worlds he'd found himself here. And how in the Worlds he'd get everyone out of it.

38

LUCIAN TOOK A BATH, luxuriating for at least half an hour and almost falling asleep before he heard the door to his chambers open. He hastily dried off, dressing in some new clothing he had left beside the tub. But when he went out, no one was there. However, a meal was waiting for him on the dining room table, a plate filled with what looked like steak, vegetables, and bread.

He ate ravenously. He hadn't had anything all day, so he couldn't worry about small details like being poisoned. The Queen would have killed him by now if she wanted, anyway.

No sooner than when he was done, there was another knock at the door. Jarvis himself entered with four servants behind him. The head butler cleared his throat, as if he didn't already have Lucian's attention.

"The Queen has asked me to prepare you personally for the soiree tonight. She intends to take you as her consort."

Lucian nearly choked on his food. From Jarvis's tone, there was no room for refusal. "Uh . . . are you *sure* about that?"

"Quite. It is an honor usually reserved for the highest – and most handsome, I might add – Mage-Lords of the Empire. I'm sure you are quite pleased."

Well, this certainly would not go over well with his friends. Was this the Queen's way of driving a larger wedge between them?

He thought of how to respond. "I suppose I can't refuse."

Jarvis's face paled, clearly horrified. The Queen would probably have his head if he returned with that news.

"All right, then," Lucian said. "Let's get this over with."

"I'm pleased, sir. When the gentleman has finished eating, please come to the mirror, that we might attend to you."

Lucian put his fork down. Better to get this over and done with.

Jarvis and his servants attended to him immediately, with Jarvis whistling a merry tune. Lucian was dressed in vestments worthy of a king. First, they measured him efficiently, and within moments, found him a black dress shirt and black pants, of quality as fine as anything on Earth. Even finer. Over the shirt went a tunic of red with gold trim, with a Septagon of seven colored jewels on the breast – ruby, spessartite, citrine, emerald, sapphire, amethyst, and diamond. Lucian's eyes popped as the gems sparkled at him from the mirror. He wondered whether they had been mined or created atomically, such was their size and purity. The tunic was cinched with a black belt with a silver buckle, studded with diamonds and rubies. Black leather boots were fitted to his feet, his hair cut, combed, pasted, and his face shaved.

The face staring back at him from the mirror was shocking. It belonged to a man ten years older than the one who had left Earth – all hard edges, fierce brown eyes, with new lines and wrinkles. He even had a few scars he hadn't known were there – one on his head, just below his hairline, and the other on the right side of his jaw, about two centimeters long. In short, he was unrecognizable. When he had left Earth, he was all of twenty years old, and on Volsung, he had turned twenty-one. If enough months had passed on the prison barge, he might very well be twenty-two, now. But the man in the mirror looked *thirty*-two, and he felt much older than that after the events of the past two years.

And he looked tired. So very tired. But there was still a determination in those eyes. He hadn't given up, despite everything that had happened.

He could never let that fire die.

Despite the fine clothing, something seemed to be missing. And Lucian realized what it was when it was brought to him.

Jarvis himself handed Lucian his shockspear, fitting a sheathe for it on his back.

"It is not proper for the Queen's consort to go without shockspear to any social gathering," Jarvis said, watching him neutrally. "It is for you to protect her, should the unthinkable happen. She has placed a great deal of trust in you, sir."

All Lucian could think was she couldn't have chosen a worse person.

"I see." It was all he could manage to say.

The other servants worked at his clothing, fixing minor details Lucian couldn't even see, adding a kerchief to his breast pocket. They even added a dash of cologne before he could tell them to hold off. The sharp aroma made him cough.

"When is the soiree, anyway?"

"In less than an hour. It will be a small gathering. No more than fifty of the Queen's most trusted lords and ladies. Quite exclusive."

"The last thing I want is to play politics. What's her game?"

Lucian had mostly been speaking to himself, something that the butler must have sensed, because he remained silent. It was not for him to speak against his Queen. In fact, Lucian had better be quiet himself. Every word he said, Jarvis would certainly faithfully report.

"That shall do it," Jarvis said, with a final bow. "I shall fetch you when the Queen has called. Until then, Master Lucian."

With that, he left, leaving Lucian alone in his chambers with his shockspear.

Immediately, he unsheathed and extended it. What kind of damage could he expect to do? Could he find the others in time and make an escape? Could he ever hope to outrun the Queen and the *Zephyr*?

The answers to that question were: almost no damage, they couldn't escape in time, and even if they did, the *Zephyr* would hunt them down within the hour. The Queen already knew where he planned to go, so all of it was useless.

Lucian reached for his Focus, streaming Dynamism along the shockspear's length. The spear crackled as he practiced his footwork, creating the space to deal with an imaginary foe. He poked and jabbed, swinging the spear in a wide arc to cut down multiple enemies, dancing away to create space again. He lost himself in the movements and sequences taught to him at the Academy, enough to work up something of a sweat. It was probably the opposite of what he *should* be doing, but he didn't care. He branded the Dynamistic Magic to the tip of his spear, allowing it to last all the longer.

By the time the brand petered out half an hour later, Jarvis had returned with a retinue of bronze-armored guards, each with their own spear and rounded shield. Lucian knew these were to be his escort, probably some "honor" he was due as the Queen's consort, but it certainly didn't seem an honor.

Jarvis's eyes widened upon seeing Lucian's state, but Lucian kept his spear out, feeling a flash of irritation at the interruption. "Yes?"

"It is time, Master Lucian."

Reluctantly, Lucian sheathed his spear with a flourish. "Lead the way."

Jarvis took a minute to straighten out Lucian's appearance –

the man wouldn't let Lucian do it himself. Once done, the butler led the way as the guards formed a box around them. For minutes, they walked through lamp-lit halls filled with sculptures, paintings, and rich carpets. The darkness outside was nearly absolute. Hours had passed since their arrival.

Anytime they passed a servant, they bowed as if Lucian were a Mage-Lord himself. He didn't know what was going on, until he realized he probably looked like one.

At last, they came to the final entry hall, a grand space with three floors with twin spiral staircases. It was in this reception area that Lucian was greeted to the sight of several dozen Mage-Lords and Mage-Ladies, all dressed richly in gold, red, blue, violet, and every color of the Spectrum of the Septagon. At once, each group and conversation stilled as Lucian stumbled inside. The Mage-Lords' eyes narrowed as if in challenge, while the ladies' eyes went wide at the sight of him. Lucian reached for his Focus to steady his nerves, while he resisted the urge to reach for his spear. He noticed some of the other Mage-Lords had armaments, too – spears, rapiers, even some hand-axes.

Lucian knew from one look that he was in a room full of jackals. The oldest ones might have even been in the Mage War, surviving until this day by wile and magic. The middle-aged ones might be their children, or those Psyche-born who had the spark of magic in them. There were few mages of an age with Lucian. This seemed to be an older crowd, and he could feel them calculating his strength of position, their minds mechanizing on how Lucian might be used to their advantage.

It was a good five seconds before they returned to their conversations, though they cast plenty of surreptitious glances his way. Lucian just wondered where his friends were.

"Please, wait here," Jarvis said. "The Sorceress-Queen Ansaldra Dara will arrive soon."

Jarvis withdrew, weaving through the lords and ladies with many-a-bow before entering the banquet hall beyond.

Lucian stood alone, doing his best not to feel like meat at a market. Though none would talk to him, that certainly didn't stop them from talking *about* him. He deepened his Focus and was relieved to see that his magic waited for him beyond. He refreshed his Psionic ward, knowing he couldn't be too careful. That should keep him at least somewhat safe.

At last, their voices stilled. From the third level above, a pair of doors opened, revealing the Sorceress-Queen, in a black dress festooned so thickly with red rubies that it might as well have been a red dress – a color of red that perfectly matched Lucian's vest. The dress had a bejeweled Septagon emblazoned on the front. It was similar to Lucian's, only the gems were much larger. The Queen, clearly, was not to be outdone. His throat clamped, not at her magnificence or beauty, but at the fact that they wore matching clothing. He knew what kind of signal she was trying to give with that, and if he had seen it coming, he might have put up more of a resistance.

The crowd of lords and ladies oohed as she descended the stairs, like an angel descending from heaven. The long tail of her dress floated with an anti-grav brand, while her burning violet gaze met Lucian's. It was hard to decide whether she was more beautiful or terrifying.

Every person turned to him, seeming to wonder how this no-name Rifter had caught the eye of the Sorceress-Queen. Eyes reweighed, recalculated, and presumed a new balance of power. Half of the lords and ladies now offered gracious smiles, as if they hadn't completely snubbed him moments ago.

Jackals, all of them. He wondered whether they were really so admiring of her Majesty, or if this simpering was simply political expedience. This soiree would be an opportunity to feel that out. It was hard to say if the information would be useful, but it wouldn't hurt to keep his eyes open.

At that moment, Lucian's friends appeared from an archway close to the banquet hall, each dressed in their own colors.

Serah wore a new gray dress. Even if the dress was far more understated than the Queen's, it kept more of the focus on Serah as a person. To Lucian, she was radiant with her blue eyes and honey blonde hair. This dress had no sleeves, so like him, she'd had no part in its selection. She had her arms folded in a way that hid her frayed skin.

Cleon was dressed in a red tunic, too, though nowhere near as fine as Lucian's, having no jewels. Coupled with his red hair and freckles, it almost made it look like he was on fire. Fergus was dressed in a green tunic, hardly fitting his size and heft. To Lucian's surprise, the Queen had allowed Fergus and Cleon to carry their own spears. Serah was without one, but none of the other Mage-Ladies had weapons. She could not have been happy about that.

His friends gazed at him with the same shock as everyone else. But eventually, the attention refocused on the Queen, who was gliding down the last few steps of the staircase. She seemed to float toward him, the levitating hem and train of her dress giving her ghostly grace. The lords and ladies parted, all smiles and manners, with looks of approval even sent Lucian's way. Lucian couldn't get out of here fast enough.

When she stood before him, Lucian had to keep icy concentration on his Focus. She lifted a hand toward him.

This required delicacy, and he had to play her game and beat her at it. As impossible as that would be, he had to make it through this in one piece.

He took her hand, and drew her to his arm in a single movement. She smiled, seeming delighted on the surface, but something burned in those violet eyes. She pulled him somewhat roughly, despite the fact he had taken the leading position, which elicited some chuckles from the nobles. From his peripheral vision, her pale cheeks colored ever so slightly. It felt good to embarrass her for once.

He stumbled over something on the floor, but when he

looked down, nothing was there. He glanced her direction, her eyes glinting with mischief. He kept his gaze forward, his expression stoic. Her message was clear: push me, and I'll push you back twice as hard.

He kept his face placid, his mannerisms cool. He forced himself to nod at a couple of Mage-Lords as he and the Sorceress-Queen strolled toward the open doors of the banquet hall.

The massive Lord Kiani, wearing an emerald surcoat over his bronze armor, stood by the door. The beautiful woman hanging on his arm was at least half his age, and half his size. Could this be Cleon's sister, Lynne? Lucian didn't see much of a resemblance, and he had to suppress the urge to search for Cleon. The woman wore a shimmering white and blue dress that left her delicate shoulders bare. Her icy blue eyes twinkled as she watched him pass, and she gave a small curtsy to both him and the Queen, her ringleted brown hair bobbing at the movement. For some reason, Lucian got the feeling this woman wasn't Cleon's sister. She seemed to be in her early thirties at least.

The Sorceress-Queen and Lucian entered the banquet hall first, where a long table was filled to the brim with food: meats, plates of breads and sweet treats, trays of hors d'oeuvres with meats, pastries, and glassware filled with bubbly, colorful drinks. In the corner, a small orchestra began to play a lively tune on stringed instruments, each of them wearing white puffy tunics. It was as if he had stepped backwards in time to the Renaissance.

"This way," the Queen said.

They didn't make for the food, but a pedestal across from it. She led him to the top, and Lucian couldn't help but feel like a dog whose leash was getting yanked. He had to lay down his pride, as difficult as it was, and keep playing the game. He made his way to the podium in his own time, and faced out to the rest of the banquet hall.

Couple by couple, the lords and ladies filed in, each standing before the Queen and Lucian. His friends entered last of all, hanging at the periphery. From their blank expressions, it was hard to tell what they were thinking. If they didn't think him possessed by the Queen's magic before, they almost certainly did now.

By the time all had gathered, the Queen shifted beside him. Lucian noticed Cleon staring murderously at Lord Kiani, who seemed oblivious. His wife wasn't looking at Cleon, but at him and the Queen. No, definitely not Cleon's sister.

"Be welcome, Mage-Lords and Mage-Ladies," Queen Ansaldra said. "I thank you for attending my little soiree on such short notice."

Little? If this were little, then Lucian didn't want to see what a big one looked like.

"Tonight, we have honored guests among us." She raised a hand toward Lucian's friends. "A delegation from the Far Rift-lands is here, who have agreed to accompany me to court and work with me on an important matter – one that stands to strengthen and unify all of Psyche. Tomorrow, the delegation will be setting sail aboard the *Zephyr* for the Westlands, as far as the border of the Burning Sands."

This elicited excited murmurs from the crowd. Apparently, it was either a high honor to fly with the queen on her airship, or the Westlands of Psyche were as exotic as the Riftlands to these people.

"As my very closest friends," she continued, with a winning smile, "I thought this delegation could regale you with tales of life in the dangerous Rifts of Psyche. Cleon Dowe, once a Mage-Knight, now fights for Kiro Village of the Deeprift." At being mentioned, Cleon's face reddened, either in embarrassment or anger. "The beautiful Serah Ocano, an expert Gravitist." Serah's face paled at the mention of her name. "Fergus Madigan, captain of the Kiro Watchmen, a Radiant of renown."

Lucian wondered where she had learned all this information. Could she have sifted it from their minds? What *else* had she found out? At that moment, Lucian realized why she wasn't afraid of them turning on her, or of even allowing them weapons. She could probably read their intent long before even *they* realized what they were doing.

How could you fight someone like that? Was she aware of his thoughts, even now?

She gave him a sidelong glance. Lucian faced forward, to keep those knowing eyes from seeing into him.

"And last of all," she said, pausing for emphasis. "My consort for the evening: Lucian Abrantes, the most powerful Binder in all the Worlds."

This got the biggest reaction, some even going so far as to applaud. What was he, her monkey? But it was best to play it cool. He tried not to let his anger show, nor let the Sorceress-Queen know how she was grating at him.

"So, my friends. Eat, drink, and be merry," she said. "The Riftlands delegation is at your disposal."

She clapped her hands once, and the orchestra began to play anew. Immediately, the nobles began to mingle as servants weaved in and out, serving drinks and hors d'oeuvres.

"Stay near me, and you'll be fine," she said.

Without waiting for a response, she strolled into the crowd, engaging a group of nobles with a charming smile. She immediately had them under her spell. They tittered at some joke as Lucian awkwardly approached. He scanned the crowd for his friends, but they were already getting swarmed by their own nobles.

This was going to be a *long* night.

39

THANKFULLY, Lucian did not have to talk much. He did have to answer questions, and tried some of the food offered by servants, more to blend in than anything else. He held a drink in his hand but intended to nurse it all evening. His goal was to not stick out, but of course, that was impossible when he was the object of attention and "the Best Binder in the Worlds." The Queen had needed some justification to take him as her consort. He hadn't liked the sound of that at all and hoped this companionship did not extend beyond this evening.

He answered questions about Earth, which no one had visited save the Queen and some of the older Mage-Lords. He spoke of the Volsung Academy but didn't volunteer information beyond what was asked. The Queen's eyes weighed him with every word he spoke, so it was best to speak as little as possible.

The Queen offered her arm, and even if he didn't want to take it, he only did so because it was expected. The last thing he wanted was for her to take offense and have every Mage-Lord and Lady come down on him in her defense. It was easier to pretend. This night would be temporary. If he had to make concessions to reach the Orb of Psionics, he would. What was his pride in the grand scheme of the galaxy?

They were approaching Lord Kiani and his wife. Lord Kiani, who Cleon had called "the Butcher of the Westlands." From his size alone he could do a lot of damage, notwithstanding his magic. Standing with his beautiful wife in her pearlescent dress, Lucian felt something was off as he and the Queen entered their space.

"Mage-Lord Kiani," the Sorceress-Queen said. "I'm pleased to see you once again."

The Butcher offered a winning smile. "Your Majesty. You honor my wife and me with your kind words."

The wife gave a deep curtsy, spreading her skirts wide while inclining her head. "Your Majesty. You're positively radiant this evening."

"As are you, Lady Catherine," the Queen said. "Perfectly lovely, as always."

Catherine? This wasn't Cleon's sister at all. Lucian tried not to show too much curiosity. He also noted some tension in the Queen's voice. These two weren't on good terms, despite the pleasantries. Jackals in dresses.

"Lord Kiani," the Sorceress-Queen went on, "I believe Sir Cleon was under your purview, yes?"

She already knew that, so Lucian didn't understand why she was pretending. Just some game she was playing, he supposed.

Lord Kiani's smile strained. "Yes, quite so. His was a . . . troubling case. Of course, he is no longer Sir Cleon."

Catherine's face reddened. Lucian was now positive she wasn't Cleon's sister.

The Queen pressed on. "It is time for the Golden Vale and the Riftlands to make amends. And likewise, perhaps it is time that you . . . ameliorate . . . any tensions between yourself and your former Mage-Knight. I would be glad to have him in my personal guard. Any man who survived the Darkrift has a welcome place in the Daran Empire."

Lord Kiani smiled, though the smile didn't reach his eyes. "If he survived the Darkrift, perhaps I underestimated him. Of course, I would doubt the loyalty of any man who abandons his post."

"His poor sister," the Queen said, sadly. "But I suppose some things cannot be helped."

The Queen watched Lady Catherine, whose blue eyes were icy.

"Farewell," she said. "Enjoy the party."

The Queen flashed a toothy smile as she led Lucian to the next group.

Lucian couldn't get out of there fast enough. Clearly, there was some sort of rivalry between the Queen and this Lady Catherine . . . whoever she was.

He leaned over to the Queen once they were out of earshot. "What happened to Cleon's sister?"

To his surprise, the Queen gave him the answer. "She died in childbirth six months ago. Something of a scandal, for he was married to Lady Catherine not two months later."

Cleon's sister had *died*? Lucian's stomach sank. Cleon couldn't find out – at least, not tonight. If he did, this little soiree might turn into a big bloodbath.

The Queen never stayed long in any group, flitting around from one to another like a butterfly, making surface-level conversation and banter that always elicited laughter. Nothing she said was particularly witty, but the nobles laughed all the same. The fakeness made Lucian want to barf.

She made sure to talk to each party attendant. Lucian was little more than eye candy. One of the women, with her husband no less, asked the Queen where she might "get one of those," pointing right at Lucian. He was about to mouth a response when he remembered these stupid, simpering people didn't matter. Only the Orb of Psionics did. Let them laugh, chortle, and diminish him. All he had to do was survive this night, and the Orb could be his.

He wanted nothing more than to go back to his chambers, but that wasn't to be. It was only a matter of time before he ran into Fergus, who was being goaded by a tall, wiry man with long, twirly mustaches.

"I don't care what you say, Lord Fergus," the man said, with a dumb, drunk smile on his lips. "You could not stand half a *minute* to a Mage-Knight in a proper Daran duel. A Rifter is no match for a man bred from the soil of the Golden Vale. Isn't that right, my Queen?"

"I don't know, Lord Sabine," the Queen said. "I'm told Lord Fergus has fought fiercely, and his spear work is second to none."

Lucian didn't know where she had gotten that information. Again, he was worried she had the ability to sift through others' thoughts. It was either that, or she was incredibly gifted at reading people.

Lord Sabine's face went blank for a moment before he recovered. "We should settle it with a bet, Fergus. I know just the place to carry it out—"

"I'm afraid not," Fergus said, coldly.

Like Lucian, Fergus wanted nothing more than to get out of here. The Sorceress-Queen left the men to their devices, wandering to a group where Serah was surrounded by the only three young men who happened to be in attendance. They were dressed dandily, all wearing superior smirks that made their faces instantly punchable. They carried canes rather than spears.

They laughed at some joke amongst themselves, but Serah's face remained carefully neutral. Their backs straightened as the Queen approached, and they stopped talking.

"What?" the Queen asked, her face displaying mock

chagrin. "Don't stop on my account. What was the joke? I love a good joke."

One of the young lordlings cleared his throat. "That was . . . as I was saying—"

"Yes?" Serah asked. "I believe you were asking about the physical properties of Rifter girls, and whether I was a prime example of them."

The young man's face reddened. "What? No, that's not what I said at all! I mean . . ." With the Queen's eye on him, he cleared his throat, too embarrassed to answer. "That's not what I said, your Majesty, I can assure you. I was merely asking about her *family*—"

"And no, I would not like to join you at your estate tonight. I'm sure you have a wonderful wine collection, but judging from the way this conversation has gone, I'm more likely to end up locked in the cellar."

He looked as if he might have apoplexy. "Any poor girl like you would be lucky to have *any* association with me, the Mage-Prince of the Three Forks. Don't even *dream* you are my equal, rift rat."

"Don't worry," Serah said. "I would never dream of stooping that low."

The others chuckled nervously, afraid to have a laugh at the dandy's expense. The young man's eyes were murderous as he stalked off. Other nobles, hearing the exchange, were laughing.

Lucian was glad she was handling herself well. That was one of them, at least.

Cleon, however, was making no pretense of mingling. His face was one of rage, weaving in and out of the crowd like a man on a mission. Lucian had a feeling he knew who he was trying to find.

This was going to be bad.

"I think he's trying to find Kiani."

The words were out of his mouth before he realized what had happened.

"This should prove interesting," the Queen said.

She followed Cleon's trail as he made his way closer to the Butcher.

Lucian shook his head and took off after him, leaving the Queen behind. He had to stop this before it was too late. But he wasn't going to make it.

Cleon grabbed Lord Kiani by the shoulder. "Where is she?"

The man spun, face enraged, and upon seeing who it was, immediately created space while reaching for his shockspear. The room went still as everyone stood back.

"Stand down, Cleon," Kiani said. "Don't do anything you regret."

"Where *is* she?"

Lady Catherine watched coolly from the sideline, her blue eyes glittering as she took a sip of her drink.

"I'm afraid you're too late," Lord Kiani said. "By several months, in fact. Had you not fled like a coward, you might have comforted your sister in her final moments." He gave a sharp smile. "I'm told she asked after you."

Cleon's face had gone white. "Lynne . . ."

"Her life was not in vain," Kiani went on, mercilessly. "She bore me a son. Healthy. A worthy heir to the Kiani estate." Catherine's face darkened at this, but Kiani seemed blind to it.

Cleon reached for his spear. "Her life was not an extension of your ego, Kiani!"

He shrugged, as if he had long put her out of his mind. "What can I say? Your sister was already quite weak. There was simply too much blood."

The surrounding faces became horrified as these gruesome details were revealed, but Cleon and Kiani seemed blind to all but each other. The Sorceress-Queen now stood beside Lucian, watching on with the rest. Was this *entertainment* for her?

"Do something!" Lucian said. "Or I will."

The Queen seemed to not hear as she continued listening to the exchange.

"I will not rest until I have satisfaction," Cleon said. "Lord Kiani, Butcher of the Westlands, I challenge you to a duel! Your blood, or my blood, for hers."

A collective gasp went through the crowd, even as the Butcher examined his fingernails. "Cleon, put aside these childish games. I haven't the time for them."

"Coward! This is no game. I will spill your blood before the night is out."

"Not at my soiree," the Sorceress-Queen said, *finally* stepping in. "I haven't a ring set up because the table is in the way."

There were several nervous laughs, but not enough to diffuse the tension. Lord Kiani released his hold on his spear, at the least. Cleon had yet to let go of his.

At that moment, Cleon's eyes suddenly widened while his body went stiff. Fergus and Serah stepped at his side, pulling him back and away. Lucian went to help them.

"This soiree was designed to ease tensions, not inflame them," the Sorceress-Queen finally said. "Guards! Stand back. There will be no trouble tonight, and if there is, let it fall on me to defuse it."

When he reached the others, Lucian was surprised to see that Cleon actually *was* calm, his eyes becoming hooded as he sheathed his spear. Lord Kiani watched him with smug satisfaction. What was going on?

That was when Lucian noticed that Cleon's eyes had a violet sheen to them.

"I think it's time the entire delegation went back to their rooms," she said. "Lucian, can you see it done?"

Her manner was cold, as if he had disappointed her in some way. Had she expected *him* to step in and stop Cleon from challenging Lord Kiani? That was probably why she had waited so long to do anything.

"We'll take him back."

The Queen nodded, and that was all the permission he needed.

They escorted Cleon away from the banquet hall.

40

ONCE THEY WERE BACK in Lucian's rooms, Cleon was still in a stupor, as if drunk. But Lucian knew his state had nothing to do with alcohol.

"She calmed him," Fergus said. "Quite brutally too, I might add."

Cleon was leaning back on the sofa, his mouth hanging agape and his eyes blank.

"Will he be okay?" Lucian asked.

Fergus nodded. "It'll take time for him to snap out of it, but yeah. He'll be fine."

"What's her *game*?" Serah asked, kicking off her sequined stilettos and putting her feet on the coffee table. From the way she had balanced herself at the soiree, it was as if she had worn shoes like that her whole life. "Is she with us, or against us?"

No one had an answer for that. Cleon was just drooling now, his back swaying. Fergus kept him supported.

"Why would he make a scene like that?" Lucian asked. "I mean, I understand *why*. But so much is at stake."

"His mission is not our mission, Lucian," Fergus said. "He wants revenge on this Butcher fellow."

Cleon groaned, seemingly trying to agree.

"We have to figure out our *own* game plan," Serah said. "What happens if we actually get to the Orb? Does she really expect us to keep going along with her willingly? How does she force that, and what do we do when she does?"

Fergus shook his head. "I don't know. I never expected us to make it this far, much more for the Sorceress-Queen to play this part."

"She has her own plans for the Orb, *and* for us," Serah pointed out. "Lucian, she's trying to soften you up with all these clothes, soirees, and parading you around like some pet." She gave him a pointed look. "And you better not be falling for it."

"I'm not," Lucian said. "I'm just playing along."

"You better be," Serah said, looking somewhat doubtful.

"We can't let her drive a wedge between us," Lucian said. "Can't you guys see that's what she's trying to do? She's testing us."

"Okay, then," she said. "So what's the plan? Keep kissing her ass, then stab her in the back?"

Cleon groaned.

"I didn't think the plan was *that* bad."

"It's not a plan," Lucian said. "It's just a gamble. We somehow need to get the Orb and get off Psyche altogether."

Fergus and Serah looked at him blankly.

"But . . . *no one* leaves Psyche," Serah said.

"I have a plan. I don't know if it'll work, but it's the only thing I've got."

"I'm all ears," Fergus said.

"There's . . . someone I know, who I've spoken with Psionically before. If she is who I *think* she is, then the Orb might give me enough power to reach her, even if she's far away. And if I am who *she* thinks I am, she will do everything she can to reach me."

Serah and Fergus stared at him blankly.

"That makes absolutely *no* sense," Serah said.

Lucian then reminded them of Vera, of what she had told him aboard the interstellar liner – that he had been "marked" by the Manifold, and that she had foreseen that he was to become her Psion. If she believed that prophecy was true, then it also meant that Lucian *could not* stay on Psyche.

It was a long shot. But if Vera were truly the most powerful mage in the galaxy, then she might be capable of pulling it off.

Once done explaining, both of them watched him, their expressions worried. Cleon groaned again.

"To sum it up," Lucian said, "we can't find the Orb without the Queen. We may have to work with her . . . temporarily. But from my short conversations with Queen Ansaldra, she and Vera are not on the same page. If we can *somehow* get Vera here, then she would offer us a way off this world. And she would most likely challenge the Sorceress-Queen directly."

After a long, considering silence, Fergus was the first to speak. "How do you know this . . . Vera . . . is any better than the Sorceress-Queen?"

It was something Lucian hadn't even considered. Emma and the Transcends had certainly thought she was dangerous. But if Lucian had to make a choice, it was easy.

"Even if she *is* more dangerous, she would have a way off this world. That's something we need if we're going to continue finding the Orbs."

"That *wasn't* the plan," Fergus said. "You were to find the Orb and use it *against* the Sorceress-Queen. I can't abandon Psyche. That isn't the oath I swore."

"The Queen wouldn't have a reason to target the Riftlands with me gone," Lucian said. "I'd rather avoid a fight, because I don't think we would win."

"This isn't your home," Serah said. "It's just another stop for you while you add to your alien artifact collection. Why am I even helping you?"

Lucian threw up his hands in the air. "I don't know! I told you that you could leave if you wanted. What you don't seem to understand is, *I can't save Psyche.* Even if we killed her, which you're suggesting, it would throw everything into chaos. Tens of thousands could die in the upheaval."

"But she would be gone," she said.

"Don't you see?" Lucian asked. "What we're doing is so much bigger than that. This fight will go beyond Psyche. I need you guys to come with me when the opportunity presents itself."

Both of them were quiet for a while. It wasn't a conversation Lucian wanted to have. Asking for help was always hard.

Serah's blue eyes weighed him carefully. "So, you need our help?"

Lucian almost didn't want to admit it. The old him certainly wouldn't have, but he had come too far. Risked too much. "I can't do this alone. I need the three of you. Not just for Psyche, but for the future. I'm still weak and untrained. I have one Orb, but it isn't listening to me. I have a Queen who is trying to manipulate me, and then there's this damn voice in my head . . ."

"Voice?" Serah asked. "What Voice?"

He hadn't told them that part yet. He was afraid they would think he was fraying.

"I hear it sometimes in my dreams. I haven't for a while, but this Voice wants me to find the Orbs. The Queen's telling me it's . . ." He trailed off, then shook his head. "Well, it's quite unbelievable who she says it is, and who the Oracle of Binding says it is. But I have no reason to think either is lying."

"We're listening," Fergus said.

Lucian took a moment to collect himself. "Remember everything I told you about the Immortal, the one who gathered all the Orbs during the time of Starsea?" At their nods, he continued. "Well apparently, when he died, he didn't exactly . . . die."

"Being immortal tends to do that," Serah said.

Lucian ignored the joke. "Apparently, something about him fused with the Manifold. And . . . he's somehow survived all this time and is speaking to me from there. *He's* the one who has chosen me. To find the Orbs and bring them to him. At least, that's what I think."

Both of them went quiet as they considered that. Serah's face had gone pale, while Fergus simply looked sick.

"I don't like the sound of that," Fergus said.

Serah's expression tightened with worry. "You're not . . . fraying, are you? That can be one of the signs. Hearing voices."

"I don't think I am. But then again, I've been using far more magic than I should be. When I wake up in the mornings, sometimes I feel this fire beneath my skin. Not as bad as a few nights ago, but it's there. Burning."

Serah nodded, her expression solemn. "That's how it starts. You have time, still. Time enough, maybe, to find these Orbs. The whole part about giving them to this Immortal guy, that sounds a bit iffier."

That about summed it up. "I don't know what to make of any of it. I'm not even sure how I would do that, or how what the Oracle of Binding told me fits into all of that." He sighed. "I'm in way over my head."

"I will help you, even if it was not my original oath." Fergus said. "Feels bad to say that to someone twenty years younger than me. But this is bigger than me, bigger than my pride. And . . . I've always felt like my life was missing something. This is a chance to do something big. Something that matters. That's all I ever wanted as the Mage-Captain of Kiro."

"What about the Elders?" Lucian asked.

He waved his hand. "I'm swept up in this now. I don't think I could get back there even if I tried."

"Me neither," Serah said. "Unless the Sorceress-Queen is kind enough to drop us off. Which I don't see happening."

"So, you'll help, too?" Lucian asked.

Her eyes softened, and there was something in her face that seemed to feel pity for him. From that one look, he already knew her answer.

"Well, someone has to stop you from doing something stupid. And you've done plenty of stupid so far."

"Thanks a lot."

"But, to your credit, you've also saved my ass a bunch of times, which is more than I expected from a soft-bellied Earth boy."

Cleon grunted, and drooled a bit.

"Is that a *yes*?" Serah asked.

Cleon moved his head and would have lost control if not for Fergus holding him up.

"He'll let us know tomorrow," Serah said. "I have to say, all this sounds so far-fetched and impossible. Just to go over it one more time, your plan depends on getting the Orb of Psionics in the first place and trusting that the Queen isn't just using *you* to get to it. All that rot about prophecy and you being the Chosen is just a distraction. Anyone can claim prophecy, it doesn't prove anything. She needs you compliant for as long as it takes for her to get the Orb."

Lucian had to admit that was a likely outcome, even if his gut said that the Queen had plans for him that went beyond the Orb of Psionics. "That's why we need to figure out a way to grab it before her."

"*What* way?" Fergus asked. "We're going on her airship, surrounded by her Mage-Knights and hoplites."

"I don't know," Lucian said. "I'm just laying out what *needs* to happen."

"And then there's Vera," Serah continuing her previous line of thought. "Assuming you *do* get the Orb, you'd still need to contact her. And we don't even know if the Orb of Psionics is capable of that, as powerful as it surely is. I've only used Psionics to communicate across a rift or at most two, so it's hard to imagine anything farther than that."

"I have a reason to think it is powerful enough," Lucian said. "Back on Volsung, I almost drowned during one of my Trials."

"Wow," Serah said. "You really *weren't* a good student, were you?"

He ignored that observation. "I heard Vera's voice underwater, speaking to me. At the time, she was lightyears away. If she could do that without the Orb, then I could probably do the same thing *with* it."

She nodded. "Okay, assuming all that, then yeah, it becomes more likely. But then she would have to have her own spaceship. Nothing flies to Psyche aside from prison barges. The space around it is restricted to League warden stations and vessels. If she had her *own* ship, what was she doing on that interstellar liner in the first place?"

That was a good question to which Lucian didn't have an answer. "Putting it that way, yeah, it all does sound far-fetched. And then on top of that, she would need to find a way through the blockade."

"The only other option we have is the one we laid out before," Serah said. "My vote is to use the Queen. Get to the Orb first . . . and then use it on *her* before she can hurt us."

"But that guarantees a fight," Lucian said.

She scoffed. "You *are* falling for her ploys. Lucian, she's just using you. You said you wanted our help, right? Well, this is me helping you, and saying for the millionth time: *don't trust her.*"

"So, you just want to gamble everything?" Lucian asked. "Go for the Orb and attack her with it, even if I don't know what the rotting hell I'm doing?"

"It's a chance! We'd be fools not to take it."

"In case you forgot, the Orb of Binding isn't helping me," Lucian said. "What if the Orb of Psionics is the same way? I doubt I'd know how to even use it on her. I would die, and then that's *two* Orbs for her. Are you saying you want that to happen?"

Fergus frowned. "This isn't helping. We're on the same team. Remember what I said a few days ago? If we can't work together, then we've already failed."

"I don't want to fight, either," Lucian said. "But you have to admit, my training is severely lacking."

"You'll have us," Serah said. "You're acting like this is your fight alone. We've already signed on, remember? Sure, maybe the four of us can't hold our own against the Queen. But if you can ward us all, Lucian, and do so with the power of the Orb, she can't Psionically control us. That's the reason she has her power, the reason no one has been able to overthrow her. If anyone openly rebels, she just turns them into a puppet. Now, *no one* challenges her."

"You're right," Lucian said. "I guess it's possible, but if you're counting on the Orbs to come through, all I'm saying is not to expect it. We almost died falling down that shaft in the Darkrift. The Orb didn't want to work. Whatever we were doing down there, we weren't on the right path. The Queen said as soon as I started doing what the Orb *wants* me to do, it'll start working again."

"Let me guess. What she wants to do just so happens to be what the *Orb* wants you to do? That's convenient."

"What if she's right?"

The others had no answer for him. He wished they did. It would make things so much easier.

"There's too much at stake to risk our lives and two Orbs," Lucian said. "We're at a severe disadvantage and don't have enough information."

"If you don't risk something, you can't gain anything," Serah said. "You have to be bold, Lucian. What other chance will we have?"

"I can wait until I become stronger."

"But by then, the Sorceress-Queen will have you fully convinced she has the right of it. You'll be completely turned against us."

"I'm sorry," he said. "I don't know what to do. What's right, what's wrong. I don't know how to get the Orb of Binding working again. I've fallen off the right path. Following the Queen doesn't seem right, but I don't see any other option. I'm in over my head."

Serah reached across and touched his hand, a move that surprised him, especially after her earlier harshness. "Who *isn't* here? We're all still alive, which is amazing in itself. What's the next thing we can do? Don't think about the Orb of Psionics. What's something we can do right now to better our situation?"

"I mean, we're doing it," Lucian said. "Trying to talk and plan. We need agency, but that's impossible when we're inside the Queen's palace." He looked around the room. "And for all we know, she has someone in the walls listening to every word we say."

"I have us warded," Fergus said. "And if someone were trying to dismantle that ward, I'd be the first to know."

Lucian nodded gratefully. "Good to know."

"We have a choice to make, as I see it," Fergus said. "Abandon our original mission and join forces with her. Or . . . the other option. Trying to get to the Orb first and then do what we originally planned. Or as Lucian said, work with her and wait for this Vera to come and settle the score. I don't much like that one, because it depends on too many unknowns."

Cleon's mouth opened and he leaned forward, as if to say something. He started to fall, and would have had Lucian not caught him.

Lucian sighed. "It's hard not to feel like we're just going right into the jaws of doom, so to speak."

"That's an apt way to put it," Serah said. "Well, rest assured Fergie and I won't leave you to this spidery bitch. We've been through too much, have come too far, the stakes are too high. Et cetera."

"Thanks," Lucian said.

She looked down at the frayed skin on her arm, drawing Lucian's attention to it also. Was it his imagination, or had that marring grown since he'd met her?

"I've only got a little time left," Serah said. "It would be nice to find all these Orbs before *this* does its work." She nodded down at the frayed skin. "And it's not like I have much to live for here."

"I know this isn't easy," Lucian said. "The last thing I want is to work with her. But she does have resources, an airship, and an entire empire at her disposal. We have to use it, but we'll always be looking out for the first opportunity to go our own way. I'm not sure if it'll come down to a fight at the end. I hope not. I believe an answer will reveal itself. We just have to watch for the right opportunity."

"We're really doing this, then," Fergus said. "I see no other way forward."

Cleon gave an angry grunt but was unable to form words.

"Are you sure he's okay?" Lucian asked.

"She calmed him hard," Serah said. "I'll have to get her to show me how she did it. Seems like a good trick."

Cleon grunted again.

"We should stick together, in any case," Lucian said. "There's no reason for us to sleep separated tonight. We've got two couches here, plus the bed."

"The floor's fine for me," Serah said. "I can't sleep on anything soft anymore."

"Let's let Cleon have the bed," Fergus said. "All of us should sleep now. We will need our wits to survive tomorrow."

———

LUCIAN DREAMED of the Orb of Psionics. It shone violet in the darkness, thrumming with power. It was as if it could *sense* he was getting close.

Find them . . . the Voice said. *Bring them to me.*

Just hearing that voice again, after so many months and after just talking about it, sent a chill down his spine. But this time, he wasn't a scared child stunned into silence.

He intended to find answers, despite his own fear.

Who are you?

The Voice was quiet. So quiet, that Lucian was sure that it had gone. The violet Orb continued to pulse with power.

I am the Voice of the Manifold. I have chosen you to fulfill my purpose.

You mean, you are the Immortal.

The Voice was silent for a long time. It was as if it were watching. Waiting.

I am all *that is Immortal. I am the Unmoved Mover, the reality that casts the shadow. Anything Immortal is me. But I am not a particular person or place. The Immortal is a part of me, but I am not the Immortal.*

So, *the* Immortal, the Chosen of Starsea who last held all the Orbs, was now a part of the Manifold, but he *wasn't* the Manifold itself.

As I have chosen you, the Manifold has chosen me to speak for its sake. The Manifold wishes for you to find the Orbs and return them to the Heart of Creation. The Balance must be restored.

The Balance? What do you mean by that?

The Starsea Cycle must end. And it will end when the Orbs have been returned to the Manifold.

To the Heart of Creation.

Yes, the Voice said. *The Heart of Creation.*

How?

The First Gate beyond the Dark Space. It will take you there. Find the Orbs. Bring them to me.

And destroy them?

No . . . not destroy. Never destroy. Magic itself would end. Your species would be left stranded, desolate. The Gates would go dark, and travel between them impossible. That would be apocalyptic for your society. Almost as bad as the fraying . . .

Of course that would be one of the effects of ending magic, besides countless others. It was not something the Oracle of Binding had mentioned, nor something that had even crossed his mind. If that was going to happen, then why would he *ever* destroy the Orbs?

Everything was even *more* confusing now.

Magic need not end, Chosen. It must *not end. It has always been, just as it always must be. The Starsea Cycle can end, and you need not carry the burden of the Orbs. Not forever. Return the Orbs to the Manifold. To me. That is all I require of you.*

Lucian didn't bother mentioning that "all" the Voice of the Manifold required was a practical impossibility.

You want me to give you the Orbs, and that will stop the fraying?

Yes. It will stop the Time of Madness. I can use their power to keep the fraying at bay. I can repair myself. Make myself work again.

Why me? Why not someone powerful, like Vera?

There was a moment of silence. *It is not her part to play. She has her role. But not as Chosen. And you were the more likely . . . candidate.*

What was that supposed to mean? *I have so many questions. I need help. I can't do this by myself.*

You will have help. Just get the Orb of Psionics, by whatever means possible. Trust in the plan.

The plan? What plan?

Follow your purpose, and everything will be as it was meant. You are Chosen, Lucian. It is your destiny. You will become the most powerful mage in the galaxy, mastering magic even the Ancients believed impossible. You will bend the Worlds to your will. Even now, you can listen to the Heart of Creation and hear my Voice. If that is not evidence, what is?

Where does the Sorceress-Queen fit into all this?

You must let her help you.

That's it? Is she going to kill me, or not?

I've told you all you need to know. Trust in the plan.

He wanted to scream in frustration. *You enjoy this, don't you? You're like some capricious god torturing a mortal. How do I shut this off? I won't have it anymore!*

The Manifold is everywhere, Chosen. And the ether follows you, like mass to a star. Wherever you go, I can follow. The ether wants to be used. The more Orbs you gather, the clearer my Voice will become. You are a Vigilant of Starsea. My Chosen.

I want to find all the Orbs and stop the fraying. Nothing more or less.

Then do as I've said, and your wish will be granted.

Lucian knew he was missing something, that this Voice of the Manifold was only telling him what he needed to hear. But all the important details, the motivations, were lacking. He was nothing more than a pawn in a game larger than his imagining.

And if I don't?

Then the Madness will take you, and your species will be ground to dust. And the Starsea Cycle will have added to its graveyard of races.

At that moment, the dream ended, and Lucian awoke.

41

THE NEXT MORNING, Cleon was woozy, but coherent. The four of them were quiet as they got ready. Lucian felt gloomy, not wanting to talk about his dream. The last thing the others needed was more bad news.

They dressed in travel clothes far richer than anything Lucian had worn in his life, aside from the outrageous ensemble from last night. He wore a loose button-down travel shirt with plenty of pockets that came with a similar jacket, sturdy pants cinched with a fine leather belt, and supple boots that fit him perfectly. On the belt, there was even a holster for his spear, large enough to hold his weapon in the retracted position.

The others dressed in similar attire, grumbling about needing to depend on the Queen even for clothing, but what they had worn before was so dirty and grimy that it was beyond repair. They packed a few other articles as well, not knowing how long the trip would take.

The servants delivered breakfast, rice porridge in a savory red sauce spiced with the native caro pepper. The mood was somber, and for that Lucian wasn't surprised. It seemed they were stuck in the Sorceress-Queen's web with no possible escape.

Hardly anything was said as Jarvis led the four of them to the airship. They were given their own cabins, a rare luxury on a ship that easily crewed two hundred people. Just around the corner from their berths was the Sorceress-Queen's own private quarters, not twenty steps away. It was hard to tell if that was supposed to be an honor, or so she could keep an eye on them.

Also traveling with them was Mage-Lord Kiani, the Butcher of the Westlands, who was staying in the cabin adjacent to the Queen's. How the Queen expected peace with both him and Cleon aboard her ship, Lucian couldn't guess. In truth, he was more preoccupied with the dream he'd had last night. He'd tell the others eventually, but for now, he just didn't have the heart. He was deflated, and at this point, it seemed there was little they could do to regain control of their mission.

Thankfully, the Sorceress-Queen didn't wish to see any of them – at least, not immediately. There was nothing left but to wander the deck and watch the passage through the Pass of Madness, into the Westlands and Psyche's Planetside.

The *Zephyr* cast off just when the golden morning sun alighted upon the Golden Vale, rising above the eastern mountains. The wind was cool and fresh as they ascended over Dara, its streets thrumming with life despite the early hour. The ship veered west, rising higher and higher. Lucian craned his neck, but even so, the peaks of the spindly Mountains of Madness were lost to the haze of blue sky. He marveled that even on a clear day, he *still* couldn't see their tops. Their slopes were brown and bare, seeming to hold little, if any, life except for the terrace farms above the city.

The pass itself, nothing more than a wide, square tunnel – seemed to be located several kilometers above the valley floor. As the *Zephyr* approached, Lucian could see dim daylight at the end. Due to the height of those mountains, their shadows would keep the other side in twilight until at least the afternoon, the shadow extending far beyond the horizon. Below, he could see a narrow road cut into the mountainside, leading from the city to the pass. There were so many switchbacks that it would take an entire day to ascend, if not longer. Various towers and small villages straddled its length, villages he supposed survived off the trade that passed through the mountains.

The *Zephyr's* shadow fell upon the mountainside. The Binders at the bow tethered the mighty vessel until it was swallowed by the tunnel. Now inside, it was much larger than Lucian had initially thought. The *Zephyr* had plenty of space to maneuver, and below, Lucian could see a sizeable town had been built on the pass's floor. A long wall of rock bisected the tunnel east to west. It seemed the town was guarding that wall, defending the Golden Vale from the Westlands. Was there something on the other side that was so dangerous?

Serah stood next to him, watching the passage with awe. "I never thought I'd see Planetside. They say it's a wasteland, full of terrible monsters and the roughest people on all Psyche."

Planetside. Lucian remembered the gas giant Cupid could only be seen from one side of Psyche, since the moon was tidally locked. And because of the extra light supplied by Cupid, along with its tidal forces, Planetside was said to be much warmer than Voidside. But Lucian supposed he would be seeing for himself soon enough.

It didn't take long for the *Zephyr* to pass through. Lucian's breath caught at the sheer change of scenery. Beyond the Mountains of Madness stretched a shadowed, barren wasteland. Rugged hills empty of vegetation stretched as far as the eye could see, broken only by a wide river running from the lower slopes of the mountains from somewhere in the north. For the first time since his arrival on Psyche, the terrain was flat enough for Lucian to notice the nearness of that horizon – and being so high up, it was all the more evident. It felt as if they would fall off the edge of the world.

But just beyond the horizon was what appeared to be a long, white hill.

"What in the Worlds is that?" Lucian asked.

"Don't you know? That's Cupid."

It was huge, dominating the majority of the horizon. And Lucian knew that every day, it would only grow larger until it took up most of the sky. By that point, they would be in the Burning Sands– and close to the Orb of Psionics. Wherever it happened to be in that vast expanse.

A modestly sized city clung to both sides of the wide, brown river they were approaching. The city's buildings were short, squat, and made from mud brick. To the south, the river was lost to the curve of Psyche's horizon, claustrophobically near. Lucian felt a sense of vertigo just looking at it. To the north was terrain even more forlorn, twisted mountains with pointed peaks. The only green was by that river, which Lucian figured to be the lifeblood of the region. Far to the west, he could see nothing but the curved line of the horizon.

The ship dropped lower. Lucian figured the Binders were too high up to find focal points, so they needed to be closer to the ground. Once a few hundred meters above the dusty land, the airship leveled out and was pulled forward. Lucian looked back at the mountains, a veritable wall of rock that closed them in. It was hard not to feel completely separated from everything they'd left behind.

"It's like an entirely different world," he said.

The sudden clanging of spears made Lucian turn. He placed a hand on his own spear and was readying to extend, when he saw it was only Cleon and Fergus sparring on the deck. Apparently, sightseeing wasn't on their list of priorities. The bout drew the eyes of the crew, who didn't exactly pause their duties administering the airship, though they were clearly less attentive to their tasks.

Cleon flurried his spear three times, his face a mask of intent concentration. Fergus danced aside, creating space and not breaking a sweat. Fergus circled around, knocking Cleon's spear aside with ease as he placed the point of his own at the tip of Cleon's scrawny neck.

"Your form is too aggressive," he said. "Your anger makes you goaded by any feint."

"I'm not angry," Cleon spat. "Again!"

Fergus shrugged, and the two men dueled once more. Cleon's form, if anything, was even *more* aggressive, while Fergus's were practiced, almost lazy. His lack of effort only seemed to enrage Cleon further. To Lucian's surprise, Cleon came close to stabbing Fergus a couple of times – although, it was clear that Fergus was allowing Cleon to get that close for some reason or another. Perhaps to enrage him further? Reaching his Focus, he could feel that the tips of their spears were branded with reverse bindings, which would keep them from tearing into flesh at the last moment. Still, it seemed a deadly dance that could end with someone getting unnecessarily hurt, or even killed.

"*Why* are they doing this?" Serah asked.

Cleon gave a shout, going all in with a leaping attack that left his stomach exposed. Fergus easily went for the kill with a quick and efficient stab. Cleon flew, pushed back by the force of the binding, and collapsed to the deck.

"Well done," came a gruff voice. Mage-Lord Kiani had emerged from the belowdecks, his shoulders broad and bronze armor gleaming, despite the lack of sunlight. "Perhaps you might be raised to Mage-Knight under my banner. Sir Fergus has a nice ring to it, no?"

Fergus sheathed his spear, his stern face putting an end to that notion. He did not favor the Mage-Lord with an answer.

Cleon by this point was scrambling up, his spear at the ready. "My challenge stands, Kiani. Your life, or mine."

Lord Kiani guffawed. "Please. After that display, you'd only be *forfeiting* your life. And what would be the fun of that? Besides, I'd rather clear the air with you. Your sister lived a good life, as short as it was. It is a noble cause to bear the seed of a Mage-Lord."

Cleon ground his teeth and charged. Even as Kiani readied his own spear, Lucian sprang into action, reaching for the Orb of Binding without thinking. It obeyed him instantly, maybe due to his decisiveness. He streamed two tethers and drew their weapons into each of his open hands.

Both looked his way. Cleon's chest heaved with anger, while Lord Kiani stared coldly.

"Never stand between a man and his prey, Lucian," Mage-Lord Kiani said. "Or you might find yourself the new target."

Lucian felt a pushing at his Psionic ward, and he instantly increased its strength to match the attack. But it was only a distraction. Lord Kiani attempted to draw his spear back with Binding, though that tug was weak compared to Lucian's own tether. There was no way the Mage-Lord could get the spear back. Not unless Lucian allowed it, or the Orb of Binding failed him.

The Mage-Lord's face reddened as he realized his predicament. Nonetheless, Lord Kiani streamed harder, not wanting to be shown up.

At last, he relented, and a dangerous smile spread across his face. "I guess her Majesty wasn't lying when she said you were the best Binder in the Worlds."

"I wasn't."

All turned to focus on that melodic voice. The queen glided forward, today wearing a violet dress and cape, with a laced bodice with an opening that left little to the imagination.

"Your Majesty," Lord Kiani said, giving a graceful bow. "You honor us with your presence."

"And you are attempting to honor me by . . . killing each other? How manly."

Lord Kiani gave an embarrassed cough. "Err . . . no, your Majesty. Merely practicing our forms. Rifters against Darans, as it were."

"Indeed?" Her droll voice told Lucian that she doubted that very much. "Well, if you were truly practicing, don't stop on my account."

Lord Kiani cleared his throat, turning back to face Cleon and arching an eyebrow.

"I think I'm spent," Cleon said. "I'm not your dancing monkey." At the Queen's intense stare, Cleon added sarcastically, "Your Majesty."

"What about you?" she asked, looking at Lucian. "Were you a part of this impromptu tournament? It wasn't a bad idea. In fact, it could be quite diverting."

"I wasn't, your Majesty." Lucian said. He didn't like acknowledging her as Queen, but Cleon had done it. If Cleon could play along, then so could he. Then again, his tone communicated in no terms was he going to put on a show for her. And from the Queen's icy stare, she fully got the message.

"Very well," the Queen said, all but giving an exasperated sigh.

She left them there, her face pale as she retreated belowdecks.

Once she was gone, Serah whistled. "Damn. The balls on you."

"That was a mistake, wasn't it?"

"You bet your ass it was."

Lucian sighed. "Well, she doesn't deserve any better. A *tournament*? Has she lost her mind?"

"That rejection was almost enough for me to feel bad for her," Serah said. "Almost."

She and Lucian were no longer the focus of attention. Instead, most were on the starboard side of the *Zephyr*, looking north across the cracked badlands at a brown mountain range to the north. A great dust was rising at the foot of those mountains.

Lucian ran to that side, placing his hands on the railing with Serah right behind him. The wind was blowing harder now, enough for the wooden hull to creak under the increased force.

"What is that?" Lucian asked.

"That would be our doom if we don't shift course," Cleon said, coming to join them. "Not much for the Binders to grab onto out here."

Another five minutes passed, and the wind had picked up even more, enough to make the great hull of the *Zephyr* sway uncomfortably. Lucian had trouble keeping his feet, and the turbulence almost made him feel like he was trying to water-walk. Particles of sand stung his face, though the bulk of the storm was minutes away. As insane as the thought was, he wondered if the Sorceress-Queen had conjured this storm because he had pissed her off.

"Doesn't look good," Serah said. "The ship needs to find shelter, and fast."

The crew was scurrying about, following the orders barked by Captain Rawley. The sails, which were usually furled, were let loose and they filled with wind from the north. The ship veered south, but Lucian knew there was no way they could escape the storm entirely.

"Better get belowdecks," Serah said. "Won't take much of a gust to send you flying."

Lucian imagined she was right. Before he took shelter, he noticed many of the sailors were donning metal boots, which he imagined would help them remain rooted in place, though it greatly slowed their movement on the deck. By now, though, most were in position to brace for impact.

Lucian watched the oncoming storm one last time, no more than a hundred meters distant. It was advancing *fast*. He and Serah ducked belowdecks, the last of the non-sailors, right before the wall of wind pummeled the *Zephyr's* starboard side.

42

LUCIAN LOST his footing and flew into the air, crashing against the wooden wall. He was tossed about the heaving corridor, only to be thrown down a staircase leading to the crew cabins.

Lucian found his feet, finding himself alone in darkness. He streamed a light sphere, the aura pushing back the shadows.

"Serah?"

His voice was barely audible above the din of wind outside. Shouts emanated from belowdecks as the ship heaved to and fro. The deck was angled, as if the ship were going down sideways.

He had to find Serah and the others. If this ship was crashing, then they needed to save themselves.

He clawed his way up the deck, tethering himself to a door frame at the top of the stairs. Lucian surged forward, just in time to see the double doors of the Queen's cabin burst open with Psionic force. The Queen herself emerged, staying rooted to the deck with a Gravitonic stream. She cast him a short glance before climbing the stairs and going out into the storm. What in the Worlds was she doing?

Lucian followed, but not easily. He tethered himself toward the exit. Peering down the dark corridor, he saw no signs of Serah. Could she have taken shelter in one of the cabins?

The ship heaved yet again. This time, however, the deck was leveled out rather than pitching downward.

Lucian pushed his way toward the deck, thinking Serah might have come out this way. When he pulled himself outside, there was no crosswind, no blinding sand. That sand instead fell like gentle rain, with nothing but Psyche's light gravity pulling it down. The ship was surrounded by a violet, protective shield, outside which the storm still raged. And at the center of the deck, with her feet rooted to the surface with Gravitonic Magic, stood the Sorceress-Queen with her arms outspread, her entire form bathed in violet light. Her posture was one of defiance, of power.

All the crewmen watched in awe, and it wasn't a moment later that Serah stumbled out from the forecastle, joining Lucian at his side.

The *Zephyr,* now on an even keel, descended toward a high mesa, which the captain probably meant to use as protection from the wind. Was the Queen powerful enough to hold the shield that long?

It wasn't even a question. The shield held over the next two minutes as the ship took shelter behind the rock formation. The Binders kept the ship steady long enough for the crew to lower the anchor. The deck became a hive of activity, the crew working to resecure the lines and furl the sails. Even back here, there was still enough wind to push the *Zephyr* back into the storm sweeping around the mesa's sides.

Only once all was secured, the Queen released her stream. There was no sign of stress on her face. The crew watched in awe, even as the wind whipped across the deck. The lee of the mesa was not a perfect shelter, but it was enough to ride out the storm.

Her eyes went to Lucian before she returned belowdecks.

"Rotting hell," Serah breathed.

He knew why she'd said it. Attacking the Queen, at least directly, simply wasn't an option. For the first time, they had seen her power. How could a mage be so powerful without the benefit of an Orb?

Serah joined him at the bow, and the two stood silently for a while. The *Zephyr* stayed behind the mesa for hours, enough for the afternoon sun to rise across the Mountains of Madness. When the dust settled, Lucian looked toward the west, noting the outline of Cupid taking up the entirety of the horizon.

"We could have never crossed this on our own," Lucian said.

"It would have been a challenge for sure. I wonder what happens if we go through all this fuss only to find Arian's prophecy was a lie, or that there *is* no Orb of Psionics."

"It's getting closer," Lucian said. "I can feel it."

She looked at him. "You really think you can find it, don't you?"

"I can't think of anything else I have besides this mission."

"Really?" she asked, amused. "You can't think of *one* other thing you might have? Or even *could* have?"

What was she getting at? "Be serious. You know what I mean."

"You never struck me as the noble type. Being the Chosen. Finding all the Orbs, all that rot."

"It's not rot. If it is, then I've wasted everyone's time."

She shook her head. "And why should it be *your* burden? Why don't you take that nice Orb you have and retire? Find a nice girl and all that."

Lucian saw immediately where she was going with that. And the way she was looking at him made him unsure of how to answer. The feeling wasn't unwelcome, but it did make him feel conflicted.

"Only one minor kink in that plan," Lucian said. "How long can that nice life last if all of us are dead in ten years? It might take longer, or not. But too much weird shit has happened for me to deny it now. Until I'm proven otherwise, this is what I need to do. Besides, I can't retire. Psyche isn't home. It's too—"

"Uninteresting?"

"No, definitely not. How are *you* able to live here? No offense, but it's pretty rough, with all the wyverns, slavery, mad queens, and whatnot."

Her blue eyes became distant. "Perhaps because it's the only thing I've ever known. But even to my eyes, there's beauty beyond the ugliness. There always is if you look for it."

"This world has its moments," Lucian admitted.

"Life is short on Psyche," Serah said. "Especially for people like me. We have to do all our living in a short amount of time. There's no time for frills, rot, or batshit."

She lowered her eyes, then laid her head on his shoulder. He felt himself soften to her touch and pulled her closer to him. It was nice to have someone. To be wanted.

He'd missed that feeling.

"Is this okay?" she asked.

Lucian nodded. "More than okay. I'm just . . . no good at these things."

"What things? Vulnerability?" He could hear the smile in her voice. "I hadn't noticed."

"Well, you certainly don't make it easy. It just feels like you're waiting to take a shot every time I . . ."

She looked at him. "Every time you what?"

"Every time I want to tell you how I'm feeling."

"Oh? And how is that?"

"See? There you go again."

"It's a real question."

"I never know with you. One minute it feels like you see me that way, and other times, it just feels like you're poking at me."

"Poor Lucian," Serah said. "You know what flirting is, right?"

He couldn't help but laugh at that. "I guess I'm just too serious."

She put a finger on his chest. "Yes. You are very much that. You are perfectly dark and brooding. I mean, it has its charms, but it's only interesting for so long, you know? I much prefer laughter, smiles, and rainbows. Life's too short to brood."

"Is that so? Well, maybe you need someone broody to balance you out."

"Hmm. I hadn't considered that."

They watched the westering sun as it sunk behind Cupid's rim. That light emblazoned the planet a fiery orange, making it seem as if the gas giant were a sun melting into the desert.

"In the spirit of honesty and not taking shots at each other," Serah said, "I should tell you the real reason I haven't left yet."

He couldn't help but watch her, the way the wind tugged at her hair, her blue eyes reflecting this alien sun.

"I'm not one for causes, quests, and saving the human race. I just do what I feel like doing. Always have, always will. That's who I am. We probably only have a few days of life left. I'd . . . like it if you were there for me for these last days. For once, it would be nice to not have to worry."

Lucian's throat clamped up. "Worry about what?"

"Being afraid."

Lucian couldn't deny that he wanted that, too. Serah was strong, brave, fiercely beautiful. That should have been answer enough for him. But he kept thinking of Emma. He knew there was no chance he'd ever see her again, and they had never truly been together, anyway. He had experienced more with Serah in a few short days than in months with Emma. So why did he feel so torn, especially when he *was* likely to die in the next few days? He hated how confusing things were.

"It's fine," Serah said, deflated. "There's . . . someone else, isn't there?"

How had she read him so well? "We were never really together. We both wanted that, but at the Academy, that's forbidden. She's just someone who was there for me during a hard time." He smiled. "Sort of like you."

"You wish it could have been something, though."

Lucian had to nod. There was no point in lying about it. "Of course I do."

She closed her eyes for a moment. "I'm sorry. There's hardly been any time to process anything. For any of us."

"And how are you holding up?"

Her eyes widened, as if surprised he'd asked that. "Usually, no one cares about a fray. They just want us to go off and die alone."

"That's what happened to me when they sent me here. As far as I'm concerned, you and I are one and the same."

She watched him for a moment, guarded. "Well, if you really mean it, where to start? Everything in my world is spinning. It feels like when we were falling into the Darkrift. I thought we were going to die. But then I held onto you, and I was . . . okay." Her cheeks flushed. "I don't know. I'm not good at all these rotting words, either. I feel like an idiot. Maybe that's why I like to take shots. It's easier. What I'm used to." She sighed. "I don't know. What do you think?"

"I think you're being too hard on yourself. And . . . it would be nice to have you there for me, too. It would certainly make the next few days easier to get through."

"What about my skin? It's only going to get worse, until I look like those people in the Darkrift."

He reached down and touched the wound. Her eyes widened, and he was afraid that he had crossed some sort of line, or that it might even hurt her. But she kept her arm still and let him touch her. It felt no different from any other skin.

"Does it hurt?"

She shook her head. "No."

"It doesn't feel any different. It just looks different on the outside."

"It's ugly, though."

"It's the best thing about you."

She gave a short laugh. "Wow. I must be really ugly, then."

"You're definitely not that. You're beautiful, strong, honest—"

"Then what are you waiting for, Lucian Abrantes?"

He pulled her face close, and her lips melted into his. This was his first chance to slow down in ages, to embrace feelings buried by responsibility. His heart pounded as he gave himself to the moment, as she responded in kind. Why couldn't they have something more? Something to give them the strength to face everything in the coming days? There were no naysayers, no Transcends or Talents looking over his shoulder. It was just him, her, and what they wanted.

When they parted, he was grateful for the mast blocking them from view, but that was no guarantee of privacy. They were on the Queen's airship, after all, and she would almost certainly not look favorably on this.

"What was that look in your eyes just now?" Serah asked. "I don't like it."

"I don't either. It's just . . ." He didn't have to finish his sentence.

"Rot that bitch," Serah said. "She doesn't own you. Don't you want to *prove* that?"

"What do you mean?"

She smiled and pulled him across the deck, mischief glinting in her eyes.

"Serah, what are you doing?"

"Oh, you'll see in a minute."

Lucian knew instantly what she meant. Part of him wanted

to protest, but who was he kidding? He wanted it, and needed it. And for Serah's part, well, she was doing exactly as she'd said. She did what felt right to her in the moment. She might feel differently tomorrow, or the next day, but for now, he was content to be caught up in her storm.

The truth was it felt good to be pushed by something else other than destiny for once. To be human instead of Chosen.

———

THEY HAD FALLEN ASLEEP EMBRACING. For the first time in months, maybe in years, Lucian allowed himself to relax. All the sensations he had forgotten, all the reasons life was worth living, he'd experienced anew. He watched her back, which bore scars from he knew not where, as the last of the golden sunlight set below the window. He watched as she slept, her breaths even and calm. He wanted her to sleep like that as long as she needed, to experience peace and forget fear, at least for another moment.

But it was not to be. She suddenly thrashed in her sleep, her body twisting and throat whimpering. When her eyes opened, they were wide and fearful. Her chest rose and fell madly, and she only calmed when he held her close. She buried her face in his chest, where she nestled warm and soft.

"Bad dream?"

She nodded against him. "You're not the only one having nightmares."

"What happened?"

"I'd . . . rather not say. Nightmares are common with frays, but mine have been getting darker lately. I try to forget them. What else can I do?"

He held her closer. "I'm here for you."

She parted from him, then wiped her eyes. "I'll manage. I always have." She looked out the window, noting the evening light. "We should probably get back out there. We're probably missed."

"I don't want to go back out there. That's the real world, and the real world sucks."

She smiled. "All right. Not that I needed much convincing." Her face suddenly became dark and contemplative, like a cloud passing over the sun.

"Another bad thought?"

She sighed. "Nothing we can fix. I was just thinking that whatever's behind magic is not a good thing. Just look at what's happening to me." She looked down at her arm. "It's larger, now. Twice as big as when we met a few days ago."

Lucian felt guilty about that. If she'd never met him, that likely wouldn't have been the case. "Well, if the dream I had last night is to be believed, something about magic is broken. Maybe we can fix it. At least, I hope so. That's the whole reason we're doing this, right?"

Serah was quiet again. His heart ached that she seemed to be going back to that dark place. He waited for her to speak.

"I don't have long. I've been using too much magic. I never meant to come this far, but it seems my fate is tied with yours. Whether I want that or not."

It felt as if he were a tornado, and every person he came in contact with got sucked into his schemes and struggles, whether they wanted it or not. Is that what it meant to be Chosen? Was the gravity of his destiny too great for anyone to escape?

"It's not over yet," he said, taking her hands. "Not until we say it is."

"How?" she asked. "How is it not?"

"I'll find a way. We can get off Psyche. We can find the Orbs, stop the fraying. You'll be saved, then."

She looked out the window. "How likely is that to happen?"

"Who knows? We might find a way we didn't see before. We've got to try, right? We're in this together, now."

She gave a small smile. "I was wrong about you being just broody. You're a broody optimist if there is such a thing." She heaved a sigh. "All this about saving humanity. Well to be honest, humanity can rot for all I care. What has humanity ever shown me besides the *lack* of it?"

She had a good point. Lucian found he didn't have a response to counteract it – not that he was looking for one.

"To hell with what other people think. I'm here because it feels like the right thing to do, even if I don't understand everything. But this has grown to be so much more than I thought. I can't make sense of anything anymore. And worse . . ."

Above came the creaks of footfalls on wooden planks and shouted orders. The ship was getting ready to depart.

Serah broke away from him and Lucian watched her dress. She went to the small vanity in the corner and straightened her long, honey-blonde hair.

Lucian took that as his cue, dressing himself and straightening his own appearance.

She took his hands and looked at him seriously. "Look. I like you and all, and I hope you don't take this the wrong way. But . . . I'm happy with things staying the way they are."

"You mean, the way they were before we committed these unspeakable acts?"

She didn't smile. "Come on, be serious. Not to say we can't do this again. It was . . . nice." She watched him closely. "I don't know. I just don't want you to think it was something more than it was."

"What was it to you?"

She bit her lip nervously. "Um . . . two friends comforting each other during a dark moment? Can we agree on that?"

"Yeah. I mean, sure."

"Sorry. I'm shit at explaining things. Let's put it this way. Yes, it meant something, yes, it was good, and yes, I like you. Just . . . don't get all lovey dovey on me, okay?"

Lucian laughed. "Is *that* what you're worried about? Putting labels on things?"

"Maybe? I don't know. Let's just let this be what it is. We already have enough going on without feelings to complicate it."

"Well, I agree."

She blinked. "Oh. Well, that was simple." She let out a sigh of relief. "As long as we're on the same page as far as that, I think we can put this awkward conversation to bed."

She opened the door slowly and peered both ways down the corridor. She nodded, the signal that the coast was clear.

Just before he slid into the dark corridor, she grabbed his arm with surprising strength and pulled him in for a final kiss.

"Remember. This never happened."

He winked. "What happened?"

She patted him on the chest. "Good boy. Now get out of here."

With a final slap on the rump, she sent him on his way.

43

THANKFULLY, the days passed without incident. It was hard to pretend things were normal with Serah, but it seemed no one was the wiser to what had happened. She was incredibly good at pretending, which made Lucian think the whole thing really *did* mean nothing to her. He wasn't sure how he felt about that. Despite their conversation, he needed more clarification on where they stood. He'd been hoping it'd meant at least *something*, but from her behavior, it seemed it really was just comfort for a single night and nothing more. Because of their previous conversation, he didn't want to bring anything up. That would just make things weirder.

In the end, though, he figured Serah was right. It was something they both needed at the time, and they had bigger things to worry about than feelings, although Lucian had to admit feelings had a certain way of gumming up the works, sliding into every nook and crevice of thought and action.

So, he did his best to put it out of his mind, even if it was difficult.

What few times Lucian saw the Queen was for training. She treated him no differently than before, evidence that perhaps she didn't have a spy following him around everywhere. That was, she treated him as a teacher who was somewhat annoyed at her student's lack of progress. From her, he learned more about wards and brands, and how to combine different Aspects for different effects. He got more education in the few days' journey across Psyche's Westlands than he had in months at the Academy – perhaps because with the Sorceress-Queen, no knowledge was forbidden. He could ask whatever he wanted, and she would show him how to do it.

As time went on, he became even more convinced she actually *did* believe in her prophecy about him being the Chosen. Why else go through all this trouble? That left Lucian in a bind, too, because it naturally meant she might be right about things. What if he really *did* have to work with her, for years on end, for the Orbs to work? What if he had to become the kind of person that could stand to work with her, to have no qualms about ruling a stratified society with slavery?

Either now or in the future, there would be conflict with the Sorceress-Queen. And he was nowhere near ready for that.

With Fergus, he trained his spear work, while Cleon showed him some tricks with Thermal Magic. He showed Lucian how to stream fireballs, both stationary and moving. Stationary fireballs were no different than branded sphere light – it was just heat with some Gravitonic Magic to hold its shape. The trick to get it moving was a flash of Binding, or alternately, a second Gravitonic stream, though that method was less common. Cleon also showed him how to make ice spikes, which can be shot like projectiles using the same principle.

And Cleon also taught Lucian something he always wanted to learn: creating a Psionic brand powerful enough to cut off a mage's magic at their source.

"It's not easy," Cleon said. "It involves creating a brand around another mage's Focus, and trust me, *no* mage in their right mind will let you do that if they know how to defend against it. And almost every mage will be expecting you to try if they know you're gifted at Psionic Magic."

"So, how is it done?"

"Two ways," Cleon said. "You can do it sneakily, or you can do it with sheer power. But the problem is, it takes so much magic to do it right that if you fail, you'll be left weak and at the mercy of the other mage, who can just come right back at you and surround *your* Focus with a Psionic brand."

"Makes sense," Lucian said. So basically, he could kiss his prospects of cutting off the Sorceress-Queen goodbye.

"You need at least a dualstream, as with any brand," Cleon said. "Ideally a tristream if the mage you happen to be branding has a particular gifting for Psionic Magic."

Both of them looked at each other, knowing full well who they were talking about.

"The streaming of a Psionic brand is similar to that of a Psionic ward. But since you're streaming it around another mage's Focus, it will take much more magic. And the more powerful the Focus of the mage you're dealing with, the more powerful the magic. Any Focus outside your own repels the magic of another mage if it gets too close, if that makes sense. So, the brand has to hold together strong, even considering that repelling force."

It sounded complicated. "Okay. When can we practice?"

"Now, if you want. It's all for a good cause, right?"

Cleon was right; it *did* take a lot of magic. Lucian could only make three or so attempts before being completely spent of his naturally accrued ether. He chose to create his brand with Psionic and Binding Magic, and even if his Binding Magic was unlimited, it was still draining.

Lucian practiced with Cleon every chance he got. He wanted to be ready for anything, to know how to do something to another mage that had made him feel so powerless.

The days passed like that – watching, waiting, and training.

The *Zephyr* sailed farther west, across bone-dry mountains, lakes of lava, and sharp peaks more akin to spikes than mountains. If there was a literal hell, this was probably pretty close to it. The air was sweltering, even at the high altitude. On the surface, it must have been an unbearable oven. The white giant of Cupid loomed above, its baleful crimson eye increasingly dominating the pale blue sky. Even night was no relief from its gaze, as the planet's light kept the fiery land in half-twilight.

And then one day, the mountains and lava flows ended, and what lay before them was a vast desert of shifting dunes riven with cracks. It stretched for hundreds of kilometers, north, south, east, and west, a seemingly endless expanse.

On the fourth day, with the white giant of Cupid dominating the sky above, the Sorceress-Queen summoned Lucian to her stateroom. When the doors were opened for him, she stood looking out the glass windows. She wore a glimmering dress set with pearls that almost blended with her creamy skin. Her violet eyes seemed to peer deep into Lucian's thoughts.

"Stand beside me," she instructed. "There is much we have to speak of."

There was nothing but to humor her. He stood at her side, looking out the window at the passing desert below. Those red dunes, some almost as tall as mountains, stretched toward the far eastern horizon.

"Something we must address," she said. "As a man, I understand you have certain . . . needs. I also understand if you need to act upon them. But you must never let it become more than that. Your destiny is greater, and you must always be mindful of that destiny. Your focus should always be the Orbs; all else is secondary. You are the Chosen, and there are few women who will be a match for you in strength."

Lucian kept his face forward, and when he answered, he did his best to keep his voice controlled. "That's not for you to decide. And whatever I do on my own time is not your business."

"There, we beg to differ. Too much is at stake, Lucian. I've a mind to forbid you from such future . . . meetings. They are a distraction."

He wanted to defend himself, but it would be a waste of breath. Better to change the subject entirely. "Is this all you wanted to talk about?"

Her eyes refocused on the expanse of dunes before him. "Tell me. Do you feel anything?"

"What do you mean?"

"We should be close to the Orb, now, and this is the first time I've been this far into the Burning Sands without being forced to turn back due to a storm. An auspicious sign. Access your Focus, Lucian. Feel what you can."

"As you wish."

He held his Focus, and the image of the Septagon formed clearly in his mind. He reached out, trying to feel . . . *something* out there in the sands.

He shook his head. "Nothing."

Her gaze went above, to the planet and its malevolent red storm. "At any moment, we will be directly under the planet's eye. The planet's eye shifts over time. It's a tempest, after all, prone to movement. That means the Orb could be anywhere in these deep sands, really, so I'm waiting for some sort of sign that we're close." She faced him. "How is it you found the Orb of Binding?"

"I stumbled upon it," he said.

"You . . . stumbled upon it?" Her expression registered disbelief. "This mighty artifact of Starsea Empire, that hundreds of mages have sought with great patience and study, including Xara Mallis herself, and you just . . . *stumbled* upon it?"

Lucian cleared his throat. "That's right."

She shook her head and gave a light laugh. "What a joke. Let's hope that your luck still holds, even on Psyche."

There was a knock at the door. The Sorceress-Queen's delicate brows lowered in annoyance. "Yes?"

The door opened, revealing the broad-shouldered Captain Rawley, who gave a slight bow. "We are directly underneath the eye, your Majesty."

"So soon?" At the Captain's nod, she sighed. "Very well. Drop anchor. Prepare the away team. I intend to go down myself, along with Lucian and his companions."

"Your Majesty, the sands today are treacherous. Perhaps it would be better if you remained here, where it's safe."

"You *dare* question me? Begone, Captain. I'm *not* to be trifled with today."

He bowed so quickly that Lucian thought he'd keel over. "Yes, of course. At once, your Majesty."

He shut the door softly while the Queen rolled her eyes and sighed. "Imbecile."

Within the minute, the ship began lowering over the sands beneath. The landscape was warbled through the undulating heat waves. It looked like hell and a half down there.

And this was where he was going. There was nothing but to be mentally prepared for it, if such a thing was even possible.

———

THE SURFACE WAS like standing in an oven. Lucian had no real way to tell the temperature, but it was certainly far hotter than anywhere on the surface of Earth. It was so hot that the Queen's Thermalists were forced to combine streams to create a ward powerful enough to protect the party of thirty or so mages.

The surrounding ward shimmered red with radiated heat. It only served to cool the air somewhat. And of course, it would do nothing to steady their footing in the loosely-packed sand.

"Reach for your Focus," the Queen told Lucian. Her face seemed to not feel the heat, not to break in a sweat at the slightest. Not even this harsh terrain could steal her dignity. "The Eye of Cupid is directly above us. I would see prophecy fulfilled before the day is out."

Well, she was going to be sorely disappointed. Lucian really had no other choice. He reached for his Focus, expanding its reach until it encompassed the surrounding environment.

"Anything at all?" the Queen asked.

He shook his head. "I'm afraid not."

"Are you certain?"

"Yes," Lucian said, with forced patience.

She huffed, as if she didn't believe him. "Well, let us at least scale this dune in front of us. We may see something from the top."

As good as her word, the party climbed the dune ahead, a veritable mountain of sand. Everyone walked, but the Queen used a moving gravity disc to speed her ascent, while the two Gravitists in the party did so as well, the capes attached to their gray robes streaming behind. Well, let them. Lucian wasn't going to waste his ether on frivolities.

It took half an hour, but he made it up with the rest of the party, huffing and puffing. Despite the lowered gravity of Psyche, the dune was high, and the sands beneath his boots treacherous.

He turned in a wide circle, scanning everything in sight. Just dune, dune, and more dune, all with that same reddish tinge that was only amplified by the Thermal ward. Everyone was looking at him, only adding to the pressure.

"It all looks the same," he said. "It all *feels* the same."

"I did not come here for excuses," the Sorceress-Queen said. "The Orb is out here. Somewhere. It's your job to find it."

"Perhaps it is buried," Lord Kiani said, wiping his brow with a kerchief. "It's said the Burning Sands are as deep as any ocean in the Worlds."

Cleon stared at him balefully but did not say anything.

"If that is so," the Queen of Psyche said, "perhaps it's time we started digging."

Everyone looked at her as if she were insane, but her eyes held steely determination. "Psionics, to me!"

At once, four violet-robed mages approached her.

"That depression over there," she said. "Blast it."

"At once, your Majesty," the eldest of the four said. He nodded to the other three, and as one, faced the depression between the dunes on the opposite side from which they came.

"On my mark," the lead Psionic said, raising his palms outward. "Combine streams with me."

After a moment, their hands became wrapped in violet light. The sands shook, causing several to lose their footing, including Fergus. A massive hole formed between the dunes, into which the surrounding sand immediately tumbled. It was useless. Whatever sand was excavated would only be buried a moment later. The Psionics increased the power of their combined stream, causing the base of the surrounding dunes to crumble ... including the one they were standing on.

Some glanced her way nervously, but the Sorceress-Queen showed no signs of giving up. Her violet eyes shone with dangerous slight.

"Everyone at once! I don't care what your primary is, I don't care how long it takes, I don't care if it frays you. Stream!"

Tentatively, the other mages joined in. The original four Psionics' arms were tremoring with the effort, awash in violet light. But as more power was added, more magic, the hole at last was widening faster than it could be buried. Lucian wondered whether he should join in, but none of his friends were streaming, nor had the Queen asked him to, so he just watched. He couldn't help but watch the cliff racing up the side of the dune they were standing on. If the mages kept this up, *they* would be the ones falling in that hole.

Lucian was about to shout for the Queen to stop this madness when she held up her own hand. "Stop. Stop at once!"

Instantly, every mage cut off their streams, panting as if they'd just sprinted a marathon on a high-G world. The cliff advanced up the dune, only slowing once it was halfway up. The dune rumbled once, then twice, before growing still. Lucian readied the Orb of Binding, just in case he needed to pull he and his friends to safety. He looked at Serah, who watched him worriedly.

But the dune stood steady. There was a moment of disbelief, and then nervous chuckles, as the surrounding mages realized they were safe. The heat shield, which had fallen during the collective streaming, was reraised, and the heat of the Burning Sands was defrayed.

"Rot it all," the Queen said, fuming. "Where is that Orb? I will have it!"

Lucian looked at her. "*You* will have it?"

"It's here, Lucian. Do you truly not want to find it?"

"And how am I supposed to do that? The Orb of Binding revealed itself to me. Maybe the Orb of Psionics doesn't feel the same way."

Or maybe it wasn't here at all. But Lucian kept that thought to himself. If she ever believed that, then she might actually kill him.

"Confound it all," she said.

One of the men beside her collapsed, eyes closed.

"What's wrong with him?" she demanded of Lord Kiani.

"He likely overdrew. And combined with the heat . . ."

She shook her head as her angry violet eyes turned on Lucian. "*You*. Are you trying to make me look like a fool? You know where it is. Show me!"

"I know as little as you," Lucian said. "What do you expect me to do?"

"I don't know," she said. "Find it? Is that really so difficult? Just . . . do something! You're the Chosen."

"Hey, lady," Serah said. "He said he didn't know where it is. Why don't you just relax?"

The Queen screamed as she swept her hand, and Serah shot backward into the air in the direction of the *Zephyr*. Lucian's heart lurched as he reached for the Orb of Binding. To his relief, he found it readily enough and tethered her. That slowed her speed greatly, and only once she came to a stop, he reset the focal point on himself and drew her toward him.

Once close, he slowed her and pulled her to the ground next to him. Her eyes were wide and her form shaking. The Queen wore an amused smirk on her face. It was all some twisted game for her.

"I will suffer no more insolence. That goes for all of you!"

Serah's face blanched as the Queen once again regarded the depression. By now, it had been completely reburied with sand.

"We'll repeat what we just did," she said. "Only for the depression toward the south, here."

Lord Kiani gave a gracious smile. "Your Grace. If we do that, half our Mage-Knights will be out of commission."

Lucian couldn't help but note his wording. It was as if the mages were machines rather than people, but none dared raise a voice in their own defense.

Her eyes were violet fire, but in the end, she gave a slow nod. "Very well. What would you suggest, Lord Kiani?"

"A two-hour reprieve, at least, to allow ether to regenerate. And to leave the Thermalists out of the next streaming since they need to maintain the ward."

"As sensible as ever," she said. She looked around at the mages, who did not betray a single emotion. Lucian realized these were men and women well-schooled in hiding their true feelings from their sovereign.

"An hour's rest," she said. "No more."

"Or we could wait until night," Cleon said. "That way, we would not need to use the heat shield."

"Fool," she said. "There is no time to lose, and we must continue our work while the weather is fair. And the moon-quakes grow worse at night, so that shows how little you know. Do you know how many times I've come out here only to be turned away by the weather or tectonic shifts?"

"Wait," Lucian said.

The Queen looked at him. "Yes?"

"I noticed this dune looked a bit strange on our way up. It's steeper and taller than the others. That's why we climbed it."

"Your point?"

"There must be something beneath it that's causing it to hold its shape."

"How could a tiny Orb do that?" Lord Kiani asked.

Lucian shook his head. "Not the Orb itself, but maybe the building the Orb is kept in. The Orb of Binding was inside this sort of shrine, and this dune seems about the right size to bury something that size."

The Queen's eyes widened in realization. "Of course. And you're only mentioning this *now*?"

"It just occurred to me. We should return to the ship. Get the ship close enough by air and then stream from there."

The Queen watched, as if suspecting some trick. But in the end, she turned from him and faced the others.

"You heard him. Back to the *Zephyr*." When she turned back, she added, "This had better not be a delaying tactic."

"It's not," he said. "I want to find that Orb just as much as you do."

And probably more. But he kept that to himself. In truth, he didn't know if his theory held water, but it would get them off the ground and give him time to think of what to do.

He was out of ideas. But if he was patient, the right opportunity would come.

He had nothing else.

44

WITHIN THE HOUR, the entire party had returned to the main deck of the *Zephyr*. All had gathered near the bow, where Lucian stood at the fore, just a meter from the bowsprit carved in the likeness of a wyvern's skull.

From the sky, the strange shape of the dune was even more apparent, so much so that Lucian couldn't see how they'd failed to notice it before.

The only question was what came next?

"Can your mages blast that sand away, your Majesty?" he asked the Queen.

The Queen shook her head. "It's too far. That was the reason I wanted us on the surface."

"And we can't pull the ship any closer?"

"Not without risking losing it to shifting sands."

It was as he had feared. It would be on *him* to peel back the sand from this dune. He didn't know if it were possible, and truth be told, he didn't even know if he was right about the Orb of Psionics being down there in the first place. But there was only one way to find out.

He drew a deep breath and assumed his Focus. The Orb of Binding couldn't fail him now. Not if this was truly his destiny.

Once he got the Orb of Psionics, he could figure out the rest later. How to deal with the Queen, how to get off Psyche, where he stood with Serah . . .

"My Queen?"

Captain Rawley approached, pointing a tentative finger north, where the horizon was obscured by a wall of violet-tinged dust and flashing, purple lightning.

"Now, Lucian!" she said. "We don't have much time."

"It's in the south, too!" one of the Mage-Knights shouted.

Lucian took time enough to have a look. The approaching storm wasn't just in the north and south. It was *all around them*, a converging noose from which there would be no escape.

"Well, shit," he said.

"Stop cursing, start streaming!" The Queen ordered.

Lucian nodded and faced the dune again as people began to shout and panic. How was he supposed to get everyone out of this? He realized that he couldn't. All he could do was try to blast that dune away in time.

Assuming his Focus, he reached for the Orb of Binding. Magic streamed. It was a trickle at first, but its intensity picked up as he created an anchor point that covered the *entirety* of the side of the dune. In his deep shell of meditative silence, he barely registered the chaos outside his Focus. He was doing something that should have been impossible, and he had yet to set the focal point toward which all that sand would go.

He did so, streaming a focal point off to the south. At once, a layer of sand at least a meter thick was stripped away, flying toward the dune on their left.

"It's getting closer," Serah said.

"Faster!" the Sorceress-Queen said.

Lucian restreamed, stripping away another layer of sand.

Binding Magic burned through him in a torrent. The first wave of dust was already hitting them, and the surrounding mages put on masks to keep the grit out of their noses and mouths. Lucian streamed again and again, the dune getting smaller as the sand was methodically shifted away. Lucian's mind was fried with the effort. He could feel the Orb pulsing within him, ready to unleash more power. He could actually *see* ether swirling around him, as if his consciousness had partly shifted into the ethereal background. Streams of blue magic, drawn by the Orb, infused into his body, only to be streamed outward toward the dune. His mind was heady with vertigo, and the job was nowhere near finished.

He had to believe this was possible. He had to believe in his reasons. The Orb of Psionics was in there somewhere. And he would unearth it.

Lucian stripped away another layer when a sudden force *pushed* him from the direction of the dune, as well as every person on the ship. Lucian's stream was cut off, his vision blackened. For a moment, he believed himself blind as an unholy roar surrounded the ship. The storm was upon them, but through the darkness was a violet glow in the distance.

"The Orb! Captain Rawley, put us down."

Despite the buffeting winds and shifting sands, the good captain gave the order, shouting above the din of wind. Apparently loyal unto death itself, the crew obeyed. The *Zephyr* dipped down, even as it heaved to and fro due to the deadly, dust-filled wind.

And all the while, the purple radiance that had once been the dune extended outward. It was clearly some sort of ward or shield, but when Lucian reached for it, he found the complexity of the stream confounding. And its rate of expansion only grew faster.

Whatever it was, it would hit them soon.

"It's a kinetic wave," the Queen said, with growing trepidation. "Turn around! Ahead full! Binders, get us out of here!"

"Anchors aweigh!" the Captain shouted. "You heard her Majesty, bring her around!"

But the wave would catch them long before they got moving. And from the Queen's wide eyes, it seemed she realized that, too.

The ship gave a sudden heave, causing the Queen and a good number of Mage-Knights to lose their feet. Lucian just barely managed to remain standing.

As the Queen struggled to rise under the pressure of the maelstrom, he realized that this might be their only chance. In the chaos, the four of them could get off the ship and down to the Orb before the Queen got the same idea. The ship would be lost, anyway. The only concern was getting through that kinetic wave without getting ripped to shreds. With luck, the Sorceress-Queen wouldn't realize what was happening until it was too late, and would go down with the ship.

Masked by the storm, Lucian immediately abandoned his post and searched for his friends. He found Serah first, whose blonde hair was easy to pick out. "Where's Fergus and Cleon?"

"I'm here," Cleon said, stepping forward. "Fergus is more sternward. That blast sent him reeling back pretty far."

"We have to find him and get out of here before the ship goes down."

More screams emanated from the direction of the bow as the roar of the storm only increased in volume. The darkness of the storm, combined with the incredible brightness of that violet light, threatened to overwhelm all. Getting to the Orb before the Queen was no longer the top priority.

Survival was.

"Run!" Lucian shouted.

The three of them ran sternward, finding that they were not the only ones fleeing. Mage-Knights and sailors had abandoned their posts, seeking refuge from the advancing kinetic wave. The ship heaved as the front of the wave reached the bow, splitting timbers as it punctured the helium-filled envelope above them.

"Serah, gravity aura!"

"On it!"

"Fergus!"

He was dead ahead and running toward them. Serah streamed her aura, and instantly, Lucian was light on his fleet, lifting off from the deck below them. Were they going up, or was the ship sinking? It was impossible to tell. But all four of them were together now, clasping to each other and borne by the wind, sharing the aura streamed by Serah. She would not be able to maintain this magic for long, and worse, they would fly right into the disintegrating envelope above unless Lucian found something of sufficient mass to tether themselves toward. But that was impossible to do in a storm where he couldn't see more than five meters ahead of him.

Fergus's eyes shone vibrantly green, and not a moment later, something was shining in the direction of the Orb – what looked like a pillar or a column. It was beyond the kinetic wave, the only visible thing of mass onto which to tether himself and his friends.

Still streaming the Orb of Binding, he tethered the four of them to that pillar, shining like a beacon in the darkness. From before, he knew doing this would require an insane amount of ether. And he knew if the Orb failed to supply it, all of them were as good as dead.

Don't fail me now. I'm either Chosen, or I'm dead. You decide.

As if in answer to those words, magic roared out of him, and every limb shook with that power. Lucian streamed power into all four tethers. Just as Serah's gravity aura dissipated, all four of them rocketed forward, past the falling deck of the *Zephyr* and before the collapsing envelope above could ensnare them.

A rope nicked at Lucian's shoulder, sending him into a spin, but the tether set him straight as he continued on his path forward.

But there was still the expanding kinetic wave. It was mere seconds away.

"Stream with me," he shouted. "Psionic shield!"

As a single unit, they joined his stream, entrusting their Focuses to him. Serah was the first to add her Psionic Magic to Lucian's. Soon after, Fergus and Cleon added their own strength, each of those streams weaker than Serah's. Every little bit of magic would matter.

For the first time in his life, Lucian was controlling four streams from four people. The sheer amount of magic ripping through him made him want to faint with euphoria. *Anything* felt possible. Despite the excruciating inferno beneath his skin, the sheer bliss of that amount of magic made it all worth it. He streamed the shield, directing every bit of ether he could into making it strong enough to withstand the wave. But despite that amount of magic, it might not be enough.

Their shield winked out as soon as contact was made, but that split second was all they needed. Lucian felt faint at having that amount of magic suddenly extinguished, but he refocused and maintained his Binding streams on the pillar. They could still die if he lost his concentration. A fall from this height would kill them just as surely as the kinetic wave.

Lucian had just enough energy to look over his shoulder and see the wave tearing the rest of the *Zephyr* asunder. Men and women were jumping overboard, flying into the air, screaming and dying.

Serah pinched him. "Focus!"

Lucian turned back around. They were almost there. He kept the Binding stream steady. Fergus's eyes were still green, his face strained with the effort of keeping the pillar lit. He had to keep it up long enough for them to make it.

"Almost there," Serah said. "Don't give up."

He felt her hand reach his. It was enough motivation to continue. He couldn't give up on her, nor on Fergus and Cleon. They had followed him across an entire moon on this mad, stupid quest. They deserved to see what lay at the end of it after everything they had gone through.

The storm and dust whipped around them. It was just the four of them floating down in the maelstrom, inching closer and closer toward that spire.

Lucian could feel it, now. The Orb of Psionics thrummed with power, with potential.

And it was waiting.

With the last of his strength, he sped the rate of their descent. Within seconds, they were landing on an ancient floor of stone, which must have been buried under all that sand. Lucian almost wanted to kiss the ground, but he didn't have the strength. His vision was dark at the sides, and it was a struggle to look up, to see an ancient spire stretching at least two hundred meters above them, a building of clearly non-human origin.

Serah and Fergus helped him stand, both of whom had their shockspears at the ready. A tornado of sand surrounded them, swirling with violet Psionic Magic. It surrounded the entirety of the spire, protecting it from the outside. Lucian watched in awe. He felt as if he were in a trance looking at it.

"We can't stop and gawk," Fergus said. "We're here! Let's get the Orb. We don't know if that wave got the Queen. If we reach it first . . ."

A blinding, violet light shimmered from the direction of the Psionic storm. It could only mean one thing. The Queen was coming, and her Psionic Magic was surely strong enough to endure the Psionic wall, just as theirs had been. A blue tether bound itself to the base of the spire just fifty meters away.

"They're coming!" Serah said.

The four of them ran. Lucian tried to reach for the Orb of

Binding again, to undo the focal point set by the Queen, but his mind was so fried that he couldn't even reach for it. And the others were not strong enough in Binding to do so, either.

Their only hope was to outrun the Sorceress-Queen and reach the Orb of Psionics first.

45

THE ENTRANCE of the Spire swallowed them, and within it, they found a massive empty space extending all the way to the top, with a glowing crystalline staircase running up the room's circular perimeter. A purple light shone at the top of those stairs.

The Orb was waiting.

"The three of you go," Fergus said. "I'll guard the entrance."

Was he serious? "What? You'll die!"

"I swore an oath to see you safely to the Orb. Now, Lucian, you must do your part. Use it to end the Queen's reign of terror! Promise me!"

"Fergus—"

"Do it!" he bellowed. "I can hold them off long enough."

Lucian saw that there was no point arguing with him. He ran, and Serah joined him. He glanced over his shoulder to see that Cleon, too, was staying behind.

"I have unfinished business with Kiani," he called. "I have a feeling he's with the Sorceress-Queen now. And two will last twice as long as one."

Fergus nodded gratefully, before both men pointed their spears outward toward the entrance.

These two would be dead long before he and Serah reached the Orb. And now, Lucian had no choice. People were already dying for his cause.

"Run, slow-ass!"

Serah charged ahead, taking the steps two at a time, almost skipping up them in the low gravity. They were running for a couple of minutes before Lucian dared to look down again at the floor, where Cleon and Fergus still stood, spears wreathed in electricity and a Psionic ward deployed.

"If it comes to it," Serah said, between breaths, "I'll have to stay behind, too."

"Stop talking like that," Lucian said. "We'll make it before the fight even begins."

"Can't you tether us up there?"

Lucian reached for the Orb, but his Focus was unresponsive, and he couldn't latch onto anything. It was if everything in this Spire was warded in some way, keeping his Binding stream from attaching. "I can't."

They didn't waste any more breath. They charged up the stairs until they were about halfway to the top. The violet radiance was becoming so bright that Lucian was blinded to the floor below them. The only sounds were their footsteps, the hum of the Orb above, and finally, shouts and the clash of spears and shields below.

So much for getting there before the fighting started.

Not a moment later, Lucian felt ten times heavier. He collapsed to the stairs, like a fly caught in a trap.

"Damn her!" Serah said. "She's strong!"

"Ward it!"

"I'm trying!"

They were reduced to a crawl with two more spirals left to go. It might have been Lucian's imagination, but he thought he could see the Sorceress-Queen circling up the steps far below them, along with several of her Mage-Knights. Of Lord Kiani, there was no sign. Had the fight ended so soon? Or was time simply flying at the speed of light?

"Fergus . . . Cleon . . ." Lucian said. "I'm sorry."

"Stop apologizing, start running!"

Lucian was suddenly light on his feet again. He bounded up the steps, with Serah ahead of him. At least, until she collapsed with a gray gravity amplification disc glowing below her.

Lucian reached her. "Serah!"

"Go! She thinks you'll stop for me."

"No. I won't leave you here."

"You idiot! Get the Orb! If you can get it, you can save me."

She was right. As bad as it felt, he had to leave her behind and go for the Orb.

He felt his legs being pulled – someone was trying to tether him. He reached for the Orb of Binding, which he used to shield himself. Instantly, the tether disintegrated. He continued to run, keeping the Binding shield alive, a shell of blue surrounding him. A ward in this situation would not be strong enough to stand up to repeated attacks. Multiple tethers grabbed at his back, his legs, his feet. They slowed him down, but he only streamed his shield stronger to dislodge them.

He looked down to see the Sorceress-Queen advancing at incredible speed, no longer walking, but gliding. She was just meters from reaching Serah.

Her voice entered his head. *Stop running, you fool! You can't use the Orb of Psionics without me.*

He ignored her, and instead drew deeply from the Orb of Binding. What he was about to do would take a lot of magic, and he was already near the breaking point. But he simply couldn't leave Serah to her fate.

He'd learned little enough about brands, but he saw no other option. Using the Orb of Binding, he redirected the stream protecting himself to Serah, surrounding her with her own branded Binding shield. He somehow knew the effect would only be temporary, but it should help her last a few more seconds. To reach her physically, they would have to break the shield first.

He was making the final spiral – now directly above the Queen and her Mage-Knights, he was lost to sight, and safe from direct magic attacks. The violet light emanating from the Orb was blinding, but there was no time to wonder at it. He ran toward that blindness, and he couldn't think about the consequences. He cleared the last step and galloped in low gravity across the flat, marble floor. He could see the pedestal, the prize before him, surrounded in a purple aura that had to be some sort of shield.

He was tripped up, either by another tether or a kinetic push. He crawled across the floor, entering the Psionic aura, feeling a curious coolness overwhelm him.

He stood, and before him saw the pedestal holding the glowing violet Orb of Psionics, just as the Orb of Binding had been on Volsung. Standing directly behind it was a bearded, hooded figure, arms folded, with completely white eyes set in a wrinkled face.

The old man raised a hand, and the purple motes of light swirling around the Orb went still in the air. All sound ceased, save for Lucian's heavy breaths and the slight breeze that swirled around the Orb. Looking back at the stairs, he stood alone. No one was chasing him any longer – and peering through the open ceiling above them, even the Psionic storm had come to a dead stop.

Somehow, time itself had stilled for this moment. All that was left was Lucian, and the old man.

He could be none other than Shantozar, the Oracle of Psionics.

46

LUCIAN WATCHED THE FLOATING, violet motes streaming from the Orb. He stood about five meters away. With just a few more steps, it could be in his hands. But if this were anything like the Orb of Binding, he could not simply walk up and take it.

He had to prove himself worthy.

"You must be Shantozar," Lucian said. "Unless I miss my guess."

Shantozar nodded. "That is certainly the name Arian gave for me in his *Prophecy*. And that name will suffice."

"Did you speak with Arian?"

The Oracle watched him carefully. "Not as you and I are speaking now. But we had . . . conversations. And those conversations formed much of the basis of his *Prophecy of the Seven*. As the Oracle of Psionics, it was easier for me to communicate with him. And perhaps I had more motivation to."

"What do you mean by that?"

Shantozar gave a rueful smile. "You are not ready for that knowledge, Aspirant for the Orbs. I daresay you seek to claim my Orb as yours by right. No doubt you have traveled far and have endured many hardships. And now, the moment of truth. Will I give it, or not? Will I find you worthy to bear the Amethyst of Starsea? Are you the Chosen of the Manifold, or merely another pretender?"

Lucian wasn't sure how to respond to that. He didn't see the Orb as his "right," but he did see himself as the only one he trusted to hold it. "That about sums it up."

"You certainly have proven something by finding this place," Shantozar said. "The Psionic maelstrom I created with the power of the Orb could not hold you back, showing me that you are well-versed in Psionic Magic. Either that, or my storm was too weak."

"I had help," he said.

"Ah," the Oracle said. "That is not something I counted on. You see, we Vigilants worked alone, not trusting even family to help us. To see your friends fight for you so . . . is strange to me." He raised a quizzical eyebrow. "And in accordance with my own prophecy, you've come here with one of the Seven Jewels of Starsea."

Lucian nodded. "Yes. The Orb of Binding."

"The Vigilant of that Orb's name might roughly translate as *Rhana* in your tongue," he said. "She was a warrior of great beauty." He smiled in reminiscence. "And my bitter rival."

Lucian looked over his shoulder. "Look, I don't want to rush you, but I have a friend out there who needs my help."

Shantozar held up a wrinkled hand. "As soon as you entered the aura, time stopped. It is powerful Radiant magic that will abide until this Orb passes to another. It was sealed with the Seven Aspects and will not pass until the last suns die and the universe is a graveyard of black holes." He smiled bitterly. "I daresay we have time. As much as we need to figure things out."

"Okay," Lucian said, hardly comprehending magic that powerful. "What must I do to gain the Orb of Psionics, then?"

"Understand that this is not a light thing you ask of me. I would see it in the right hands. The price of failure is too high."

"Wouldn't the right hands be someone who already has one of the Orbs?"

"Not necessarily." He gave a frigid smile. "The right hands belong to the one who is most capable. The one who is wisest, who is mature enough to see the task through to the end. One who has a strong vision and plan for the future, and a dedication that will sacrifice anything for the fulfillment of that plan."

Lucian went cold at that, since that last line especially seemed to describe Queen Ansaldra, and not him.

"Do you know how far I've come?" Lucian asked. "How hard I've worked, how many times I almost died to reach this point? For this to end with you telling me *I'm* not good enough . . . I'm sorry. I don't buy it."

"Ansaldra is powerful indeed. For her to even *contact* me with Psionic Magic, despite my own powerful wards wrought with the Orb, speaks to her skill. She could do a hundredfold more than you with the Orb in her hands. The Manifold has blessed her greatly with the Gift of Magic. With this Orb, she could command armies and fleets, bending them to her will, scouring every world in Starsea until every last one of my companions' Orbs is uncovered." Shantozar watched Lucian for a reaction and sneered. "What could *you* do? Even with the Orb, you cannot hope to defeat her."

Lucian felt the hairs on his arms rise. He had a feeling he knew what Shantozar wanted, what he was being goaded into.

"The Sorceress-Queen said she wanted to work with me, for me to have the Orb while she trained me. She says I'm the Chosen."

"And are you?"

Lucian paused. "I have no choice but to believe that."

Shantozar guffawed. "Maybe, maybe not. It doesn't seem as if you're too sure, which doesn't help your case. Of course, it's impossible to say who the Chosen truly is until all the chips are down and the cards have been revealed, to borrow a metaphor you are familiar with. She may believe you are the Chosen of the Manifold, boy, but prophecy is a tricky thing, especially where it concerns the Chosen. In other words, I wouldn't count on that, were I you."

"She said the prophecy came from you."

"Yes," Shantozar said. "But who says you're the only one with an Orb to have ever visited this world, in the past or in the future?"

It wasn't something Lucian had considered. And it didn't do much for his confidence.

Shantozar waited, seeming to expect something more from Lucian.

"You want the Queen to have the Orb," Lucian realized. "Not me."

Shantozar nodded. "I do. Unless you have a better argument for why *you* should hold it?"

This was going to be harder than he thought. Saying he was here first probably wasn't a good reason. He had to fight to keep his voice steady, because what he was about to say scared the rot out of him.

"Give me the Orb. If I defeat the Sorceress-Queen with it, I will prove myself worthy. If I die, well, then it only proves *you* right, and she will not only gain the Orb of Psionics, but the Orb of Binding, too."

Shantozar's wrinkled eyes widened ever so slightly, the only sign of his surprise. "You can't be serious. You will surely die."

"I'm dead either way," Lucian said. "And if am the Chosen, maybe I have a chance."

Shantozar scoffed. "You're no Chosen until you hold all the Orbs, boy."

"This is my path," Lucian said. "The sooner I accept that, the easier things will go for me. Give me the Orb of Psionics,

Shantozar. The Queen is a madwoman who can't be trusted to do the right thing with it. The only thing that motivates her is revenge. Me? I actually intend to go through with it. To find all Seven Orbs and bring them together. Isn't that what you want, too?"

Lucian felt the presence of the Orb of Binding. And the call from the Orb of Psionics. Shantozar frowned, seeming to sense that same resonance. Lucian knew ether was swirling around him, being drawn to him. He felt his reserves replenished, with none of the attendant fire of the toxin.

"I will have that Orb, Shantozar," Lucian said. "If you please."

Now, Shantozar was scowling. "It wasn't supposed to be like this. *She* was supposed to gain the Orb, not you."

"The Manifold has plans for us all," Lucian said. The words made him smile; it sounded like something Vera might have said. "Not even an Oracle can stand against the will of the Voice."

Shantozar's expression grew darker, but then he gave a yellow smile. "All right, fine. If you are so confident, then take it. The Orb is yours. But no doubt, not for long."

Shantozar spread his arms, and the purple orb floated right into the air toward Lucian. He reached for it, knowing that the moment he did so, not only Shantozar would disappear, but the time ward surrounding the pedestal. As soon as the Orb was his, he would have to turn around and use it, to defend his right to have it.

He clasped the Orb of Psionics in his hand, and it thrummed with power, brightening like a violet supernova. Its lines bled into his arm, streaming toward his heart, until its essence was bound to his very soul.

And he felt its presence in his Focus – felt its power drumming with potential. The frozen motes resumed their dance, their light fading with the removal of the Orb.

Lucian turned, bathed in a violet aura.

It was time to embrace his destiny – to behave as the Chosen would.

————

FOR THE FIRST TIME, Lucian had no doubt that each of his Orbs would work. And also for the first time, he knew the reason why.

He had accepted that this was who he was . . . fully. He was an Aspirant for the Orbs, the Chosen of the Manifold, and now held Two of the Seven. As long as he continued on this path, believed in himself, then the Orbs would continue to be useful to him, so long as he had the mental fortitude to stream them.

And now, it was time to face the Sorceress-Queen and save Serah before it was too late.

He heard shouts from the staircase. He ran, reaching for the Orb of Psionics. Unadulterated ether infused into his Focus as he streamed a Psionic shield around him, so strong that it was practically unassailable. It wasn't elegant, but what it lacked in elegance it made up for in raw power.

And that was the only way he knew he could defeat the Sorceress-Queen: raw power. For she had elegance and skill in spades.

The time aura that had surrounded the pedestal had disappeared, leaving Queen Ansaldra standing at the top of the steps, about twenty meters away. She stood with her Mage-Knights of varying colors. There looked to be two Thermalists, four Binders, two Gravitists, two Radiants, and one Dynamist, all armed with shockspears. Holding the Orb, Lucian could see their Septagonal Focuses floating in their minds, and noted each of their primaries in fact matched the colors of their robes. Mage-Lord Kiani was not among them. Either he had not survived the crash, or Cleon had gotten his vengeance.

But most shocking of all, Serah was levitating behind them in a gravity aura streamed by the Gravitists, her blue eyes wide with fear.

"Put her down," he said. The ether within him begged to be released, and it was all he could do to hold back the tide.

"You're forgetting your prior commitment, Lucian," the Sorceress-Queen said, her voice filled with gravitas. "The Orbs will not obey you without my help."

"You're wrong," Lucian said. "I am the Chosen, and if there's anyone who needs to be following orders here, it's you."

There was a moment of frigid silence, as even the Queen's Mage-Knights' eyes widened at the challenge. Likely, they had never seen anyone stand up to the Queen like this.

"You are clearly not fit for the Orb, Lucian. Stand down, and I may have mercy. Your friend's life hangs in the balance."

Serah screamed something at him, but she was somehow silenced. He opened a Psionic link to her, which he felt instantly blocked by the Queen. Lucian brute-forced the link, drawing more and more magic from the Orb of Psionics. At last, the connection was made.

Lucian! Don't worry about me. Kill her!

Lucian didn't want to risk Serah's life, but he also knew that she was right. If he limited himself out of concern for her life, they might both be lost.

He had to get at the Queen, but that wouldn't be easy.

"You artless worm," she said. "This isn't how it's supposed to happen!"

"Last chance," Lucian said. "Let her go."

The Queen snarled. "Kill him."

Instantly, he streamed the Orb of Psionics with all its power, sending out a kinetic wave aimed precisely at every Mage-Knight that stood before him, along with the Queen. Before they could even let off a single volley of magic, the Mage-Knights flew backward at incredible speed, smashing into the interior wall of the Spire. Only the Queen was able to block the wave's power with her own shield, but even she was struggling under its force.

Lucian blinked in surprise, unable to believe the amount of power he had unleashed. With no more Mage-Knight Gravitists streaming, Serah's gravity aura dissipated and she sunk to the floor, landing with a thud. Her eyes remained closed, but there was nothing Lucian could do to help her for now.

The Queen, with a scream, streamed her own counter, a kinetic wave of great power that rippled against Lucian's shield. Lucian's breath caught, fully expecting it to tear him to shreds. But it didn't make so much as a dent. The Queen's eyes widened, and then narrowed in anger as she streamed another wave, this one more powerful. Lucian streamed his shield stronger to match. And there was yet more power to bear from the Orb.

"You can't touch me," he said. "The Orb won't allow it."

"It obeys you!" she said, fear creeping into her voice. "*Why* does it obey you?"

Lucian now stood a few meters from her. "You said it yourself. Because I am the Chosen."

He reached inside the Queen's mind, where he saw her in her true state – an old, shriveled woman with yellowed skin and long, greasy hair. That husk of a woman was not here in this spire. Only her mind was. Instantly, Lucian realized why the Sorceress-Queen appeared so young – and he could only see the truth due to the power of the Orb.

The woman standing before him wasn't truly the Sorceress-Queen.

The violet eyes should have been his clue. This young woman, whoever she was, was possessed. A powerful brand surrounded this woman's Focus, a brand that allowed the Sorceress-Queen to control her from elsewhere, probably the Golden Palace in Dara.

But for all purposes, the Manifold was treating this woman as if *she* were the Queen, with all her attendant power.

In short, killing this woman *would* kill the Queen, too – her mind and her Focus. But it would also mean killing the woman being controlled by her.

She gave a cruel smile, a smile that seemed to realize what Lucian knew.

"You rotting bitch."

Lucian sent out another kinetic shockwave, but it was easily countered by the Queen with a shield. She smiled.

"A one-trick pony, aren't you?" She chuckled coldly. "It's over, Lucian."

He kept his shield up, a flood of ether keeping it powered. Her various attacks against him were deflected – attacks against mind and body. She couldn't touch him, as far as Psionics was concerned. But Lucian had trouble attacking *her* with the same intensity, knowing the truth.

There had to be a way to save the woman possessed by the Queen, but how? It would not only take brute force, but delicacy. The mind was a fragile thing and forcing the Queen out in one ruthless blow might destroy the helpless person she was controlling.

A lance of blue light shot from the Queen's right palm, latching onto Lucian's leg. Lucian quickly countered, but the Queen's Binding stream was only a feint. A gravity disc bloomed below him, and immediately he was forced to his knees. His shockspear felt as if it weighed a hundred kilos, and it dropped to the floor. Lucian knew he couldn't match her Gravitonic stream. It was only a matter of time until he was crushed like a bug underfoot.

He had to stop her at the source. He wasn't even sure the Orb of Psionics could handle blocking her Focus. No mage in their right mind would ever allow access to that most vital aspect of themselves and would defend it to their very deaths.

But perhaps the Sorceress-Queen would not anticipate a move so bold. But the window of opportunity would soon close. He had to make one final attack. Even now, the force of the gravity pulling him down was relentlessly increasing.

He drew as much ether from the Orb of Psionics as he could – untold power that kept collecting in him, growing and growing while demanding release. He was halfway tempted to unleash another kinetic wave, one so powerful that it would rip her to shreds. But that would kill Serah, too, not to mention the woman the Queen's mind was occupying.

There was only one solution that was acceptable to Lucian. Cut off her magic entirely.

He let the ether manifest into magic and directed it right at her Focus – her eyes widened at the incursion, the violation, and what Lucian found was that her Focus was a weapon tempered over decades of practice and meditation. Even with the Orb, it wouldn't be an easy thing to create a brand around. The Queen screamed as she pushed back. Hard. Gravity pressed down on Lucian more intensely, until his vision darkened and his muscles shook. Lucian could hardly draw breath, as if a ten-ton stone were pressing into him from above.

It was as he feared. Even with the Orb, the magic was still not enough to overcome the Queen's Focus. She smiled in triumph. He would be crushed long before he could overwhelm her. Hope was draining faster than his own consciousness. Shantozar had been right, in the end. His last image before his death would be of the Queen's gloating face as she became the owner of two Orbs of Starsea.

But from nowhere, the gravity pushing him down became less intense. He didn't understand why at first. Was the Queen weakening?

But it wasn't that. He had wits enough to see that Serah was now standing behind the Sorceress-Queen, working to counter the Queen's Gravitonic amplification disc.

The Queen shrieked in fury, but she couldn't afford to switch her attention on Serah. If she did so, it might give Lucian the opening he needed to break through the last of her shield. Lucian gasped for breath as his vision returned. The gravity was still intense, but at least he could concentrate now.

At that moment, he remembered something Vera had told him – with the Manifold, magic stemmed from belief. He had to *believe* it was possible, and the Orb would supply the rest.

The rush of magic increased, until the purple stream emanating from Lucian's hands was blinding in its brilliance, entering the Queen's mind. It intensified until that light was everything, until the world itself faded and was replaced with a matrix of purple streams. All those streams were converging on the Queen's Focus. Lucian knew what those streams were – ether itself. He was so deep in his Focus that the Manifold itself was manifesting before him, the ethereal background that formed the bridge between Manifold and reality.

Slowly but surely, the Sorceress-Queen's Focus was shattering. Her shield collapsed, and she screamed as he gained access to the vital core of who she was, her Focus. He controlled it now as if it were his own. He set a brand over it, preventing any magic from entering or leaving – and to secure it, he reached for the Orb of Binding, cohering it with the magic from the Orb of Psionics, creating a brand so powerful that even the Sorceress-Queen of Psyche could never hope to break it.

With that final stream, the real world returned as the magic from both Orbs petered out. When his usual vision returned, it revealed the Sorceress-Queen of Psyche, stripped of power, her dress in tatters, her dark hair askew, and violet eyes wild.

Her eyes widened as if she were naked. From her expression, she did not know what to do with that feeling of vulnerability. She had probably never experienced it before. She looked like prey who had just seen the hunter, who was about to take his shot.

The Queen ran, attempting to brush past Serah.

"Oh, no you don't!"

Serah extended a hand, which emanated a silvery aura. The Queen slowed at the increase of gravity, her knees buckling. Not giving up her hopeless prospect of escape, she crawled on the ground like a worm. Lucian could feel her trying to break the block he'd formed in vain, but an ant might as well try to break a wall of pure graphene. Even so, he held his Focus, with both the Orb of Binding and Psionics near to hand. He didn't want to leave anything to chance.

He stumbled forward, picking up his shockspear and using it as a support. Serah waited by the Queen, who could barely even breathe from the force of gravity forcing her down.

She cut a pathetic figure, but Lucian had to remind himself that this wasn't truly the Queen. Serah stood above her, the point of her spear at the Queen's throat. The Queen raised her hands in surrender, her expression one of pure loathing.

"Don't kill her," Lucian said. "This isn't the Queen."

Serah looked at him incredulously. "What?"

"I mean, the mind is hers, but the body belongs to someone else. Someone the Queen's possessing. That's why she looks so young. Everyone else must have known – Lord Kiani, all those people at the party. They all knew, but we never thought to ask."

Serah looked at the Queen with wide eyes, as if she didn't believe him. "Well, rot me. How do you know?"

"I felt it when I cut her off," Lucian said. "I . . . saw her as she really was. If we kill her, the person she's possessing dies, too."

"I don't get it. Would the Queen die if we killed her, or would she live?"

Lucian shook his head. "I really don't know. The Manifold is treating this woman as if she is Ansaldra, both her Focus and her mind. So yes. Probably."

Serah edged the spearpoint closer to the woman's throat.

"And I don't suppose you'd share that information with us, your Majesty?"

The Queen – or rather, the woman she was controlling – spat.

"She can be exorcised. I can do that with the Orb of Psionics. At least, I think I can. After that, this woman – whoever she is – will be free again."

Serah frowned. "Can you really do that?"

Lucian watched the woman. It would be far simpler to kill her and be done with it. The Queen's mind was trapped, stuck here due to Lucian's block. Presumably, her mind would die along with the woman.

But he didn't have it in him to kill someone like that. How did this woman come to be possessed by the Queen in the first place? Who was she? Lucian would never learn those answers unless he spared her life.

He was sure with the Orb of Psionics helping him, he could drive the Queen's Focus out of the woman for good. That would force the Queen to return to her own body back in the Golden Palace, or wherever she happened to be. Or at least, he could only assume.

The Queen watched his moral dilemma play out, her violet eyes cunning. "If you kill her, then yes, you kill me, too. But if you want her to live, you must drive my Focus right out of her. I won't be able to reach her again. Or better yet, release my Focus and let me do it myself. That way you don't bungle the whole thing."

"That's not happening," Lucian said.

"We should just kill her," Serah said. "This woman was likely one of her lackeys who willingly gave herself up. Powerful mind control magic doesn't work unless the target is somewhat complicit."

"We don't know her reasons for being mind-controlled,"

Lucian said. "She may be innocent." He looked at the Queen. "Who did you possess?"

She gave a small, treacherous smile. "If I told you, would you believe me? You can find that out easily enough by saving her."

Lucian sighed. "True enough."

"More is at stake than one woman's life here, innocent or not," Serah countered. "There's no court here. No judge, jury, or executioner, save us. We will never get this chance again."

Lucian had no idea what to do. Was Serah right? He knew it made a certain logical sense, but his heart railed against it.

"I can't kill an innocent woman," he said. "Even if it means missing the opportunity to kill the Sorceress-Queen."

Serah's mouth twisted in disgust. "Lucian! This is our only chance! Psyche will be free from her terror once and for all. Don't show her mercy. Never leave an enemy like this alive or they will hunt you down to the ends of the galaxy!"

Lucian watched the Queen, whose violet eyes peered at him with interest. She was feeling the power shift back to her, like oxygen to a flame. Those mischievous eyes belonged to a complete sociopath – unempathetic and uncaring. She already knew what Lucian was going to do, because a little duplicitous smile was stretching across her lips. A smile that said she had won.

Lucian roared in frustration, slamming the butt of his spear against the crystal staircase. Letting her go was a terrible mistake, especially if the woman she possessed happened to be some ally of hers. But Lucian just couldn't take the chance. He wasn't a killer, and didn't have it in him to end someone who might be innocent.

Before he could second-guess himself, or before Serah could take matters into her own hands, he drew ether from the Orb of Psionics. He had never felt so conflicted. Why did doing the honorable thing have to feel so bad? Was there *even* a right thing to do? Serah had a point too, after all. Her way might even cause the least amount of suffering in the end.

He had to put that out of his mind. He reached for the Queen's Focus, which was completely at his mercy. He couldn't destroy it – somehow, he knew that to be impossible. The Focus only died when the body itself died. But he could force the Focus out of this woman and snap it back to its source, remind the Manifold that this wasn't where it belonged. The Focus would return to the real Ansaldra, wherever she happened to be.

So, he prodded against the brand the Queen had made. The Orb allowed him to not only see the brand's inner workings, but also the complex instructions that made it function. He instantly saw those instructions specified that this woman *was* Queen Ansaldra, that the Manifold would treat this woman's mind and magic as if they were her. It was a sickening, twisted perversion of Psionic Magic – and it made his skin crawl knowing such a thing was possible. Lucian found the source of the brand's power, a sort of switch. Tickle that switch with a thin stream of Psionic Magic, and the brand would dissolve. This woman would be herself again, and the Queen would be gone.

He drew a deep breath and streamed. The brand dissipated, and Lucian felt the Queen's presence depart. Queen Ansaldra's eyes – no, this young *woman's* eyes – became lucid, their color shifting from violet to green.

Serah released her Gravitonic stream, mouthing a curse. The unknown woman immediately stood and backed away from them, her eyes wide and fearful and her breaths panicked. It was hard not to see her as the Queen, but there was something about her posture that was different. It was hard for Lucian to place a finger on it, but the way she stood was more solid and less airy. The young woman's hands were clenched into fists, as if she expected a fight at any moment.

"Who are you?" she asked, her voice tremulous. "Where am I?"

This would be a long story indeed. But it wasn't one Lucian had the energy to tell right now. He reached into the woman's Focus using the power of the Orb, just to be sure the Sorceress-Queen was gone. It was only her, whoever she was. Queen Ansaldra was thousands of kilometers away from here, with no way to reach them without her airship – which was gone, anyway. They were safe, at least for the time being.

Lucian fell to one knee, only supporting his weight from his shockspear. He was tired. So very tired. He fell forward.

Serah grabbed him by the torso, just in time to catch him before he descended into darkness.

47

SNOW WAS FALLING. Lucian looked into the star-studded night sky, seeing a molten moon providing light. Ahead stood a village of wooden cabins, windows lit and smoke rising from chimneys. It was a cozy scene, and the memory of it was returning.

Vale, on the planet Aurora. This was from the simulation, the place Emma had grown up. What was he doing here?

He ran until he was inside the village, his heart thundering. The streets were empty, and there were no sounds coming from within the buildings. He felt pulled by a familiar force, until he saw the great tree that overshadowed the village's entirety.

Standing before it was the woman he thought he would never see again. Emma turned as his boots crunched over the snow toward her. She was as stunning as he remembered. Even more so. The year or so since he had seen her had added a maturity to her face that only enhanced her beauty. Her dark hair and heavy coat were laden with snow, but her brown eyes were the same, warm, sad, and happy all at the same time as she looked at him. A smile spread across her face, like the memory of the sun long forgotten.

He drew her close, and almost cried to be holding her in his arms. He questioned for a moment whether he was somehow dead, but he knew that wasn't so, somehow. This was a dream, and Emma was far away on Volsung, while he was on Psyche.

But just because it was a dream didn't mean it wasn't real. Certainly, the bittersweet happiness he felt at seeing her was real enough.

When she pulled back, there were tears in her eyes. "I *knew* you were still alive."

"This is real, then?"

"Seems like it." She watched him closely. "Where are you? What are you doing? I felt you trying to reach out for me across the stars. And somehow, I was pulled here."

"How can that be possible?"

She shrugged. "Who cares? It's . . . good to see you, Lucian. So much has changed, but at the same time, a lot is still the same. Time stands still here."

"Are you at the Academy?"

She nodded. "I'm a Talent, now. Technically, I have another half year to decide my Aspect, but I already know I'm going to be a Radiant."

"Seriously?"

She nodded. For a moment, the image of her warbled. Lucian frantically tried to reach her again, and only just managed to keep the dream alive.

"You're far," she said. "I can feel it."

"I'm . . . on Psyche," he said. "It would take days to explain everything that's happened to me. Listen, Emma . . ."

He wanted to tell her everything then. How much he missed her. How he wished he would have just chosen one of the Transcends so he could have stayed. But he stopped himself short. That would only bring him pain – and her, too, if she felt the same as him.

Their lives had moved on. She could be nothing more for him than a memory.

"What is it, Lucian?"

He opened his mouth, but his words were caught in his throat. With her looking at him like that, it was so hard to speak. So hard to say what was important.

But at that moment, the dream's power began to fade. Lucian felt panic as he tried to rekindle it.

"What is it, Lucian?"

Her voice was fading, and so was the snow, the village, the tree. A light shone from that tree, illuminating Emma with green radiance. She watched as he was pulled away, as if into a black hole . . .

———

"There you are," Serah said. "Thought I'd lost you for a second."

Lucian blinked, finding himself in the last place he wanted to be – the Spire. Somehow, Serah had dragged him down the staircase, and now they were before the tall, open archway leading out into the desert. The Psionic storm was gone, but all the dust it had kicked up still hung in the air. Night had fallen, and the breeze blew cool through the entrance. Of the crashed airship, or any survivors from it, there was no sign.

The other woman – the woman who had once been the Queen – huddled against the wall, her green eyes lost. It was unreal to see her like that, but those haunted eyes made her seem a different person. Her white dress of pearls was in tatters, dirty, and bloodstained. Her empty gaze seemed to see nothing.

"Won't even talk to me," Serah said. "But she does follow me around and do what I say."

"She's shocked," Lucian said. "I might have pushed the Queen out of her mind too hard."

Serah frowned. "I can't believe you let her go."

"It felt . . . right. Then again, it'll probably bite us in our collective asses later."

"Yep."

"Now, the Queen is out there somewhere. Planning."

"If the Queen is capable of possessing the mind and body of another person, she's far more terrifying than I thought." Serah looked over at the unknown woman. "And . . . I do feel sorry for her. She tried to run away, but came back when she realized there's only desert out there."

Lucian's throat clenched when he remembered Fergus and Cleon.

"What about Fergus? Cleon?"

Serah's face fell as she shook her head. "They're . . . at the base of the stairs. I laid them out, side by side. I'll . . . need help with the rest."

It was as he expected, but that didn't take away from the sick wrenching at his gut. Lucian followed her. As good as her word, both men lay side-by-side at the base of the stairs. Bloodied, but with the bodies of at least ten Mage-Knights around them, many of them severely burned. Among the dead was Mage-Lord Kiani, who still had Cleon's shockspear jutting from his chest. Both were simply *dead*, with no discernible wound. As if the Queen had simply reached into their minds and . . . turned off their lives.

"No doubt they gave us enough time to get to the Orb," Serah said. "And . . . it's good that Cleon got his vengeance."

Lucian's stomach fell. He hadn't even considered that letting the Queen go would be a dishonor to his memory. Guilt clawed at him like a thing alive.

Serah knelt beside Fergus, tears in her eyes. "Sleep well, Captain. I wish you'd stayed alive long enough to see the mission through. This whole thing . . . this was what you wanted. To make a difference." The tears fell, wetting his dusty, begrimed clothing. "Well, you did. I just wish you were alive to see that."

At that moment, Fergus coughed and Serah jumped back as if he were an adder.

"Fergus!" Lucian said, hope swelling in his chest. "You're alive!"

The Captain started to prop himself up but was forced back down by Serah.

"Oh my God. Fergie, I can't believe it!"

"Did you get it?" Fergus rasped. "Is the Orb safe? Is the Queen dead?"

"How are you even alive? What happened?"

Each of their questions went unanswered as Fergus's eyes roved upward, toward the unknown woman sitting against the wall by the open door.

"It's a long story, but the Queen is no longer any danger to us." Lucian paused. "At least, not for a long time. I have the Orb."

Fergus's eyes questioned, but he was simply too tired and in pain to ask more.

"I'm weak, Lucian," he said. "I . . . don't think I can even *think* straight."

"Just relax," Serah said. "Rotting hell, you're alive!"

He turned to look at Cleon beside him, his eyes watering.

"He must be alive, too," Serah said. "Let's see if we can wake him up."

Lucian felt for Cleon's pulse. His skin was colder than Fergus's, and there was no sign of life – no pulse, no breath, and he just felt . . .

"He's gone," Lucian said.

Serah looked at him. "How do you know that?"

"He killed Kiani, in the end," Fergus said. "And he said something about that being enough for him. He told me to go to stop her, but I couldn't move, and I thought I was dead, too.

Now, though, I understand what happened. He drew the Psionic ward onto himself, made it into some kind of magnet. It drew most of the power of the Queen's attack, and I got something of an . . . aftershock, which I apparently survived."

Lucian saw what he meant. Cleon had sacrificed himself, that at least one of them might live. It just deepened the sorrow he felt.

"He had a hero in him after all," Serah said. "I . . . underestimated him. And freely admit that I was wrong about him."

It seemed so amiss that the person who had never wanted to be here in the first place was the one to have died. Lucian wiped his own tears, the heaviness in his heart making him sink to the floor.

"Thanks for everything, Cleon," he said, his voice thick. "It's . . . my fault this happened. But without you, without your actions, your lessons, your bravery . . ." He shook his head. "None of this could have happened. I won't let your sacrifice be in vain."

Serah and Fergus nodded at that.

"He annoyed me, if I'm to be truthful," Serah said. "I'm going to miss that. Somehow."

"He was a good watchman," Fergus said. "A former Mage-Knight of Dara. Knightlier than any of these ones sent after us. And the best Thermalist I knew, and I've met many." He gave a slow nod. "And one day, Ansaldra will answer for his death."

Fergus's eyes went up to focus on the woman, who was watching them from across the Spire's entry hall. Her green eyes were wide, her face curious.

Fergus sat up, and with help from Serah, managed to stand fully. "And what of her?"

"That's not Queen Ansaldra," Lucian said. "She was controlled by her. The real Queen is probably back at the Golden Palace."

Fergus's eyes widened a bit at this revelation. "How is that even possible?"

"Really powerful and corrupt Psionic Magic," Lucian said. "I can vouch that this woman isn't the Queen anymore."

"She's refused to talk to me so far," Serah said. "Shocked, I guess."

"I imagine so." Fergus considered. "Is she blocked at least?"

It was hard for Lucian to remember the details – things had gone hazy at the end. All Lucian did remember was casting out the Queen. So, he reached out toward the woman's Focus and found the block was still there, working as intended. She was indeed a mage, which was probably required for the Queen's magic to have worked.

"The block is still there," he confirmed. "She won't be able to stream until I dismantle it."

Fergus nodded. "Until we interview her, we cannot be sure of her loyalties. It's possible she was some ally of the Queen's. Or she may be a victim. But we have an important matter to attend to first."

Lucian knew what he meant. "Feels wrong to bury Cleon here, in this place . . ."

"I know what you mean," Fergus said. He looked up at the interior of the Spire. "Maybe we can think of this place as a mausoleum for the greatest warrior Psyche has ever known."

Serah sniffled. "I like that."

Fergus went over to Lord Kiani's corpse, and unceremoniously yanked out Cleon's shockspear. "At least this might go with him into the afterlife."

They lifted his body – an easy thing to do in Psyche's gravity – and carried it outside the Spire. Each of them confirmed that he really *was* dead, and not just sleeping under some strange, demented Psionic Magic. There was no heartbeat, no breathing, no electrical impulses, all confirmed by them scanning him with their Focuses.

So there, under the light of the gas giant Cupid, they buried him deep in the sands, along with his spear. There were no rocks or anything else to mark his grave, so they did the best they could to honor him – telling stories, conversations they'd had, the things they would remember most about him, and how they would carry him with them into the future.

"I'll always remember what he taught me," Lucian said. "I won't ever be as good a Thermalist as him, but he taught me about brands. And without his lessons, I would have never been able to block off the Queen's magic. This victory is more his than mine. And . . . I will remember his loyalty, what it means to fight to the last breath for what you believe in. I'll never be the same because of his sacrifice."

There was a moment's pause before Serah stepped forward, reflective. "He was a good man. Cursed almost as good as me, and he knew how to call it like he saw it, despite what others thought. That's a good quality to have, and something I'll remember for myself in the future."

Fergus watched for a moment, his tears drying quickly in the desert air. "Rest in peace, great warrior." It looked as if he wanted to say more but couldn't find the words.

They stood there for a while, Serah resting her head on Lucian's shoulder. He wrapped an arm around her, grateful for the comfort. Something had shifted between them – just what, Lucian couldn't say.

Fergus looked at them, a small smile on his lips. "At least some good has come out of this whole thing." He glanced back at the Spire. "We should head back. Find out who that woman is."

Fergus was right. There was still work to be done. Together, they returned to the Spire.

48

WHEN THEY GOT BACK, the unknown woman was asleep, curled up behind a stone pillar on the opposite side of the entrance. The three of them kept an eye on her while they did the grisly work of going through every corpse. There were no survivors, and none of them had much in the way of supplies. They picked up six canteens, some full and some not, about two days' worth of full rations for all of them, including the woman, as well as twenty shockspears, all cast from bronze – though Lord Kiani's, like Lucian's, was made from graphene.

"Take it," Serah said to Fergus. "You'll get more use out of it than me."

For a moment, it seemed he was about to argue with her, before realizing he couldn't argue with good sense.

Once everything of use had been collected, they gathered the bodies and took them outside. It was gruesome, disgusting work, but it needed to be done. The Spire would be their shelter, at least for now, and Lucian didn't much like the idea of sleeping next to the dead.

Using magic, they were able to create a mass, shallow grave, into which they placed the bodies. By the time that was done, the light of the sun was beginning to rise above the dunes. They washed their hands with the canteen water – not ideal when they needed true disinfectant, but there was nothing else to be done.

When they returned to the Spire, the woman was still asleep.

"I can keep watch," Serah said.

Lucian was too tired to argue. As soon as he lay down on the stone floor, sleep took him.

———

LUCIAN SLEPT like the dead buried outside, swimming through dreams unending. Emma's face swirled among nightmarish visions of the Sorceress-Queen. Cleon shook his head disapprovingly. The Orb of Psionics glowed, seeming sinister in the darkness.

When he awoke, it was still morning. No, it couldn't be morning. *Evening* then. The light was different, and it felt he'd slept for a long time.

Serah and Fergus were already up, sitting around a branded fire floating a few centimeters off the stone. It had grown chilly. Lucian looked around, but there was no sign of the woman.

"Where is she?" he asked. "Has she talked?"

Serah shook her head. "She walked outside an hour or so ago. Your block still seems to be active because it looked like she was trying to stream."

Lucian nodded. "Maybe I can try talking to her."

Serah shrugged. Lucian got the feeling she was still displeased he let the woman live. Fergus was drinking a bowl of soup, a blanket wrapped around his broad shoulders. He didn't seem in the mood for conversation. After everything, Lucian didn't blame him.

Lucian went out into the night. He was surprised at the

chill, considering how hot the desert was during the day. A long walkway of paving stones, lined with broken columns, led into the desert. At the end of that walkway stood the woman, her white dress shimmering under Cupid's reflected light. Lucian almost felt a chill watching her. It was as if the ghost of the Queen were still among them. He had to remind himself that this wasn't her, and that the real Queen was alive somewhere.

But he couldn't lower his guard. After all, a new person meant new potential dangers. His decision to save her could backfire massively.

There was only one way to find out who she was, and whether he had made a mistake in letting her live.

Lucian cleared the distance in about two minutes. He stopped about ten meters away from the woman, who gave no sign of knowing he was there. He was wondering how to break the silence when she turned. Her face was sorrowful, but only a little of the haughtiness of the Queen remained. She looked Lucian up and down, her green eyes narrow and mistrustful.

"Can I get you anything?" Lucian asked. "Food? Water?"

She shook her head.

"Can you speak?"

Silence.

"Is there anything I can do to help you? Anything I can tell you to clear up confusion?"

More silence.

"Your mind was possessed by the Sorceress-Queen of Psyche. I don't know how much of that you remember, but that's over now. My name is Lucian. I'm the one who drove her out of your mind."

He offered a hand. The woman looked at it for a moment, and then back at him.

"What can I do to get you to talk? Do you want me to undo your block?"

The woman, at last, nodded. At least they were getting somewhere.

"Do you promise not to attack me? Will you at least talk to me, tell me who you are? No one can survive alone out here."

After some hesitation, she nodded. Lucian supposed it could all be a trick, but he was the one who had decided to save her, after all. It was only fair he assumed the risk of unblocking her. With the Orb of Psionics at his disposal, he could recreate the block in an instant if he needed to.

At least, that was what he hoped.

Before he could second-guess himself, he unraveled the block. It was gone in an instant.

The woman blinked a few times, a small smile coming to her face. "Thank you. Although perhaps I shouldn't be thanking you. Death would have probably been a kinder fate."

Her accent was hard to place. The words were smooth, almost melting into one another. It reminded him somewhat of the way the Queen spoke, as well as the nobles at the soiree. She was someone among Dara's upper classes, then, further evidenced by her magical ability. From her age, she was likely born and raised here, too.

"What's your name?"

She watched him closely, carefully. "Selene de Mordred."

"Do you mind telling me what happened, Selene de Mordred?"

Her expression became grave and pale. "Just call me Selene. It's easier."

"Selene, then." After a moment of silence, Lucian realized he would be asking all the questions. "What do you remember?"

She shook her head. "I don't want to talk about it. I don't trust you."

"I suppose that's fair. I don't really trust you, either, which is why I'm trying to talk to you."

"Is . . . she dead?"

Lucian shook his head. "Unfortunately, no. I was only able to drive her out of your mind."

She nodded, as if she had expected that answer. "That's what I thought you said. I was hoping I misinterpreted." She looked around. "And where is this?"

"We're in the Burning Sands. Under the Eye of Cupid."

She laughed bitterly. "I . . . was afraid of that. I've just been staring at that planet above, thinking I'm in a nightmare. But after hearing it from you, I think it might have been better to die."

"Why do you say that?"

She looked at him as if he were stupid. "Because we're in the Burning Sands, with no way out."

Yes, that was a good point. "We're working on that. How are you associated with the Queen?"

Her lips curled in distaste, and the action didn't seem to be forced. That was a good sign. She clearly hated the Queen, and that made her a potential ally.

"I'm the Psion of the Atomicist, Nostra. Other than that, no association at all. We've barely spoken. At least until . . ." She trailed off.

So, Selene was someone in Queen Ansaldra's circle, if only on the periphery. Perhaps she even had quarters in the palace.

"How did the Queen take control of you?"

"Must we go over this? I barely even know you."

"I saved your life. Don't I deserve some answers?"

"Perhaps my life wasn't yours to save."

Was she *serious*? "Most would be grateful to have their life saved."

"Not if you've just given me a worse fate." She shook her head. "You should've just killed me along with the Queen. At least my life would've meant something, then."

Her, too? It was hard not to throw up his hands in frustration. Or to even agree with her.

"Whatever the case, this is where we stand. It's the four of us now. You probably noticed we had to bury our friend back there. Unless you were sleeping through that."

She nodded, seeming to look down her nose at him the entire time she did so. She seemed stuck up, but maybe that was to be expected of a noblewoman. "I saw."

"And you probably can't go back to Dara, seeing as the Queen would probably just want to take control of you again."

"Yes, I surmised as much. I don't need you to explain things to me as if I were a child. You can't be much older than me, anyway, and I'm probably better educated."

Lucian had to swallow his first response. "Just trying to help."

"Then stop. I don't need a rescuer. However, I am willing to work with you in order to get out of this mess. If such a thing is even possible."

That was something, at least. "We would be grateful."

"Well, you can't get out of here alive unless you or your friends understand basic Atomicism. Which most mages don't." She sighed. "Even if I *did* get out of here, is there any point? Every option that matters has been taken from me."

"Don't you have family somewhere?"

She shook her head. "Dead."

That might have made her a target of the Queen. And if she were the Psion of an Atomicist, she must have had enough potential for the Queen's Focus transferal to work. And of course, Selene was exceptionally beautiful. If the Queen had to pick someone to possess, beauty would have been requisite. Beauty was power, especially when power backed that beauty.

"Look," Lucian said. "Atomicism is the only Aspect I have no experience with. And it probably means you're a fair

Dynamist and Thermalist, too. Those talents will be useful in getting out of here. Fergus is a Radiant, and Serah a Gravitist."

"Which would make you a Psionic," she said, with a secretive smile that said she knew more than he thought. "And a damn good one at that, to challenge the Queen."

Lucian decided a change of subject was in order. He wasn't ready to tell her about the Orb of Psionics, though if she knew anything about Arian's prophecy, then she might figure it out, anyway. "I have a potential way of getting off Psyche for good. If that path ever comes, then you're welcome to join us . . . at least until we find a decent-sized port for you to get off at. I'm sure you probably don't want to hang around any longer than you have to."

"How generous of you," she said, drolly. "And how do you plan to leave, exactly? Even assuming you do, your solution is just to throw me at the first port you come across? My blood means *nothing* beyond Psyche. I'd be fated to be some dockyard strumpet for as long as my looks lasted. And no doubt, some mage-hunter would detect me and send me right back here, anyway."

Lucian frowned. When he had saved her life, he certainly hadn't expected all these complications. He hated to admit that killing her would have been far simpler.

But even so, Lucian could feel the truth. She was scared, and her contrary nature was just a shield. After what she'd been through with the Queen, that made sense. It would be best to give her the benefit of the doubt, unless she did something substantial enough to lose that benefit.

"Maybe we can find an Academy to enroll you in, I don't know," he said. "This is all pointless unless my plan works, anyway."

"You still haven't *shared* your plan. Out with it."

She was a woman used to getting what she wanted quickly, especially from those she deemed socially inferior. Well, she had another think coming. She knew nothing about the Orbs he held, and until she proved herself in some way and stopped berating him, telling her would be supremely stupid.

"I have a plan," he said. "I just can't tell you."

"A secret plan." She smiled. "Aren't those the best kind?"

His face flushed. "Well, I'm not going to just tell you. I don't know if you can be trusted yet." He looked back toward the Spire entrance. "Look. Would you at least come inside and meet the others? They helped me to rescue you."

"Ah. So they are to blame as well."

"If you choose to think of it that way, sure. It's your life. We have food, but not much. Maybe we can find some more where the *Zephyr* went down."

"So *that's* how everyone got out here," she said. "Shame about that ship. We might have sailed it to the Riftlands. It wouldn't have been an easy life for me, but certainly better than drying out like a prune in the Burning Sands."

Lucian had another dark thought about why the Queen might have selected Selene. As a disagreeable person, she might not have been much missed.

"You can join us. Or stay out here. We'll likely set out tomorrow at dawn."

"That's ill-advised," Selene said. "The sun will burn you to a crisp, and I can't hold a Thermal ward that long."

Lucian nodded. "Fair enough. Tomorrow night, then."

At that moment, the ground rumbled, causing the sands ahead of them to shift. It was a good half minute before the moonquake had passed. The sudden movement made Selene grasp onto him like a life raft in a storm.

As soon as the quake had passed, she let go of him as if he were toxic sludge.

Lucian shook his head. "You're welcome."

"And we have these wonderful quakes to look forward to, too," Selene said, as if she hadn't offended Lucian in any way.

As if his feelings didn't matter. "If you get me back to the West-lands, past the Fire Rifts, maybe then I will be glad you spared my life."

Lucian scoffed. "Come inside and eat. Or not. But if you do, mind your manners. You're not in charge of anything out here, and you'll need us to survive just as much as we need you."

He returned to the Spire at a fast pace. Selene did not follow.

49

OVER A BOWL of watery soup that did little to satisfy his hunger, Lucian shared his conversation with Selene.

Once done, Serah nodded. "Yep. Should've killed her."

"Killing her would've done no good," Fergus said. "An Atomicist would be incredibly useful. She can make water for us. Any Atomicist worth their salt can do that, and we certainly don't have the water supplies to make it all the way to the Westlands."

"Can Atomicists make food, too?" Serah asked.

Fergus frowned. "I'm not sure, but that seems a bit more complicated."

"I might forgive her if she conjures us a full dinner here. Wyvern skewers spiced with caro, slathered with plenty of butter and herbs, some roasted potatoes and cave mushrooms . . ."

"*Not* helping," Fergus said.

Their conversation was cut off when Selene stood in the wide-open archway. She joined them at their fire, warming her hands.

"I'm Selene."

"We know," Serah said, somewhat coldly.

Her green eyes watched Serah, somewhat amused, but she said nothing more.

"Would you like something to eat?" Fergus asked.

Selene watched him a moment, her eyes placid. "If you please."

Fergus passed her a bowl of soup, even throwing in a few extra chunks of meat. Selene looked at it, all but pinching her nose as she stared at it.

"What is this?" she asked.

"Dinner," Fergus said. "Beef, caro, and potatoes mostly."

Lucian watched Serah nervously. If Selene turned down this meal, she might actually kill the woman.

Selene took a small, dainty sip. "It's not . . . *terrible*."

"Well, eat up," Fergus said. "We've only enough food for two days. Four, if we stretch it."

"We need to head out to the crash site tomorrow night," Lucian said. "It can't be far, and there were stores of food for two hundred. Some of it has to be intact."

"It's probably five meters deep in sand by now," Serah said.

"We'll find it. We have new tools at our disposal."

That one vague line was enough to communicate to Fergus and Serah that Lucian hadn't told Selene about his Orbs.

"It's time for sleep," Fergus said. "There's no monsters out here that can bother us, right? No wyverns, giant sand worms, anything of that nature?"

"Nothing like that," Serah said. "The climate is what kills."

"No point setting a watch, then," Fergus said.

"Someone might have survived the crash," Selene pointed out.

Serah shook her head a little too vehemently. "If they had, they would be here by now."

Selene pursed her lips but said nothing. Lucian supposed it

was naïve to think drama would go away with the Queen's expulsion.

"There's one more thing I have to do," he said. "I'll be back."

Without waiting for an answer, Lucian went up the crystalline steps circling the interior of the Spire. He realized then how high they rose. The three of them at the bottom looked small indeed even halfway up. The top of the Spire was certainly higher than the dune that had once covered it. Either it had grown after being unearthed, or it had risen up from beneath the sand. The second option seemed more likely.

Once he reached the room where he'd found the Orb, he discovered it wasn't a room at all. The time aura had only made it *seem* like a room. In fact, it was the top of the tower, in the shape of a Septagon with seven sharp points, each denoting an Aspect of Magic. Each of those points had a carved line leading to the center of the roof, where the empty pedestal stood. Looming above was the gas giant Cupid, its bands pearlescent, its bloodred storm sinister. Several smaller moons were silhouetted against it, like moles on a face.

Lucian reached for the Orb of Psionics, trying to impart his purpose onto it.

Reach across lightyears, across stars. Find Vera, wherever she is.

Ether rushed into him as the command was enacted. His Focus expanded outward, far beyond the atmosphere of the planet. It did not find Vera in the Cupid System, nor did it find her in the vast space beyond it. Lucian's Focus spread farther and farther, stretching thin even as more magic streamed from the Orb. Multiple stars entered its awareness, along with their planets, thousands of millions of souls. The ethereal field thrummed before him, and though he could now see a thousand stars, it was but a grain of sand in the context of the galaxy.

It was all too much. An existential dread overwhelmed him,

THE RIFTS OF PSYCHE

of his smallness in the universe. All he could feel was that vast darkness, his insignificance against it.

He needed to find Vera before it broke him. She was somewhere out here. If he could just get a message out . . .

Then, there was a connection. He saw her form, huddled around a fire in what appeared to be some ancient ruins. As with every time he had seen her, her dark hood was thrown overhead, her eyes black as she stared into the flames. From this image, there was no telling what planet she was on. All Lucian knew was that she was far, far away. Just seeing her brought back all his misgivings, all his doubts about her. He almost cut off the link.

But he had to go through with it. He saw no other option.

Vera . . .

When Vera looked up at him, her eyes widened, but she recovered quickly, as if him being there was the most natural thing in the Worlds. Nothing could phase her for long.

Lucian. I wondered when the Manifold would make good on its promise to bring us together again.

Her voice was the same – like the wind rustling over dead leaves. It sent a chill down his spine. Magic roared through him, a hurricane of ether. He could not keep this up for long, even with the Orb of Psionics.

I need help, Vera. I'm on Psyche, and I need you to come get me.

She watched him closely, her eyes dark and seeming to hold many secrets.

I daresay you do need help. This link you've forged is a clumsy thing. It should be . . . impossible. I can show you how to do it better.

I have the Orb of Psionics. And the Orb of Binding. Please. You must help me.

Her gaze grew intense as she peered into him. Something told Lucian that those words had reeled her to the core, despite her lack of reaction.

Indeed? It's clear we have much to speak of, but already, I feel your link slipping. And how did you know I have a ship at my disposal? I never told you about that.

I didn't know. I just figured the prophecy you told me might be true. That we would meet again. That . . . you would train me. That's all I had to go on.

I see. I remember you not believing me. But people only cling to prophecy once they've lost everything else.

She was going to say "no." Lucian could feel it in his bones. All of this had been for nothing.

Fear not, Lucian. I will be there as soon as I'm able. You have but one job until then.

What's that?

Her eyes bored into his, and it was as if she had grabbed him by the shoulders. *Survive.*

The connection severed, and Lucian's vision blackened as sound retreated. When the world returned, he was on his knees and the wind was gusting over the rooftop. Footsteps approached from behind. He whirled to see Serah, whose eyes were wide while her blonde hair was blown by the wind.

"You okay?"

Lucian forced himself to nod. "It's done. I contacted her."

"Vera? It worked?"

"It did. Only . . . I'm not sure it's a good thing."

"I'm not in the mood for riddles."

He stood. "It's nothing. She said she'd be here as soon as she's able."

"That's good news, right?"

Lucian shook his head. "I'm not sure. I just have this weird feeling about it. The connection broke, so there wasn't time to ask any more. Whatever I did to reach her, though . . . I never want to go through that again."

Serah came forward and held him. He wanted to break down and cry like a child. The image of all those stars, all that space . . . it was enough to drive someone mad. People weren't meant for such vastness, to know so many things. They were meant to stay rooted to a single, small world, clinging to a single idea and way of living. People's minds couldn't conceive the enormity of existence. And Lucian had only sensed a small fraction of it all at once, and it had nearly broken him.

He would just have to trust Vera was coming. Weeks, months, he couldn't say. But she would be here. Of that he was sure.

Hopefully, when she arrived, she wouldn't find his corpse.

He and Serah stood at the precipice of the Spire, looking east across the dunes. That way lay the Westlands, however many hundreds or even thousands of kilometers beyond the near horizon. And in the Westlands would be habitable lands – villages, food, running water. There they could survive, for months if need be.

But before they could reach the Westlands, they had to cross the Burning Sands and the Fire Rifts. Lucian vaguely remembered that area – lakes and rivers of lava, deep fissures. Impassable terrain.

But the Orbs would help them cross it. He had convinced the Jewels of Starsea of who he was – at least for now. And he had convinced himself. There were moments of doubts still, but he was almost there.

It would have to be enough. Two of the Orbs were his now. If he wasn't the Chosen, then who else could be? At least one other Orb had been found. Otherwise, the Starsea Cycle would not have returned, and along with it, magic. But who could have found it?

The answers were out there, somewhere, beyond the sky of this world.

Lucian's hunt for the Orbs was just beginning.

EPILOGUE

VERA WATCHED as the ghostly apparition of Lucian faded to nothing. What was the boy thinking, streaming himself so far? Psyche was four Gates away – a journey of some months. Likely, trying to rescue his careless hide would be an exercise in futility. It was said no one survived the Mad Moon for long, and from what Vera had seen of it, that was true.

She never thought she'd have occasion to go back. But she, above all else, knew that the Manifold worked in unfathomable ways.

And yet. The boy had the Orbs of Binding *and* Psionics. Or at least, he *claimed* to. No, he wasn't lying about that. What reason did he have to lie? And it would explain how he had managed to project himself at such distance. Still, it was hard to imagine how *two* Orbs had fallen into his hands. That was fortuitous. Or unlucky.

Then again, nothing was more beautiful than the will of the Manifold, seeing its plans come together in an infinitely complex tapestry, thousands of threads creating a picture still incomplete.

"The Manifold is in control of all," she mused, with a

chuckle. "Always. I should know that better than anyone. It's happening. All of it is happening, faster than I ever thought possible."

"What was that, Master?"

Vera considered a moment. How much to reveal? How much to hide?

"Something has happened. Something momentous. It requires my immediate attention."

"You're leaving, aren't you?"

Vera thought a moment, staring into the floating orb of fire, the only source of light in this dark place. "I'm afraid I must."

"But we've only just begun! All those weeks of travel, all those near-deaths. We stand so close."

"I've had a revelation. It could be everything."

"A revelation?"

"Yes. Things are moving along now. They're moving along very well indeed." She looked at her disciple, her gaze intense. "You must continue your work here. Prepare yourself – heart, mind, and soul."

"Will you be back in time?"

Vera considered. "I must be, if the Manifold wills it."

"Then let it be so."

Vera allowed herself a small smile. There was no greater feeling than the fulfillment of a plan decades in the making.

The Chosen of the Manifold was coming.

THE END OF BOOK THREE

THE STARSEA CYCLE CONTINUES IN BOOK FOUR

THE CHOSEN OF THE MANIFOLD

ABOUT THE AUTHOR

Kyle West is the author of a growing number of sci-fi and fantasy series: *The Starsea Cycle, The Wasteland Chronicles,* and *The Xenoworld Saga.*

His goal is to write as many entertaining books as possible, with interesting worlds and characters that hopefully give his readers a break from the mundane.

He lives in South Florida with his lovely wife, son, and two insanely spoiled cats. He enjoys hearing from his fans, and invites them to connect with him through his Facebook group, Kyle West's Readers Guild, to hear the latest on his books.

ALSO BY KYLE WEST

Made in the USA
Middletown, DE
01 October 2023

39878739R00283